To Malcolm, beloved Man of Kent
To Tony, beloved Kentish Man
And to Jim, beloved Man of Kent
One born in Africa,
One born in London,
One born in America—
But all men of Kent.

ELIZABETH GIBSON

Men of Kent

A NOVEL Of The ENGLISH CIVIL WAR

Zondervan Books
Zondervan Publishing House
Grand Rapids, Michigan

MEN OF KENT: A HISTORICAL NOVEL
Copyright © 1988 by Elizabeth Gibson

First U. S. paperback edition 1990.

Zondervan Books
are published by
Zondervan Publishing House
1415 Lake Dr., S.E.
Grand Rapids, MI 49506

Library of Congress Cataloging-in-Publication Data

Gibson, Elizabeth.
Men of Kent.

1. Kent (England)—History—Fiction. I. Title.
PR6057.I246M46   1988   823'.914   88-37873
ISBN 0-310-32221-9

Edited and designed by Judith Markham

Printed in the United States of America

90 91 92 93 94 95 / AK / 10 9 8 7 6 5 4 3 2

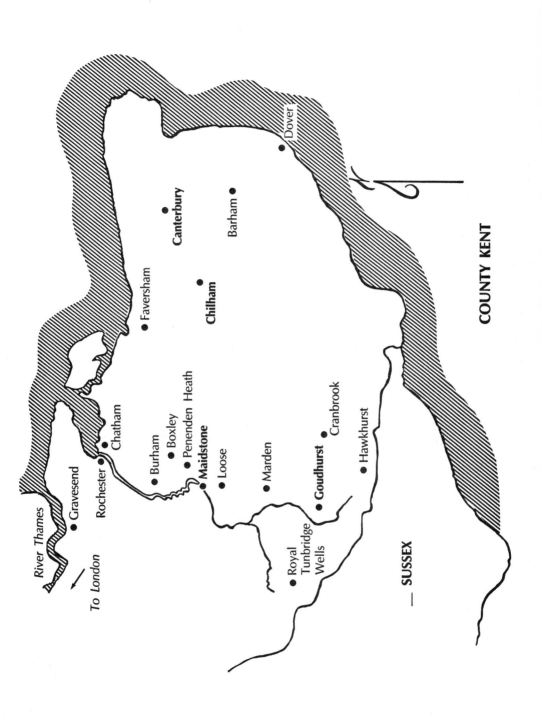

River Thames

To London

Gravesend

Rochester

Chatham

Burham

Boxley

Penenden Heath

Maidstone

Loose

Marden

Royal
Tunbridge
Wells

Goudhurst

Cranbrook

Hawkhurst

Faversham

Chilham

Canterbury

Barham

Dover

COUNTY KENT

— SUSSEX

The Fessendens

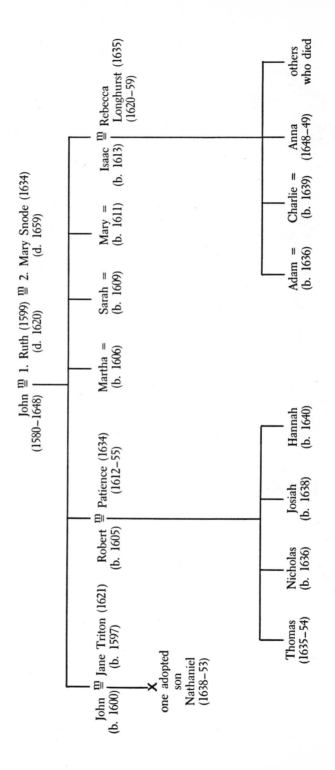

Part 1
for god and kent

I have house and land in Kent
And if you'll love me, love me now.
Two-pence half-penny is my rent,
I cannot come every day to woo.

One time I gave thee a paper of pins,
Another time a tawdry lace;
And if thou wilt not grant me love
In truth I die before thy face.

I will put on my best white shirt
And I will wear my yellow hose
And on my head a good grey hat,
And in't stick a lovely rose.

Wherefore cease off, make no delay,
And if you'll love me, love me now;
Or else I seek some other where—
For I cannot come every day to woo.

Melismata, 1611

Chilham, Spring 1619

Robert

Through the dry, bricked vaults of the wine cellar Robert followed the voices of the kitchen wenches. The bolt of cloth under his arm had become a dead weight, and not knowing his way through the new castle, the boy had lost his way already. *The steward should have accompanied me,* he thought resentfully.

The cellar suddenly opened out into the wide space of the under-kitchen, into light, heat, and merriment. Two girls of his own age were plucking fowl, shrieking and giggling as the feathers flew in clouds round them. The cook stood at the wooden board, flour dusting her hands, cheeks, and cap as she pounded the dough and watched the kitchen maids with tolerant amusement.

Robert thought fleetingly of his mother, of her horror if she could have seen the slackness and laxity of the cook, the foolish laughter of the girls. She would never have suffered such a brawl in her own kitchen. But neither would she have had maids to do the work for her.

He stepped forward with what he hoped was a civil bow to the cook. "I'm here to see m'lady, ma'am, and the steward bade me come here."

The cook thumped the grain-speckled dough louder than before and ignored him.

One of the girls stopped her squealing and turned toward him. "Did 'e, now? Well, ain't 'e the fool, then. Madam'd never deign to walk in 'ere, you may be sure of that." With a blood-stained hand she reached to tuck a greasy tendril of hair into her cap, simpering as she did so. "But you look like a handsome cock." She turned to the other girl. "Be 'e old enough, this lad, d'you think, Prudence, for us to pluck his feathers?"

Robert backed away uncertainly. The smile of gratitude for their interest froze as he heard what she said.

The second girl made faint sounds of rebuke to her companion and sent

9

him a pitying look. "Leave off, Joan. Can't you see 'e's got something for the lady?"

The bold girl clacked her tongue, eyeing the bolt of cloth pointed toward her. "Lackaday, I thought 'e had something for *me!*"

The thumping of the dough suddenly stopped. "Give the lad some ale, Prudence. And take that great parcel off him afore he drops it in the flour and feathers." The cook glanced up briefly from the pans into which she was pressing the dough. "I'll see she gets it. Don't you fret."

Flinging a triumphant smirk over her shoulder at Joan, Prudence came forward with her eyes down and offered to take the parcel from him.

He backed away. "Nay, 'tis my father's will I give it to the lady myself."

She fluttered her eyelashes at him, and he felt the heat rise into his face. "Ah, poor lad. 'Tis a heavy thing he's got." She bustled off to fill a tankard of ale for him.

Robert watched her retreat, trying to gauge where her sympathies really lay. He liked the flattering way she had looked at him, almost as if he *were* a good-looking young fellow. He enjoyed the way her neatly patched skirts swished over the tile floor this way and that as her hips moved.

She returned with the ale and gave it to him. Afraid of soiling the cloth, he nervously laid the bolt down on a vacant chair, then took the tankard with an unsteady hand. His father had recently declared that there would be no more ale in the house, that ale was a tool of Satan, and that henceforth they were to drink nothing but water and milk.

He knew he would run the risk of a birching if he drank it. Still, the saucy looks of both girls stirred him to risk it, to enjoy the inevitable wait before he could see Lady Digges. He sipped the ale slowly as the cook sent Joan to find her ladyship.

By the time Lady Digges came to the kitchen door, shadowed by Joan, who leered at him from behind her mistress, Robert was heady with the ale on an empty stomach. Prudence's insinuating looks provoked him even more as she returned to plucking the birds with coy innocence.

He tried to rally his wits as he presented the cloth and bowed. Her ladyship received him kindly and seemed not to notice his agitation. After she had given him a small parcel of eggs for his mother, Robert was at last free to escape from the kitchen and back through the wine cellar to the frosty out-of-doors.

Almost out of the castle, he realized that he had been followed. A shadow darted out from behind the last keg of wine by the door, and Prudence blocked his way. She pulled off her cap, and her hair hung in loose curls round her face. Despite the smear of poultry blood across her cheek, she was pretty and she knew it.

His throat went dry. "What is't?" he rasped hoarsely, beginning to tremble but nevertheless determined to show himself a man.

She twisted her shoulders and looked at him slyly. "Cook said I might go and beg a kiss of thee since I'd shown you kindness."

He grinned. "So that's your game. Well, have it, and welcome. Then let me pass, pray." He leaned toward her, intending to escape with a brush of his mouth across her face, then to push her aside and be gone.

But she caught him by the arms, and in his befuddled state, his sense of space, time, and distance became suddenly distorted. He was kissing her with a hunger he did not know himself capable of after years of cold kisses from his mother and sisters. He shuddered and broke free of her, a vision of his parents suddenly looming large before his eyes. "You're naught but a harlot," he spat.

She reached up quickly and wrenched the small neckband off his jerkin, her eyes sparkling with laughter. "Then I'll have a keepsake of thee."

Robert tried to tear it out of her hand, but she was too quick for him. Realizing he could not follow her, he shoved the door open and fled out of the kitchen gardens and down the long walk to the front gates. There he stopped, quaking inwardly, suddenly sobered by the rush of cold air and half-darkness. He must set himself to rights before he dared go home.

As he halted by the well, he tried to decide whether to draw water. Setting down the parcel from Lady Digges, he leaned over the edge of the well and listened to the faint dropping below, smelling the familiar dampness and welcoming its comparative warmth in the March frost.

But the knowledge of the long walk home and the ache of his body spurred him on. Disregarding the bite of the cold Wealden iron in his palm, he gripped the crank and forced himself to turn it. At last the winch brought the bucket to the mouth of the well. Swinging it over, he grabbed it clumsily. Water spilled out, soaking his breeches and hose.

He groaned in dismay, gritting his teeth as he pictured his parents again. *Drunk*, his father would say, *and smelling of wenches*. And *You'll be starved with cold, you foolish boy*, his mother would say. *Whatever possessed you? And where is your neckband, pray?*

Robert bent his hands to scoop the water, swilled the first numbing mouthful round his tongue and teeth, and spat it out. He had to wash away the smell of ale first. Then he drank greedily, shivering. Eventually he dropped the bucket back into the well, retrieved his parcel, and headed across the dew-soaked village green.

As he passed the church, he gave its battlements only a half-glance, flung without thought over his left shoulder. On the other side of the narrow valley ahead of him he could discern through the twilight of this spring afternoon the movements of the cottagers against the dimness of rushlights and wood fires. In the forge a smith clanged his hammer on the anvil, the glare of the fire behind him. The banality and sameness of the scene reassured him as he walked in the shadow of the churchyard's great yew tree and long stone wall.

An old man leading a goat left the muddy alleyway between two of the Poor Row cottages and shuffled past Robert with only a nod at him. The man jerked the rope round the animal's neck as it snorted and swerved skittishly toward the wall. An infant in one of the cottages near the bottom of the hill let out a thin, mewling cry that was answered by the screech of an owl. Unthinking, he watched the bird flap silently toward the cloud-blurred moon.

At the end of the lane, outside the alehouse, the sweetish smell of the charcoal burners' furnace drifted toward him from somewhere in the woods. Its orange glow stained the sky above to a livid, ghastly color. His brother would have been uneasy, gabbling beside him about witches, or pagan bonfires, or evil spirits. John: the dreamer, the fanciful, they called him. And now John had gone to live in Leyden, with the Pilgrim Church on the Kloksteeg.

Newly resentful, Robert thought, *If I were the elder, I could be there. I'm the one should have gone. He's the elder. My father needs him, not me, to work for him. John may be no man of business, but mayhap I'm not, either. We'll not satisfy my father . . . not I, especially.*

He frowned. Surely John wasn't as zealous as he was. *Surely not.* His letters had been full of details about the wool industry in Holland: the way the Dutch in Leyden wove and dressed their cloth; his own interest in the new draperies—softer, finer clothes of silk and Spanish wool dyed by clever craftsmen whose work, John said, could not be bested by Kentish dyers anywhere; the organization of the Dutch guilds; the growing respect, grudging at first, won by the Separatist church from the men of Leyden for their commercial deftness and energy.

Yes, John spoke of the church there in every sentence, but more of the members' work and prosperity than of their religious life. Yes, he quoted from the sermons of Brewster and Robinson, but he wrote much more about the witness of his elders among the foreign merchants and craftsmen than about the inner workings of God in his own heart. For sure, he, not John, belonged in Holland.

No, he was not worthy, not spiritual enough after all. He had just polluted himself at the castle, and he had enjoyed it. He would get that collar back from that wench if he was branded for it, and he would settle his account with the girl once and for all. *Prudence!* What an unfit name for such a girl!

A thud of hooves beat across his mental picture of her. Unthinking, he drew back into the hedgerow. The horse was panting, in a lather. Robert could hear the rider's grunts as its hooves struck the uneven ruts and flints of the road, and the slight creak of the saddle leather. Mantle flying, the rider drew nearer. The messenger obviously knew the road well to ride so recklessly downhill in the dark. He passed Robert, a sack of what might have been mail bouncing on his back, a horn gleaming beside it in the light of the moon, the smell of oats and sweat and stable permeating the air, a splatter of mud spraying Robert's surcoat.

He walked on, faster now. No witches or ghosts abroad, perhaps, but footpads and other rogues. One never knew. Muttering a hasty prayer for safety, he rounded the last curve before his cottage and searched for the first glimpse of home.

Candles in the kitchen window, the sweet scent of bacon curing in the smokehouse, the acrid smell of tallow rendering in one of the outshots behind the washhouse: all the familiar signs of his mother's busy, well-ordered life. He and his brothers and sisters were fortunate to have parents who worked so hard and taught them as well as his parents had.

His father was now his own master, a successful clothier who chose not to leave his yeoman's roots—the village of his father and grandfather, both weavers. Though he had built the timber-framed cottage where they lived, and could have built a grand Wealden hall had he wished, he chose to live in simplicity without household servants and without all the luxuries of neighboring gentlefolk.

Perhaps someone had heard the gate, for the studded oak door of the cottage suddenly flew open and his sister met him on the threshold.

"Robert, you're home at last," Martha cried. "Come in, come in! Such news there is!"

Her cap sat slightly askew and her broadcloth skirt was as dusty with flour as that of the castle cook. At thirteen she already carried herself like a young matron: as brusque and practical as her mother; and, unlike her mother, plump and comely, rapidly filling out her bodice.

"What, Martha? What is it?" He reached to tilt her cap further over one eye, for he knew it would annoy her. Then he turned to place his parcel on the settle by the door.

Narrowing her eyes and pursing her lips, she made a great show of straightening her cap again before hurrying down the passageway, through the buttery, and back into the kitchen. "Now you shan't find out, you naughty child."

"Child!" he sneered. "And, pray, what are you?"

He was answered by three pairs of clear eyes and heads of dark curls shining in the firelight of the kitchen. Esther, Abigail, and Isaac sat side by side on stools in front of the fire. Clearly, Martha was making supper for everyone—mother for the evening.

"Where's our father?" he asked stiffly.

Martha resolutely stirred a thick broth in the brass pot over the fire. "In our mother's chamber." She nodded toward the ceiling. "There's much ado."

He shifted impatiently and looked down at Esther. "What's ado, Esther?"

"Our mother has the ague. She's abed." Her serious face broke into a great smile.

Now he guessed the news. His mother never had an ague, was never one to lie abed at six of the clock in the evening—not unless—*John nineteen, himself fourteen, Martha thirteen, Esther, ten, Abigail, eight, Isaac six. . . .* Aye, quite likely Providence would be bestowing another child in the months ahead. His mother had lost a child between himself and John, and another after Isaac. And still she wanted that seventh child.

He grinned uncertainly at Esther. "So *that's* the news. Good news, aye. She's not too poorly, I hope."

Martha clicked her tongue as if resigned to his inclusion in this women's talk. She sighed. "Nay, weary, though. But there's more news yet. As good news as the other, mother said."

Robert studied the faces of his brothers and sisters.

"They know nothing more," Martha cautioned him. "And nor will you till we sup." She turned to Esther. "Pray set out bread on the board, and two candlesticks, and spoons for all. And fetch me the trenchers from the cupboard. I see Robert is hungry, and no doubt our father is, too." She at last looked at her brother. "Our mother told our father her news this morning—early, though. 'Twas after you had gone. And they did not break fast today, till now, in thanksgiving for this mercy of God."

He frowned. "No wonder mother feels weak now. She will sup, I hope, at last."

"My father said so. I doubt it not."

Robert left the room, retrieved his parcel, and placed it on the bench beside the hearth. "Eggs from the Lady Digges for our mother," he said.

Martha swept them up without a glance and went to deposit them in the buttery. "What, does she think our hens know not how to lay?" Her voice rose indignantly, and she clapped the buttery door shut behind her.

Robert laughed. His mother would have said the same. "She must think so, surely, you sour little maiden."

Behind them, Esther moved quietly round the table with the spoons, then took a taper from the fire and lit two more brass candlesticks.

"Be not ungracious," Robert went on. "Perhaps the lady knew of our mother's state."

"Nonsense! News travels not in the wind."

"How knowing you are, dear sister."

"And how discourteous you are, dear brother—" She stopped, frowning at his jerkin. "And where's your collar, you rascal?"

He glared back, deciding to ignore the question. "In truth, the lady sent the eggs, besides the money she owed, as a gift of thanks. Very kind she was." He raised his voice to a higher pitch and shed for a moment the thick Kentish accent in which the family always conversed at home. "'Give your father my thanks,' said she. 'The seal on his cloth, 'tis what I look for nowadays. Wool of the best. And mannerly, too, to send his son to bring it.'"

His sister scoffed, though he knew she was impressed. "Happen she might have liked it better had our father taken the bolt himself . . . had he not enough to do!"

"Enough of what to do?" The elder John Fessenden had quietly opened the low door at the foot of the stairs and now stood watching Martha thoughtfully. Already flushed from the steam of the kettle, the girl flushed a deeper red and began to stammer out an answer that he stopped with a wave of his hand. "Nay, you and Robert are full of idle talk." He met Robert's eyes. "What account can you give of yourself, son?"

Robert licked his lips and stood straighter than before. He dreaded having to answer questions about his neckband or the goings-on at the castle. "I delivered the cloth you wished, sir, and the lady was well pleased. She bade me pay you five shillings and give you two dozen eggs." He threw a quick glance at his sister.

"'Twas well done."

Robert continued, gathering speed in the hope of forestalling awkward questions. "And before that I went to my lessons, and this morning I saw to it that the weavers were paid as you bade me, and that their looms weren't idle. Abraham and David had a hundred-weight of cloth or more ready for the fulling. David says he thinks some of the spinners lack wool. Abraham says the weavers in Loose and Maidstone wanted—"

"Never mind what Abraham says. He wouldn't know, never having been out of Chilham. But you've traversed much ground today, I see. Good lad. Is your purse safely under key?"

For a moment he panicked. *What if the wench got it off me, got more than my collar and now sits laughing at me . . . ?* He fumbled at his belt. The purse was safe. "Nay, I forgot to put it away."

"Then give me what you took in today, and later you'll give me a full accounting"—he fixed him with a stern glare—"every item. Martha, you're ready to wait on us? Come, sit up for prayers and supper, as you're bid, children."

As the family pulled stools to the table and Martha ladled broth into bowls, Ruth Fessenden moved into the room behind her husband—weary, as Martha had said. She did not smile as she took her place. Robert eyed her through his fingers as his father prayed long and earnestly over the food.

He had not seen his mother since the night before, and in just a day she seemed to have changed. Some of the force had left her. He remembered clearly her carrying the second child that had died. Even more clearly, though it was when he was only eight, he remembered her being great with Isaac. She hadn't slowed her pace then. He felt strangely anxious for her.

The vigorous, stern mother he'd known for fourteen years wasn't always as he had wanted her to be, but she was mother. His mother. Fear seized him for a moment. Only for a moment. Grace over, her quietness vanished as she reached quickly to chastise Isaac for dabbling his fingers in the broth. There. She was with them again: indomitable, untiring after all.

The family customarily spoke little over food, so the room fell silent except for the crackle of the fire and the soft scraping of wooden spoons in the trenchers. From time to time Ruth met her husband's eyes, looking down the full length of the table to where he sat at the opposite end. Robert caught the glances and smiled inwardly. His mother would be all right. Pray

God this child would be born strong and healthy. Pray God it would be another boy who could grow up to relieve John and him—and later Isaac—of all the responsibility their father was slowly shifting onto them.

At last Ruth spoke. "Martha, you made a good supper. Thank you."

Martha bowed her head with uncharacteristic meekness. "I had good meat and vegetables to put in it."

Her mother sighed. "Aye, the harvest was good last year."

Martha smiled. "Yes, all the fruit, remember? And the apples are fine and crisp, even the pears. . . ."

Robert stared at them both, not wanting the conversation to wander far from what occupied his mind. His sister had a fine way of talking of trifles.

"What is't, Robert?" his father suddenly asked.

Robert looked sharply to the other end of the table, though he shouldn't have been surprised by the question. His father had an uncanny knack for sensing his moods.

"Something's troubling you, for all the good work of the day."

He started guiltily but then saw concern, not condemnation, in the lines of his father's face. "Nothing to do with my work, sir," he mumbled.

"What, then?"

Martha flashed him a spiteful look. *Now you'll catch it for losing your collar.*

He ducked her look, thrust the wench out of his mind again, and assumed an air of injury. "There's news, I hear, and none to share it."

"News indeed! You'll know it presently. Isaac, fetch me the Scriptures. And another candle, pray."

Robert suppressed a moan, confronting afresh his spiritual poverty. Of course his father could never forget prayers, not even in the height of the summer when magical daylight enticed them out-of-doors until late in the evening, when woodpigeons called, and those cutting the hay on the hillside sang until dark. Prayers: an unrelenting pattern, winter and summer, a ritual his three sisters endured in uncomplaining, even attentive silence, but one that he and Isaac fidgeted through. Especially when there was news to hear.

Perhaps, he thought as his father opened the large volume to one of the Books of Moses, *perhaps I'm not the one who should live in Leyden after all, with talk all the livelong day of God's laws and Moses' laws and sacrifice, sin, and sanctity. Not I!* But he did not know, either, where he'd rather be.

"Robert, you'll read to us, please," his father said.

Taking the Bible, Robert swallowed hard and began at the beginning of the twenty-fourth chapter of Genesis. *The man at the well for his master,* *Isaac,* he thought irritably. *And a beautiful girl gives him to drink.* He remembered Prudence again, glanced up at his father questioningly, then read on.

Even as he read, his mind ranged to other subjects: his sisters going to school with their mother all day, learning in the kitchen how to cipher and write, how to read aloud from the Gospel stories. His mother would be up to her elbows in flour making the week's loaves, or pickling vegetables from the garden, the benches and floor awash with vinegar. A patchwork sort of education!

He had started his own in the same way—as had his brother John— chanting numbers or letters in order or verses from Scripture. John had once undertaken tongue-in-cheek to count to one hundred and forty-four thousand as God would do at the great marriage supper of the Christ. He had also memorized an entire chapter of the book of Revelation to please his mother. Then he had teased her because she could not con the Greek alphabet besides *alpha* and *omega.*

And for his pains· John had been packed off to board in Maidstone to attend the grammar school there as a William Lamb scholar. But that was years before, and his parents had prospered. No longer would their children need scholarships. "It was the right thing for John," his mother had said. "He wanted studiousness and discipline, and one day you'll both take over from your father. But as for you, Robert . . . no . . . you'll learn at home."

Robert had not remained at home, however. The village priest had singled him out a few years after John had returned from Maidstone and had tutored him in elementary Latin, the Catechism, Psalter, and Bible. Only at the Prayer Book had his father balked and threatened to bring him home to lessons with his mother again. "A popish book," he'd grunted, words Robert still didn't fully understand. "They chant it off as if they were parrots."

Robert faltered suddenly on a sentence that seemed to have no end. His mother checked him. "You're not minding, son."

He read further, then listened as one by one Esther, Abigail, and Isaac recited verses they had learned that day. At last with his brother and sisters he bowed his head to his father's familiar voice pronouncing solemn invocations, petitions, and prayers for God's mercy on his own sins and those of his family. As his father prayed, Robert convinced himself that he could actually see between his fingers the candles burning down inch by inch.

He moved restlessly on his stool and caught a glimpse of Isaac twisting and fretting even more. His father's voice intoned with greater urgency than ever, suddenly punctuated by the sharp slap of flesh on flesh. His mother had pounced, and Isaac was stifling sobs in his sleeve as the prayers droned on.

When they ended at last, Martha and her mother began ushering the younger ones to the upper chamber. There in the uncertain warmth which crept between the cracks of the stone chimney piece and that afforded by flock bedding, by sacks of malt and corn stacked for warmth against the walls and under the lead-paned windows—there they would soon fall asleep.

Robert could no longer restrain himself. "Father, I beg you, what *is* this news?"

"I see I should have told you before our devotions. You might have learned something. But no, you'd have thought of naught else, either way." He inhaled deeply. "The news is this: your brother John will sail in April or May for England. A letter came by the post from him this evening. He's coming home with Robert Cushman and William Brewster."

Robert sighed. "Oh, would I could have gone with him, only to sail on a real ship across the sea and back again!"

"Hush, that's childish talk." His father looked grave. "Your place is here, I'm certain of it. John was called to go, as now he's called back. I don't yet know what his coming means—whether he'll stay, or go. He says changes are afoot. The Pilgrim Church is not as settled in Holland as we thought. It seems that God may call them to make a farther journey, still."

"But where, my father, and why?" Robert burst out.

Fessenden held up his hand. "You're hot-headed and rash tonight, in a fever about everything. As to why— Only the Lord knows why the Pilgrims cannot all remain in Leyden. But that they must move—that the Pilgrims know for a surety."

"Then where should they go?"

"They've thought of the Virginia Plantation, so your brother tells us. Mr. Cushman and Mr. Brewster are to see some men in London at the Virginia Company. They want a patent for another venture to Virginia."

"Then my brother has come to help them obtain it?"

"Nay, I think not." Fessenden frowned, looking away for a moment. Robert recognized caution in him, an unwillingness to say too much.

"Truth to tell, John is not satisfied now with Leyden. The ten-year truce with Spain has almost run its course, and the Pilgrims fear the Inquisition."

Robert scoffed. "A group of silly, superstitious old men asking them questions about God, you mean? Why be afraid? The Pilgrims walk more closely with God than any other men in Europe."

"Bravely spoken, but spoken in ignorance." Fessenden's face hardened. "The Spanish Inquisition sets terror into the hearts of the Christian church in all of Holland. You cannot, being but a lad, imagine the horror and evil those men of Spain bring with them—from Satan himself."

"But to throw away so many years of labor—?"

His father nodded. "Aye, but we cannot see God's purpose in all this. For John 'tis only a year, and other things are at work to hasten the move." He stopped, frowning again. "None wants to return to England. They remember too well, I suppose, what they'll face if they do—hatred at best. Forced to swear oaths that go against their conscience, and stocks and pillories and floggings if they go not against their conscience. More persecution unless many things change."

Robert was puzzled. What did his father mean? He and others who called themselves the honest folk had never suffered for their beliefs, not as far as he knew.

Rumors ran rife, as always, especially in a village where the principal gentleman rode to and from London with his retinue to serve King James at Court; where one of England's greatest architects had just finished for that knight a resplendent brick castle—an edifice that required the labor of glaziers, plasterers, stonemasons, bricklayers, carvers, carpenters, and gardeners from much farther afield than Chilham. The building had gone on throughout Robert's childhood, a source of never-ending fascination for all the lads of the village and a source of contradictory and puzzling rumors tossed about by all the village gossips.

His father, perhaps catching his bewildered look, continued. "You have no idea what may happen to God's people in the next few years. We may *all* pray to leave England! So Virginia must seem to the Pilgrims to be an answer to prayer."

Robert digested this, still uncertain, wanting to get back to the firm ground of things he knew and understood: the Christian brothers in Leyden, John. . . . "And John—you say he's disappointed with his lot in Leyden?"

"He says so, but only between the lines. There's been argument between the families all along about the bringing up of children. Some are influenced by what they've seen of the Hollanders. Even the God-fearing

Dutch are not such strict parents as our own countrymen. Now there are serious quarrels."

"With the Dutch?"

"Nay, I meant among the brethren. And things are made worse by their separation." Leaning his elbows on the board, Fessenden rested his chin on his knuckles so that his face was only inches from the candle flame. "That's why I don't hold with being so separate, myself. It makes you too ingrown and weak in the end."

Robert had lost the meaning again, but he listened all the same.

"The community's so closed, you see," Fessenden went on. "Most of the English can speak no Dutch. In many ways the brethren are cut off, more or less. John doesn't like it any more than I would. I wasn't . . . going to tell you all this . . . but I suspect Brother Cushman's journey is providing an escape for John, an opportunity to leave without deserting."

All evening Robert mulled over what his father had told him. As they sat working together on the day's account books, he found himself distracted. What did John's return home mean for John himself? Would he come back disillusioned, full of ridicule for the church? Would he turn back on his spiritual brethren and their beliefs, setting a course toward his father, toward success in the cloth industry? Or would he—with all his freshly acquired knowledge of new dyeing methods and the fashioning of new draperies—scorn his father's well-established system of business and thus anger him? Would he refuse to work as his father's factor—a post Robert himself had reluctantly begun to fit into—overseeing distribution of the wool to local cottagers for spinning, weaving, and finishing?

And what would John's homecoming mean for himself? He had no idea, yet, what God would want of him. The future was clouded, hidden.

Canterbury, June 1619

John

London lay two day's journey behind them, and Rochester almost a day behind. Ahead stretched the almost straight chalk and gravel ribbon of Watling Street, rising and falling over the northern edge of the Downs. They had passed through Faversham already, a town familiar to John since it stood quite near Chilham. But they had continued without stopping toward Canterbury, determined to reach it before nightfall. To the south, orchards gave way to sheep pastures, and they in turn gave way to sparser land, patches of heath and wild gorse still yellow with blossom. For the most part the three men enjoyed a companionable silence, all intent on walking as fast as possible and avoiding the ruts.

"I'm glad you're with us, sir." John looked warmly at Brewster and unconsciously wished Brother Cushman weren't with them.

"And I'm glad I came with thee," Brewster asserted. He still spoke with the thick accent of the North Midlands, foreign to John even after a year in Leyden where almost all the Pilgrims hailed from Scrooby, Gainsborough, or Sturton-le-Steeple—places John thought of vaguely as "up north." Even Brewster's Cambridge education had not softened the accent. It was an endearing characteristic, something John associated with the ringing clarity of Nonconformist preaching, something that moved him week by week as no ritual trammeled by Acts of Uniformity could ever do.

Brewster's fingers, gripping his staff, were permanently dyed with printer's ink. He seemed as unaware of this as he was of his beaver hat and cloak, tossed on carelessly as they had left their lodgings that morning; unaware, too, that his white neckband and wristbands were now somewhat frayed, dusty with chalk and grit thrown up by passing packhorses and wagons loaded with timber and fish. But life shone in his eyes and in his voice, despite the pain and danger he faced.

As he watched Brewster, John reflected that in the same circumstances he would have been joyless, tearful, and complaining. Brewster had suffered for several weeks now with a nagging pain in his stomach. And the King's officers were searching for him for the crime of printing a supposedly seditious pamphlet. This pamphlet, directed against a new oath being forced by the King on Scottish Presbyterians, the godly folk, and others who disagreed with rites of the established church, had been sent from Holland to be circulated in England, much to the King's displeasure.

"You'll be welcome indeed in Canterbury," Cushman put in, though without warmth. "And safer, I warrant, than in London."

Brewster chuckled. "Had I indeed erred in printing that pamphlet, I'd fear not to stay and face my retribution. But as long as I live, if there's truth to be declared—be it in England or Holland, or even far away in Virginia— I'll see it declared." He shrugged. "And, as I erred *not*, it matters not whether I be in London or Canterbury." He laughed aloud.

Inwardly, John applauded. No bravado, that. Brewster spoke as he lived—forthrightly, seeing truth as something to be lived, not merely defended.

"Ah, Virginia," Brewster went on. "I hope and pray it brings our freedom. I believe it will, Brother Cushman."

"If we be not devoured by cannibals or driven out by the smell of that wicked weed, tobacco," Cushman muttered.

John wanted to laugh at Cushman even as a few moments before he had laughed with Brewster. Always so morose, Cushman was respected, trusted as a deacon of the Pilgrim Church for the past ten years, but frequently disliked. "Waspish," some of the brothers and sisters called him behind his back. "Mind lest ye step on his tail and be stung for your pains."

Still the Separatists had chosen him to go with Brewster, taking their request to the London Virginia Company; they could count on him. And now when matters were out of their own hands—as the members of the Company had quarrelled to a deadlock in London, thus reaching no settlement for the Leyden Pilgrims—it was Cushman who had suggested that John accompany him to Canterbury. They were to lodge with the Cushman family and to meet a man who had just sailed home from Virginia. Then John could return, if he wished, to Chilham.

Apparently having none of John's tender conscience, Brewster did laugh at Cushman. "Come now. You're as anxious to go as the rest of us. We can't give up hope now."

Cushman drew his mouth into a grim line. "True. But neither can we rush ahead, foolhardy and uncircumspect." He shook his head, forestalling protests from the others about all the obstacles that had already delayed their attempts to obtain the necessary patent. "I cannot help but remember what happened two years ago. We thought then that our way was sure."

John looked questioningly at Cushman. As he did so, he noticed, beyond the heath, the towers of the cathedral now only a few miles away under the evening sky. *Not far, now,* he thought in relief.

"You should explain that to our young companion," Brewster said. Then he winked. "Though briefly. He looks done for, poor lad."

Cushman inhaled quickly as if meditating a sharp reply, but then tempered his expression and tone. "You surely know some of what happened."

John flushed. "Little, sir."

"Well, then." His voice became deliberate, slightly stilted. "Brother Carver and I went in secret to London a little over two years ago. The Church charged us with proving to the Virginia Company governors that we could ably support ourselves by fishing and trade in the Colony"—he cleared his throat—"and, a harder task, that though living separately in Holland, we were still loyal subjects of His Majesty and obedient to the Church of England."

"A harder task!" Brewster laughed, interrupting. "Nay, nigh impossible."

"Aye, even with Sir Edwin Sandys's word on our behalf to King James. His Majesty played the tyrant with us, referred our articles of faith to the archbishop of yonder city for his inspection"—his voice turned bitter with sarcasm—"then turned on him, as well, and had us all accused of setting up a free state, defying the laws of God and England. Monstrous!"

John murmured in sympathy, beginning to see what lay behind Cushman's bitterness—all the years of struggle and frustrated dreams.

"Well, never you mind, young John," Brewster reassured. "God will not leave us comfortless. See, Canterbury lies ahead. We're Pilgrims truly today, to go from London to Canterbury."

"Though not to see the bleached old bones of Becket," Cushman sneered.

Ignoring him, Brewster went on. "I'm sure Sir Samuel will have good news for us. Just think. Perhaps within a year our church will dwell in a place where we need not fear Spanish armies, or Acts of Uniformity, or arrest for printing the truth. Surely a community of God lies just ahead."

"Amen, I pray as much," Cushman said fervently, sweeping off his hat for a moment and raising his eyes toward the sky.

"And if the Virginia Company of London stand not as our surety, then we can go to the Plymouth Company. And if not now, then soon, I believe." Brewster smiled. "The trade between England and the Colonies is increasing. The King cannot afford to lose the revenues entailed. Sooner or later, we shall sail." He nodded to himself, beating out the rhythm of the words with his staff. "We shall sail."

The three went on in silence for a while, their eyes fixed on the city walls ahead. Brewster's words of encouragement and prophecy sounded repeatedly in John's head. "Virginia?" he said quietly. "'Tis the only place in America the Pilgrims may go?" He was careful not to say *we*.

Cushman looked at him contemptuously, as he would at a child in a grammar school who had asked a foolish question.

Brewster, though, answered him patiently. "We do not know for certain. At the moment, yes, I fear it is the only place we may go. The English settlement on the River James has prospered."

"Tobacco," Cushman grumbled.

"From tobacco," Brewster acknowledged. "But the land is vast, we understand. We need not live close neighbors to any save those we choose. And the land is rich, too. We'll learn to use it—learn from the others who've settled already. We need not plant tobacco, I'm sure." He glanced at Cushman. "Then if we want their help in times of plague or famine, we shall have it. And when the other settlers want help and preachers, too, then they shall have them—men unafraid to leave the comforts of Europe and preach in a heathen place."

John could have predicted Cushman's response. "Aye, unafraid, and rightly. But let's hope not unready, as well. Do not forget that of a hundred and fifty who first went to Virginia, only two score lived to see a harvest. We'll have to be better stewards than that if we're to prosper. Provisions must be laid by with far greater thought than before. And the brethren must learn to live as the ancient church lived and share their property."

Brewster did not reply immediately, and John guessed why. Of all the Pilgrims at Leyden, Cushman was one of only a few who believed in communal property. Had Cushman suggested or explained his convictions more gently, he might have won their ears; as it was, he had offended most of the brethren.

Brewster, however, was long accustomed to Cushman's acerbity and well able to blunt the sharpness of the conversation before it injured them all. "Aye, Brother Cushman," he said. "Though I can't agree with thee about sharing, necessarily, you're right about the need for careful stewarding. I'm thinking you'd be quite the man—once we secure a patent and have ourselves a stout, sound ship—to be in charge of provisions."

Cushman first paled, then colored. "I'd count it an honor," he replied with a slight smile.

John now raised his eyes from the city to the sky. Within a mile of the walls, they followed a way that led gently downhill into the Stour Valley. Below the sky's china and chalk pastel, the Canterbury meadows spread out, glistening under the sun that fell almost directly behind them. The angle of the light gave the view an almost ethereal quality as fleeces of fog rose from the fields and wrapped themselves round the twin towers of Westgate.

Ethereal, yet deceiving, John thought. Westgate was notorious as a prison, and even from this distance he could see the loopholes where guns were mounted behind the walls. *No New Jerusalem this,* he reflected, *for all that Archbishop Abbot lives here. No heavenly city here.* Though he knew he might be awed by Canterbury's grandeur, he trembled inwardly for a moment to think that in leaving the Separatists he was effectively handing himself back, body and soul, to the vagaries of the Church of England as represented by Canterbury. For even the godly folk, who could not espouse the divine right of the monarch to rule the church and set up godless bishops over the people, would be subject to the Anglicans as long as they feared to break away and join the Separatists.

John trembled. He no longer belonged to the Separatists, nor did he belong to the Church of England. But if he belonged only to God, how then was he to find freedom of faith in England, since he would not find it, he believed now, with the Pilgrims in America?

Light was failing as they passed the watch at the Westgate and went over the Stour Bridge toward the High Street. The smell of the city breweries and the clatter of late weavers at work in their candlelit cottages came to them clearly in the still air. John looked round with lively interest and forgot the rough flints and cobbles rubbing his raw, blistered feet through his leather boots.

He craned his neck upward. On the sides of St. Peter's Street, jammed as tightly together as skeins of wool in a spinner's basket, houses climbed jetty over jetty, almost tumbling over each other, to second, third, and even fourth stories topped by gables. Vagabonds in rags stood singly on corners waiting for the unwary. Weavers and victuallers in small groups jostled their way down the narrow pavements, all trying to avoid the foul and slippery gutters on their way to an alehouse. Others passed them more thoughtfully, stepping aside though the three strangers were obviously no gentlemen.

Occasionally, John caught the low murmur of a foreign language—not the Dutch he'd grown used to in Leyden, but another tongue. *Flemish or French*, he thought. And these Huguenots with their serious demeanor and skilled work in fine cloth might one day change the English cloth market entirely, reducing forever the importance of wool! A year in Europe had convinced him of that, and he must bring all the influence he could to bear on his father's business before those changes came about.

At the church of St. Alphege, Cushman turned to Brewster. "Sarah and I were wed here, you know."

"Not at the cathedral then?" Brewster asked mildly.

"Shame on you, Brother Brewster," Cushman said with a frown, "Your tongue is full of devilry today."

"God forbid, but a little mirth doth shorten our way."

"Short enough. My wife's parents live but a few yards from this place—in the precincts behind that inn there." He pointed, and John saw a small hostelry, poorly lighted within by candles. "The Mayflower Inn," Cushman added. "'Tis the place appointed for our meeting with Sir Samuel tomorrow, I believe. And yonder we'll find my mother, I trust."

The following day John almost forgot that he would be saying good-bye to Brewster and Cushman within a few hours and returning to Chilham. Against their advice he left them at Widow Cushman's house in the morning and set off to see the weavers' hall and the cathedral.

In the cathedral's towering vaults of golden Caen stone the boys of the Kings' School were practicing an anthem. The sound rose in shafts like the clustered perpendicular columns of the cathedral—in perfect harmony, blended together, smooth and polished. Again he was struck by the ethereal beauty of the place, but as he remembered the squalid narrow lanes and alleys outside, the richness of the tapestries and the colored window glass troubled him, too. How did these speak of God?

When he returned to the Cushman house again, Widow Cushman sent him on to the Mayflower Inn. "That gentleman has arrived from Gravesend," she told him. "You'll find my son at the inn now, with others no doubt." He hurried away, eager to listen to Captain Argall though he would probably never go to Virginia.

Before he entered the inn, he realized how hungry he was. He noticed a pump on the opposite side of the road, where housewives clustered to fill their buckets and jars. Squinting up at the sun, he saw that noon had already passed; he ought to eat and drink. But unwilling to spend his last pennies at the hostelry, he joined the crowd of womenfolk at the pump. They eyed him strangely, their talk ebbing away, but went on filling their buckets in turn before trudging dully away in bands of two or three. He waited patiently, longing to go into the inn, but also longing for water.

The women stepped forward, bent down, and worked the pump. One by one they filled their buckets, swung them up from the tiled pavement beneath, and went away. As if by common consent they made no room for John in their midst. It became a sort of game. One by one they moved away. "Your turn, Leah." "Now you, Lizzie . . . Susannah . . . May. . . ." One by one they nodded to each other, yielding place to one another, but not to him. And he had no cup, either.

The splashing of the clear water on the dusty tiles and the droplets on the women's gowns began to madden him. Still, he hung back, feeling for his purse at his side and thinking, *Drink I must, but perhaps 'tis foolish not to drink at the inn after all.* Then, to his horror, he realized his purse was missing. The leather thongs that usually held it dangled empty from his belt.

He groaned aloud, turning his head quickly to see if he could discover the culprit. No cutpurse here, though. No rogue fleeing away on quick, quiet feet. No, he must have lost it as he went up to the cathedral or down again. He would have to return to Chilham with no more than the surcoat on his back. Angry with himself for not heeding Cushman's warnings, he reconciled himself to thirst and turned to cross toward the Mayflower Inn.

"Pray wait, sir," a woman's voice said.

He swung round quickly to face a young woman as tall as he. Pale, slender, and pretty, with wheat-blonde hair, she was clothed modestly in a clean cap and an unadorned kirtle laced high under her chin and tied with a loose girdle. The fabric was soft, well made, but fraying at the wide wristbands and in need of mending. She held a bucket before her, empty, her two hands clenched white-knuckled round the handles.

"Forgive me, sir." Her brows drew together.

He had to step nearer to hear her voice as she now spoke barely above a whisper. He noticed the slight smell of soap about her, and the tiny lines at the corners of her mouth and eyes. He judged her to be only a year or two older than he. Still sore from his own lack of watchfulness and the loss of his purse, he answered more rudely than he would usually have spoken to a woman. "What? What do you want?"

"Nothing . . . only I saw your distress . . . and my companions' want of kindness." Her voice was soft, free from the distinctive Kentish accent, the speech of a woman brought up in a gentleman's house, perhaps.

John glanced down at her hands again. No wedding ring. Then, ashamed of his discourtesy, he looked back at her solemn face. *She'd wear no ring anyway*, he thought, *if she were one of the godly folk.* He stammered out an apology for his sharp reply.

She shook her head. "Nay, think nothing of it. You've been robbed, and you're athirst." She turned toward the pump, now strangely deserted.

"Let me—" he said, quickly recovering his senses. "Pray let me fill this for you."

"Then you may drink, too." She did not smile.

"I thank you." He worked the pump, aware now that she watched him, not brazenly, but gratefully; for the sun beating down between the houses now created a stifling heat, and beads of sweat had formed on her forehead so that loose strands of hair stuck to it.

When the bucket was full, she handed him a small tin cup that she had pulled from a pocket in the folds of her dress. Dipping it under the stream of water that flowed from the pump, now slowing to a trickle, he filled it and drank greedily.

"You saw the thief, perchance?" he asked when satisfied.

"No . . . only that, as I said, the wives would give you no room."

He nodded, handing back the cup. "Thank you, anyway. A cup of cold water in Christ's name, this was."

Her chin went up quickly, an answering spark in her eyes as he spoke the name of Christ. "You're welcome."

"Who may I say gave it me?"

She hesitated, and he knew he had presumed too far.

"Well," he hazarded, "I shall tell you my own name at least. John. John Fessenden of Chilham."

"And I—" she faltered again, looking round uncertainly as if caught as a thief herself. "Jane Tritton, of Canterbury."

"Farewell then, Jane, of Canterbury." He saluted her, but found with surprise that she followed still close behind him as the crowd of the street closed about them again.

"I lodge with my kinsman, serving as one of his maids. Mr. Tritton, by St. George's." Her voice was still low, but urgent now, the words rushing out.

He stopped again, puzzled by her forwardness and yet certain that it was uncharacteristic, borne of innocence, not coquetry. "I won't forget," he managed.

"God be with you, sir."

Again he steeled himself to move away from the pump square. But this time he saw not the sign of the Mayflower hanging over the door of the inn but the sweet face of Jane Tritton before his mind's eye. As he lifted the latch, glancing round, however, he discovered that she had gone.

If the air had been breathless and hot outside, it was worse within. The oak-panelled walls of the inn seemed to press against him, and the increasingly familiar smell of Virginia tobacco hung heavy in the airless rooms. Startled, he looked round quickly. Had Cushman truly intended this as the meeting place with Argall?

John searched the room again. His eyes, blinded by the brightness of outdoors and by smoke, gradually became accustomed to the dimness. He stood still on the sawdust-covered floor amid the chestnut stools, benches, and tables. Wooden stairs rose into the pipe smoke to his right. Suddenly he realized that the boisterous talk and laughter round him had ceased and that he was as much an object of study to the inhabitants as the inn itself was to him.

"Come here, you pretty fellow," a woman called from one corner.

Through the haze he discerned the robust figure of a girl of no more than eighteen. Smirking, she sat on the knee of a fat knight who wore his hair in lovelocks flowing over an exaggeratedly large white ruff. He was dressed in the flamboyant fashion of Queen Elizabeth's day with bright doublet and slashed sleeves.

"Come here, pray," she repeated, earning a cackle of laughter from all the onlookers.

"Nay, come not near that dangerous wench," a bearded man warned him, thumping his coarse hand on the board so that the ale slopped over. "Not unless you want the French pox."

She raised her fist in mock fury. "I'll see you paid for that!" Then she subsided against the willing knight in peels of laughter.

John recoiled in horror. He had expected an inn, not a bawdyhouse. "Thank you, but you'd pay me no court if you knew I'd just lost all the money I own."

The laughter renewed. "Oh, so have we all!" the drunken knight roared. "To ale, and wenches. So join us, do."

Bewildered, John backed away, thinking he would escape quickly and return to Widow Cushman's. "Nay. I have come to the wrong place."

Another girl sidled past him. "The right place, you mean," she said.

"Oh, look at him. He's one o' them Puritans," the bearded man derided. "No wonder he looks so serious and solemn. Faith, he is in the wrong place, as he said. Too good for the likes of common folk."

John lifted the latch, then heard a scuffle behind him. Turning, he saw the innkeeper in a stained apron burst out of a door at the back of the room. Unceremoniously catching both the girls by the shoulders, he boxed their ears.

"Be gone, you saucy wenches, and let these gentlemen alone." He caught John's eye. "Friend, if you're John Fessenden, the other gentlemen await ye. Pray, come with me." He glowered at his unruly patrons.

John hesitated but then saw that the two women had vanished and that all the men in the room were making a close study of their ale mugs. He stepped back and followed the innkeeper up the stairs.

"I'm sorry, sir, for my daughters. 'Tis vain and idle they are, and never a fine-looking young gentleman like yourself comes a-courting. But that's no surprise, I suppose. Well-a-day, I'll get no honest sons-in-law while I'm an innkeeper, for all I may get grandchildren." He shook his head, still plodding ahead of John, who could scarcely catch his breath before the man continued. "You *are* John Fessenden, I warrant? For 'tis truth, you look like the young gentleman they bade me watch for. Your face is an honest one, and your eyes be"—at the top of the stairs he swung round, breathing heavily in John's face—"blue, as they did say. And you do wear the garb of the plain people. Sir, you *are* John Fessenden?"

Anxious not to be rude, but still wanting to stem the man's garrulousness, John hastily interrupted. "John Fessenden, I am. But no gentleman. A man of Kent, like yourself."

"But you speak like a gentleman, sir, and your garments be finely made, of better stuff than yonder knight below stairs who wastes himself in here by day and year alike." He stopped in the middle of the corridor into which they had passed. "Your place is here, sir, at this door."

Without thinking, John reached for his missing purse.

"Nay, the good Sir Samuel has provided all. I need not your pocket."

Relieved, John thanked him and knocked faintly at the door.

Brewster immediately opened it. "Welcome, John!"

He stepped in, again aware of many eyes on him. But the looks were different this time. No mockery or ribaldry. The men within were all except one dressed like himself in dark surcoats with small white falling bands, their hair cut short and their faces sober and watchful.

The man who stood apart, John thought, must be Sir Samuel Argall. He wore a small immaculately clean ruff—nothing like the knight's ridiculous encumbrance downstairs. Above his grave eyes, neatly trimmed beard and moustache, he wore a Monmouth cap. A sword hung at his side, half-concealed by his cloak. If John had expected rough, weather-worn skin reddened by sea gales, and the bowlegs always attributed to sailors by envious landlubbers, he was disappointed. The man instead had about him an air of self-possessed refinement, even aloofness, a cool but not forbidding dignity. His skin was tanned but not rough, his hands sinewy but not coarse.

In turn Sir Samuel's eyes traveled over John. He stood still under their cool scrutiny, waiting for him to speak.

"Find a stool, lad. Your friends have been at their prayers till now."

Prayers? Was Sir Samuel joking?

"For our venture." Cushman explained.

"And for you, too," Brewster added. We thought you'd fallen to some band of cutthroats by now."

Plainly, Brewster—not Sir Samuel—was joking.

"No, sir, but a cutpurse. I fear I should have heeded your warnings." He showed them the loose purse straps.

The men murmured in sympathy, but Brewster continued. "Well, never mind, John. We'll mend it presently. Come, we waited for you. Sir Samuel has been telling us a little of the progress in Massachusetts Bay, but we wanted you to hear about the journey of the folk from Amsterdam, so he has put off that part of his tale."

John pulled up a stool next to Brewster's and looked up at Argall, whose face had taken on a pained expression.

"Like you," Argall said, turning his head slowly to be sure of his whole audience, "those good people were anxious to go." His face darkened. "But, listen well, and learn of what I'll tell you now. Get a sturdy ship, and sail in the spring—or better yet, the summer—and be certain you're working with an honest man." He held up his fingers, counting off the three points as he made them. "The Amsterdam Church contracted with one Francis Blackwell. You've heard his name, perhaps?"

A few heads bowed in response.

"Aye, black indeed, his name is to me. He it was who was to take the last of the Ancient Church to Virginia. The ship was to sail from Gravesend, and when the emigrants saw that ship, they groaned aloud"—he stopped, smiling slightly—"like the children of Israel going into captivity. That ship was never meant to carry a hundred and eighty souls. The women on the quays, both travelers and their families, fell to weeping and lamenting, every one. The men grew angry, but Blackwell determined to see them all aboard and therewithal line his pockets." He cleared his throat. "But he lined his own coffin, instead. And others' too."

John bit his lip. Brewster, Cushman, and he had come with no inkling that Sir Samuel brought anything but good news. Argall had returned safely himself, after all. Could the crossing be as terrible as he suggested?

"'Twas folly, in the first place, to leave in September. Mark well, and if you go not by July, wait until the following year. When the ship left the estuary, even then she was low in the water, listing not a little. One of the men who reached Virginia told me he feared for their lives even in the very Straits of Dover.

"But things grew worse." Argall emphasized his words. "They met squalls and gales the hour they left the sight of land. The waves were mighty and the skies dark, so the master—he was Captain Maggner—lost direction. The boat went south of its intended course, they thought, and drifted day after day. The mast cracked, and the ship wallowed in the waves, drifting aimlessly till all feared they would go down. The crew was worked to the marrow, and the supplies began to fail. 'Twas then that many died. The frost, the hunger, and thirst—'twas all more than many could endure— and Maggner and Blackwell died with them."

Argall's listeners groaned. John found himself recoiling from the horror. He wanted to withdraw, turn away, and go back to Chilham. Surely, surely, crossing this terror of a winter ocean could not be within the will of God? Surely not within the will of God for him.

Argall had again paused. John wondered fleetingly if the man's expressive face, gestures, and habit of pausing were for dramatic effect. But as he looked at those eyes burning in indignation and heard the cold harshness of his voice, he doubted it.

"One hundred and eighty souls, I said," Argall grated out, "and one hundred and thirty perished. Buried at sea, all of them, in the tumult of the waves."

John thought of the Psalms, all of which he had memorized at his mother's insistence years before. "*The floods have lifted up, O LORD, the floods have lifted up their voice; the floods lift up their waves.*" He shivered.

"Fifty made landfall in March of this year of our Lord. Just before I left, they sailed in. I know not if all those fifty be alive or how they prosper. My own crossing was smooth and easy. Three months, not six, and a hearty crew. Would I could have captained another ship to bring all safely to America—in the summer."

The room fell silent. Argall stood with his head bowed and his hands clasped out of sight under his cloak. John glanced quickly at Brewster's face to see his cheeks wet with tears; then he looked down at the wide beams in the floor. *"The LORD on high is mightier than the noise of many waters, yea, than the mighty waves of the sea."* . . . *Yet I can never go with them. I want to stay in England, trade in cloth, and get a wife.*

Jane Tritton's face swam before him, her luminous eyes, blue as the Venetian glass he'd seen in Leyden. He tried to blink away her image—a chance encounter in a public watering place—but the dark oak wood floor seemed awash in swirling, luminous blue. Massachusetts Bay would have to wait this crossing.

Chilham, Autumn 1620

Robert

Ruth Fessenden had died in childbed in early January. Never having called a midwife for the other births, she had refused to allow her husband to call one this time. "Foolish, superstitious old women," she declared, turning her stony face to the wall as another wave of pain swept through her body.

Helpless, Fessenden knelt at the foot of the bed and cried out to God. His prayers and her pain went on for two nights; then on the third morning she gave birth to a daughter—dead. Fessenden locked the other children out of the room, for he expected his wife to rally as she had done before. White and dazed, however, she died in a violent hemorrhage that left him stricken with amazement and sorrow.

Life in the household changed. When the mother and child were laid next to the other dead children in the churchyard and visits of mourners had ceased, Fessenden lost direction for a while. He drifted aimlessly in and out of the house, in and out of the cottages of his weavers and spinners, back and forth to the staple.

Martha tried to take over her mother's tasks, but she was not wise enough for them and fell into hysterical anxiety each time Isaac crossed her or the supper burned or congealed. The brothers saw now how much their father had depended on their mother, their anchor. The family listed, but did not yet founder. John became his father's main mast, and Robert his inexperienced navigator.

Lady Digges, hearing of Ruth's death, called several times at the cottage with baskets of bread, cakes, and ale, and bundles of clothing for the children. Then, seeing that the family was more self-sufficient and prosperous than all the other yeomen families in the parish and not likely to sue to the poor houses for relief, she came no more. Instead, John took it upon himself to go to the castle for advice on domestic servants.

He told Robert he almost expected Sir Dudley to send a steward with a rebuff for the impertinence of his questions; instead, Sir Dudley himself met him courteously in one of the anterooms. Genuinely moved, he offered to help in any way he could. There was not talk of the inappropriateness of a yeoman's family looking for a maid or housekeeper. Sir Dudley inquired after the clothier's business and the other children as well. He then recommended several young women to the Fessendens' service.

The choice rested finally on Widow Snode, a woman of thirty from Boughton Aluph. Her husband, Christopher, had once served as a falconer for Sir Dudley but had recently been killed in the German war. Childless, Mary Snode delighted in the children. Though she never neglected Fessenden and the two older sons, she devoted most of her time to the younger children. As a result, they followed her round the house and the garden, never tiring of hearing her sing or instruct them, and she apparently never tiring of doing so.

Fessenden leaned increasingly on his sons for support. No longer was he suspicious of John's advice on the new textiles. No longer did he resist ventures into the manufacture and sale of cloth and garments for which he himself was not entirely responsible. And no longer was Robert a mere child to be sent on trivial errands. With John, Robert had become his father's factor.

While John oversaw changes in his father's business—for example, the use of some foreign weavers in Canterbury for the first time, and the production of new draperies—Robert rode farther and farther afield on the bay mare his father had given him and took over most of the purchasing from staplers, threadmakers, and weavers.

Robert came to love the freedom of his new job: the early morning rides to Cranbrook to see a wool broker, to Canterbury to purchase bolts of baize and flannel made to order by the Flemings and silks from the Huguenots (though for some reason John always begged to do the Canterbury work), even to London to act as an agent for his father with some particularly important customer. He learned to appreciate the warmth of the Belgian flannels, the fine softness of the Huguenot silks, and the sturdy durability of English broadcloth made locally by their own weavers.

New draperies sold well for them, but so did the traditional woolens. The Fessenden seal on a bolt of cloth began to acquire greater reputation. At first, Robert was surprised. Hadn't his brother said on return from Holland that the English wool market was in decline? Hadn't his father spoken grimly of the wool-trade recession a thin five years before, and of the growing superiority of Dutch fabric finishing? Still, they had produced and sold more cloth in the last twelvemonth than ever before, and the weavers and fullers could hardly keep up with the demand.

"'Tis the mixture that gives our cloth its strength," John maintained. "Buy all your wool from one market and your garments may look well for a month or two, but they won't last, and they won't hold their color. That's why you and I have to be alert all the time. We must insist on the short-staple wool fibers of our reliable fullers. But we've also to find new ways of making stronger thread out of finer wool. Softness isn't everything, yet we can't afford to ignore the new stuffs or the market's demand for them. That's the way we'll keep our trade up."

Family councils between father and sons became common—sometimes into the late evening hours when the younger children and Mary had retired to their chambers—even when John expected to be gone to Canterbury all the next day or Robert to one of the Cinque Ports to examine imported cloths.

They held such a council one night in the late autumn. Mary, unobtrusive as usual, had put away her mending as soon as light failed, and without so much as a good night she had left the three men by the hearth. They heard her upstairs settling the children: the shrill demands of Esther or Abigail for another kiss, the scamper of Isaac's feet overhead as he jumped out of his covers insisting on another lullaby or prayer, and finally the creak of the bed as Mary herself put out the candle in her narrow bedroom, once a storeroom, over the front of the house.

Fessenden raised his eyes toward the beams. "Widow Snode's a good woman, but those children are getting beyond themselves. Your mother—"

"They're happy again, Father," John cut in. "Let well enough alone. We should thank Providence for Mother Mary."

"Your mother would turn in her grave if she knew the goings-on."

"Maybe, maybe not," John replied. Robert threw him a quick glance. "Mother had far too much to do when we were little. She did the work of two women."

"Aye, we'll not replace her. No more fine bacons or hearth swept spotless every day."

Robert nodded in vigorous agreement.

John grew bold. "Nay, but Mary finds more time for the little ones, and they're thriving. She's grand, Father, and never a word of bothering to us.

Why, if you forgot her twelve pound a year for months on end, she'd never say a word."

"The more fool Widow Snode, then," Fessenden grunted. "But this is vain chatter, John, and you need your bed if you're to be up at daybreak. But I have yet business with you, Robert my lad."

Robert, who had been lulled by the casual drift of the conversation, jerked forward. He noticed his brother's mouth turn up at the corners as if he were party to what was to come. But then the room fell still, and his father's brown eyes focused on his intently. He gulped, managing only a faint, "What is't?" Something important was going to be said, and it concerned him.

"I've been pleased with all you've done for me, Robert. You've shown good judgment. You've grown in confidence in your own abilities, and rightly. You're only fifteen, I know, but you're a man in my eyes now."

Robert sat up, brightening with pride.

"I know how much you've wanted to work more independently. John's told me you even longed to take the place he might have had with the Pilgrims and sail on *The Mayflower* this September." He broke off, smiling. "Though only heaven knows where those souls are by now, and I'm glad you're with us, not away with them. But I want to give you a chance to set out on your own a bit."

What was his father saying? Was he going to suggest that Robert go to the remaining Pilgrims in Leyden or London as his brother had done, and study for himself the ways of the European craftsmen? Or was he to set up a shop for his father—perhaps in Canterbury, where John liked to spend his time? He watched his father's face intently for a clue. The answer came immediately.

"You'll go to Maidstone and lodge there a while—as a trial—to see how you get on." Fessenden glanced at John, then back at Robert. "Your brother has a notion that Maidstone's going to become more important than it is at present. And he thinks someone in the family should be there. Then there are the mills at Loose to oversee—you'd be right handy for those—and that'd take a worry off me." He leaned back, resting his palms on his knees. "There now, what do you think of my plan?"

Robert opened his mouth and laughed breathlessly. "Sir, I hardly know—"

"You look as winded as if you fell off a horse," John teased.

"No—" Robert smiled back at his brother's dry expression. "I think I just found myself mounted on one that's galloping away with me."

Fessenden smiled, but there was no humor in his eyes. "A very pretty conceit, boys. But I want to know what you think, in truth. Your mother'd never forgive me if I sent you off before you were ready. Younger boys than you, though, have gone to sea and done battle, and you're wiser than most. Speak up, now."

"I'm fair speechless."

"But he's your man, aren't you, Robert?" John prompted.

"Aye, Father. I'd like to do it."

Fessenden reached out and put a dish under the candle to catch the tallow that began to drop and spill onto the board. "Then let me explain," he began thoughtfully. "When you were just a lad—I mean about five years ago when the trade was falling off and we were all worried about it—there was a move afoot in London to stop all exporting of unfinished cloth, especially cloth that went to Amsterdam. Some of the gentry thought they knew more about the trade than we do, and they said all the money was to be made in dyeing and finishing, and even though only the Dutch could do it properly, they would still insist the cloth be kept in England for finishing. John, you'll pardon me, for I know we differ here, but they forgot that the English made the best cloth in Europe."

He laughed scornfully. "The gentry lost pride in their own weavers and ranted and raved at their own dyers." He grimaced. "Treating the men that way didn't work. English wool profits didn't increase, and English dyers were no more and no less skilled than ever. They were going at it backwards. You can't change the quality of a whole bolt of cloth by finding fault with one thread in the warp, and neither can you make the English wool trade the best in Europe by shunning the Dutch or by refusing to train the English craftsmen properly. So I think it's time we did something in our own little corner of the trade, time we took our best dyer and gave him some journeymen—Maidstone men—and did more of our dyeing at Loose. What do you think?"

Robert shifted nervously. "But I know nothing of dyeing and fulling, sir."

His father nodded. "But you can learn. You're quick-witted enough. If your grandfather could full the cloth by trampling it with his own feet, and if I could full it with my own hands at the mill, then you can learn to do it—or at least oversee it—yourself."

Robert watched his father carefully, containing his enthusiasm as he caught the unintended exaggeration of his father's argument. His grandfather had certainly worked in the days when fullers had laid their cloth in troughs and walked on it until matted together in the soap and fuller's earth, but his grandfather had been a weaver, not a finisher of cloth. In the same way, his father may have been a journeyman at Loose for a short time, but with all the modern equipment the fullers used, surely his father had never turned the wheels by his own effort.

"I'll learn as much as I can, sir, and willingly," he said.

"That's right, son. I knew you would. It'll give you the chance to work even more on your own and see more of the country. Well, then, it's settled. You'll start on Tuesday. We'll travel to Maidstone the day after the Lord's day, and we'll see you lodged there and your horse stabled—"

"But won't it cost too much?" Robert began to frown, biting his lip, the doubts trickling back.

Fessenden's mouth twitched. "You'll more than earn your keep."

"But where shall I stay?"

"A wise question, lad, and I've given it much thought. I met a victualler there not long ago, an upright man, once from Goudhurst. He was a landman there, but restless, and felt Providence wanted him in a town where he could preach to more souls. Peter Longhurst by name."

Robert frowned. "A blackcoat, sir?"

"Nay, not a priest. But he preaches in the open air. His shop supports him now, but some squire or other helped him start. He's a man of our sort, Robert—pious, God-fearing, a yeoman. He'll treat you as a son."

Robert was pleased though he remained silent.

"We'll go early and inquire until we find him," his father concluded. "Away with you now to bed. I've a word or two for John, as well."

John

John's mouth dried as his father turned toward him questioningly. He stumbled over the secrets of the past year and found himself blundering on as he had blundered through the streets of Canterbury almost a year before.

Careless of his surroundings, he had walked right before a horse so that the animal reared up and the carter flashed out with the whip, cursing both John and the horse.

After that, shaken, he tried to gather his wits and attend to where he was going. He spoke to the Huguenots about the next parcels of silks his father intended to purchase from them, but the conversation was halting, made slow by the lack of a common tongue. Hence he arrived too late at the weavers' hall and missed the master weaver he had wanted to meet.

Now, three months since his last time at Canterbury, he wanted only to find Jane Tritton, not that he had any formed idea what he would say or do when he found her. Her eyes, her face had faded to a spectral memory, half dream. He remembered more clearly, however, what she had told him. "*I lodge with my kinsman, serving as one of his maids. Mr. Tritton, by St. George's.*" He remembered, too, the urgent sound of her voice as she pressed after him in the crowd, and the sense of certainty he'd felt about her. "*This is the way, walk ye in it.*" He must find her.

But what if she were a sorceress? What if she had bewitched him with her brilliant eyes, convincing him falsely of her purity and sweetness? What if she, older than he, were wiser in the world's arts? What if she herself had stolen his purse, then mocked him afterward to her friends as a fool and a gull?

Then he remembered the cup of cold water, the kindling in her eyes as he spoke the name of Christ. No, surely she could not fabricate that.

The clock tower of St. George's tolled the hour. He stood uncertainly at the foot of the tower and looked round in the twilight. Laborers were leaving their work for home. He panicked. Why hadn't he tried to find her at noon, in daylight? Ah, but he had done all he could in Canterbury, and he could hardly have tried to find her first. No, he would find her if the Lord willed it.

He stopped a passerby first. "Will you tell me, pray, where a Mr. Tritton lives, somewhere hereabouts?"

The man rewarded him with a sly, derisive look. "Nay, no such in St. George's parish as I know of." The man walked off without a backward glance.

John thought of inquiring at an alehouse next. However, remembering his discomfort in the Mayflower Inn, he thought better of it and turned round to face the church. *If her kinsmen be near the church, no doubt they could tell me at the rectory where Mr. Tritton lives.*

Under the brick arch next to the churchyard stood an iron gate, and a path led to the rectory. Having pushed open the iron gate, he ran up the pathway to lift the door knocker.

He was still catching his breath with nervous excitement about his nearness to Jane when she herself opened the door.

Shock, disbelief, joy—a multitude of feelings surged through him and left him hardly able to speak. Taking off his felt hat, he looked up into the same blue eyes that had looked up at him in his dreams for three months. He gazed into the same face he had seen in the flesh only once and had not clearly remembered: a face now far more open, sweet, and beautiful than the one he had pictured.

The color came and went from the girl's cheeks as he stared up to where she stood with one hand on the lintel and the other on the door. Plainly, she remembered him, too.

Perhaps only a few seconds had passed, but to John it seemed longer before he was able to stammer out a few words. At last, he said, "Miss Tritton, I was coming here to see if I could find you. I didn't expect—"

Laughter creased the corners of her eyes. "To find me here?"

Was she scorning him? John met her eyes doubtfully. "No, indeed, I came here to find Mr. Tritton, your kinsman. I thought the rector would know where I might find him."

He floundered, at sea in the blue of her eyes. She stood with the warmth and light of the hall (or was it a parlor?) behind her, apparently enjoying his bemusement as he stood in the damp twilight. But he was not to be dissuaded by her mysterious smile. See her he would, and her kinsman as well. Recovering, he said, "Then, pray, let me speak with him if he is in." He tried to sound authoritative, more self-possessed than he felt.

His tone of voice evidently made some impression. Her teasing smile gave way to anxiety, the same pleading expression he remembered at the crowded pump opposite the inn. She backed away from the doorway, hovering within.

"Then you've not . . . you've come to see my uncle?"

He ascended to the top step so that the slight advantage of his height showed. "Nay, you know that's not it. I came to see you." He took a deep breath, struggling to keep the fear out of his voice and to assume the same lightheartedness she had just forsaken. "But since this is your uncle's house and he is a man of the cloth, I suppose I must see him first."

"And what—?" Her eyes were suddenly lambent, full of hope.

"Did you think I would forget, then?"

"Nay . . . yes . . . I know not."

He laughed. "Pray, let me speak with your uncle. Treat me as you would any of his visitors. 'Tis better that way."

She hesitated, her hand to her hair in a quick gesture of self-awareness. "Truly? Then come this way, pray." She held the door wider so that he could pass her and enter the house. "He's at his supper. I'll wait on him and bring him to you if he will." Her face fell suddenly, as if she would add something—a word of warning, perhaps. Instead, she left him silently in a small room lined with books, left him there to stare at the empty grate.

He studied the shelves to blunt the apprehension that had frozen his hands and dried his mouth. Perhaps the bookshelves would yield a clue to Reverend Tritton's personality and theological leanings. If he were a high churchman, John realized with a chill of foreboding, that might suggest that Jane herself was not one of the godly folk and that her uncle would be cold toward any addresses to his niece.

Was that what he had come for, then? To pay court to a young woman he had met once in a public place? A woman he knew nothing of save her address and name? What else! And if not, then for what reason had he come to search for her, and what could he say to her uncle? *Sir, I met your niece at Canterbury in the summer. . . . Confound your insolence, you young pup! What mean you, "met my niece," pray? Or this? Sir, I beg your leave to woo Miss Tritton. . . . Which Miss Tritton, pray? Helen is already betrothed, and Rachel is too young. . . . Oh no, sir. I mean your niece, Miss Jane. . . . But that's preposterous! Our maid? Why she's . . ."* His mind clamped down on that last thought. Married already? Betrothed? Promised? He could not bear it.

Well, he would say whatever the Spirit prompted him to say when he had taken Reverend Tritton's measure. He forced himself to look at the books. He knew hardly any of them and could pronounce even fewer of the titles. Ovid—*Metamorphoses*. The works of Chaucer, Tottel's *Miscellany*. The plays of Ben Jonson. The works of Richard Hooker, and St. Augustine, Virgil, and Sir Philip Sidney. Now there was a name he knew. Didn't the Sidney family live in a splendid castle of a house at Penshurst? But who were the others? And why was there no Bible? Lancelot Andrewes, Aristotle . . .

Absorbed in reading and thought, he had forgotten for the moment the reason he would not reach Chilham before midnight, the reason he had come at all, the reason he was waiting in this never-to-be-forgotten room. Then the double doors opened. He swung round and saw Jane first. Keeping her eyes carefully averted, she murmured, "Mr. John Fessenden to see you."

Then John came face to face with William Tritton.

The man was powerfully built with wide shoulders over which hung long, fashionably curled hair. His eyes were the same deep, Venetian blue as Jane's, though shadowed by thick eyebrows and a savage beak of a nose. But while his face conveyed shrewdness, even coldness, his dress seemed to gainsay it. Out of his top pocket protruded a crumpled kerchief—good linen, but soiled. His black clerical coat was darned and patched, his shoes shabby. His was the dress of a man who thought appearance of no significance whatever; the dress of a vague, otherworldly man?

"You wanted to speak with me, Mr. Fessenden? I beg your pardon, but I believe we are not acquainted." A cultured, genteel voice, deferring, yet not obsequious. And his face—watchful, perhaps even a little suspicious, the eyes darting up and down in assessment over John's plain, travel-soiled broadcloths. But his words were courteous, at least—intended, seemingly, to put him at ease. Perhaps he anticipated a new parishioner, or a man in want of a priest to read the banns and perform a wedding.

John collected himself. "Thank you, sir. No, we are not acquainted. My father is John Fessenden, a clothier of Chilham. We do business with some of your Canterbury weavers." He broke off, unsure, but then decided to press on. "The Strangers, that is."

"Ah—" The rector's lips curled in obvious distaste. "Yes, strange ones indeed, foreigners who hold aloof from divine service in all of Canterbury and meet for some strange ritual of their own." His chin went up abruptly, and John saw the expression of a man who might be proud, intolerant. "But now, I was supping. How may I be of service to you?"

How may he be of service to me? John echoed mentally. *He asks that as if wanting to know how I may serve him!* He fidgeted with the hat in his hand. "I'm sorry, sir, to interrupt you. Truth to tell, I've come to beg your leave to woo your niece, Miss Tritton."

The rector turned sharply and moved toward the door. "Have you indeed?" His voice was cold, satirical. "Then you should never have come. Jane is but a poor simpleton. She's your senior—that I can tell by looking at your smooth face." He paused, all inner hostility now unveiled. "And I give her no dowry. In short, she is here to serve our family since my brother died in penury for his fantastical Puritan notions of preaching to the poor and bailing them out of debtors' prison. But I need say no more. 'Twas I redeemed his debts and took his orphaned daughter as a servant. 'Twas the understanding when he died."

John's temper rose. "Then she's no more than a slave to you?"

The rector's face turned cruel. "And what else would she be to a husband, pray?"

For a moment he blenched, misunderstanding the words completely. No, of course she was not married to her own uncle. No, Tritton meant something else. "Not if she were *my* wife," John began hotly. "I'll have no slave. And if it's money you want to free her from her servitude and your bond, then it's money you'll have."

The rector was apparently struck by the forcefulness of John's convictions. He hesitated, but only briefly, for his huge hand crashed down on the nearest shelf. Two books fell to the floor, and all the shelves shook. "Be gone. You're an idiotic dreamer. Jane has a soft life with us. After her father's foolishness, she'll want no Puritan for a mate, and she'll never marry anyway. Neither cleric, nor gentleman—nor yeoman."

John stood his ground, narrowing his eyes. "You say Miss Tritton's my senior, and I doubt it not. But that makes little difference. She's an honest maid, and true—that much I know. And as she's of age, she may decide."

"Not Jane. She abides here."

John's blood ran hot with indignation. He wanted to strike the man. A man of God? "She *shall* decide, I say." Immediately he knew what he must do.

He strode to the end of the room, risking and prepared for a blow from Tritton as he passed, but trusting in the thin hope that the rector might expect him to be leaving the house.

Flinging open the double doors, he called out for her at the top of his lungs. "Jane—Miss Tritton!" His voice rang up the curved staircase and through the hall.

From behind, Tritton caught his arm in a grip of shuddering brutality and twisted it backward. "You blackguard! I'll see you whipped and pilloried for this. Get out of my house!"

Bent double under the rector's weight and the torment of the ligaments in his shoulder, John looked to another doorway at the far end of the hall and saw Jane half-concealed behind the door. Though scarcely acquainted with her, he knew she was shaking in fear and anguish. He cried out for her again as Tritton began wrestling him toward the front door.

Then he caught sight of her over his shoulder. Coming out of hiding, she gestured frantically to him, her left hand down in a fist, and her right arm swinging up and down at the elbow and shoulder in a movement he could make no sense of. It was just a glimpse—her arms signaling and her face pleading—then Tritton jerked open the front door and John was teetering on the top step, no longer able to see her.

"I'll have the constables on you. What sort of a raving, ill-bred lout are you to brazen in here and shout out like—"

Beside himself, John lunged backward with his boot, but to no avail. He shouted for the last time, "Jane I've come to—"

Tritton cut him off with a vicious twist from behind. "What, you weakling! Think you that trembling wench'll rescue you? Nay, she's wiser than you. If she come a step nearer, she'll be beaten, and she knows it." He hurled John down the steps. Then, hair askew, he stared down as John staggered to his feet in dull amazement. The door slammed so hard that the echo clapped back from the church and from the houses on the other side of the road. And it still echoed in John's head a year later.

"I'm certain of her, sir." John stared at the yellow-white flame of the candle and thought of Jane's hair. "I know it sounds absurd. I know I should never have gone as far as I did, and I'm ashamed of the way I lost my temper."

Fessenden answered his oldest son's look of despair with a look of compassion. "Young blood," he muttered. "Hot blood." He sighed. "Thank God I never had to woo your mother with a pike or musket in my hands. 'Twas all arranged when we were in our cradles."

John only nodded. He saw his father's eyes mist over but did not want him to lose the thread of their conversation.

"And all this happened a year ago, you say?"

"Yes. Almost to the day."

His father let out a small, tight laugh. "The man was right. You're a dreamer, John, and always were."

John looked down in disappointment and shame. Was his father going to offer no more counsel than this?

"But dreams that last so long acquire a substance. And I've seen your other dreams at work this twelvemonth."

John blinked a puzzled response.

"Your plans for our draperies. Your dreams of better weavers and dyers. . . ."

"Oh, those—?"

Fessenden's hand touched John's shoulder in a rare display of pride and affection. "Yes, those. And if those dreams prove substantial, you're not the madman he took you for. This, too, may prove substantial." His look suddenly became penetrating. "You're sure she's maid, not kept woman?"

John flushed darkly. "Never a kept woman, sir. I know it in my soul."

"So you've seen this maid again, have you?" His father was smiling again, his face softening. "Risked yourself to see her every time you went to Canterbury? Small wonder you journeyed there more oft this year than I in a lifetime."

John returned the smile, relieved that his father seemed to understand. "Aye, I've seen her several times—at a distance. But she's never seen me, until today, though I've learned her times for going in and out." He flushed again under further scrutiny. "I was near the Mayflower Inn again, passing the pump where I first saw her, and I suddenly realized what she meant that day when she was waving her arms at me. All this year she's waited and hoped to see me at that same place."

"At the pump? Poor lass, with a lover too dull to know what she meant."

John was surprised by his father's levity. Irritated, he said, "'Tis of no consequence now. No one takes account of a maid drawing water with a crowd of others and passing the time of day with a traveler who's nearby."

Inwardly he shook with excitement as he remembered it. He wanted to throw himself at her feet and beg forgiveness for the year that had elapsed. He wanted to flout all that his mother had taught him about courtesy and press his mouth onto hers in the middle of the road, then and there.

"You spoke to her, then?"

John nodded. "Aye. Told her I wanted no other, and would she consent to be my wife if we could find a way round that dragon who lives under the nose of St. George without being vanquished—"

His father burst out laughing but instantly became sober again. "That's a popish, pagan tale, son. Apt for nothing."

"I'm sorry."

His father heaved a deep sigh. "But something must be done, I see."

"Aye, but what? I dare not endanger her. She's not as hearty as she was, and paler."

"You think her ill used?"

He shook his head. "I doubt it. Her uncle's too public a man for that."

"It's happened before. Blackcoats be not immune to beating women and children."

"Not Jane, pray God—"

"Miss Tritton, son."

"Aye, Miss Tritton."

"Well, I hope you're right." His father fell silent for a short time. Then he continued, "And her knowledge of God, my boy? Think you she knows aught, dwelling in a benighted house? Could she accept our ways, do you think?"

John's reply came back in a rush. "Aye, I'm certain of it. If her father was a godly—"

"Salvation's not inherited, John."

"Nay, but . . . her face when I spoke of the Lord . . . and when I told her today that we were godly folk. If she's been with her uncle these many years, she's untaught, maybe, but not against us."

Fessenden shut his eyes, his brow furrowed in thought, and John waited anxiously. "We know too little about Miss Tritton for my liking," he said at last. "And yet there's something about what you've told me that rings true. If I were guided by my baser impulses, I'd say we should endeavor to talk further with this gentleman. But I must seek the Lord first. And John, you're young. Very young. Most lads your age these days aren't thinking of marriage yet."

"I know I'm young." He met his father's eyes steadily. "But two years ago I was not too young to go to Leyden for a year. And now I'm not too young to work for you as any man of thirty would."

"Nay, better." Fessenden sighed deeply once again. "'Tis true. True." Then, tremulously, "I'm sending Robert away, too. You knew that I planned it, and yet you said nothing to me about your hope of a wife until now? Would you have left me here alone with the children?"

John frowned, surprised at the new undertone of sadness, the sudden hint of his father's own loneliness. "Forgive me, sir. What could I say to you until I had seen Miss Tritton again? But . . . if it would come to pass that we be wed, then . . . I'd not think of leaving here. I want to serve you. You know that. The new world—I couldn't take a wife there. Not yet, anyway. And I wouldn't go there now." He held his father's eyes with his own. "I belong here. I want to stay here, Father."

The heaviness in his father's face lifted again. "If that be so, son, then unless the Lord counsels against it, I shall see Mr. Tritton myself. It shall be done." He smiled. "And I'll see this paragon of sweetness and beauty, too—to be sure—before I agree to any match."

"Sir, I'm twenty."

"Twenty, not twenty-one."

John made a slight noise of exasperation, then caught a glint in his father's eye. "You'll like her, sir, no doubt wish you'd seen her first."

Fessenden grunted. "Not I! What you see with the eye, 'tis but the appearance." His face turned wistful again. "No, I'll not find another like your mother."

Masking his excitement about his father's decision to help him, he tried to mirror the change in mood. "Nay, but you ought to marry again."

His father turned away. "Who'd have me, pray?" He bent to stir the fire, his face hidden. "An aging man with six children?"

"Four now, with the eldest girls gone. And thou'rt not old."

"Four, then."

"I know who'd have thee, Father," John said slyly.

"Only the Lord knows that," Fessenden scoffed. "I'll give you counsel, John, but I'll none of yours, I thank 'ee."

May 1621

Robert

Robert slowed the mare to a walk. He felt no inclination to hurry along the Loose Road today. In the short time it took him once a week to travel the lanes between Maidstone and Loose he enjoyed rare moments of peace that were generally crushed out of his life. At least out-of-doors he could observe the changes in creation: the subtle shortening of the shadows; the flutter of nest-building birds in the high hedgerows of holly, cobnut, ivy, bramble, elderflower, and privet; the lazy movements of the sheep under the apple trees; the scent of the apple blossoms; the vivid uncurling of the sweet chestnut leaves. Not that Chilham had not beauty to show beyond its stiles and along its footpaths, but until now, he'd never had the inclination to study it.

From his vantage point on horseback he could see over some of the shorter banks into the orchards. Clouds of blossoms foamed on the trees, pink and white, though soon they would be shaken down, bruised, and trampled into disappearance. The freshness of the colors—the arc of sky above the hedgerows, blue as the chalk moths that flew in the summer on the Downs; the pinks and whites of the petals and the faint green-gold spikes of young grain—all made him think suddenly of his brother's bride.

John had married in April. Their father had gone to Canterbury on John's behalf more than once to see the Reverend Tritton. Apparently struck by Fessenden's forcefulness—a will equal to if very different from his own—the Old Dragon (as John insisted on calling him, to his father's dismay) had finally been persuaded by the clothier to relent and release Jane to marry. Privately, John had told Robert that he doubted whether it was their father's persistence as much as his means that had finally won Jane away. The Fessendens, not the Trittons, had given her a dowry.

Until the two were married Robert had given little thought to women: a distant species who, like his mother, worked unceasingly; or like Mary, busied themselves with the children all day long; or like his sisters, always talked or played or interrupted the menfolk; or like that wench in the castle, were saucy and wicked. Women might be human, he decided, but not people one deliberately chose to live with for the rest of one's life. In general, they were creatures one might almost discount.

And yet Jane belonged in different company. He could see what had drawn his brother to her. Even in the sober blue dress and high white standingband she wore on their wedding day, she looked as beautiful as a pagan princess of corn. His mouth twisted. John would not be flattered by the comparison. A pagan, indeed!

But that wheat-gold hair tumbling from her cap, those eyes like cornflowers in a wheat field, that skin as perfect as the apple blossom petals before they fell. A rare beauty. He found her puzzling, a creature to idealize, not a woman like dull Widow Snode to mend and cook and teach the children at the kitchen table. And yet . . . she was not fairy or enchantress, after all.

He knew now, after a few days at home since the wedding, that Jane did as much as the widow to help his father and the children. Between the two women, all the work of Ruth Fessenden went on. Not, however, in a dreary, drudging way anymore, but with laughter striking out like sparks in the old forge at Chilham between the eyes of lovers.

He looked up suddenly and fancied he saw Jane's face in the apple blossoms over the hedge. Suddenly his jaw set hard. He knew the taste of jealousy.

His thoughts turned to *The Mayflower*, which had reached America in November. Stories had already returned of the horrors of the journey—the stench and dampness below deck, the storms that rolled and pitched the boat like flotsam in the troughs and crests of the waves, the narrow escape from disaster when one of the ship's main beams cracked. . . . Could John have endured the plague and fever that claimed many of the lives the seas had not.

Had his brother married before, could Jane have endured that journey? No, it was unthinkable. Thank God they were both in England! He hated to imagine Jane in the dark, foul hold of a ship, flung through the waves in the grip of winds that shrieked like dead spirits escaped from hell. Thank God they had never gone to America with the Pilgrims!

But what of himself? What if Jane were his? And how would he have fared, had he fallen in with the Pilgrims—Brewster and Carver, Winslow and Bradford—all the men of which his brother had spoken? He could not imagine Massachusetts Bay, nor could he imagine himself in that settlement. Not that he had lost hope of seeing America for himself one day, but for now it seemed entirely remote. *As remote as Jane*, he thought bitterly. He would never be anything to her but a younger brother.

Instead, life was tied to things much more concrete, present, and mundane. In Maidstone: the clatter of carts, the shouts of vendors, the chiming of bells and clocks, the noise of the pretty Longhurst children below stairs, and the long-winded stories of Mistress Longhurst, his landlord's wife, about her husband's patron, the older Squire George Tolhurst. In Loose: the rhythmic pounding of mallets and the splash of water in the troughs. At the staple: the bleating of sheep and the haggling of men. All these were what made up his life now, and though they gave him no peace, they satisfied him in many ways.

The road dropped downhill now, with higher hedges and the sound of rushing water beyond them. One of his father's mills lay ahead; he could see the white-washed clapboard exterior against its background of early summer greens. Then, a few moments later, the rush of the stream could no longer be heard, replaced now by the pounding within the mill.

Outside the mill, he dismounted and led his horse into an adjacent field to crop the grass. He shut the gate behind him, climbed up the outside steps, and stopped to enter the mill's low doorway.

Immediately, the master fuller was beside him, knowing Robert's usual arrival time, and doubtless having expected him for some time already. His coarse apron and the sleeves of his smock were permanently bleached by the chalky earth he worked with every day. He looked at Robert warmly. "You're here, then, son."

Because Robert liked the man he did not resent the indulgent tone he always used. "Aye," he said. "'Twas such a blithe day."

"To be sure." The fuller winked. "But what would your father say if 'twere one of my apprentices getting here three hours past the cock's crow?"

Robert was used to the teasing, but he could not laugh. Within the hour he would change from the son of the master to a clumsy apprentice, shoulder to shoulder with the others at the trough. "Ah, but his apprentices don't ride all the way from Maidstone for their day's work." His voice sounded sharper than usual.

"Maidstone? Is that all, lad? I thought for certain thou'd come all the way from Chilham by now."

Suddenly Robert wanted to raise his fist to the fuller's round smug face, but he restrained himself. "Nay, nay . . . but come, what's ado here?"

The fuller folded his arms and sat down on a sack behind him. "All's well. Young Ralph's a sharp one. He's learning faster than any apprentices I've given Matthew before. Or else Nathan's just a better teacher than before."

Robert nodded briskly, secretly wishing (though knowing it would be impossible) that the fuller could honestly say the same of his own attempts to learn this end of the trade. He took out the note he had carried inside his surcoat bearing reminders to himself of what he was to do this day. "And the cloth we've been bringing you? You're satisfied with the weavers' work, I hope?"

"Aye, it's been fine stuff you've got me. Your father knows a good weaver, all right."

"And what of the earth? Have you still sufficient, my father wants to know?" His voice was growing confident.

"Come and see for yourself," the fuller said. He lumbered off to the storeroom on the other side of the mill, carefully walking round the trap door that opened to the floor below.

Robert counted the bulging sacks of fuller's earth and made a note of the weight of soap remaining. Then, with the fuller, he examined the latest batch of finished cloth, checking it for close matting of fibers and uniform color. This was the routine to which he had accustomed himself over the six months he had been his father's factor in Maidstone.

At first he had felt particularly helpless and self-conscious. It was absurd for him to examine and make pronouncements about the finished work of master craftsmen! But the fuller, sensing his discomfort, had eased him into his role by showing him exactly what to look for, by teaching him (as he taught his apprentices) how to full and dye the cloth, how to make best use of the mill's equipment. Without crossing the boundary of disrespect, the fuller was able to laugh and tease Robert into competence. Now when Robert looked at the cloth, he missed no flaws.

With the master fuller he went below to join the other apprentice lads for his weekly lesson. He feared their censure and needed their friendship far more than he did the fuller's. As—with them—he laid the cloth in the damp felting troughs, he was acutely aware that they watched him closely, as though searching for some opportunity to ridicule. Matthew, the journeyman, was intolerant of any inattention to work at all, however. He shouted lustily at any of his apprentices, even Robert, who dared to exchange looks and take his eyes off the cloth.

Once the cloth was laid evenly in the trough, Nathan would open a sluice which allowed the water to run over the wheel again. The mallets would turn and begin the steady pounding of the cloth as the apprentices measured careful amounts of soap and fuller's earth into the trough. Soon Robert was oblivious to all save the splashing of the water and the slap and stamp of the mallets until the sound ceased at last and the cloth—now compressed—was heaved out to be dyed, dried, and pressed.

By the end of such a day, his back would be aching and his head still roaring with the noise of the mill. At dusk he would catch the mare and canter off to the north. He was doing what he loved; he was independent without having complete responsibility; and he was learning the path God had chosen for him—that of a clothier.

Barham Down, Summer 1625

Robert

Robert took a deep breath of sweet air: the hot, clean smell of newly cut hay from lower down, the tang of the heather and gorse that covered the hill where they sat. The fragrance renewed him, for he rarely found the opportunity nowadays to notice his surroundings. "'Tis grand to be out of Maidstone for a while," he acknowledged.

His brother's wife turned to him. "Aye, brother Robert. We're glad you're away here. Especially now." She turned her eyes toward the road down which the new King and his bride were shortly to come. Widened and smoothed for the occasion, it stretched below them like a dusty length of undyed wool that grew wider as it climbed level with them, then up again to the summit of the Downs.

John stretched out his legs. "Never mind all this pomp," he grunted. "I'm thankful you've escaped the plague, my lad."

Robert looked down. Surrounded by other local families—men and women he had grown up with who now had children of their own—and by the variegated ivories of linen shirts and smocks, wool jerkins, hats and caps, by striped shawls brought for comfort on the uneven ground, in such serenity it was hard to contemplate the growing seediness and dissoluteness of the town he now thought of as home. The plague, absent nine years, had returned to claim several lives already this year. His father had called him home until the pestilence subsided, and he found himself unexpectedly relieved to be back in Chilham. Here, in the beauty of the Downs—fields of ripening oats and barley below and garlands of gorse and heather above—the ugliness of the town was almost inconceivable.

He smiled uncertainly. "Thank you. I'm glad to be here, myself."

The pealing of bells in the village warned that the King would soon approach. A noticeable change took place in the crowd. Men stood and shaded their eyes against the glare so as to be the first to see King Charles.

Women gathered their children onto their laps or leaned over to point out the way the royal party would approach. Robert noticed Jane watching the women with children and knew what her sad eyes expressed. He wondered fleetingly what sin she or John might be guilty of that the Lord had still bestowed no children. He moved to stand shoulder to shoulder with his brother.

"I'm hopeful England will improve," John ventured softly to Robert.

"So may it," Robert returned, though without conviction. His mind traveled away from Jane again and back to the conversations he heard in Maidstone at the staple every week.

"You sound doubtful, Robert."

"Aye, I am. You've heard the tales yourself. That man Buckingham will rule as long as Charles will tolerate him. I doubt Charles will prove much different from his father."

John's eyebrows rose. "I think he will. What I hear is that the court's a more decent place already—that none of the profanity and profligacy James Stuart tolerated is now permitted."

"I hope 'tis true. But think you, truly, he can reverse all the years of ill his father did to godly folk?"

"You mean—?"

"I mean the *Book of Sports*—an affront to any Christian. And the chains he put on men who'd preach the truth, or write or print the truth—like your friend William Brewster."

John's face fell. "Aye. These are hard times to follow Christ."

"James—he was aptly named *deceiver!* If some would make a god of him for his fine Bible, they're sadly misled!" Robert shook his head.

John looked round anxiously. "Hush, you're speaking treason, I'm sure."

Robert only laughed. "Nay," he said bluntly, thrusting his thumbs in his belt with a shrug. "Nay. 'Tis all between himself and his Maker, now. 'Tis naught to me."

John watched him for a moment. "But you'll be proven wrong about his son, I trust. They say he's devout, genuinely so."

"Devout about the right of kings to rule by God, I'm sure," Robert said flatly.

"Come, what's the mordant in your jerkin that makes you so sour today? What know we of such things?" John searched his brother's face earnestly. "You should have gone with the Pilgrims after all, perhaps, if you wanted none of kings."

"Not I, brother!"

"And you've heard, have you, of the new King's grant to the Strangers?"

Robert grinned back at him. "How should I? I go not to Canterbury as oft as you. What is't?"

Jane looked up but said nothing, her blue eyes resting on each of the men in turn.

"They may keep all their rights and freedoms. His Majesty favors them."

Robert cleared his throat. "Good news, that, I agree." He rubbed the wooden sole of his boot in the chalky earth of the ridge on which they stood. "But, he favors the Papists, too, John."

John's face clouded again, and Jane returned her gaze to the road uneasily. "Aye. There's no arguing that."

"It's that scoundrel Villiers—Buckingham—again. When the King's suit fails for a Spaniard, he runs straight into the arms of a French Papist."

"A princess."

"But a Papist, nevertheless."

"Ah, Robert, you've been too long in the town. You talk like a bitter, worldly courtier, full of hatred and intrigue and vain politicking."

"God forbid!" Robert flushed. "But I've been there long enough with their lordships and ladyships coming in and out at assizes and the gentry talking at the staples and the inns to hear what others besides myself think and know."

"Look!" Jane scrambled to her feet dusting off her gown in haste. "I see them coming, I'm sure." She came to stand close beside her husband, and he put his arm round her waist.

"Aye, I see a cloud of dust . . . and banners . . . and, listen—"

"Trumpets on the wind!" a man nearby called to his wife.

Robert listened intently but at first heard nothing. He could, however, see men on horseback attired in splendid cloaks. The horses moved in a slow trot with heads raised, seemingly mindful of the royal presence not far behind. As they drew nearer, beginning the climb, the whole party slackened pace. Robert watched the horses' tossing heads, the drummers, the pipers, the infantry marching close behind with their pikes ceremonially mounted in leather slings, and the flags of the King and—notably—of Kent with its white horse emblazoned over the word *invicta*. Then, in the middle of the procession, came two figures mounted on horses as white as the Kentish horse, closely followed by another on a great black stallion.

Robert strained to see the details of face and form, but the distance was too great.

"Do you hear the drummers, brother Robert?" Jane asked in excitement.

He frowned, puzzled. "I hear the trumpets faintly, aye, but not the drums."

John glanced swiftly at him. "Yet *I* can hear them. How strange."

Robert shook his head. "'Tis strange, indeed." He leaned forward but caught only the low babbling of the families near them, the breeze rustling over the brush and grass. "Well, never mind. Ah, but would I could see their faces." He laughed ruefully. "I suppose you can, brother."

"Nay, they're too far off. There's naught wrong with your eyes, Robert." He turned to his wife. "Jane, your eyes are bright and clear. Do you see them better than your menfolk do?"

She smiled back. Her face always lighted when John consulted her, and for a moment Robert felt the flickering of envy that had dogged him ever since the marriage. Childless though she be, Robert knew she brought more joy to John than did anyone else on earth.

"His Majesty's hair is dark," she reported.

"'Tis a wig, you ninny," John teased.

"No," she said firmly. "His brows are dark, and his hair is dark, too, with a wave in it. A very handsome man."

"Prettily said, love." John smiled.

"But not as handsome as you be. Never. His nose is too large and his beard too pinched for my liking."

John squeezed her arm. "You're a saucy wench today. Go say it to his face, pray."

"Nay, nay. He wouldn't notice me at all. Look at his wife. All blushes and black ringlets."

"Aye, now I see her as well as you do," John put in. "She's just a slip of a thing. Looks no more than fifteen. Poor lass, married to England."

"Poor lass!" Robert scoffed, becoming uneasy about the light-hearted vein of the talk. "Her father was the King of France, and the Pope is at their beck and call. And no covering on her head to speak of. Pity not the new Queen, John."

"I do, though, from the bottom of my heart. And the King, to boot. The kingdom in disarray, and a never-ending war in Europe, and Spain hovering like a hawk waiting for the kill, and debts, and bad harvests, and Villiers breathing down their necks. Who'd be King?"

"Now who sounds like the cynical courtier?" Robert asked mildly.

They watched the procession reach the highest point of the road then disappear behind one of the folds of the Downs, quickening as they began to descend. The tail end of the procession—more infantry and two horseguards at the rear—disappeared from sight. Robert wondered how a man so obviously enamored of pageantry could set to rights a country besieged by the Devil himself, a country whose church called on Christ but that martyred Christians as rebels and traitors to the King. What would become of King Charles and his England?

George Tolhurst

Just over the other side of the hill an enormous pavilion had been erected for the royal party. Long canopies extended at either end of the pavilion, and on all sides hung the standards of the new King, the new Queen, and Kent. The scalloped edges of the tent cloth undulated in the slight breeze, and round it moved many of the local gentlemen. A few of their wives had accompanied them out of curiosity, but they sat together in the shade of one of the awnings, conversing quietly and fanning themselves against the heat. Servants and laborers from the village, hired for the day, hovered anxiously within the tent, eyes agog. A *picnic*, the gentlemen had said. A *picnic for the King?* This was no picnic. It was a veritable banquet.

Within, the pavilion tables were heaped with venison and smoked meats; fresh breads; wheels of cheese made by women in Canterbury, Great Maydeacon, and Barham; two boars' heads garnished with bay leaves and rosemary; bowls overflowing with cherries, strawberries, and raspberries; flagons of cider; butts of sack and wine; and barrels of beer. Within the hour, most of this would be consumed by the King and his courtiers and by the lords and ladies waiting without. And though these laborers, as men of Kent in the lushness of Kent's fruitfulness, had never starved—even in the recent famines—nevertheless they could not conceive of so much food.

George Tolhurst was one of the many gentlemen waiting outside the tent to pay respects to the King and his bride. Unlike most of the other knights, courtiers, burgesses, and gentlemen in attendance, he had no wife to bring with him. At twenty-five he had just lost his parents and now found himself alone, save servants and laborers, to manage his newly acquired court in Goudhurst with its hop gardens, fruit trees, and fields of barley.

He would never have left his farm and come all the way on horseback with only a groom and one manservant had not Sir Henry Oxinden of Barham invited him. All the gentry of the county were there today, or so it seemed, and those he did not know well he knew at least by name and by sight from hunting parties and from the assizes in Maidstone. He had gone to these court sessions with his father for years before he had actually held responsibilities there.

He felt a little unsure of himself in this august body of men, though he could not account for the feeling. The gentlemen of Kent were known for their easy familiarity with their tenants and with each other. After all, most were related to each other, and no one lorded it over another. The gentry—and the yeomen—all prided themselves on independence and freedom. They depended on each other for the perpetuation of the ancient rights and privileges of what was once the Kingdom of Kent, so there was never more than friendly rivalry among the families, and they stood together in crises.

For this reason, Tolhurst was proud to be a man of Kent. Still, he found himself uneasy with all the ceremony and pomp and with the company of so many older men of great experience and influence.

There was Sir Dudley Digges, for example, a friend of Sir Henry's, who had left Digges Court some time earlier and built himself a fine castle at Chilham. Seventeen years older than himself—not much, perhaps, but enough for Digges to have befriended the Archbishop of Canterbury; to have traveled as an ambassador to Russia, Holland, and Ireland; to have been imprisoned in the Fleet for his speech against the Duke of Buckingham; and to have made an enemy of a certain Bishop William Laud, who was reportedly a favorite of the new King's.

And what of Edward Dering, the son of Sir Anthony of Surrenden? Only two years older than Tolhurst, he was already well known as a King's man. Not a man who blindly yielded to the whims of King James, nor to the demands of his son, but a man whom royalty trusted, a man who was already lieutenant of Dover Castle, who was sure to be knighted within the year.

And besides these men there were the Twysdens, Tuftons, Astleys, Sondeses, and Culpepers—all the main threads of the Kentish network of family ties—most older than he was, all wiser.

Since the King had still not come, Tolhurst stood with Sir Dudley and Edward Dering outside the pavilion. A group of musicians inside the tent began to practice an air, and he found his foot tapping as he listened to the other men's conversations.

"What think you, Sir," Dering was asking, "of our new monarch and his bride?"

Sir Dudley turned aside to cough into a lace-edged handkerchief, and when he looked back at Dering and Tolhurst, his eyes were full of laughter.

"It matters not what I think, gentlemen," he said suavely. "I serve the King, be he James or Charles."

"Nay, and so do we all, sir," Dering replied. "But you have been in Whitehall and Westminster these long years, and you surely—"

"These long years?" Digges echoed with cool amusement. "You make me sound like a hoary old kingmaker." He ran his hand through his thick, wavy hair. "Hoary I may be . . . but no kingmaker. I'd rather be at home in Chilham to wait upon my lady and the common folk of the village, truth to tell."

Tolhurst watched Dering's keen eyes search the older man's face in bland assessment. "Nay, play not the country squire with us, good Sir Dudley," Dering teased.

Digges's eyebrows rose. "I knew not that I did." He linked his arms through those of the two younger men. "Then since you press me," he continued, "come, let us walk a little, and I'll put my head upon the block. Repeat not my opinions, however, for I will deny them to the death if treason's the word. I've seen enough of prison bars already to be more cautious now than I was at your age."

The three men strolled round the pavilion, past an enclosed field where the horses were tethered, and up another rise in the Downs. "In truth," Digges began again, "I fear for England." He gave a quick, grave smile—a glimpse of faltering sunlight between the dark clouds that gathered in his eyes. "Not as our Puritan brethren fear for England with all their cant of the Antichrist at war with the Body of Christ and the great Millennium on the horizon, with Christ Himself coming as their Captain to blast the Papists and the High Church party to hell." He drew breath, smiling faintly again. "Not, I say, as my neighbors the John Fessendens fear for England."

Tolhurst nodded. "Aye, I've heard of Fessenden—the clothier who has a son in Maidstone? Robert . . . Robin . . . or some such?"

"The very same. Robert, it is."

"And Robert's at lodging with some Goudhurst folk—the Longhursts—people my father foolishly patronized. Peter's turned preacher. He's in the stocks as often as he's out, and not even able to write, let alone read the prayer book or heed the catechism. Fancies himself a Prynne or a Lilburne, doubtless." He shook his head. "'Tis a scandal, such a beggar pantomiming as a man of the cloth—"

"You were saying?" Dering interrupted.

Tolhurst flushed with embarrassment. "Forgive me," he put in quickly. "'Tis a sore matter with me, that Puritan nonsense."

"Aye, nonsense," Digges agreed. "Nonsense that'll soon be knocked out of their heads if Laud has his way."

"Or if the Queen has hers," Dering parried.

The corners of Digges's mouth turned down, and he shook his head again. "Nay, she's a poor little waif, I'm sure. The King will tolerate the Catholics more than his father, I've no doubt, but England'll not go back to the Pope in Rome. No, that's not what makes me afraid."

Dering and Tolhurst looked at Digges, and as they did so, each caught the question in the other's eyes.

"It's this matter with Buckingham and the King, and the King and Parliament, these things I fear. Buckingham will rule, I fear, and the King, who like a little child with a spoiling uncle thinks he's getting his own will all the while, will be led from one folly to another to please his favorite. Then Parliament will rise against them, and Charles will protest they interfere in what they know not of, and we may have war."

Tolhurst dropped his arm. "Bleak prophecies indeed, sir."

Dudley stood still on the grass beside them. "Aye, bleak, but I see it coming. And we poor men of Kent will know not where our hearts should lie—with our King, who wastes the realm in his associations with dangerous men—or with the common folk His Majesty thus defrauds—or with their Parliament! Aye, we may have the worst war of all when brother raises sword against brother."

His sober words hung in the silence broken at last by the faint sound of the King's trumpets in the wind.

Chilham, April 1628

Tolhurst had ridden too far and too fast, and now his gray gelding was lame. Chilham was near, at least, but the long, slow climb up the Pilgrims' Way—to a haven for his horse at the forge and to food for himself at the castle—seemed unending.

He cursed himself every step of the way for bringing no servants with him, but it had seemed a pleasant enough jaunt, at first, to set out alone with nothing but a portmanteau slung over the back of his saddle and the spring wind off the Downs in his face. And so it had been—at first. He had stayed with some distant cousins on the way. And he had met Elizabeth.

Now that he had to walk the rest of the way to Chilham, he had plenty of leisure to think both of his reason for going to Chilham and of Elizabeth.

The two things most on his mind, one expected and the other unexpected, rivaled for his attention. As he marched along, occasionally whistling an air or a jig, he tried to concentrate on one or the other of them. Instead, his mind willfully swung from one to the other. If he thought of the letter from Sir Dudley that had summoned him to Chilham, he inevitably thought of another letter, arriving the same day, inviting him to spend a few days with his cousins. The coincidence was perfect. He could hunt with his cousins, for a day or two enjoying a respite from Tolhurst Court and the sowing of the barley, then he could go on to Chilham.

If he thought of Sir Dudley's seat in Parliament for Kent, ruminating on the influence that position was already bringing to bear in London on behalf of the county he and Sir Dudley loved so well, then inevitably he thought of Elizabeth's father, who sat in the House of Lords. *Nay, rather—* he laughed to himself—*he does not sit, but sleeps, the old fool.*

And if he thought of Dering and Twysden and Sondes and all the other young men of Kent he expected to see at the castle, and of the earnest political discussions to which they had all been summoned, then inevitably he thought with chilling uneasiness of all the young men who came and went at his cousins' house with no other reason than to woo Elizabeth. He ground his teeth when he remembered them.

The girl's father was doting and careless. She was his darling, the only daughter among a houseful of sons, the last child of his first wife. But even as the old man doted on her, he gave her what Tolhurst considered too much freedom for a modest young woman. The men came and went, flirting and bowing and talking nonsense to his cousin. Cousin! No, hardly that. Her father was his own father's second cousin, so that made them third (or fourth) cousins. No, not cousin. She was his sweetheart.

But he couldn't talk nonsense to her or curl his hair and perfume himself with pomade as some of these other gallant gentlemen did. These things were not part of his nature. As Elizabeth crossed and recrossed her father's great hall—her dark, reddish hair braided round her head, pearls gleaming at her throat, her waist slim beneath the embroidered bodice of her gown, and her full skirts brushing the floor—he had tormented himself, worrying about whether she actually liked these men.

Was she as careless as her father, a spiteful kitten who minded not how many hearts she broke, playing without interest the same coquettish little games that so many gentlewomen played nowadays? God forfend it! He could not imagine that she would be as light as that, young though she was at eighteen. But could she be interested in a dull old bachelor of twenty-eight who liked to hunt, fish, dine with friends, and tramp about in the muddy fields of Tolhurst Court? A farmer, after all, that's what he was.

Only on one occasion had her father's laxity worked in his own favor. After the young men had departed and the old father and stepmother had retired for the night, Tolhurst had found himself unexpectedly alone with Elizabeth in the candlelit splendor of the family's dining room.

The serving maids had removed the last platters and dishes, but Elizabeth herself had shown no inclination to rise or retire, so for a blissful hour they had faced each other across the table. His eyes never left her face. He took in the high, smooth brow revealed by the old-fashioned, simple way she dressed her hair—innocent of any Puritan cap—the wide cheekbones, the tapering oval of cheeks and chin illuminated by the golden light of the candles, the semicircular arch of perfectly even brown eyebrows, and the greenish-blue fire of her eyes.

During most of their time together, she did not look at him directly unless she was answering a question. Otherwise, her eyes gazed downward or focused on the Dutch sideboard behind him, which was adorned with vases and china plates. So when she did look up, the color of those eyes struck him so forcefully that he began to fidget and sweat uncomfortably and had to loosen his neckerchief.

He had felt more foolish than ever then, and more certain than ever that she must think him a country oaf with no better manners than to stare at her like a gawking yeoman in the lane. Even now, vividly remembering her expression, he felt hot with longing and excitement.

Perhaps he would have left his cousins' estate convinced of her disdain, had there not been one exchange between them near the end of the conversation that had left him musing in wonder and joy.

"It grows so dreary now," she had commented. "My brothers are rarely here, and I have little enough in common with my stepmother."

"Then I'm glad I came," he said softly. "But you have so much company here. Surely 'tis never quiet."

"No, I wish it were. That's not what I mean. 'Tis not the quiet I'd mind." She looked up briefly, blinding him again with her eyes.

He swallowed hard. "Then what?"

Thoughtfully, she ran her fingers round the stem of a goblet. "'Tis the mindless prattle of my father's acquaintances that I find so dreary."

Relieved, and seeing her now in a different light, he took courage to probe further. "But they admire you so, 'tis obvious."

She made a scornful noise at the back of her throat. "In their simpering way, yes. But I suspect they admire my dowry more." Her face clouded. "'Tis unfair that a woman's naught but a ewe in the marketplace to be quarreled over according to the depth of her fleece, poor creature. Not all women have empty heads bent on house and husband and infants."

She flushed, and that revealed more about Elizabeth than he had dared hope or imagine. "Some of us grew up listening to stories of good Queen Bess—nay, were *named* for her—and some of us wanted to be as shrewd and clever as she was, or as a man is in politics and the ways of the world." Elizabeth shook her head. "Instead we're mured up in our courts and houses waiting for the best bargain in the marriage staple to cross our fathers' thresholds and rescue us from one pen just to put us in another." Her voice had grown high, and she had looked him fully in the face again. But there was no anger directed at him as one of the male captors, only something . . . might it have been an appeal?

Tolhurst reached out now and absently stroked the neck of his horse. What *had* that look meant? And what was it he had replied, awed by her passion and by the originality and strength of her convictions? "*I've* never thought that way of women, I confess—"

"Why should you? You're unwed yourself and free to pursue your work and your life and your opinions without troubling over the thoughts of a rebellious girl." Then she had dismissed herself with a deprecating shrug.

He had laughed then, throwing back his head and unconsciously thrusting his feet so far under the table as he leaned backward that his feet had found hers.

He moved them quickly, murmuring an apology, then answered her. "Life isn't as interesting for us as you might think." His feet still burned from the contact.

"But London . . . Parliament . . . affairs of state . . ."

"I'm only a justice of the peace."

"Then at least you go to Maidstone."

"Aye, but most of my time is on the farm. I'm a yeoman, in truth. Just a yeoman with an old name, 'tis all."

"'Tis all?" Her eyebrows arched. "Then why, if you be yeoman only, do you go to Chilham to see Sir Dudley?" She fired the question back as smartly as a musket answering the slow fire of a cannon.

He saw he was contending with a woman of quick wits, a woman as different from his dead mother as his pedigree mare was from a tinker's donkey. He shrugged. "His lordship did not say."

She pierced him with her look. "I don't believe you'd ride all the way from Goudhurst for naught."

"Nor would I." He felt ashamed, as if he'd been caught playing the same little word games he so deeply scorned in Elizabeth's wooers. "But I cannot tell you the matter of our meeting."

She leaned forward. "Would you if you could?"

His heart beat fast, then, and he longed to leap up on the table, wrest her from her seat, and feel her mouth under his own. "Aye—" It was all he could manage to say.

Then one of the servants came in—Elizabeth's own maid, perhaps—an older woman. She drew the curtains and lifted the candle snuffer with a meaningful look at Elizabeth. There ended the magical encounter, which now assumed the quality of a dream in his mind.

Would you tell me . . . why do you go to Chilham to see his lordship? Would you, if you could? The words ran round and round in his head, repeating themselves in her honest, musical voice until they obliterated all other sensory impressions and almost all thoughts of what he was now doing on the road to Chilham.

In fact, he knew quite well why Sir Dudley had written no particulars of his meeting at the castle. If the nature of the meeting he anticipated were discovered, there might be outcries of sedition, rebellion, and treason from certain quarters. And Sir Dudley did not have to list details for Tolhurst to know precisely what would be discussed. The theme stated three years ago on Barham Down would be played again in all its variations, now with the knowledge not of prophecy but sad hindsight.

They had met Charles Stuart briefly that day. The King was slight, small, and spoke haltingly in a Scottish accent, with a tone that suggested shyness. Courteous he was, with a curious magnetism that both drew and repelled Tolhurst, and courteous he had shown himself ever since. That same quality, though, bore with it dislike and scorn for anything discourteous, for anything that smacked of commonness or coarseness. The King was fastidious, in fact. He had shunned Parliament, calling it only reluctantly and occasionally in the last three years. He had tolerated his wife's Catholic emissaries (and practices) at court and had favored the High Church party's policy of intolerance of all dissenters. The intolerance had magnified since Laud's appointment to the Dean of his Chapel Royal, to the Privy Council, and now to the Bishopric of London.

Though Tolhurst looked down on Puritans, considering himself a high Anglican and Royalist, he still rejected the crude, extreme punishments for dissenters that were allowed by the King. He could not be uncritical, even of a King appointed by God. Yes, this meeting might well open the way for yet another rising in Kent.

Amusement creased his face. *Wat Tyler, Jack Cade.* Would the names of Sir Dudley Digges and George Tolhurst yet be among the chronicle of Kentish rebels?

In a room bare of all ornament save candles, an oak table surrounded by stools, and heavy damask curtains pulled over the windows, Tolhurst bent forward to listen as Sir Dudley stood at the head of the table.

"I've spoken to you all before," the knight began. "And we've all seen the paths the King has chosen. Buckingham has disgraced himself in France. Stade is lost. Rochelle is still unsuccored, betrayed by Buckingham. The Exchequer has exhausted its money and its patience for four years, first for the Palatinate, and now for Rochelle. But truly"—he shook his head grimly, his voice turning harsh—"for *nothing.* And now the King will use his 'divine' right to imprison those who do not grant him what His Majesty calls loans. He will billet men on innocent householders, obliging them to put up with ill-bred ruffians who abuse their property and even commit foul murder. 'Tis not right. 'Tis *not* just. Parliament will brook no more. I will brook no more. And I say, we cannot brook these policies or delays any longer. If other counties and their men in Parliament be silent, Kent shall not."

A few of the men nodded and mumbled in agreement, and Tolhurst surveyed Sir Dudley's face in surprise. Always so mobile and sardonic, it was now impassioned and solemn.

"I represent the men of Kent, as well ye all know, and I've been persuaded by Sir Edward Coke that Parliament needs to speak more strongly. You know Coke's position well enough, I warrant."

"Nay, Sir Dudley," one man spoke up. Then he flushed in embarrassment as all stared at him.

Sir Dudley inclined his head deferentially. "Forgive me, Walter. I take the affairs of Kent with me every time I go to London. I forget sometimes that I take not the men of Kent, also." He cleared his throat. "'Tis this. The King is God's man. That we all believe. But he's God's *lieutenant,* no more. We cannot rely on messages and promises delivered to us by word of mouth alone. We must have written confirmation of his will to change his policies. 'Tis time we present a formal petition to His Majesty."

An older man than Digges was frowning. "You distrust the King, then, do you—you and all yon men in Parliament?"

"Nay, rather, we distrust his ministers. And we cannot take his trust but in a parliamentary way, as Sir Edward Coke says. There must be some limit to *iure divino*. His Majesty is obliged—he must—listen. Or if not, at his peril. 'Tis time the word of Parliament regained its power." He paused, passing a hand across his brow. "Surely, surely you remember what happened two years ere this, when we opposed the loans forced out of Kent to support the war?"

"Aye, clearly enough," answered one man bitterly. "Clapped in prison, and I'm not like to forget."

"Nor I," Digges agreed. "But I'll lay the King turns a deaf ear to voices from the provinces—be they squires' voices or justices'. Yet he can't do that forever. He wants to win the war. But without Parliament, and without money—yea, without the men of Kent, he can do little there."

A wizened man at the foot of the table nodded vigorously. "Aye, when Spain was on our doorstep, Her Majesty listened well to us. She knew right enough that if Kent stand not as bulwark, England hath no defense. But Charles, it seemeth, is less wise than his good cousin Bess."

"True, too true." Digges stroked his beard. "But here's the rub. We're a free people, and thank God for that. We bow the knee to no man save the King. All well and good. This betokens, however, that we band not together or choose a leader when we have a cause. We take our rights for granted, and we take our family connections for granted, too. We scarcely think of joining together because we believe ourselves already joined. We never think of leading one another because in Kent we all be kings on our own land."

He narrowed his eyes. "Some of that must change. That's why I called you here. God knows I'd rather be sitting by the fire or working the falcons and the hounds, but here I sit. Here you sit, and I beg your support. We must get our tenants and our yeomen on our side also." He waved a parchment on which were inscribed the tentative clauses he and Coke had discussed already with fellow members of Parliament. "For if they be not with us, being without a cause, they'll follow the Brownists, or dreams of Eldorado on the far side of the Atlantic. Fever, plague, and despair—all for nothing. And the yeomen of Kent are where the power lies, verily."

Tolhurst nodded vigorously, though he heard a few voices of dissent.

"Then tell us, Sir Dudley, what this petition will advocate," one man said timidly, "and whether we should promote it ourselves."

"Whether you should promote it yourselves," Digges answered with a soft laugh, "that I'll not say. 'Tis on your consciences. But we advocate naught but what is reasonable, moderate. Kent has a history of changing kings' hearts, if you recall."

A few of the men laughed.

"Hear, then, what this petition pleads. Then let us discuss the reasons for it." His eyes searched the room. "Item: no man hereafter shall be compelled to make any gift, loan, benevolence, tax, or such like charge, without common consent by act of Parliament. Item: no free man shall be imprisoned or detained without shown cause. Item: soldiers and mariners shall not be billeted upon private parties against their will. Item: commissions for proceeding by martial law shall not be issued in the future." He stopped, looking round the intent circle of faces. "That's all we ask, and thus far the lords are with us."

Immediately, loud discussion broke out, but Digges quickly quelled it. "Listen," he urged. The room fell silent again. "The Crown has taken more and more power unto itself. The bishops and the justices seem to think it their sole cause to extend and magnify the King's royal power at the expense of all that we hold dear in our constitution, at the expense of common law, at the expense of Magna Carta itself. He creates new offenses that were never offenses before. He gives Buckingham a free rein in France so that the war—"

"Aye, and the marriage made to cement us to our enemies has done no good," one man grumbled.

Digges nodded, then went on. "And Buckingham, sent to make 'peace,' incenses the King of France by his indulgence with the King's wife. In short, unless we stand for our rights, we shall be ruled by dangerous fools. At their mercy, too, aye. And *taxed* to pay for their folly."

The men all murmured in agreement, but the timid man spoke up tremulously again. "Sir, what if our lands be forfeit for this petition? What if this be treason?"

All eyes turned on the master of Chilham.

"They cannot take our lands when we demand rights that are ours by the constitution of the realm, and when we do it lawfully, within Parliament." He sighed. "And if they do, well then, we live under tyrants, and naught that we do will be right. But if we do nothing, as Sir Edward has oft reminded me, we forfeit our substance anyway—in taxes." He searched the faces of all men in the room. "Who's with me, brethren?"

Tolhurst saw himself yet again as the naive countryman who knew too little about court intrigue, Crown policy, and parliamentary debates of the day. Like the others, however, he remembered painfully the "loan" he had been obliged to make to the King only two years before. He answered Sir Dudley's raised eyebrows and questioning eyes with quick energy. "I, for one, sir." And then he thought of Elizabeth and knew that she would applaud his decision.

Goudhurst, 1632

For the first time since Tolhurst had met Elizabeth, no barriers divided them—no hovering maiden aunts, no perfumed suitors, no men pouring out full glasses of sack while pouring out too many words in those rare moments they had tried to be alone together. Now, on their wedding night, they lay close together in the flocked ease of the canopied oak bed at Tolhurst Court, the bed in which George himself had doubtless been conceived. The wedding festivities behind them—the heat and the crush in the family chapel; the rude country jokes that had assaulted their ears; the homely music of the shepherds' tabors, pipes, and voices (too rarely heard in these new days of frowning Puritan disapproval); the platitudes of Elizabeth's overwise cousins and brothers; the flowing butts of claret—all dissolved as they rested in the drugged warmth of each other's arms and explored each other's bodies.

He held her face inches from his own, shaking his head in amazement at the depth and steadiness of her eyes, the smoothness of her skin. "I never saw how you could love me," he said softly. "And now that I know you do, I curse myself for waiting all this time to make you my wife." He shifted to cradle her head on one arm. With his free hand he pushed her tumbled hair from her face.

She moved closer to him. "I did not know I loved you," she said, her voice low. "All I knew was that I had found a man—a sympathetic man— to whom I could talk, who wouldn't censure me for having all my wits about me."

He threw back his head to chuckle and gave her cheek a quick pinch. "Who wouldn't censure you anyway, since he has fewer wits."

"Nay, 'tis not true."

He hesitated. "Then when was it you knew you loved me?" He knew the smile had left his face, and suddenly the room seemed terribly still,

69

hovering on the edge of words he couldn't quite believe, truth he couldn't grasp.

Her eyes left his face and rested on the curtained windows. "Two years ago, I think." Then she looked back at him. "The second, nay, third time you came to see my father."

"'Twas not to see your father, love, and you know that well enough." He leaned over her, his hand smoothing the curves of her shoulders and breasts, his heart thudding in his ears again. "'Twas you."

She smiled, her cheeks reddening slightly. "And after you stayed with us—the first time, even—the men I already found dreary seemed worse. I felt insulted by them. They talk to a woman as if she's just a pretty shell, a china thing to mind lest one break it. Pretty and empty." She wrinkled her nose. "But you were my first real friend, and you never treated me like that, and I never want you to."

He laughed suddenly at her definiteness and sat up, leaning back against the bolster and looking down at her. "Small hope of that, Eliza Tolhurst. I've made a woman of you, and you're a squire's wife. Worse. You're a farmer's wife."

She reached up and pulled him down beside her again. "So you'll make your poor little coz' into a dairywoman? Like all the pretty maids of Kent who serve you already, who set their caps at you when you were a lad? You'll teach me how to shear and drive a horse and plow, will you?" Her eyes danced with mischief.

He exaggerated a shudder. "Never!" Then he winked. "But you shall go to the assizes with me and help me oversee the constables and wardens and surveyors. And the folk hereabouts will call you Good Queen Bess of Goudhurst—a shrewder judge than her husband of politics, of right and wrong." He tightened his arms round her again, and bent his mouth to the softness of hers. What did all those civic affairs mean now that he had the woman he wanted in his arms? His longing for her obliterated everything else.

She smiled again. "Now I know why all those songs are about love. I lay the yeomen know more about it than we poor deluded gentry all puffed up with our estates and what not." She stroked his hair, her eyes blazing steadily into his. "And at this hour, in spite of all we've said, I care not a fig for politics or assizes or constables." Her voice dropped, and her hands moved over his body, stirring his desire for her again.

"Nor I." He pushed himself up on his elbows to cover her, still dizzy with the wonder of a wife in his bed.

Chilham, March 1634

Robert

Robert's brother Isaac poked at the fire and came to sit beside their father on the settle. Taller than his father, and broader in the shoulders than both John and Robert, 'little' Isaac had become strikingly handsome with the black hair and dark eyes of all the Fessendens, save John, though Isaac's features were more even than theirs. Wherever he went nowadays, on business for his father or with his brothers, the maids turned and stared.

Robert watched as Isaac picked up *The Plain Man's Pathway to Heaven*, which he had been reading fitfully throughout this Sabbath afternoon. *Too handsome by half for his own good*, Robert mused, staring. The thick curls of dark hair, the slight mask of freckles, the chiseled nose and chin, the sensual redness of his mouth. *Thank heaven the boy is too innocent to know his own danger*, he thought. Robert remembered the morning worship at the fellowship that day, when the brazen girls of the village—doubtless ill-bred wenches who served the foppish Sir Dudley at Chilham Castle—had ogled over the pews at his brother. Surely they had heard none of the sermon that day!

Then he recalled his new love, Patience, and he thanked God for her. No bold maiden was she! No fluttering eyelashes, faint blushes, or silly talk. No lewd garments designed to tempt the unwary to their destruction.

He glanced quickly at Jane, sitting across the room in the window seat with John, and Mary Snode, talking with them in low whispers he couldn't hear. Still without children, Jane had acquired none of the matronly caution in her dress that he remembered in his mother. Not that she was immodest—the Fessenden household would never have brooked that, but she seemed to have an inborn sense of artistry and design in her choice of fabrics, bodices, and skirts. And John, of course, indulged her.

Jane's enduring radiant beauty somehow went against Robert's grain. It was not seemly, surely, for a woman of her mature age to dress like a

71

courtier. He frowned. *No, she doesn't*, he thought. *All's plain and simple, and yet. . . .* He stared hard at the lines of her body beneath the materials. Supple and strong from all the work she did about the house, she managed to be elegant, princesslike. Even the somber colors she preferred showed off the gold of her hair escaping from under her coif, as well as the clear brilliance of her skin and eyes.

She caught his eyes briefly, and he glanced down, clasping his hands round his knees in a quick gesture of guilt. It occurred to him suddenly, and to his chagrin, that he was staring lustfully at his own brother's wife as had the girls at Isaac this morning, the very girls he had condemned.

Remaining still, he shut his eyes, hoping to shut out Jane's image. Was he too condemned, then? He tried to summon the face and form of Patience, but he could not. Was he destined thus to lust after other women as a betrothed man, even as a married man? God forbid!

Opening his eyes, he jumped up and gave the logs in the fire a push with the fire irons, sending a shower of sparks and soot dancing under the mantel.

"What is't, Robert?" Isaac inquired.

Robert did not hear him, so Mary Snode, sitting nearer, repeated the question more loudly.

He swung round toward the settle and caught the eyes of all the family on him: his father's and Isaac's; and over on the window seat, Jane's, John's, and Widow Snode's. Unlike John and Jane, he had never really liked Mary—the interloper who had tried to take his mother's place, who had spoiled his sisters and Isaac, and who now took her place in the parlor as if she were one of the family. But he had never really known her, either, having left home to spend most of his life in Maidstone soon after she arrived.

He tried to answer civilly. "Oh . . . naught," he mumbled. Castigating himself for lying, he turned round to face the fire again.

"Where's young Patience?" John asked loudly.

Robert repressed a sharp retort. They all did that now—this shouting at him. It was a curse to be going deaf, and only Patience understood how lonely and bitter he often felt. And worse still, he could never be sure if his own voice were a shout or a whisper, and this uncertainty only heightened his resentment. But now he regarded his brother with what he hoped was a face of accustomed friendliness. "She be in her chamber." In spite of himself, he thought suddenly of her slenderness, mentally disrobing her as he longed to do on the day of their wedding. But then he pushed the thought away, angry with himself for desecrating in his mind what he loved with all his heart.

"She's . . . she's reading, I believe. She says 'tis her custom on the Sabbath afternoon to read some godly book. She reads aloud with her aunt. A very edifying way to spend the day, I do believe."

His father, looking up from the open Bible, mumbled his agreement, though Robert sensed a slight constraint in his father's approval.

Isaac waved his own book with a mischievous grin. "She's right, dear brother."

"Mock not, Isaac," his father growled.

"But it seems strange, does it not, my father," Isaac began guilelessly, "that she and her aunt have traveled all that way on Robert's account just to sit at books all day, hardly to show their faces to Robert, let alone his family."

Robert opened his mouth to rebuke Isaac, but Mary intervened. "Nay, Isaac, you do overreach yourself in discourtesy to your brother."

Robert noticed his younger brother's surprise at her sharp words. Mary Snode rarely corrected her beloved these days and had never before taken his own part against Isaac.

His father joined in support of Mary. "Have done, lad, and read your book." He glanced at her, but she was drawing a thread through her smocking and did not look up. "'Twill soon be time for prayers and a light repast, and I'd like peace enough this day to read the Word of God, if you please."

"I'm sorry, Father," Isaac murmured. Then he raised his voice. "And I'm sorry, brother, for my thoughtless words."

Robert bowed stiffly. "I do forgive you." He went back to his seat again. Unwilling to look at Jane again, or at Isaac, he retrieved a devotional pamphlet he had begun reading by candlelight the evening previous and tried to lose himself in the teaching it contained. Before, when he had wanted to think of his betrothed, she had eluded him. Now, when he wanted to purify his thoughts, her image would not leave him alone— Patience unhooking her bodice and discarding her petticoats; Patience in a linen shift, her hair (always tightly covered by a cap) unbound and rippling through his fingers; Patience in their bridal bed. . . .

His mind stopped there, bridled by a severe conscience, and he silently bade the Devil cease troubling him. Well, thank God, they would be wed within a few weeks, and then he would not live in fancy anymore but have her for himself in the flesh, as God willed man to take his maid.

Perhaps his father sensed his restlessness, for he looked up from his reading again and caught his eye. He called out. "Nay, Robert, but you *are* troubled." He stood up. "Come with me, son. Let us walk in the garden a while."

Fleetingly, Robert felt like a boy again, a boy who, when times of melancholy assaulted him, had sought out his mother for comfort. It had been the same then—a walk between her herb borders down beyond the outshots and the chicken run to the rose garden. That rose garden was now Widow Snode's province. Grudgingly, Robert admitted that she tended it with more skill, care, and devotion than his mother had ever given it. But then, his mother had borne eight children, had done all the churning of butter, starching of collars, smoking of meat, and brewing of small ale. Mary was no more than a paid servant with time of her own to play at gardening and making physic.

The two men, wrapped in heavy wool cloaks, seated themselves under the arbor, bare now of all but a few dark-red knobs that would soon burst into leaf.

"Are you not easy in your mind, Robert, about your choice of a wife? I'd thought—"

Startled, Robert interrupted sharply. "Not easy, Father?" He gave a short laugh. "Nay, I'm . . . I'm glad of her." He struggled against self-betrayal, against revealing to his father all the base fancies that seemed to taint his relationship with Patience when she was not actually present. "I'm as glad of her as I can be." He grimaced, taking a deep breath. "But our wedding day seems over-long away."

If he expected censure for his eagerness, he received none. "Ah, so that's it. And when Isaac jested with you, he touched you on the quick."

Robert nodded. He looked down absently at the tulip plants poking up through the leaves and earth.

"Isaac's young, and you must forgive, as you said you did." Fessenden paused. "He's never yet known what it is to desire the woman you love, never known what it is to wait. But he will one day."

Robert stared at his father, wondering at the depth of feeling in his voice. "But I fear . . ." He felt the color rising to his face. "I cannot speak of it."

His father laughed. "You think I know not what you mean? You think, do you, that an old man like your father wars not against the flesh as his son does?" He spoke loudly so that Robert could hear, but his voice was gentle. "We are all of one flesh, Robert, so harken well. Evil is real, as well you know. But your longing for Patience is no evil. 'Tis a longing God Himself has given you. Learn the difference, son. How else shall He give you fruit to her body—fruit he commands to you both?"

"But my thoughts . . . I can't . . ." He wanted to bare his soul to his father but stopped short. It wasn't Patience alone who aroused him. It was Jane. It was even, God forbid, the hussies in church this very day.

Fessenden put his hand on Robert's knee. "Hush, I shall beseech the Lord in my private prayers for thee. But thou hast waited too long, perhaps, to marry. You're twenty-nine, are you not?"

Looking at the newly dug earth round the rose bushes, Robert said sullenly, "Aye, twenty-nine."

"And your brother was barely twenty-one. I told him he was too young, but now I see he wasn't. I married your mother when I was younger myself. And you've contained yourself these many years, Robert, waiting for the will of God. He cannot but bless your union."

Robert looked up again, gathering fresh courage. "Thank you. You've heartened me. I felt condemned."

Fessenden smiled. "You wonder not why I understand so well?" His eyes were warm.

"I confess . . . I did not expect . . . but it must be mortal hard to lose the woman you love and never see her more."

"You're thinking of your mother."

"Of course." He looked up sharply. "Who else?"

Fessenden smiled again, a small, inscrutable smile. "I grieved for your mother for many a year. But like you, Robert, I'm made of flesh, and bone, and blood. And God takes not away a man's longing for a bedfellow just because his wife dies."

Robert flushed indignantly. "Sir, you profane—"

"Nay, 'tis pride makes you think otherwise, as I have learned," Fessenden said easily.

The relief Robert had felt from his father's kindness gave way. The man was becoming altogether too soft in his judgments, too mellow. Robert began to mistrust the very source of his own comfort.

But his father went on. "I was going to tell you and John this evening, in fact, that I will wed again." He stopped, seeing the color drain from Robert's face. "'Tis something I have peace about, and I doubt she'll refuse me. With Jane and John sailing to America after all, and you to be wed, and your sisters all grown and married, there's only Isaac—" He stopped, laying weight on his next words. "—and Mary Snode—left at home."

Robert stared at his father in shocked disbelief, and some unnamed resolve within him hardened against Mary.

"'Tis not right for Mary to be turned out after all these years, and Isaac shall not do the work of women. Nor is it seemly for her to dwell with me and Isaac alone. I mind what evil tongues will say in the village once Jane and John set sail, and I'll not give house-room to the Devil." He smiled yet again. "But that's not all. Mary's won a place in my heart as never I thought woman would do again."

Robert jumped up, aghast. "You'll wed *her*, Father?" Mary had cast her influence on him, then, she who had always been so lax with Isaac and the girls.

"Aye, I will. And, like you, most gladly." His father's eyes were slightly amused now.

Robert looked back into them, thunderstruck. Was his father as weak as he was—the man who had scourged him for kissing a lass under the pagan mistletoe when he was fifteen, and again for making sheep's eyes at a new sister-in-law at Martha's wedding breakfast? Was his stern father weaker than he was? "Sir, you amaze me altogether."

His father leaned back so that his cloak fell open, his fingers splayed over his knees. But then, in a gesture Robert never expected to see, he laid his finger alongside his nose and winked. "Mind you," he said cheerfully, "I've not asked her yet. I'm a little forward in telling you, perhaps, so I'll thank you for your silence until she's answered me."

Robert gazed at his father in blank bewilderment. His father marrying Widow Snode? *Pray heaven she will not take him*, he thought. Anger rose and he sought to hide it.

Fessenden

"I've a few things to tend to ere morning," Jane said.

"'Tis the Sabbath, lass," Fessenden prompted gently, not moving from his place by the fire. Except for Mary Snode, John, Jane, and himself, all the others had now retired for the night.

Jane looked across the room at him with answering warmth. "Aye, I know it, Father. Forgive me, but what with the extra company in the house—" She stopped, glancing at Mary with what John recognized as a hopeful look of request and mutual understanding.

Mary stood immediately. "I'm sorry, Jane. Forgive me. I do forget myself." She flushed and averted her eyes from his. After years in the house with her, he suddenly felt awkward.

Fessenden held out a restraining hand toward her. "Nay, Mary, Jane will manage, for I have need of a word with thee." He shifted and looked up at John. "Son, go with your wife, or else retire, if you please."

John stood to follow Jane, but she stopped in the buttery doorway and smiled back at him. "It matters not, John, I'll be finished in a winking, and I know thou'rt tired. Do you go to bed, love."

Fessenden's nervousness increased as he listened to the exchange. John was nodding, pushing a hand through his hair. "Aye, tomorrow'll be a weary coil." He closed the stairway door behind him.

Without a look at his father, John climbed the stairs. He knew that his father meant to speak to Mary tonight, and his heart was light with joy for them both since he had long hoped for their match.

At last they were alone, but Fessenden waited until the latch of the buttery door had fallen behind Jane and until he knew by John's booted footsteps that his son was in the upper chamber. He cleared his throat and felt a new, unfamiliar warmth spreading through him.

Fleetingly, he wondered if he had ever loved his first wife, for he could remember nothing of his feelings for her, save the hunger, that which Robert had spoken of, for this had never changed nor left him. Now, though, his hunger had a direction, its sharpness tempered by a new wave of tenderness. Mary had unknowingly taught him the gifts of compassion and sympathy. Without sentiment, without laxity or godless license, she had shown love to him and his children for the past fourteen years.

Constraint had grown up between them of late, however, and at first he misinterpreted it. *She's forty-three,* he said to himself, *and eager to shift for herself now Isaac's the only one left. She's restless, wanting to be gone.* It had not occurred to him, then, to question his assessment of her mood. Instead, he found himself watching her more and more closely when they were at home together, found himself sitting by the hearth more of an evening to keep her company.

If he had wondered before at her blend of cheerful good will and quiet usefulness, he wondered no more. She had always spoken more to the children than to himself, maintaining a reserve toward him that he had expected and understood. Now, though, he learned more about her and about her long-dead husband, Christopher. He learned what she thought of Thomas Jackson, the minister at Chilham's parish church, and what she thought of each of his children. But she had never, of course, vouchsafed an opinion of him, and that silence piqued him.

His curiosity deepened as she seemed to resist his presence in the kitchen. In private prayers he searched his heart for an explanation, while she found ways to keep Isaac or Jane in the room with them after evening prayers. Again, he concluded at first that she must resent him. But in studying her closely, he found that she watched him often when he was, perhaps, supposed to be unaware of her eyes on him.

It dawned on him, suddenly, that far from being eager to leave, she was fearful about it. It dawned on him, too, that there might be more to her dread of leaving than had met his unobservant eyes until now. It dawned on him, in fact, that there might, after all, be a woman who would want to marry an old man of fifty-four—and not out of pity for his remaining children, either.

He watched her now. There had been a stillness about her all day, a restraining calm, as if she awaited some word or revelation from him. Each time she lifted her eyes from her needlework, they had been full of questions.

Fessenden was confused, bewildered, even afraid of his sudden rush of feeling for her. The confidence he felt in the rose garden with Robert had evaporated, and along with the warmth that ran through him came uncertainty.

"Mary?" His voice sounded a few tones lower than usual.

She folded her hands on her apron and looked away from the fire toward him. "Aye?"

"I'm wondering"—he bungled the question he had tried to frame in his mind all day and instead, in spite of himself, diverted their talk to another channel–"if ye are well pleased with Robert and his betrothed?" He swallowed, irritated with his own clumsiness. He had known her long enough. Could he not speak out and ease the strain once and for all?

A shadow fell between them as the flames died down on the last big log in the grate. The searing pinks and oranges of the flames gave way to a faint glow.

Mary sat forward in her chair, her gray eyes finding his at last. "I'll be sorry to see John and Jane depart. Jane's become like a daughter to me . . . but 'tis God's will, and you must make the best."

Her words came simply, yet he sensed a depth of unspoken feeling behind them. "We'll miss them, aye," he pressed on, "but Patience may fill the space that Jane leaves, and Robert has been trustworthy and upright all his life. I doubt not God will bless them. I told him so this afternoon."

Mary nodded. "Indeed, Robert is ever the obedient son to you, as is John. Patience, though"—she looked up, hesitating—"is not like Jane. And you and Robert will be hard put to it, I fear, to govern her."

He frowned. Throughout the evening prayers, he had been uncomfortable with the length of Patience's prayers, by the words she chose, by what seemed a critical, niggardly spirit. Yet he could not have found fault with anything in particular. He shook his head. "I hope not, Mary."

"I have trespassed in saying so," she began unsteadily.

"Nay, nay, Mary." He leaned forward, and his knuckles whitened as he gripped the side of his chair. "That's what I would say to you this very night. You've more than earned the right to speak in this house. So many years you've given us." He surveyed the sweet roundness of her face, the gentleness of her eyes and mouth, the matronly curves of her breasts under the wool bodice and white partlett she wore, and he marveled that he had been so blind to her for so long. "And you might have given your beauty to a second husband long ago, but for us."

She did not simper, but the color rushed to her face. "I? No, 'twas here I chose to be, and here I'll stay." But then she stopped. "Unless . . ."

He stood up and crossed in front of the fire with both hands outstretched to her. "Never say *unless*," he implored. Taking her hands, he raised her to face him.

A rattle behind them made both of them jump as Jane opened the buttery door and hesitated on the threshold. "Oh, pray pardon—" She gathered her skirts in confusion, rushed to the back door, and was gone.

Mary laughed suddenly, and he laughed with her, not releasing her hands. *No more of this* his heart begged him, and he turned to face her again. "There's no 'unless,'" he said thickly. "Aye, the children have grown now, and I suppose I'll need to send Isaac to Maidstone in his brother's stead ere long. But I do not wish you to go. I've sought the Almighty, Mary, and I find it in my heart to ask if you'll be my wife."

Tears gathered in her eyes, surprising him. She released his left hand to wipe them away. "I'll be thy wife, and gladly," she said faintly. "This is what I've asked of God but never thought to see."

He held her hands tighter. "I do not ask for pity of you," he said firmly, "nor gratitude, though I'm thankful enough for all you've done, and I hope you know it. I ask . . . because I love thee with all my heart, dear Mary."

"And I thee," she whispered.

He placed one hand on her waist and put his other arm round her. She was a small woman next to him, and he felt her trembling as he folded her to him. "We'll see the minister when Robert and Patience go," he said. She nodded.

Dumb with joy, he rocked her slightly as they stood before the fire. The warmth flowed between them, swaddling them in a cocoon of muted happiness as the fire died down to ashes and the quiet upstairs deepened to silence.

At last with a small movement she stirred against him and woke him from his daze. Looking into his face, she asked, "Do you suppose we should wait till then, John?"

He started at the unaccustomed familiarity of his Christian name on her lips, then smiled. "Oh, aye, people will gossip whatever we do, and there's the banns to be read, and the license to be got."

"Perhaps I should go away for a few weeks if you can spare me. Now that you've declared yourself, and we're together in the house. . . ."

He hesitated. "I cannot spare thee, love. We may occasion gossip, but I know not where I'd send thee, anyhow."

"What about the castle? 'Twas Sir Dudley who brought me here. He'd give me lodging till we wed."

He grimaced so that she pulled away. "No. You'll not go there, dear. Years ago all was well between Sir Dudley and me, but he's hardened now, like the rest of the gentry hereabouts, in the popish ways of Laud and his company. I'll not see you in his house, not even for three weeks."

Her eyebrows rose. "You sound like Robert—forgive me—set against all who believe not just as we do."

"'Tis not that, I hope," he protested mildly. "'Tis what the King and Parliament have done with men who dare to speak truth and preach the Gospel. That's what I abhor, though I'll have no truck with violence, persecution, and interfering in men's consciences, even as some of our own brethren do."

He broke off, and the face of Patience that afternoon, issuing condemnation of moderate men he thought godly, hovered before his eyes. "But nor can I brook the forcing of rituals down a man's throat by bishops who call themselves High Churchmen but flaunt themselves in splendor like papal legates." He heard his voice rising and stopped ruefully. "I'm sorry, Mary. What has this to do with you?"

"I'll bide where I be, then."

He tightened his arms round her. "Aye, for I have need of thee, love."

John

The little chamber upstairs was cramped: a bed raised from the floor by piles of local bricks, two straight chairs, a desk by the window at which John generally sat to do accounts if the light had not failed, and a washing basin and ewer in the corner. As a child, John had shared this room and this bed with his brothers. But for thirteen years it had belonged to him and Jane. Only a few more weeks now. Then they would exchange the little window for creaking ship timbers, the big bed for narrow pallets stacked one above another, their comfortable house and freedom to walk and ride the lanes of Kent for a hole below the deck of a ship bound for the New World.

This was no sacrifice, John reflected, sitting on the edge of the bed. This was what he had longed for. What if he was exchanging the abundance of a Wealden home for the crudeness of a wattle hut in the harsh settlements of Massachusetts Bay? Yes, it was what he had longed for. The other exchanges were small, and he spared them only rare moments of regret. The exchange that mattered was the one by which he was leaving behind the increasing persecution directed by the bishops and the Church against all so-called Independents.

In the Bay Settlement, he would find the bright light of religious freedom—distance himself from the Reverend Trittons and Archbishop Lauds of England, from the forced attendance at services that smacked more and more of the Queen's Roman Catholic practices, from profanation of the Lord's Day, from the new Archbishop's suppression of the God-fearing French Huguenots they knew in Canterbury. Aye, they were longing to go.

The timing was providential in many ways. His father might be married soon, and Robert was bringing a wife home ere long. No doubt there would soon be children again to fill the house. Isaac was a grown man: strong, resourceful—no good with accounts, perhaps, but a favorite among all those with whom the Fessendens did business.

Besides, some of the worst days in the Colony were over, it was said. No longer random outposts of huts in the hostile wilderness, communities and villages were growing up all round the Bay. They would have neighbors, markets for supplies, a church, and a minister already established. Thus his old hunger to cross the sea had returned, and he was filled with the same curiosity, hope, and idealism that had once driven him to Leyden, then to Canterbury with Brewster and Cushman.

The Providence of God, he thought gratefully. *'Twas not His will for me to go then to the Colony. But had He not bidden me to Canterbury, I would never have found my wife. And she . . .* His mind moved slowly now, heavy with an old sadness they had shared. . . . *Had she conceived, as we long hoped, we might have settled here, loath to leave for our children's sakes.* He sighed. *Yes, God is all-wise.*

He pulled off his boots and undid his Sabbath falling bands. He did it without thinking, his mind still traveling toward the future, but now full of questions. Robert would soon uproot from Maidstone and with Patience occupy this room, taking over all his responsibilities in Chilham and Canterbury. All should be well, and yet. . . .

He pictured Patience, and new misgivings needled him. What was it about her that disturbed him? She was God-fearing, pious, careful in her speech. She deferred to Mary, at least thus far, as if she had already learned of Mary's soon-to-come change of position in the household. Plainly, too, she was devoted to Robert, and he to her. *Then why this anxiety?* he asked himself uncomfortably. *The Devil tempting me to doubt?* Her thin, intense face appeared before him, her delicate hands and brilliant blue eyes.

Briefly, he smiled. He and Robert both had a taste for women with luminous blue eyes. But without censuring himself for that thought, John realized suddenly that he found Patience very ugly, except for her eyes. There was a pinched, tight look about her, as if she carried a grudge. Her manner with him, with Jane, and with his father seemed forced, brittle, no more than mere civility.

He tried to stem his thoughts with caution. Could they expect otherwise from a young woman brought up in a poorhouse, who had retained respectability by working as a spinner and occasional seamstress for her aunt in Maidstone? No wonder she was thin and fidgeted with her cap so often. No wonder after his brother and father had returned from their stroll that afternoon she had sat stolidly beside her aunt and spoken of little else but the tracts they had been reading and of the inadequacy of the preaching that morning. She had found comfort in overzealousness, of course.

John frowned. *She's right,* he told himself. *Everything she said is right.* He struggled, then, to name the cause of his unaccountable dislike for her. Was it her face? *"The Lord seeth not as man seeth . . . the Lord looketh on the heart."* No, he dismissed that. Appearance had never swayed him much except, he acknowledged wryly, when he had first met Jane. But in her he had seen inner as well as outer beauty. This seemed lacking in Patience.

Irritably, he wrenched off his smock, breeches, and hose. Who was he to judge? How could he see into her heart?

He looked round the room. The candle already burned low. Where was Jane?

She came in with a flurry a few moments after he had settled in bed. "Just think what I was witness to just now, John!" She laughed.

"For shame!" he said mildly, sitting up again. "Turning into a gossip, little wife?"

Her face fell, but not for long. "Nay, but *you* know what's afoot, I lay." Her eyes sparkled.

"Perhaps." He reached up for her. "Come, get thee to bed. 'Tis cold and lumpish without thee, and I mean to enjoy this bed while we have it."

Laughing again, she untied her coif, unlaced her bodice, and went in her chemise to the basin. "Sometimes, husband, I wonder about you. I'd be breeding all the time if I weren't . . . ." In the candlelight her eyes wavered, then steadied again. "But now, seeing your father and Mary at last, I know whose son you are."

"Jane Fessenden!"

"Aye, 'tis true. Thy father must've forgot I was off in the buttery. When I came out, he was standing by her with his face on fire and her hands in his. I hardly knew where to put myself." She stopped, her face clouding. "I fled out to the privy and then up here. Will they mind that I—?"

John lay back on the flock mattress and laughed. "Oh, love, would I had seen thy face, my poppet, and my father like the green lover I was with you at first. Oh, 'tis what I've hoped these many years." He clasped his hands together. "The Lord is a God of joy, is He not? Come, let us thank Him for His mercy to our father after all these years. He's got a jewel, he has."

As they knelt together, the candle sputtered and went out. In bed again, he made love to her slowly and tenderly. Then they lay still, their arms round each other in the dark.

But Jane could not sleep as now he wanted to do. "John?"

"Aye?" He heard the sleepiness in his own voice.

"I'm glad as you are for this change for Mary, especially now that Robert marries this . . . Patience. . . ." Her tongue seemed to stick on the name. "And now, we're away ourselves."

Her gentle voice had jolted him more surely than a shout. He lay quite still. "What can you mean, my love?"

"I feared to tell thee. I hoped you'd feel the same or know what I meant without my saying more."

His mouth went dry, and his voice caught as he answered. "I often do." He sighed. "But this time you'd better speak your part."

Her breathing quickened, and he knew she was weighing her words, not trusting herself. "'Tis hard to say. 'Tis hard." She took a deep, quick breath. "But with Mary as his wife, I think our father'll be master here yet. Without her, I fear he'd fade, and Robert would command all. And lately, love, thy brother has . . . I cannot say."

He put his fingers to her lips. "Hush, I have felt it, too. He's been so silent, so turned inward." He wanted to add, "And too stern in his convictions, as if he'd made enemies of us all," but he forbore.

She seemed to take courage from him. "Aye, that's what I meant to say. And Patience is the same, only more so. Truth to tell, John, though I'll have to learn to love her as a sister for duty commands it, I cannot like her."

He had always relied on Jane's judgments. Not about business—he would never consult her there—but about people she seldom erred. "Nor I. But I cannot say why, though I've tried. I was thinking of them just afore you came up."

"But I can see clearly why I like her not." She dropped her voice to a whisper. "'Twould offend your brother mightily if I said aught to him, and I could not." She shook her head vehemently, and her hair brushed against his face.

"Nor I. Then tell me."

She groaned. "What good will it do for me to speak my mind? I have no wish to poison your—"

"Jane, my wise darling, you'll never do such a thing."

She waited so long to continue that he thought she might have drifted into sleep, but at last her voice came softly in the dark, direct, without a trace of resentment. "It's the very thing I should most like—nay, love—her for. The reading she does. Her knowledge of the Word. Her courage to dissent so openly. But instead, I find her zeal cloying. I doubt her. She was expounding this very eve on the joy of helping our Christian brothers and sisters bear burdens, but yester eve when Mary and I had the dinner still to ready and all the Sabbath food to prepare, she gave no help at all."

Jane paused, her voice changing. "Nay, but I'm ashamed of my pettiness. She had just come by cart all the way from Maidstone, and no doubt was aweary." She paused again. "God will have to deal with me. I'm surely wrong to think thus."

He stirred, pressing close against her. "I think not, love. Unless I be wrong, too. You've only said what I had thought but knew not how to name."

"John, I could not have lived here with Robert *and* Patience, you know."

He did not answer immediately and consequently felt her body tense with anxiety. He searched for words to reply. "I know . . . nor I. 'Tis better thus." He kissed her hair, feeling her relax again. "And Mary will look after our father. God knows His purpose for us all."

They fell asleep at once, like children. And as John drifted out onto the lake of sleep, he dreamed of the new land to which they would sail in only a few weeks.

Maidstone, May 1635

George

They had been married for almost three years. From the very beginning, Elizabeth wanted to bear his children, but none came. Then she found herself pregnant, only to lose the unborn baby after a few weeks. Grief dampened her spirits so completely that George took her from Tolhurst Court in April, making a hurried journey by coach to St. Bartholomew's Hospital to see Doctor William Harvey. The doctor examined Elizabeth closely and pronounced that he saw no reason why she could not produce a whole nursery of healthy children, especially as she was still so young. "Just give her a little adventure now and then, my boy," Harvey counseled privately after the examination.

"We'll go home now, my love," George had said.

She looked at him with pleading eyes he should have known he couldn't resist. "Nay, dear heart, pray let us not. You'll turn the horses and drive straight for Maidstone, won't you?"

"Maidstone?" he queried vaguely, having forgotten all else but Elizabeth and the lost babe.

She laughed sadly. "Aye, the quarter sessions. 'Tis the first of May in two days, remember?"

He frowned deeply, his jaws tense. "Nay, I *had* forgot, though."

"Please, please may I go with thee?"

He thought immediately of the plague and wished to take no chances with her. "Never. 'Tis not safe. 'Tis not wise." Though no plague deaths were reported yet for the year, forty had died only a year before.

Then, seeing her crestfallen face and recalling her longing, even before their marriage, to support him in all his civic responsibilities, he began to weaken. She didn't understand, he thought with pity, how tedious most of his charges were—licenses to be issued to victuallers, commissions for road repairs, bastardy orders, arrangements for paupers, fines for those who had missed divine services—little of it interested him. He would much rather, like Sir Dudley, follow his hounds and oversee the stringing and training of the hop bines on their poles. However, perhaps such a jaunt would be a small way to assuage his many worries about ship tax money, and about his wife.

So Elizabeth prevailed, and now he tried to suppress his misgivings about being in a busy town at the beginning of the plague months.

They were up earlier than usual on May Day, Elizabeth clad in a glistening green taffeta gown and red stammel petticoats that he heartily approved in these days of dull duns, blacks, and blues that the Puritans insisted on. Her maid had dressed her hair to a perfection of red ringlets, too. She was beautiful, and she was his, her arm tucked through his own as they walked slowly down the High Street.

Bright spots appeared on her cheeks as they left the Star Inn. For her, he realized, the coincidence of their return from London through the county town on this particular date was a happy one. The rest of the town was astir just as early. All round the Bear Ringle a crowd had already gathered for the bear-baiting. Farther up the street, under the arches of the Market Cross and at the top of Mill Lane under the shelter of the tile-roofed Shambles—butchers, drapers, cordwainers, victuallers, mercers, and fishmongers had already set up their wares.

Tolhurst exulted in the roar of activity, the shout of the crowd round the Ringle, the crowing of the cocks at the Cock Inn on East Lane, the swirling array of color as all the women of the town, like Elizabeth, seemed to have been infected with the madness of May, the mildness of the air, and the silent withdrawal of all Puritans from the festival day.

The old days are come again, he thought happily, remembering his father's tales of the Queen's Day celebrations in the Fair Meadow, days when the church bells rang until dusk, when players and minstrels performed among the crowds, when women and children made joyful processions with candles, flowers, and fireworks. He dismissed from his mind the burdensome thoughts of the morrow's work at the Lower Court House as well as the curse of the plague. Burying his nose for an instant in the pomander of sandalwood that swung by Elizabeth's girdled waist, he determined to enjoy the day.

"Look, George!" his wife exclaimed. "Here's the Fair Meadow. And see how many people are come!"

He took a deep breath of the damp, warm air that rolled off the Medway and over the soft, green sward of the meadow. "Aye, 'tis a grand sight!"

They moved among the crowd, occasionally passing Elizabeth's maid, dispatched to enjoy herself at the fair with George's groom, and encouraged by a few extra pennies from George's purse. In one corner of Fair Meadow, a band of mummers was performing an uproarious comedy. The jokes they bawled were lewd, the costumes patched and fantastical, but the Tolhursts stopped to watch, drawn almost against their will, and laughing helplessly. The actors danced, wagged their heads, and gestured while the bells on their caps and shoes tinkled merrily. Then, linking arms, they came to the edge of their crude wooden platform and sang a May song George had known from childhood.

> *A branch of May we bring to you*
> *As in your courts we stand.*
> *'Tis naught but a sprout,*
> *But it's well budded out*
> *By the work of the Good Lord's hand.*

As they sang, a man covered in wide, flowing hessian, his blackened face partially concealed by the rough material, capered in front of the boards. His skirts adorned with sprigs of hawthorn, ivy, and lilac, he caricatured the mummers' words and gestures by his own movements. High over himself he carried the carved head of a horse, which was attached to a pole and a simple lever. By working the lever from under the hessian, the man nodded the horse's head and snapped the nail-studded jaws to show off his absurdities.

Elizabeth rocked back on her heels with laughter. "Isn't he comical?"

Laughing too, George agreed. But then he hesitated, struck by a sudden idea. "Wait, dear Bess," he said. "See what the hooden horse does? Why, I remember what my nurse said when I was an unbreeched lad."

> *If a lass*
> *But kiss*
> *An 'Hobbyoss*
> *Upon a May Fair*
> *Be she*
> *Wife or maid*
> *Mother shall she be*
> *Within a year.*

He thrust his thumbs in his belt, feeling slightly foolish and worrying that he might have pained her by the reminder. "'Twas something of the sort," he added lamely.

Elizabeth's laughter faltered. "Nay, husband, I'm amazed. You're not a one to believe old tales. And I'd not kiss that old 'ooden horse for the world." Her eyes flashed at him. "Fie, shame on thee for thinking of it!"

He started, chagrined by her sudden show of temper. "Sweet, I didn't say you should do it, did I?" But then, disarmed by her hot face, and wanting to mock her intensity, he grinned. "I knew not I was wed to so chaste and prim a wife as that! Next you'll be telling me 'tis all superstition"—he flung out his arm to indicate the entire fairground—"all of it. You little Puritan hussy!" He slid his hand down her back and gave her a playful spank.

She leaned against him, smiling up into his face. "And so it is. But I love it, all of it. I'm no Puritan, sweetheart. Rather, an utter pagan to take delight in it all."

Satisfied, he turned his eyes back to the mummers. Their song ended, the hooden horse pranced through the crowd, reaching out to grab maids and wives alike. When the horse caught one—and most were eager to be caught, squealing with delight or pretended dismay—he lapped her for a moment in his copious skirts, kissed her heartily, then set her free, red faced, to join her husband or lover.

Elizabeth now stared at the middle of the fairground, her attention arrested, perhaps by the maypole, perhaps by the colorful gypsy wagons drawn together a short distance away. She seemed to have lost interest in the hooden horse and not noticed its nearness. George made to lead her gently away, but it was too late. Unless he offered to fight the man dressed as the horse, which would hardly accord with the good-natured spirit of the day, he would have to surrender her for a moment to the enfolding arms The superstitious part of him, brought up in the old lore of an English country village, wanted her to be caught anyway. It would do no harm, he reasoned, and what if it worked a charm on them both and she had a baby to dandle on her knee in a year?

"Here's a pretty lady, now!" the hooden horse roared in a lusty, boozy voice. Approaching Elizabeth suddenly from behind, he snatched her into his arms.

She let out a scream and sent George a look of helpless surprise before she disappeared into the swirling skirts. He heard and almost felt the rough, loud wetness of the man's kiss, the struggle of her hands beating against him in rage. Then in a second she appeared again, her ringlets askew and one cheek smudged with the man's face paint.

He held out his arms with a look of resigned amusement. She flew into them, half laughing, shuddering, embarrassed by all the eyes staring and mouths gaping to see a fine lady caught by a common hooden horse.

"Thou—thou planned this," she hissed.

He laughed indulgently. "Nay, nay, how could I, love?"

"But thou did'st not *stop* it."

"Again, how could I?"

"A great farmer like you?"

"A farmer and a gentleman, not a fighter, and . . . I left my cudgel at home."

She snorted crossly, but then dissolved in laughter again, her hand shaking the sword that hung at his side. "You're a gentleman only when it suits you," she mocked.

He drew her away. "Look," he said. "See what use this fine blade would be?" He made to unsheathe his sword, pulling it only half way so that he would cause no alarm to anyone. "Rusty. Useless, I'm sure."

She scowled. "Then why wear it?"

"'Tis elegant, they say. Fashion dictates it, as well as these wretched silly feathers." He threw out his arms in a loose shrug and waved his hat irritably.

"Since when did fashion dictate to George Tolhurst?"

"Not often," he conceded, weary of the sparring match she wanted with him. "Except when I'm to town."

She seemed to catch his change in mood, for she quieted again. "Come, I'd like to see the rest of the fair."

He bent to kiss her, then took his neckerchief and dabbed at the paint on her face until it was gone. "What is thy will, fair wife?" He made a courtly bow.

She pointed ahead. "To watch the maypole dancers for a while. The day grows warm. Will they not crown the Queen of the May before the flowers and garlands all wilt?"

"Aye, they will surely. Look out. 'Twill be you they choose, I lay."

As they ambled toward the gypsy wagons, she shook her head vehemently. "Not me. They'll choose a maid, not a cross old matron of five-and-twenty who shunned the kiss of the 'ooden horse."

Before them lay the booths of gypsy tinkers, where men in garish clothes lounged on the steps of their wagons or bent in concentration over goodwives' broken pots, where fresh-faced gypsy women asked to have their palms crossed with silver to tell the fortunes of credulous maidens. Beyond all these stood the tall maypole of Maidstone. Permanently planted in the

Fair Meadow, it flourished each year with an array of flowers and brilliant streamers. And this year's was no different.

Clustered round the pole stood a pack of girls dressed in white smocks, full skirts, and adorned with the ribbons and flowers that befitted the day: reds, greens, and whites all mixed in bright profusion and highlighted by intricate rosettes.

Beside the maids stood their lovers dressed in similar white smocks (some embroidered), their breeches and hose crisscrossed with leather bands, buckles, and metal bells, and their soft hats crammed with a riot of trailing kerria, lily-of-the-valley, and violets.

Tolhurst, as much as his wife, wanted the dancing to begin.

At last a man dressed in shabby livery stepped out of the throng, swept his hat off in a low bow, and called for the dancers and musicians. The crowd stilled, and the first beats of the tabor sounded, slow at first, a flat thud lacking in the resonance of a large cavalry drum, but gradually growing in strength and speed. Soon, gitterns gave depth to the tabor: gentle strings inaudible but for the reverential hush that had fallen on the center of the fairground. Finally, pipes began to shrill.

The music interwove with itself, reeling out threads of sound that crossed and countered and pulled at each other in the perfect interlacing of a weaver's loom. The melody was of fairyland, of an older age when elves and fairies danced through flowers, blessed the growth of wheat, oats, and barley as well as the birth of lambs and calves, and the marriage beds of brides. It chased away wicked hobgoblins from the sweet, fair courts of enchantment.

The dancers loosened their ribbons and, with faces transfigured by joy, mirrored the music in their own interweaving pattern of steps. Without faltering they dipped and rose with the ribbons until a tight warp and weft of color clung to the chestnut shaft. At last the music changed, the dancers turned, and the ribbons gradually unfurled to their full length.

Elizabeth sighed with pleasure as the first dance ended.

"There will be more," George assured her.

"Aye, but not yet, I think."

He looked at the flushed faces of the dancers. Garlands had slipped on the maidens' heads, and sweat plastered hair to foreheads under the brims of the men's hats. "Perhaps you're right. Come, I'll buy thee some ribbons for thine own hair, love." He smiled at her, delighting again in her delight, and glad that they had decided to stay in Maidstone together. Later, when they were alone again, he would see to it that the charm of the hooden horse had a chance to work. How lovely she was!

They stopped a gypsy man who carried brilliant ribbons on a tray tied round his neck.

"There, love," he said, "a red one for your red cheeks, a green one for your green eyes—"

"And your green fields," she interrupted happily.

"Aye, and a blue one for—"

"Nay, no blue. 'Tis a mournful color."

"No blue then, but a bonny reddish brown one"—he picked through the tangle of color on the tray while the gypsy eyed him suspiciously—"for the color of your hair. And a gold one for wealth, and a white one for purity, and a purple one in honor of His Majesty."

Elizabeth giggled. "Fie, I didn't know," she said, mocking his words to her only a half hour before, "that I had married so poetical and gallant a cavalier. I thought I married a farmer, truly I did."

He glanced up awkwardly. Even the dark-faced gypsy was caught in the web of magic that enmeshed them both today. "And you did," he said. "But 'tis a holiday!" He tossed a coin carelessly onto the tray. The gypsy quickly pocketed the coin with a sneering look at him. George knew immediately that in his excitement he had paid too much and that the gypsy thought him a fool. *Well-a-day, never mind.* "'Tis a holiday," he repeated, "and we shan't be gay tomorrow, I fear."

They wandered through the crowds again, stopping at a booth to buy sweetmeats. The crowd flowed like a river, moving with one mind toward another part of the meadow. Stretching up to see ahead, Tolhurst realized why. "The May Queen," he said quickly. "They're choosing a lass over there to be crowned. I lay she's one of the dancers. Shall we go watch?"

Elizabeth pressed against him. "Yes, I wouldn't miss that for all the hop gardens in Goudhurst."

He laughed at her. "Oh, what a wager for a wise woman to make, little wife." All the same, he pushed forward as eagerly as she did toward the wooden structure erected near the river. They stood as near to it as they could in the throng.

Sprays of lily-of-the-valley and baskets of primroses, cherry blossoms, and forget-me-nots frothed round the stage. Above them rested a high-backed squire's chair that had been dignified for the occasion with wreaths of May blossoms festooned upon it, the white horse of Kent painted on its back, and poles lashed to its legs so that it could later be raised up as a litter.

The mayor of Maidstone, Samuel Marshall, solemnly mounted the platform and stood by the decorated throne. He wore the chain and livery of his office proudly. Not a tall man, he commanded attention by his clear speech. "Ladies and gentlemen, goodwives and goodmen, men and maids all, we have a pretender Queen this day, a fair lass of Maidstone. She is Rebecca Longhurst, daughter of Peter Longhurst, a victualler of this town, as ye all know right well."

Frowning, Tolhurst glanced at his wife. What was there in the tone of the mayor's voice that suggested untimely impudence, even doubt as to the wisdom of the choice? Had Elizabeth felt it, too? She was standing on tiptoe, her wide eyes fixed on the mayor, but registering no concern.

The people round them were murmuring in surprise. "Peter Longhurst's daughter?" they said. "He's not of Maidstone. What can the mayor mean?"

"Longhurst? Phaw! This'll send a pox on him and his house! How came she to be chosen?"

"She's fair. By the Mass, she's fair."

"Hush, that's papist talk!"

"Hold your tongue, wife. No Puritans round to hear it, are there?"

"I won't hold my tongue! You can be sure her father isn't far off."

In a flash the significance of the name and the babble of voices round him struck home. *Peter Longhurst's daughter, daughter of the man my father sent here twenty years ago and patronized till he got himself established! And now he's a Puritan preacher!* He snorted with laughter, and this time Elizabeth did look back at him.

"What is't, George?" she whispered quickly.

"I'll explain later, sweet. Watch, this will be worthy sport."

A frown creased her high forehead, but before she could question him further, the mayor again began to speak, this time sounding less certain but more pompous. "God in His wisdom," he said, "rains fair daughters on the just and the unjust, the Laud's man and the Lilburne's man alike. What say you for this blushing maiden? Shall I crown her Queen o' the May?"

Tolhurst looked over the crowd to see a tall youth, broad-shouldered and with striking, curly black hair, gently prompt a young girl to climb the steps to the platform.

She hung back, biting her lip in uncertainty, one hand on the young man in a gesture of shyness. The young man prevailed, however. Raising her head high, the girl stepped up beside the mayor. In her left hand she held a wilting nosegay of violets, but her face was transformed now from doubt to radiant joy.

The crowd gasped in wonder at her smooth fair hair, her skin unblemished by warts, moles, or scars of the pox, her blue eyes, her fine body arrayed in the white bodice and full skirts of the maypole dancers.

"Ah, but she's a fine choice, is she not?" Elizabeth asked.

His throat had gone dry. "Aye, she is." His voice caught as he answered. "Still a child, though. I'll lay she's not above seventeen." He had no memory of her. Peter Longhurst had left Goudhurst long ago, and George had known none of the offspring, perhaps unborn then, anyway.

"Still think they would have crowned your crabbed old wife?" Elizabeth teased.

He caught a faint note of jealousy in her voice, but she had obviously misinterpreted his concentrated interest in the girl. It pained him to think that this vulnerable, pretty young maiden might be made to suffer because of her father's zeal, either at his hands or by the mockery of the crowd if any of Longhurst's fanatical followers stood among them.

He shuddered, then quickly covered his misgivings and turned to Elizabeth. "Sweet, you shall be Queen of the May for me, always."

Tolhurst watched as Rebecca Longhurst, now sitting on her throne, bowed her head to receive the crown of honeysuckle and cherry blossoms. A shout went up as the mayor placed it on her head. Then the musicians struck up a lilting, boisterous jig, and four young men, including Rebecca's own partner, lifted up the throne and carried her into the crowds. A line of other girls followed, strewing flowers left and right as they went.

Tolhurst followed the steady movement of the procession with diminishing anxiety. All would be well. He led his wife back to see if there would be more maypole dancing, but the meadow was subtly changing.

The soft haze of the warm morning had hardened to the brilliant, remorseless edge of noon, and the excitement of the crowd had wilted to fatigue even as the flowers wilted. Families spread out cloaks and shawls and sat down with wineskins, bottles of ale, crusts of bread, and last year's apples. The fairground quivered in the heat and sank down under wagons, canopies, and the short shade of booths. The musicians stopped, and the May Queen stepped off her throne to be lost once again among the crowd. A respite in the day.

The Tolhursts returned briefly to their lodgings for luncheon, and afterward George endeavored to make Elizabeth rest. But she would have none of it, demanding greedily to return to the Fair Meadow to see more of the dancing.

"'Twill turn drunken as the day wears on," he cautioned her.

"More so than my father's addlepated hunting parties, do you suppose?" she asked brightly.

Disarmed again, he agreed to take her back. Entranced once again by the maypole dancers, they remained near the center of the meadow. Every so often as the dancers whirled and skipped past them, Tolhurst caught the animated expression of that curly-headed youth as he crossed ribbons with May Queen Rebecca. He found himself curiously drawn by them both, sensing somehow—perhaps because he knew of Rebecca's Puritan family—that the two did not really belong. Their graceful bearing suggested something beyond the usual scope of the Kentish yeoman.

Among the graceless yokels with lewd looks and the artificially coy girls with sidelong glances, low-bodiced dresses, and suggestive movements, those two stood out as if of gentle blood. The youth's garments were obviously well made. Perhaps he was a rich man's servant. And Rebecca's dancing gear was made demure by a white partlet over her breasts and a skirt longer than the others wore, to cover her ankles. *Little here that her father could disapprove,* he mused.

Suddenly there were shouts from the maypole and the loud voice of a man rang out. George stiffened in alarm. Had he not warned Elizabeth? With one hand on his useless sword and the other at his wife's waist to steer her away, he strained to see what was happening.

A gang of men pressed toward the dancers, their faces dark with excitement and their fists raised. It was with only slight relief that he saw they carried cudgels rather than swords.

Through the group of men pushed a short, stocky man with tow-colored hair and the wide, flattened features of a bull, the kind of man Tolhurst hated most. He knew the face—and the man—immediately.

"Have done with your wanton sports!" the man shouted. He stood still now, his arms spread and his palms lifted, his men clustering behind him. "Out upon this pagan blasphemy, for shame!"

The musicians winked and grinned at one another but kept playing. Two of the dancers faltered, however. At once the neat pattern of the ribbons was disrupted, and the pole swayed dangerously.

"Behold the children of darkness! They sport in the shameless daylight to worship at this foul terebinth of Baal, and God Himself shakes their pole as a sign of His wrath!"

The man was screaming now, and Tolhurst saw Rebecca's face crumple, caught the look of despair that passed between the girl and her handsome partner.

The ribbons tangled again, and again the pole swayed, but the musicians whistled, banged, and plucked strings louder than ever, and all but the two dancers went on with their frenzy of rising and dipping, twirling and spinning. Finally, as the music reached a wild crescendo, the ranting orator and his cohorts made a rush at the maypole with hoots and shouts as wild as the music itself. Tearing the ribbons from the hands of the dancers, they flung garlands and ribbons to be trampled on the grass, and with one great shove they sent the maypole tottering and crashing to the ground.

A deadly hush followed. The minstrels and dancers stared at the wreck of their afternoon's May games in horrified silence while the surrounding crowd moaned in sympathy.

But the peace lasted only briefly. Once again the voice of Peter Longhurst thundered out, and the crowd surged forward to answer him fist for fist, cudgel for cudgel.

Elizabeth screamed in terror beside her husband. Tolhurst pushed and pulled her away from the brawl as fast as the crowd allowed.

"Repent and be saved," screamed Longhurst. "Put away those lascivious, filthy ballads, those scurvy rhymes. They savor of raging sensuality! The way to heaven is steep, too narrow for men to dance in and keep revel-rout." He paused only for an instant. "Where is that Jezebel, my daughter?"

"There'll be broken pates and bloodshed in this day's work," Tolhurst shouted to his wife over the tumult. "Let us away quickly."

Pandemonium erupted across the fairground. Puritans, recognizable by their sober dress, starched collars, and small ruffs, rushed in twos or threes to upset booths, tear down garlands, break the May Queen's throne, and wreak havoc wherever they might.

Elizabeth stared wild-eyed at the violence and leaned more and more heavily on George, gasping as they pressed forward. In a cage by one of the gypsy wagons, a brilliantly plumed cock, stirred by all the confusion, opened its beak and crowed raucously three times.

The Tolhursts reached the gates of the fairground just as the wardens and constables arrived. By now the noise behind them had risen to a furious roar, but George knew he could not lead Elizabeth straight back to the Star Inn, so he found a bench nearby.

"We'll rest a while, my love. I'm sorry that I ever brought—"

"Nay, 'twas my doing. We shouldn't have returned." Her face was pallid, her voice coming faintly.

He wrapped his arms round her and pulled his mouth into a grim line. *She needs not these upsets if she's to breed,* he thought, grinding his teeth savagely. *In spite of what that doctor says, she's better home. Her notions of seeing "the world" are childish, though I cannot tell her so.*

She was trembling against him. "What will they do, the mayor and his constables? What will happen?"

He shrugged. "Rabble such as that will not rule Maidstone, nay, nor England. As long as we've a King and an archbishop, weak as they may be, we'll have order here. Those men are but rogues, scum, ill-bred, unlettered. . . ."

Elizabeth turned her face up to his in surprise. "You sound so harsh, so unlike yourself," she observed.

He sighed and his voice softened. "Aye, you're right, sweet Bess. 'Tis just that they've taken too much unto themselves of late, those Puritans. They think they can rule because they have a Geneva Bible, think they can stand ranting and raving in the marketplace all day." He gestured back toward the fair. "But you have seen how loutish and indecent their carriage is. You've seen it for yourself. Indecent in the name of decency! 'Twill never do."

She nodded slowly, and he tightened his arm round her shoulders. "His Grace is aweary of such fellows, and so are the judges and jurates."

"They'll be tried and punished?" Her voice was low.

"Aye, more than likely the constables will snare their conies today."

"And then what?"

"For unlawfully preaching without a license in public meeting places? Why, that alone carries the penalty of the pillory nowadays. They'll be clapped in irons tonight, at least." He shuddered. *And mutilation for others,* he thought, but he could not bring himself to say it. "These sessions will be a mite more lively than of yore, I fear." He felt the muscles in Elizabeth's upper arms tighten. She rarely missed his meaning, even if unspoken.

"Ah, poor misled—"

"Misled, aye, and blind men who would lead others who are equally blind." He shook himself. "But come, let's not brood and darken this day further. Not all Puritans are canting madmen, I dare say. And 'tis warm, still, out-of-doors. Let's up to the market before we return to the inn."

Glancing up at the gates to the meadow, he saw another couple hurrying out—a young girl in white, the hem of her skirt torn, her fair hair disheveled, her arm through that of a tall man with sinewy arms and a fierce expression on his face. She was crying, clinging to him. Shocked, Tolhurst realized that this was the May Queen, Rebecca Longhurst. Only shreds of her honeysuckle and cherry-blossom garland remained in her hair.

Elizabeth had loosened herself from her husband's hold and sat forward, ready to leave the bench.

"No, wait," he muttered. Where was Rebecca's young lover? The hawk-like menace of the other man's face disturbed him, and he felt the same desire to protect the Longhurst girl that he had felt earlier. But then he saw that she was glad to be with the man at her side. As they passed in front of the bench, he even caught some of her words. The man must be a brother, or perhaps some more temperate friend of her father's sent to extricate her from the brawl. "Thank'ee, sir. I was so afeared . . . but Isaac . . ." Her voice came in sobs as they passed, but there was no mistaking the relief and gratitude that mingled with the sorrow and terror, even if he could make little sense of what she said.

He studied the profile of the man before they vanished out of sight: a deep jaw, chin slightly jutting, clean-shaven, the dark hair close-cropped so that the man's ears, cheekbones, and nose were accentuated. He looked about thirty, perhaps older, and Tolhurst determined to remember him. When things calmed down he should go and see Peter Longhurst, try to talk him out of his foolishness, to reason with him. He would ask after Rebecca then. No doubt the girl would be well provided for—with or without her young escort.

He turned to his wife and saw that the color was returning to her face. He promptly forgot Rebecca.

Robert

The first night at the Longhursts' lodgings, well known to him over years of staying there, brought an unpleasant jolt to Robert's otherwise serene life. Marriage suited him well: he had filled out a little, felt less restless, more satisfied with life. Better still, though Patience had been prudish and frigid in their bride-bed, he was rarely troubled by the lustful thoughts and desperate hunger for the bodies of women that had bedeviled him all those years between the provocative kiss of the wench at Digges' Castle and the timorous kisses of his new wife. Patience had accepted her new role submissively, fulfilling her duties to him as a good Christian wife exactly as he had known she would, though she had never said she loved him. But he was content.

Content he was, too, to have taken the absent John's place as the eldest son of the family. Glad that John was happy in Massachusetts Bay, he admitted to himself, too, that he was glad for his own sake that his brother had gone. Jane had alway unsettled him. Beautiful—but barren. And children were a reward from the Lord to the righteous. Jane's unrighteousness lay hidden as yet, but *he* had found the pearl. Patience had presented him with one child already, Thomas, and another was due in the winter.

Trying to fall asleep without the accustomed warmth of her back against his own to keep out the cool of this late spring night, he had no difficulty picturing her now. The second child had not shown himself yet in the swelling of her body or stirring within, but her face had rounded and softened, and he found her more desirable than before. *Not just a godly reader, she,* he thought cheerfully, *but a good breeder, please God.* He reached across the bed without thinking, but of course she lay far off, in Chilham. She was not here.

And neither was Isaac. Where *was* that scoundrel? Carousing in one of the alehouses, perchance. A fine bedfellow he would make, no doubt, coming late up the Longhursts' stairs and falling onto the bed without so much as a glance at the ewer or a search for his nightsmock.

Robert turned over in bed and groped for the tinder box to light a candle. It was his obligation, he decided, to remain awake until Isaac returned, then to box his ears and issue some sound rebukes. His father would not do it, too soft in his old age, now wed to that easygoing Mary Snode. No, it was for him to chasten Isaac and stop his wicked, debauched ways. That was why Longhurst had asked one of the grammar school masters to write Robert a letter:

Sir,

> *Know that your brother Isaac doth taint himself in idle sports, no longer conducting himself in the ways of righteousness. He is riotous and heeds not my words. Though I doubt not he honors his father and worketh well for him by day, I know not how long he may continue when all the while he plays by night. I beseech you call him home and upbraid him. There is another matter besides, which I fear to write here. Pray make a speedy answer, sir. I remain your servant and your friend.*

The letter was neatly written in the practiced flourishes and stiff rhetoric of the teacher, clumsily signed by Peter Longhurst. So without telling his father what he intended to do, Robert had left the next day for Maidstone.

Here all his fears about his brother had been confirmed. Longhurst recounted, at first with ingratiating timidity, then with increasing boldness and savagery, how young women had flocked to Isaac for his fine looks and debonair, gallant manner.

"He's growed those thick black curls, you know. Looks like a swaggering Cavalier. Always so civil to me, he is, but he's a sly one." The victualler's face darkened. "Wooed my daughter, he did, without a by-your-leave to me. I'd have been proud to see her wed to him if he'd remained as he promised at the first, but he's a blighted apple, that one—rosy-cheeked and fair on the outside and rotten within, the kind my customers bring back to me and I refund them for. She swears he hath not had her maidenhead, but I . . . fear he has, and I'd thank'ee to take him away afore he sires bastards on her."

Longhurst shook his head in disgust. "I never thought to see this day with a Fessenden in my house, and all my daughters been so chaste and sweet. I'll not have such lewd, ungodly folk above stairs no more. Your brother Fessenden'll have to shift for himself if he stays in town."

Robert was struck silent by this news, which Longhurst shouted to him so that he would not miss a word of it.

So Isaac had discovered his handsome self! And in so doing, he had taken advantage of his relative freedom in Maidstone and had discovered women. Shame on him! Robert winced, thinking about him and remembering with fury the rest of his converse with Longhurst as darkness had fallen in the poky room, and lamps, candles, and rushlights had begun to glow without.

"He's off and away this very evening," Longhurst told him loudly, "and naught I could do to stop him save fetch him a clout on his pate with my stick. And that would make but little dint in his thick skull." Longhurst shuddered. "'E's a big lad, your brother, and not the likes of you and John—not a one I care to quarrel with."

"Oh, but he'll mind me," Robert burst out. "Don't you fret!" And he thought with vicious satisfaction of the pleasure he would take in beating his brother.

"Rebukes run off him like water off a foul, slimy gutter in the High Street." Longhurst shook his head mournfully.

Robert stared, felt pressure building behind his eyeballs as he meditated on Isaac's soon-to-fall punishment. "Rebukes? Nay, I'll not waste my breath. I'll do with him what my good mother would have done years ago, had she lived, and what my father should have done. He'll get a beating such as he's never had."

Longhurst's eyebrows curved up under his thick, oily thatch of yellowish hair with a hint of skepticism that he soon veiled. "Aye, he has it coming. Then I'll thank'ee to take 'im away for good. And I pray heaven he hath not violated my daughter. Why even now . . ." The man shut his eyes and screwed up his face.

Robert felt the blood rushing to his face. Anger overcame him like a red tide. "She's off with him this very night?" The scarlet waves broke over his brain, and he thumped his fist so hard on the mantelpiece that the wood splintered at the edge. "Why couldn't you *stop* her, you fool?" he barked.

Longhurst backed away. "I'm no fool. Devil take your ill tongue, Goodman Fessenden!"

Robert bit down on his lower lip until the blood oozed out. "Forgive me. I spoke in haste."

"Aye." Longhurst turned away bitterly. "Now you have children of your own, you'll soon know what a coil it is to keep order even under your own roof. Especially"—he swung round again, his voice heavy with emphasis—"when the Devil puts one of his own under your roof to tempt them away from the right path."

Robert kept silence, waiting for the man to exhaust his anger.

"If I'm to be a shepherd of God's flock," Longhurst ranted on, "then I *must* keep order in mine own house. The Word says, 'For if a man know not how to rule his own house, how shall he take care of the church of God?' Yon Isaac goes with you."

"And if your daughter—" Robert faltered. There was more he must say. "Rebecca."

"Henrietta?" He wasn't sure he had heard correctly.

"Rebecca!" Longhurst shouted.

"If Rebecca's with child?"

Longhurst scoffed. "Then she'll wed a man more fitting who can foster the poor babe. I'll none of your brother for a son. Rebecca shall learn obedience of a man who's godly, a man who shall know the truth about her harlotry but stoop like Hosea to keep her as his wife despite her wickedness."

Remembering their talk now, Robert sat forward under the bed linens and tried to visualize the Longhurst children. The eldest of them was but fourteen when he had vacated this very room to be wed to Patience, moving home to Chilham with his bride. Their young, childish faces eluded him—except one. Was she perhaps the eldest? Was that Rebecca, then?

He had noticed her always, but only because she reminded him of Jane: the same hair of flaxen gold, the same clear, sky-bright eyes, the same silvery laugh. Like Jane, the girl had been slightly built, slender. Had she grown to womanhood now, a willow beauty of fifteen or sixteen whom Isaac could not ignore? Isaac, the ill-disciplined Isaac, the beautiful one, the one he had always been jealous of. *Jealous?* A fearful, ugly thought! Shaking his head to clear his mind, he slipped out of bed, fell to his knees, and began to pray in desperation for his own cleansing and forgiveness.

When first he opened his eyes the next day, it was with the mistaken idea that Isaac had not slept in the bed at all. The bedding beside him was hardly disturbed. But as he went to the ewer in the corner to begin his toilet, he noticed a discarded jerkin that had not lain over the chair back the night before. Isaac's work boots also stood beneath the chair, old leather stained with the mud of East Lane. The lad was gone already, then, making a holiday of it. But what was he wearing on his feet?

Robert looked down at his own feet, pale and naked now on the rough boards of the room he had occupied for so long. He had never possessed more than one pair of boots, and now his brother was cavorting round Maidstone at dawn on May Day in a second pair of shoes! The thistles of resentment grew higher within him, and angry words that he had difficulty swallowing came to his lips. A plague on Isaac's cunning for escaping him this morning!

After Longhurst had presided over lengthy prayers, mainly for Isaac and Rebecca, who were caught, as he put it, in the evil enchantment of the rites of this godless day, Robert sallied out with him to find the young couple and bring due retribution upon them. He discovered, however, that Longhurst's purpose was wider than the mere punishment of his daughter. They were to gather up other men of their own persuasion and issue a public denouncement of the May Fair. Longhurst believed that they were the instruments for the message of God to the deceived and idolatrous people who had risen so early in the day to celebrate the coming of the summer.

Robert heartily approved Longhurst's sentiments and offered his help.

Resentful at first because of Isaac, Longhurst eventually accepted. "Well, you're a brawny man, and middling tall. Those graceless rogues and their wanton wives will heed me if I've thee beside me. Go with me, then, if thou wilt."

All morning as Longhurst preached in the marketplace and gathered a crowd of supporters, Robert's hands itched to clutch at Isaac's shirt and send him staggering backward with a long-due blow in the face. He paid little attention to some of the men Longhurst was bringing into their cause. They shouted agreement with all Peter Longhurst said, raising their voices in loud affirmation each time the May games were condemned, and waving their cudgels. He did not notice the vengeful, bloodthirsty looks on some of the men's faces as the mayor and corporation were mentioned.

Once he caught a glimpse of himself in the warped glass that was for sale in one of the market booths, a glimpse of a man as bloodthirsty as the rest, a man he did not even recognize.

At the Fair Meadow he saw Isaac immediately. He hadn't seen the lad for several months now, but he would have known his brother anywhere, even with lovelocks. His face illuminated with sweat and happiness, Isaac skipped in and out of the other dancers. His thick hair bobbed on his shoulders, and his huge, muscular frame was strangely graceful in movements that were entirely foreign to Robert.

Longhurst pressed close to his side. "Abomination! Wicked, lustful abomination!" he shouted.

Robert reluctantly let his eyes rest on the dancing girls and mumbled agreement, but as he noticed one in particular, his voice died in his throat, and his chest contracted painfully. She was Longhurst's daughter, for sure, and as different from the other girls as velvet from hessian. *No, if she's given Isaac her maidenhead*, he thought, *then wolves go these days arrayed as tender lambs*. She was enjoying the lewd dancing, certainly, but she danced unaware of herself. She looked at none of the other dancers save Isaac, flashing a quick, innocent smile each time they passed. She was a maid yet.

And Isaac? There was nothing hardened in him, either. The boy was absorbed completely in the dance, not in amorous glances and coarse gestures as some of the men were. But suddenly Robert hardened himself against the same wily enchantment to which his brother had succumbed. Dancing itself was evil. The maypole was a sign of crude, ancient rites of which no Christian man should have a part. Yes, Isaac must be chastened, and the girl must be separated from him before damage be done.

"Shall we wait further?" Longhurst hissed. "At my signal, one and all pull down the pole and scatter the dancers." He raised his voice to address the crowd, but the people only stared, frowned, and shifted uneasily from one foot to another.

Dull sheep in a market pen, Robert thought with distaste, looking back at the lively dancers.

The music gained momentum, its rhythm flinging the dancers in a rainbow of color and movement. Robert's eyes never left Rebecca, and he knew suddenly that he could not do as Longhurst wanted. It was his duty, because of his own brother's conduct, to save the girl, to draw her away from the wickedness to the safety of her own dwelling, to the safety of his own protection.

He could not club the dancers or wrench the ribands from their hands. He could not even beat his own brother. He must get to Rebecca, save her from the stain of Isaac's lust, save Rebecca. . . .

The men round him were jostling forward, crying and hallooing like Sir Dudley Digges's hounds in full pursuit across the Lees. He heard his own voice among the rest, but he hung back as they pushed forward.

Sightlessly, he saw the maypole reel, sway, and thud to the greensward. Sightlessly, he saw the dancing girls raise their hands in fear and rush to escape the upraised cudgels. Sightlessly, he saw the youths defend the girls with ill-placed, harmless blows or arms that shielded garlanded heads from the crack of chestnutwood on shining hair. Sightlessly, he watched his fellow Puritans seize the gitterns, pipes, and drums and dash them on the heads of the musicians.

All round him, wood splintered and snapped, women screamed, and men bellowed in fury. He was in the midst of a whirlpool, but it did not draw him down. What was happening round him was happening to someone else. He did not belong to these men of violence.

Rebecca stood helplessly by the fallen maypole, her face white and her hands clasped in agonized despair. She was frantically searching the brawl with her eyes *for Isaac,* Robert thought, suddenly driven toward her by his own conjecture.

"I'm Isaac's brother, Robert," he told her, hardly recognizing his own choked voice. "Mayhap you recall . . . I used to lodge with your father." The words died on his lips. She had not even looked at him. "Isaac's *brother,*" he said more urgently, and he grasped the soft warmth of her arm.

At last she registered his presence, but her eyes wandered from his face immediately. "Aye. His brother. But where is *he?*" Her face crumpled, and tears poured down her cheeks.

Groaning, he reached his arm round her shoulders. "Come lass, we'll find him. You must come away before you're hurt."

She did not pull away. Meek and trusting as a lamb led to its ewe in the pasture, she allowed him to lead her forward.

A fever seemed to take hold of him. The thought of Isaac with this girl became repulsive to Robert, and the currents of fire seemed to invade the arm he kept tightly round her. He dared not look at her face, for he knew he would bend and pick her up, carry her in his arms away and alone. It was like a dream, a bitter-sweet and sinful dream he had dreamed repeatedly of Jane, not of Patience. And if he looked at her face, the dream would become real, and he would fall into foul sin himself.

He moved forward with her as one transfixed, not even noticing the blows that glanced off his shoulders, not even noticing the shrieking crow of the cock or the loud screams of the other women. All was Rebecca, her warmth, her terrified beauty, her fragility, her nearness. The crushed out scent of her honeysuckle crown poisoned and maddened his senses, and his face set in the lines of a struggle that had gone on within him for half his life.

"No! No!" She was sobbing against his chest, struggling and weeping in a frenzy. He had torn off her partlet, ripped off her petticoats, and thrown her on Isaac's bed, where he now held her down with one hand while he battled with his own clothes.

She made a last convulsive effort to free herself, but he knew the house was empty now, and no one would hear her cries. "You came to save me," she shouted, her whole soul rising into her face. "Now would you damn me as a harlot or a whore? In the name of God—"

Cutting off her pleading with his mouth, he pinned her down with his full weight and acted out the rest of his dreams of Jane. She was white as fuller's earth under his hands, soft and fine, pure and untried. She struggled, fought, and clawed at him, but her resistance only made him more cruel, and at last he lay spent upon her.

He did not realize what he had done in his madness until he saw the blue lines of the veins in her neck as she turned away her agonized face in shame and despair. Now the sorrow and shame of the poor girl-child on the bed permeated the gold, white, and red haze of his trance-like state. He looked down at himself in horror: hose rolled to his ankles, breeches unbuttoned, his collar torn off, and his flaxen shirt stained with her blood. He had violated her. He had taken her maidenhead. He had sinned against her, against his brother, against himself, and against his wife. He had sinned against God.

He fell sideways onto the bed, away from her, drawing his knees to his chest in anguish. Sobs wracked his body, and he did not hear her leave the bed and creep away.

Isaac

"Marry her? Are you mad? Of course I'll wed her."

Isaac stared at his older brother, not understanding. He who had come to call him home, away from Rebecca, was now begging him to wed her, promising to intercede with Longhurst. What did all this signify?

Isaac narrowed his eyes, and suspicion grew in him. "There's something amiss here, and I mean to find out what," he said. "Since the May Fair, when she ran away, Rebecca's been as scared as a mouse in a sack of rye when there's a cat in the mill." She was all he could think about, and he had to remind himself to speak loudly so that his brother could hear.

Robert backed away from him, the color draining out of his face. Isaac followed, keeping the distance between them the same, sure that Robert was tricking him. "What's your purpose, brother?" he pressed, holding his gaze.

"Why . . . I . . . to see you content, Isaac. That's my will. I had not realized till I saw Rebecca what a fair lass she is and how she'd bring honor to our family. I'd thought she was naught but a—"

Isaac waved his hand angrily. "Thou'rt babbling. You knew well what she was like from lodging here thyself." He thought back to yesterday's fair, the shuttle of his mind and memory passing back and forth as in a loom. "There's deceit in thy voice."

Robert tried to smile, as if he had not heard, so Isaac roared his last complaint all the louder.

Robert's hand went up. "Hush! Hush, dost thou want this whole house to hear thee?"

Isaac quieted his voice. "Nay. But hear *me*, thou shalt," he hissed. The thread of his thinking grew tight enough to snap, and he lunged forward to grasp his brother's jerkin. "Tell me true, if you value your life, have you been tampering with my sweet Rebecca?"

Robert's face grew livid. "Nay, nay. I swear—"

"Swear not, you hypocrite, for I can never believe God more when men like you call on Him. You're a fiend—" Drawing his hands closer together, he caught him in a strangle hold. He would not kill him, he knew that, but he would get the truth out of him. "Speak the truth, you rogue." He shook him hard.

Robert's hands flailed uselessly. "I . . . I . . ."

Isaac shook him again, then dropped him so abruptly that he crumpled onto the floorboards, his face to the floor.

Robert's body heaved, sobbing. "Brother, forgive me. Something came over me. I do not know—"

Isaac went cold inside and walked to the other side of the room. "I feared this. This is what I knew in thee all along. Get up. Go talk to Longhurst. Tell him what you like, but protect my sweetheart's good name."

Robert raised himself slowly and wiped his hand across his face so that there was a dark smear over his cheeks and nose. "What will you do, brother?"

"Do not call me brother more." He spat. "I shall never go back to Chilham. When I'm wed, I'll give not a fig for my father-in-law's cant nor thine. And I'll not go home again. My father shall speak of me as his youngest son the tailor, for I was meaning anyhow to quit this place and set up for myself. Get out of my sight!"

He went himself, though, before Robert could gather himself together, and found Rebecca in her father's kitchen below stairs, her face swollen with crying. He took her into his arms gently, but she flinched from him. In his heart, he cursed his brother.

Part 2
for king and kent

King Charles anointed, by God appointed
Twenty years past to rule over this land
Is not subjected to the disaffected
Preaching rebellion with pikestaff in hand.
Shall we go down, then; desert our Crown, then?
When he bids us stay, boys, why then cry "Nay," boys.
Let us but follow; he'll scotch their base ploy.
Right on our side will always abide.
Then take no alarms, boys, down to your arms, boys,
Cast up your caps and cry,
"Vive le Roy!"

Now the King's bowmen take honest yeomen,
Put them in prison and steal their estates.
Though they be forced to go unhorsed,
And walk on foot as it pleaseth the fates.
In the King's army, no man shall harm ye.
Then come along, boys, valiant and strong, boys,
Fight for your rights which the Roundheads enjoy.
And when you come, boys, with fife and drum, boys,
Isaac himself shall cry,
"Vive le Roy!"

Goudhurst, July 1642

George

Tolhurst grunted and settled further back in his seat. After the commotion of Maidstone at the July assizes, the peace of his house and gardens fell round him like a cloak of fulled wool—soft, warm, secure. Joy rose up in him like a spring, not the heady wine of the early days of his marriage, but the milder ale of steady happiness, comfort, and relative ease among the upheavals of this hot summer.

Elizabeth sat close beside him suckling their third child. As usual she was completely engrossed, and not far away across the brick-paved courtyard their two other daughters, Anna and Henrietta, played with one of his bowling balls. Oblivious to their parents, the girls rolled the ball back and forth over the bricks, chuckling, their little petticoats dusty and their faces flushed with pleasure.

He watched them absently, aware that his feelings of satisfaction were connected as much with the farm itself as with the fragrant nearness of his wife and the play of his daughters. Glancing out beyond them, then, past the well-pruned fruit trees and nut trees that flanked the courtyard, he could see down the steps to the kitchen gardens. Two of the maids worked among the herbs cutting lavender, St. John's wort, and foxgloves. He could hear the snip of their shears and the babble and giggle of their voices as they worked. Beyond them lay the lane to the stable yard on one side and a row of stately poplars on the other.

And then there were the hop gardens. Yes, the bines were trained up on their twine frameworks now, the extra lower leaves pruned off, and the tops of the plants forming a "house" of green leaves and prickling stems. He sniffed. The heavy bracts of burrs had already bloomed, and the pollen blew to him in the breeze—resinous stuff that smelled like weak ale already. The bines would be ready for harvesting by the beginning of September. He shut his eyes and inhaled deeply.

The murmuring softness of the little girls' voices faded in and out of his head, and from somewhere in the dovecote a pair of birds crooned low in their throats. For a moment he drifted to sleep on the gentle currents of sound and smell.

Elizabeth nudged him, lacing her bodice with one hand. The baby lay asleep in her lap now, stomach distended, arms splayed backwards, head turned aside with a thin trace of milk trickling from the corner of her mouth.

Drowsily, he took in these little details. "Oh, I'm as bad as Charlotte, dozing like a well-fed infant." He reached over and gave the baby's stomach a light pat, and Charlotte's face puckered slightly but then relaxed again in sleep.

"Or like a doting old man." Elizabeth winked.

"An old man sated with the beauty of his wife," he parried, opening his eyes wider at last and waking properly.

"Sated? No one will think so, not if ye keep giving me babes."

He watched her face tenderly, heard the pride in her voice. "'Tis as we've wanted."

"Aye, as we've wanted." Her voice was husky.

He smiled back, but a shadow passed over him. Charlotte's birth had been long and arduous for her. He stretched out one hand and cradled the baby's head in it, leaning toward Elizabeth. With his free hand, he drew her face to his own. "Indeed, three daughters as lovely as their mother. 'Twas the magic of the hooden horse in Maidstone did the trick." He kissed her slowly, and the shadow passed.

She pushed her hand against his shoulder and laughed at him, her head thrown back so that he could see the strong lines of her throat and shoulders. "Nay, 'twas not! And well you know it, for Anna came not for three years after that."

He cleared his throat. "Oh, aye, Bess. Ever the one for thorny mathematics and logic, my lass."

Her eyebrows arched. "As are you, George, when you're figuring the planting and acreage or when you're away to the assizes determining fines and the like." Her voice was serious, but he knew the barbed tail would follow soon enough. "'Tis only when you're with your wife and babes you turn into a sleepy simpleton." She nudged him again. "Fie, 'tis time you were down in the gardens!"

"Play the shrew, would you?" He laughed. "It suits you not." He stretched out his legs and leaned deliberately against her. "Nay, I have a mind to rest this day. The assizes put me in a dreadful coil."

The laughter in her eyes died away, and she bent away from him to stroke the baby's head. "Forgive me. I have known it, but . . . I was afeared to ask." Her voice turned passionate. "Of a truth, I'm changed. I do not wish to see assizes more . . . nor go to London and look upon the King . . . nor any such thing. The times are ill. England is so troubled. Oh, how I care to hear thy comfort. But you cannot give it, can you?"

He set his mouth in a line, hating the change from lightness to earnestness. Pretense was useless. She guessed all too quickly when he was hiding from her the weight of his charges. He looked away, unwilling to let her read his face too closely.

"Nay, you cannot," she said. "I know it as well as thee. 'Tis war we'll have, and surely."

He kept his eyes deliberately on Charlotte's peaceful expression. "It seems impossible here, does it not?" He raised his head briefly so that the sun fell full on his face. The sound of the doves and the smell of the hops came to him again on the air.

"But 'tis foolish to pretend that it's not," she answered.

"Aye." He still didn't look at her. "Sir Dudley said it years ago, and we should have heeded better then. Only pray God our own land become not a place of bloodshed."

Beside him, she shuddered, and on her lap Charlotte's arm twitched up suddenly.

"We've both seen it coming, love, since the spring."

She shook her head slowly. "'Tis a wicked shame when the men of a county try to bring peace between King and Parliament and then are thrown in shackles for it."

Tolhurst thought of Dering, Twysden, and the two Richards—Lovelace and Spencer, all of whom had been imprisoned for organizing petitions to take from Kent to Westminster. One petition had merely asked Parliament why the government could not make terms with the King, and asked whether the militia were to follow orders from the King or from Parliament. The petition had been prepared and presented legally, but even Judge Mallett, the reluctant Sir Thomas, had been clapped in the Tower of London for not opposing it.

"Shame?" he echoed. "Nay, 'tis rank injustice. And Kent will not lie low under it for long." His voice rose so abruptly that the two little girls stopped playing and turned in surprise. Henrietta, the more fearful, hid her face in her apron.

Elizabeth beckoned the girls to her knee and comforted Henrietta. "Hush, dearling, thy father's not angry with thee." She pushed her fingers through Anna's hair and wiped her face. Then she turned to him again. "You make me quake when you speak like that."

"Ah, sorry, Bess. The goings-on have changed us all. I of all men in Kent have no desire to take sides." He waved his hands this way and that, trying to explain the chaos to her. "Parliament's been unjust, but so has His Majesty to Parliament. Dering supported Parliament until but latterly. Now he sends support to the King. The County Committee supports Parliament . . . but I . . . what's an honest man to do? I'm no Lovelace to go braving Westminster with petitions, though I must sign them. Neither can I stand silent when Parliament sends an unlawful committee to sit on the Maidstone Bench and to dispense justice in the judge's stead."

Elizabeth frowned. "Why would they do such a thing?"

"To frighten the knights of the shire into submission. They want no more thorns in their flesh from Kentish hawthorn hedges"—he snorted, pleased with the conceit—"no more petitions I mean."

"But I thought—"

"Aye, I mentioned it, didn't I? There *was* another petition."

"You told me not the matter of it."

He took a deep breath. "No, but I shall. Mainy, Tufton, St. Leger, Filmer, as well as Rycaut and Mr. Clark, though I had scarce known either man before, sent another petition to Parliament against the ones Sir Michael Livesey had taken ere this—fawning, wretched rogue to lick the boots of Parliament!" He would have spat in contempt, but, remembering the girls leaning against their mother, forbore. "They gave it to Augustine Skinner to take to London. All we asked—"

"We?" She bit her lip.

"Aye, all the gentry wronged by that *committee*." His voice sank to a sarcastic guttural. "All we asked was for the King to get his military provisions and his ships back. We devised a plan for bringing the two sides together for a discussion, and we said that Kent, at least, is peaceful."

"And the King knows all this?"

"He shall within a few days. Mainy, Clark, and Filmer are riding north to see His Majesty in York. He will grant them royal protection—"

"Aye," she interrupted, "since his own general turns against him."

He swung round in his seat to face her fully. "So I have chosen sides, my love, though I see wrong in both. And all this"—he stretched out his hands to include the farm, the gardens, and the house—"may be at risk." He searched her face, expecting anguish and anxiety.

It did not come. Instead, the Elizabeth he had first known sat beside him, her face alight and her eyes dancing. "Perhaps. But thou did'st well to choose thus. I'm proud of thee." Her voice was steady and clear.

Marveling at this second change in her, he breathed more freely again. Then he bent and pushed his face into Anna's hair—she was unashamedly his favorite—and lifted her onto his knee. "Here, poppet, give me a kiss."

Henrietta put her thumb in her mouth and pulled on Elizabeth's skirts with her eyes alternately opening and drooping, so while Anna snuggled against her father, Elizabeth took Henrietta and the baby into the house.

"It's nice when thou'rt home, Father," Anna whispered, her fear of his shouting now gone. Looking out from his arms she seemed brave again. She found a loose piece of braided cord on the edge of his jerkin and began to twirl it round and round in her fingers.

He nodded. Feeling against his cheek the silkiness of her hair, the softness of her babyish skin, he savored the mixture of dust and warmth that rose from her thin little body. "And I'm glad, too, love, for it seems I've had to be away too often of late. And I'm afraid I'll come back one day and find my little girls all grown into fair women who won't know their shabby, tired old father from all the other farmers hereabouts." He looked down tenderly at her, knowing that although she didn't understand all the words he had said, she understood the feeling that lay behind them.

She reached out and patted his face. "I'll wed you, shall I, when I'm grown?"

He chuckled. "Nay, Anna. Thou'lt find another man. A girl can't marry her own father, you know."

"But I love thee, my father."

"So . . . I love thee, too . . . but another will love thee more, as I have loved thy mother."

Suddenly he could not meet his daughter's eyes any longer, nor look at the maids coming up the steps, nor at the flowers or trees. He turned his face away and screwed his eyes tight shut. *What if all this be taken from us? What if I lose my womenfolk? What then?* He clung to Anna as if she were his last hope. The questions were unbearable, and the blessed peace of Tolhurst Court was already shattered.

He was not surprised then when, moments after the maids passed by to enter the house, the kitchen door flew open again and his usually cautious, seemly manservant rushed out and almost fell headlong before him in haste.

"Sir! Sir! Rouse yourself! There's news from Friars at Aylesford. Your wife just now received a messenger." The man broke into a coughing fit.

Tolhurst gently set Anna down on the bricks. "Go in, my love and find thy mother. No crying now, for all's well."

She looked back at him with eyes so full of knowing sorrow that he regretted immediately what he knew would be proved a lie. But a girl-child of four was not one to listen to urgent reports. Not now, not in these days, particularly.

She turned and fled into the open doors of the dining hall, her white petticoats foaming in the comparative darkness like small wave crests in blurred moonlight. His heart contracted as he watched her go, and he ached to protect her, to protect them all.

He stood to look directly at the servant. "'Struth, Thomas, next time save thy news until the child's away." But he could not remain angry for long. "And you'd best ask of the cook some black mustard and rosewater for that cough of yours. Catch thy breath, Thom, ere you go on."

The servant stood with his fists at his sides, opening and closing them. The veins on his temples stood out under his flushed skin as he apparently struggled for control. "Sir Percival Rycaut's sent word," he said at last. "He's being taken to Upnor Castle, and his estate is confiscated unless he pay some vastly sum."

"The petition . . . the protest, aye . . . I knew it." He ground his teeth together but hesitated, unwilling to say more, even before a servant he trusted. "There was a written message?"

"Yes, sir, and your goodwife has it."

"I thank thee. Go back in now, but bid the other servants get forward in their tasks. We may have a mort of extra work here ere the week's out, I fear."

At first Thomas did not move, then made as if to go, then stopped again. "'Twas what your lady did say, also," he ventured.

Tolhurst flapped his hands crossly. "Aye, aye. Go now." Then he hurried to find Elizabeth, himself.

The nursemaid had now gathered the little girls into her care, and Elizabeth stood alone in the middle of the great hall, her back to the fireplace, evidently awaiting him. High color flooded her face, and the soft, maternal woman who had sat with him only moments before with her rounded breasts bared to the sunlight and the tug of Charlotte's hungry mouth had vanished. She was replaced by Bess the wise woman, the Bess who had awed him from the very beginning. Once again he became— though he had never reason to doubt her love for him—the faltering, clumsy farmer-turned-wooer.

"Show me the message, Elizabeth." He was surprised by the steady confidence in his own voice.

Her eyes scanned his face. "'Tis ill news, husband." Her voice was muted.

"So I understand." He licked his lips as she passed him the paper. Sir Percival Rycaut's hand, adorned with curls and flourishes even when executed in haste, filled only a small part of the letter. He looked up at Elizabeth briefly. "The messenger has gone?"

"Gone, and flying to warn others. He had the soldiers of Parliament on his heels. Read it, pray."

"'Tis a pity. I would have asked him where else he took his news." As he forced himself to peruse the note slowly, his heart beat loudly under his jerkin, and panic seized him.

Rochester is subdued, the castle taken by surprise and St. Andrew's Cathedral plundered. In their fury these soldiers are bent on silencing Kent. I am to Upnor Castle under guard, all the arms and silver of my household having been taken, and I shall forfeit at least three thousand pounds. I doubt not others will suffer the same misfortune. Arm yourselves, therefore, and warn all others likewise. I know I may count on you. Beware Livesey and Sandys.—PR

The letter was not sealed with the Aylesford Priory seal, but he had no doubt of its origin.

Elizabeth paced restlessly before the mantel. He watched her as her back was to him for a moment: the shapely contour of her hips, the lushness of her hair, which lay unbound on her shoulders in defiance of all Puritan execrations to the contrary. What had a woman such as she to do with the coming troubles? They were an intrusion he could not forgive or face. He drew a deep sigh, and she turned.

"Think you this is true?" He inwardly cursed himself for the simplicity of his own question.

"Of course 'tis true," she replied crossly.

His heels clicked on the oak-beamed floor as he came to a sudden decision. "Then I must gather all the men—all those able-bodied in the household and in the village—to serve us here. We cannot allow a repeat of what took place at the Friars. Parliament cannot command the King's militia to raid and sack the houses of those who serve His Majesty! This house shall *not* be touched."

She stood quite still, opposite him only a few feet away, and her eyes locked with his. "Nay, George, thou speak'st without thinking. 'Tis nonsense to shed thy blood for a few old pieces of plate and armor."

"Nay, wife, 'tis thou think'st not. Dost suppose these *godly* Puritans will stop at that? Just let the fanatics and those with grudges follow after Livesey and see what shall happen! 'Twill be women and innocent babes hurt, not gold and silver and arms, if *he* be in command."

The color died from her face. "Then you would start the war here, on this very land? You'd send out Barny and Jack, Matthew and Harry, and all the other Simple Simons of Goudhurst against the madness and force of drunken—?"

"Drunken? The Puritans touch not strong drink."

"Fie!" She stamped her foot. "Have you forgot already what we saw in Maidstone one May Day? You *know* that is not so."

"Then what am I to do?" He threw open his arms helplessly. "Send out my *maids?*" If only he could undercut the deadly earnestness that had returned to her face.

She laughed without humor. "Nay, nay! Listen, I have thought. We must make all appearance of knowing naught and of conducting ourselves as is our custom here. How think you that the militia took Rochester Castle with its thick walls, unless the men were out aharvesting?"

He nodded slowly, conceding to her but not yet following her argument.

"Perhaps if we do likewise, but first *make ready*, we shall escape the loss of too much here. Do all we can to provoke no violence, and sacrifice some things we care not for, even some silver, love, so that the angels of death will o'erpass us."

"But . . . but there is no warrant they'll not do worse here than at the Friars. You may be sure they searched before they plundered."

Her chin went up. "Let them! We'll hide everything we can. Let them find some of it. 'Twould be unnatural for us to have no arms or powder in store. But let them miss most of it, and let us go in guise of willingness."

"That's well to say, wife, but I'll not pretend to be a Parliament's man and perjure myself. Besides, they know already what I've signed."

"Oh, phaw, there'll be no more petitions now, George. 'Tis far too grave for that. 'Tis war, as we've said this day." She smiled, her eyes full of fervor and hope. "And thou need'st not perjure thyself. But if thou tak'st arms thyself against them, then there's even less surety that they'll stop plundering. You'll just force a battle then. I said, let's make all haste, take up no arms, only be wily, cunning, and ready."

The room fell quiet, her last words echoing faintly from the high beams of the hall.

Suddenly he knew she was right. He opened his arms to her. Elizabeth's arms went round his neck, the scent of lavender from her hair against his nostrils as he swung her round once and set her down again.

"Thank God for thee, my darling," he said, "and for thy wits. But pray God we have time—"

"Doubt it not." She laughed breathlessly. "If Aylesford was taken yesterday, they'll be stopping at the Mote and West Farleigh and at Linton Place ere they ride south to Goudhurst. We'll have time enough."

He nodded his head against hers. "A goodly council of war, little Queen Bess. I elect thee my general."

She laughed again so that he felt her warm breath on his chest. "You'd never make a King, my love."

For the rest of the day they scoured the house for arms and treasures. Leaving some in place, they concealed the rest in an old priest hole that George doubted even Livesey's men could find.

Only the steward and Elizabeth's most trusted maid were warned of what was likely to happen, and George ordered Elizabeth to clap all ale, sack, and wine under key so that no drunken, loose-tongued servant could betray them. The maids, if kept in ignorance, would brilliantly act out their proper roles of terror when the soldiers arrived. And both he and Elizabeth would need all their wits to assume masks of surprise and to say nothing that would arouse suspicion or provoke violence.

Before they went to bed that night, he carefully burned Rycaut's letter in the fireplace of the great hall. From thence he climbed the spiral back staircase to the small family chapel, scarcely used nowadays when the family was forced by Laudian injunction to attend only at St. Mary's in the village. There he knelt for some time at the prie-dieu.

His knees seemed to grind into the threadbare cushion as he stilled himself in the chapel's chill air. A weight of sorrow and worry pressed down on his head and chest. *What will the morrow bring?*

The light flickered, and he opened his eyes to see the candle flame bent sideways by a draft from the door. Without standing, he turned sharply to see Elizabeth, another candle in hand, framed in the lancet doorway.

"Oh, 'tis thee," he whispered. *She looks like a spirit*, he thought, *in that white shift with her hair unbound.* "Come, let's pray for peace," he said.

She joined him at the prie-dieu. "'Tis peace within as well as without I'll pray for." She gave him an inscrutable half-smile, then shut her eyes.

He shut his, too, and the two candles—his own and hers—were the last things he saw before his eyelids brought darkness. Then Anna's little face rose in his mind and obscured the darkness: the child's fair skin and angelic hair, the same look of pity and understanding stamped on her face that he had seen in the afternoon. It was for Anna that there must be peace. "For Anna" he murmured unconsciously, and he felt Elizabeth's shoulder against his own.

"We come peaceably, sir," Livesey said. Wearing the russet colors of his troop and the arms of a Parliamentarian, he sat on horseback above Tolhurst, the noon sun gleaming on his helmet and cuirass. "Peaceably, unless you do some rash deed." The hand on his sword belied his words, and the men ranged behind him sat stiffly on their horses. "Nothing will be hurt. No one will be harmed if you obey us. Put up a fight, and you may answer with your life. Parliament's orders, sir."

George had resolutely begun work with his men on the upper edge of the hop gardens. Some of the bines needed to be trimmed and pruned, but he wanted to be near both the house and the lane, also near to the arrival of any troops. He had worked all morning, but not steadily. Several times his shaking hands had cut down healthy bines.

His men worked behind him, earthing up the small hills round the poles. He urged them on in spite of his misgivings, trying not to stint, ignoring their good-natured complaints about the morning's lack of ale against their thirst. "Water today, and ye'll get ale aplenty tonight," he had promised. But now Livesey and his men had come, and behind him his own men huddled, gawking at the soldiers without comprehension.

Thoughts of Kentish rights and mildly worded petitions crossed his mind. Thoughts of England's constitution and the rights of Parliament crowded his thoughts, but he swallowed hard the sharp answer he might have given without more forethought. "Then what's your will, gentlemen?"

"To search your property as we have others'. We know you to be a man favoring the King's cause, and Parliament looks now with disfavor and suspicion upon all such since *His Majesty*"—the last two words came out with venomous emphasis—"is doing all he can to divide this nation asunder and spill its people's blood." Livesey met his eyes. "We'll root out any signs of sedition in this place and take your arms, sir, will ye, nill ye, and some of your goods shall go to help loyal Englishmen meet Parliament's expenses, as pleases the Lord of Hosts."

George felt his face grow hot in fury, and his fingers clenched hard round the hook he carried. "Nay, we men of Kent have paid dearly enough ere this, Sir Michael. Paid with ships and money, aye, and men, too. If Parliament means verily to bring an end to the King's forced loans and ship money, let not Parliament force the men of Kent in the same way!"

Livesey's soldiers muttered in surprise and something else—was it disappointment?

Tolhurst dismissed his men and marched stolidly before the troop into the stableyard. "Ye can water and stable the horses here, if ye choose. I'll get the groom to wait upon thee."

Livesey's eyebrows flickered. "Courtesy? Either you're a turncoat, Tolhurst, or a shrewd man." His derision disappeared, though, as he snapped orders to some of his men to guard the horses. Then the rest of the party tramped into the house.

With an air of guileless absorption that surprised even George, Elizabeth sat in the parlor as they entered, her foot rocking the cradle by her chair. At the sight of the soldiers, she jumped up, her needlework in its wooden hoop clattering to the floor as she cried out.

"'Tis men from London, dear," he said wearily.

"Aye, here to search for arms, madam, by order of Parliament. Pray fetch your children and maids." Livesey nodded to her, then to him. "Fetch all your servants, sir, and bring them here. We want no one about as we do our task. The whole household must remain in here."

George exchanged glances with Elizabeth, then looked back to Livesey. "May I not accompany you, or my bailiff?" He tried to sound conciliatory.

"No, I want no trickery or mischief. My men aren't thieves, sir. You'll know what goes to the cause, I do assure you. Now, fetch your servants, and make haste. These men will accompany you."

"My wife goes not alone with your men or any others. We go together, sir."

Livesey's eyes passed over Elizabeth, and George caught her look of pained withdrawal as she pulled a partlet over her shoulders to cover the fair skin of her neck and breasts. "Aye, with a wife like that, a wanton who shows her flesh so shamelessly, 'twould be better you went with her. And ordered her more, too! 'Tis not seemly."

She drew up her head haughtily, and for a moment he thought she would forget her own warnings. "When 'tis unseemly for a woman to nurse her own babes, then 'twill be unseemly to dress as I do on these hot days, Sir Michael." Her voice was satin.

"You were *sewing*, madam."

"Until a few moments ere ye came in, bold and unannounced, sir, I had my baby at my breast." She gestured toward the cradle, and as if on cue, Charlotte began to whimper from within. "In the sight of God, where be the sin in that, sir?"

"In the sight of *God* . . . nowhere . . . but, pray, cover yourself. . . ." Livesey coughed and looked away.

She's bested him! George thought, glad for her.

"And see your . . . er . . . your maids . . . do likewise, even if any be . . . suckling babes." He floundered on, and George saw amusement on Elizabeth's face, though no one else might have recognized it.

"I'll see to it," she said blandly. "This would be a place of miracles indeed if maids had babes to suckle, but I'll see to it, especially if I know when ye come again."

Livesey's face darkened. "We shall not come again, but, by God, my men shall search this nest of King's men better than the rest. 'Tis by law we're here, and by law we'll act." His hand moved to his sword. "Go now, and no more insolence."

Elizabeth gave Charlotte over to the nursemaid's care, then with six dragoons in close attendance, they went first back to the hop gardens, then to the stables and outhouses, gathering men as they went. Next they descended to the kitchens and brought the cook and serving maids into the parlor with the rest of the household.

The room, large as it was, began to smell of sweaty clothes, and George saw Elizabeth looking unhappily at the clods of dung on the beeswaxed floorboards and the black smears of hop resin on the chairs. Awed by their surroundings, uneasy with the soldiers, his servants sat or stood in cowed silence and waited. Elizabeth moved round opening the windows and doors.

Deciding his wife was safe now with the others, George mounted the wide stairway to the nursery. The nursemaid sat by an open window that overlooked the kitchen gardens, and Charlotte lay asleep on the cushions beside her. "Soldiers are come, Nancy," he said to her. Three of them came so close behind him into the doorway that he knew the words were in vain.

The woman nodded. She was plain, a spinster of unknown age whose temper could rarely be ruffled, except at times of childbed. Otherwise she lived placidly, moved slowly, and took the three Tolhurst children exactly as they were.

A *solid old oak tree*, he thought, looking thankfully at her.

"Aye, sir. I saw them ride in on their fine horses." She screwed up the corners of her mouth. "Be we all arrested, then?" She twitched at the lace on her cap, but her face showed frank curiosity more than anxiety.

"Nay! We've done no wrong. How then shall we be arrested?" He smiled at her impassive face, then sobered. "But I do not want the little girls upset. The maids below are fearful enough as it is." He bent to Henrietta, who rushed to his knees. Kissing her, he lifted her onto the nurse's lap. "You have the care of Henrietta and the babe. Let me take Anna, or she may bolt like a mare in season." He beckoned his oldest daughter. "Come, love, we must away downstairs."

Anna sidled up to him, and he knew she was puzzled by his appearance in the nursery and by the talk of the soldiers. He wanted to prepare her. "Just think, dearling," he said, lifting her against his chest so that he could look into her soft eyes. "Such a pother below stairs! We must all sit in the parlor for a while—Anna, Henrietta, and Nancy . . . and Matthew, Simon, Thom, and your mother—all of us, indeed."

"But why, my father?" Her eyes searched his, bruised and blue-violet like the love-in-the-mist flowers that grew in the garden.

"It's a rare game, my love. These big soldiers are pretending to look for a deadly enemy. They want to play the game by themselves, thou'lt see, so we must just all sit together." He ceased to care what Livesey's men thought of him.

Her arms tightened round his neck, and she nuzzled against his jaw. Her voice came muffled, then. "But . . . there's no deadly enemy, is there? They won't take thee away, will they?"

He rocked her as he walked back out the door with her. "No, pet, no deadly enemy, indeed. And take me away, that they won't! 'Tis all a foolish game. But my Anna will play her part like a brave, fierce lady, will she not? Come, now." He looked over his shoulder at Nancy. "Thou hast Charlotte, too?" He saw the baby carried in the nursemaid's free arm, so the question was light talk to fill the silence and quell the fear that must already be growing in the children's minds.

As they passed into the parlor, Sir Michael was pacing up and down the middle of the room without any attempt to cover his impatience. His boots clicked on the floor, and his long spurs jingled. "Make haste, pray!" he shouted.

By the open double doors, four dragoons stood alert for any signs of rebellion. George felt his temper rising again as they entered, hot as the bodies in the sweltering room. *What right have they to disrupt my house thus?* But he fought down the anger. He wanted no carnage under his own roof, and thus far Livesey had conducted himself with fair restraint. None of his own folk was armed anyhow, and even if the household did contrive to dispose of Livesey and his men, more would come, more violent, certainly. But he was still master here, and Livesey could never take that from him. The command should come from him, therefore.

He saw to it that Henrietta and Charlotte were comfortably settled with Elizabeth and Nancy in a more airy part of the room, but although he sat near them, he did not relinquish Anna. Her pliant, warm body, even her heart beating like a wild hare's against his jacket, gave him courage. "You may begin your search, sirs, and welcome," he said coldly.

Livesey barked orders again and, leaving more dragoons posted at the doors with orders to maintain silence within, took the others out of the room. The parlor fell quiet. Elizabeth's eyes turned on George as he strained to hear the sounds that would betray the paths of the soldiers. Outside the great hall, metal clanged. *Those ancient suits of arms,* he thought. *To be melted, no doubt, for Parliament's lackeys! How dare they!* He stiffened in helpless rage.

Anna must have sensed his anger. She raised her head, glanced round the room for the first time, gave a fleeting smile to her mother, then let her eyes rest on her father's. "'Tis only a foolish game, Father," she said softly.

His own comfort coming back to him from younger lips moved him. "Aye, my lass." He turned toward Elizabeth. "All war's a game, is it not?" He had to speak very low.

Her eyes clouded with pain. How could she answer, *There is no war yet* when they both knew the meaning of these forced searches and mentions of "sedition" and "nests of King's men?" How could she answer him?

The dragoons were above stairs now, their heavy feet marching up the long halls, curtains swishing apart, doors thudding against walls, chests splintering open.

"They have no keys!" Elizabeth whispered urgently.

He shook his head and answered under his breath, "Dost suppose they'd use them even if the steward gave them to their trust? Nay, they make a sport of the destruction they do, the rending and the bursting. I'm sure of it."

At the door, one of Livesey's men raised his pikestaff and called for silence, but Henrietta set up a wail from Nancy's arms, and Charlotte's babyish voice soon answered.

"You've frightened the children," Elizabeth said imperiously.

The guard rubbed his jaw uncomfortably but did not answer.

"Dolt!" Elizabeth exclaimed.

"Bess, Bess, pray—" He started to plead with her, but immediately felt like berating the guard himself.

Anna, in sympathy with her sisters, began to wriggle and push against him. Her arms flailed, and she broke away from him to the windows at the end of the room farthest from the soldiers. Scrambling up on the cushions, she stood poised to jump out into the courtyard.

One of the maids lunged after her.

"Let her go!" the soldier instructed. "She'll do no 'arm."

Elizabeth and George rushed after her. "Not to thee, mayhap!" George shouted. "'Tis herself we're mindful of."

Anna's hands had grasped the wooden frames and one of her feet was already on the sill when George caught her into his arms again. Her crying split the stifling air in the parlor, shrill with fury, and all the servants murmured and shuffled in pity.

Then from above stairs came the unmistakable sound of shattering glass. It tinkled and rang like gold coins bouncing down the oak stairs. Loud cracks followed, as if the men were ripping up floorboards and casting them aside. Anna's crying ceased abruptly.

Elizabeth clawed at George's arms. "Oh, what—?"

He did not have to answer her. The soldiers above answered, their voices coming clearly from the beams of the floor above. "Roman idols!" Then another crash shook some plaster from the ceiling.

The chapel! They're despoiling the chapel! The chapel where his grandfather had been wed by the family priest, where his father had prayed . . . where he and Elizabeth had knelt only hours before and prayed for peace. The inner sanctuary of his family. . . .

The remorseless zeal of Livesey's men sliced into him like a sword. Elizabeth's eyes were fixed on him, and tears started out from under her lashes. Against his chest, Anna had gone limp, beyond feeling and fear. He drew her more closely to him.

And then, in through the window flew a little blue butterfly. It settled first on his arm, then, perhaps displeased with the smell of hops that hung about him, fluttered down onto Anna's hair. George caught his wife's eye; she had seen it, too.

In the sunlight that flooded through the window, the tiny butterfly appeared as blue stained glass against the rich silk of the child's hair. Its patterned wings moved up and down, speckled brown underwings appearing each time the blue sides closed together. It stayed there, luxuriating in her warmth, in the warmth of the July sunshine, though Anna seemed unaware of it.

Canterbury, August 1642

Robert

Over the blurred, blue-green rim of the Downs, Robert plodded ahead with a troop of horse and foot soldiers. The old hills dwarfed the diminutive little men in buff, tan, and russet garb, their figures almost lost in the sere browns of the dried grasses, the gray and bay horses blending into the road of chalk and ragstone. Others followed on foot, pikestaffs pointing heavenward like thorns in an uncoiled crown of Calvary.

The downward slope of the road into the city did not increase their speed. The insistent rolling of the drums had faded to half-hearted occasional taps, and no one marched in step now. The euphoria of early morning musters in Chilham and Chartham had faded to a faint memory, dulled by blistered feet, lead-heavy arms, and dry mouths. Eyes strained forward for sight of the first welcoming tavern, then withdrew uncomfortably. Livesey would brook no drunkenness, he had said, and the men grumbled against him for it.

At the back of the troop a few soldiers took up a song. The words died quickly in the hot wind, but the song sustained some of them and fleetingly brought back the excitement of joining a troop as renowned as that of Colonel Sandys. Their steps quickened as they sang, and the muskets slung on their backs bounced up and down.

> *The king by hark'ning to your charms*
> *Hugged our destruction in his arms,*
> > *And gates to foes did ope;*
> > *Your staff would strike his sceptre down*
> *Your mitre would o'ertop the crown*
> > *If you would be a pope.*
>
> *But you that did so firmly stand*
> *To bring in popery to this land*
> > *Have missed your hellish aim.*

Canterbury, August 1642

Your saints fall down
Your angels fly,
Your crosses on yourself do lie
Your craft will be your shame.

Robert Fessenden did not sing with the others, though he knew the song. He could not be quite sure, these days, which song against Archbishop Laud was being sung. They all poured out hatred on this favorite of the King's, some in lewd words, some in angry words.

But deafness shut him in now. Even the jingling of his own bridle sounded obscure and distant. He lived in a world in which sounds swished by him in soft, foaming confusion like the rush of water through the troughs in the Loose mills before the hammers overwhelmed all other sound.

But the isolation deafness had dealt him rarely pained him. In fact he enjoyed the quiet of his mind—the inner whispers of God breathing into him the words of the Psalms, which had become such a comfort to him. It was enough to watch his sons—Thomas, Nicholas, and Josiah—tussling in the garden while Hannah, the baby, trailed behind, a thumb in her mouth and a torn homespun following her inseparably over the green-staining grass. It did not matter to him that he could not hear what they cried out to him, only that they needed *him.*

His father, meanwhile, had for several years written down all his instructions. And Patience had developed her own particular way of talking to him with exaggerated movements of her lips and hands. No, the deafness scarcely troubled him. He was content with the will of God that he live in this quiet.

He turned for a moment in his saddle and peered back over the straggling column of men. Not all were soldiers. Some had joined the muster simply by laying down their scythes and quitting the fields. Even now some of them brazenly lifted flagons and bottles to their lips. He swiveled forward again in disgust. *Wine-bibbers! Rabble,* he thought uneasily. And yet, could God still use them? His dream of these men as instruments of God cracked slightly, and he wavered. Should he return to Chilham?

He had made up his mind quite suddenly to follow Colonel Sandys. The muster had been announced for several days by letters nailed to posts in the village, but he had resolutely ignored them. There was work to be done, the Lord's work, especially with his two brothers gone.

John had built a house in Cambridge in the New World, settled

128

successfully as a glover. He and Jane had obviously become quite comfortable, but their wealth was stored in the house on Eliot Street, a thriving leather trade with the Indians, and glove trade with other merchants in Cambridge, Plymouth, Charlestown, and Providence. Their wealth, he reminded himself, was not in the Spirit, not treasure stored in heaven, as he and Patience had amassed, nor in children, either. John had only a foster son, Nathaniel. How blessed was he himself in that way! Surely God had forgiven him that sin of lust all these years ago? It was the sin of another man, not something he connected with himself anymore. Now he believed himself made new, sanctified daily by Christ. At least, he could look at his life in that way now, though at night sometimes. . . .

And Isaac? There was no further connection with Isaac. Not since the boy's marriage had Robert seen him. His abrupt, sullen departure had grieved their father deeply. The old man, never guessing the truth, had blamed himself for making too many demands of the lad. Robert shuddered. Those dark days were well covered by now, but his father used often to express his longing for John and Isaac.

Robert had doubled his work to compensate, to prove loyalty and steadfastness to his father. He had said, "But I shall stay, my father."

And once, Fessenden, reading aloud at the evening family prayers, had spoken of the parable of the prodigal son. "Robert is my faithful elder son," he had said.

For a while, the venom of jealousy had lost its bite into Robert's heart. He had at last found the place he had wanted in his father's heart. He was the eldest son now, the faithful one, the prop and comfort to his father's old age.

Not so to Mary Snode, his stepmother. But he had never wooed her, anyhow. Isaac had occasionally written to Mary, and that threw up an additional fence between them. What if she knew, or guessed, what had passed between himself and Rebecca, between himself and Isaac?

He was always her pet, Robert thought bitterly. *I shall have vengeance on her one day.*

But Mary kept her own counsel, at least before him, of the contents of Isaac's letters. He knew only that Isaac had done as he wished and set up as a tailor in Maidstone. Rumors in Maidstone and Loose declared that Rebecca's father had turned soft in the head. No doubt the young couple lived untroubled by the affairs of either the Longhursts or the Fessendens. And just as well. Robert wanted no reminders of the past, no dredging up what God had washed away. There were enough reminders as it was.

Yes, there was work to be done for his father. Why, then, had his father urged him to the muster after all? He frowned, shifting in the saddle, glancing to the walls of Canterbury not far ahead. Had his father sensed his restlessness? He had never quite lost the conviction that the Lord had some higher calling for him than inspection of the mills, supervision of the weavers, spinners, fullers, and dyers.

If only Robert could discover that calling, at last he could then turn his back on the past, on the torment that had wracked him. Lust had sometimes driven him half mad, first for Jane, then for his poor wife, Patience, then for Rebecca. Without knowing the cause, his father certainly sensed this tension. Was this why he had sent him with Colonel Sandys today? He drew breath heavily. Perhaps this journey to Canterbury was all intended. Perhaps he would discover some higher purpose there.

He had tried to hide the fact from his father, but the general demand for wool was definitely falling off. Merchants now chose to buy from larger manufacturers who owned not cottage workers but highly organized mills where almost all the work was done in one place. The wool trade had fallen off twenty years before because of the wars in Europe; and now the English cloth, in comparison with that of the cunning foreign weavers, was no longer the best. The family's trade, however, had in those years increased somewhat, mainly because of John's undertakings with the Flemish and Huguenot weavers—the Strangers—in Canterbury. But he was not sure that the Fessenden trade could survive a war in England now. *A war! That's what it is,* he told himself excitedly.

Charles Stuart, it was said, had raised his standard in Nottingham only a few days before. Lovelace, Tolhurst, Astley, Dering, and Culpeper were among many prominent men of Kent who had declared themselves King's men and had sent their support to Nottingham. Kent, like the rest of the country, would be torn in half by war, as violently as a piece of cloth torn by a tailor before the stitching begins. But Robert knew on which side of the cloth he belonged: not on the garish, fluttering standard in Nottingham where the King's supporters would pay for their errors, but with the dusty, bedraggled standards of these men. The true men of Kent, flawed as they might be, marched and rode in this column. And they rode for the Lord of Hosts, not for the papist King or for the would-be Pope, Laud. They rode for God. His chest swelled with pride.

One of Sandys's soldiers, a man who had kept up unflaggingly even over the steepest tracks on the Downs, suddenly collapsed beside Robert's horse.

His musket must have clanged as it struck flint, but his body made only a dull thud. Robert, however, heard nothing—only saw the body crumple.

His reveries dissolved, and he flung himself from the saddle and loosened the cap on his water bottle. His horse ambled away to crop the grass, and he knelt quickly, offering the water. The man's mottled face was averted, his mouth gaping and his eyes black with terror.

"Rouse thyself, man," Robert urged. "You'll ride my horse to Canterbury."

A strange, choked sound escaped the man's throat, and two dirty hands reached up and clamped themselves on Robert's falling-band collar. Dismayed, he leaned forward to try to make sense of what the man was trying to say. Then he twisted backward, away from the stench of sweat and filth. The collar ripped away from his jerkin with a searing, angry sound that even Robert could hear. Then the man's eyes became glazed, fixed desperately on Robert's face as death rode over him. For a second Robert saw the screaming mouth and stricken eyes of Rebecca, but the image dissolved. With the grip of death, this man was pulling him down, not fighting him away as Rebecca had done.

He cried out himself now, overtaken with disgust, horror, and pity. But beside them the line moved past as if nothing had happened. The movements of horses and men seemed monotonous, unmitigating, especially to Robert, for whom they moved in silence. Suddenly he hated their dull purposefulness. And he hated the dying men, too.

At last another horseman stopped, one Robert knew. Looking up, Robert said blankly, "He's dead."

"Then God 'a mercy on the wretch," the horseman shouted back.

Robert pulled off his felt hat. Together they lifted the first casualty over the back of Robert's horse. The corpse slumped, and the horse snorted and shied away.

Robert rejoined the column, on foot now, leading his horse. There would be time later to find out who the man was and send word to his widow. Robert's pride had melted, replaced by a vague feeling of foreboding.

In Canterbury, Sandys set guards on the cathedral and on the houses of the dean and chapter. The townspeople rushed about in confusion until assured that no harm would come to them.

Robert's efficient arrangements for a pious burial of the dead man had attracted Sir Michael Livesey's notice, and early on Saturday morning, he was summoned to Livesey's lodging.

Informed that Robert was deaf, Livesey shouted throughout their conversation. "Few of my men are as well educated or skilled as yourself, Goodman Fessenden," he roared. "I need your support. You're not a soldier, I know, but you think like a soldier, I suspect. I want you dressed like one, in the colors of this troop, and I shall provide a helmet and cuirass myself. I shall need you with me. We must needs pay a little visit this day upon Mr. Bargrave, he who calls himself 'Dean.'" Livesey bowed his head deferentially. "Will you do me the honor of accompanying me? We have the Lord's work to do this day."

Robert hesitated, asked Livesey to repeat some of what he had said, and strained to hear. Something struck a chord in him. *The Lord's work.* Yes, this was all as God had planned. "*All things work together for good to them that love God. . . .*" He flushed with pleasure and put aside all thoughts of flattery. Of course he was better educated than most of the men in the troop! Who else but he could thus be singled out? Yes, it was all the doing of Providence.

He smiled back at Sir Michael. "Aye, sir. I should be honored."

Livesey's broad hand struck the table. "Good." He shook Robert's hand earnestly. "Have you broken fast yet?" The man mimed eating, his hands flying to his mouth and down to an imaginary trencher.

"Nay." Robert faltered but then he remembered he was addressed by another godly man. "Nay, I was at my prayers when your servant came."

Livesey's eyes opened slightly wider, his eyebrows twitching. "Quite so," he replied. Then he raised his voice again for Robert's benefit. "Well, then I'll see if I can stir the wenches of this idle place to bring us victuals for the day's work. You'll join me, I hope."

It was a command, not an invitation, and Robert gladly complied. He was attracted by Livesey's direct manner, pleased with the man's understanding of his deafness, gratified that the deafness did not, here at least, exclude him from honor and usefulness.

The two men breakfasted on bread, oatcakes, and small ale. The ale surprised Robert. The Fessenden household had consumed no ale for years. But he made no remark about it and enjoyed the lift in his spirits that a second tankard gave him.

Immediately after the meal, one of Livesey's attendants came with a cuirass, buff coat, bucket boots, and helmet for Robert. Gladly shedding his dusty white jerkin and high-tongued boots in favor of what was now the unofficial parliamentarian dress, Robert tried to temper the bursting excitement he felt. It would not be enough merely to be in the good graces of Livesey and to *look* like a soldier of Colonel Sandys. He must win their respect by loyalty, zeal, and courage.

Livesey took him with a small troop of dragoons to the deanery. There they demanded the keys of the cathedral so they could sequester all the gunpowder, ammunition, and arms known to be stored there.

His stomach tightened as he watched the great wooden doors of Christ Church swing open before them. If the people of Canterbury thought to turn their cathedral into a magazine or fortress ready for war between King and Parliament, they were mistaken. It was his hand that had turned the key in the enormous lock, his hand that had made way for soldiers to carry away the means of victory from the rebellious, godless men of Canterbury who dared call themselves men in divine office!

And now they were joined by others in Canterbury who were of his own persuasion, those who thought Laud the Antichrist and the interior of the cathedral a hellish room for Rome. In the crush of men in the church precincts, Livesey introduced him to Richard Culmer, rector of St. Stephen's and a supporter of Sandys.

Robert took Culmer's measure quickly—tall, crowlike in his black robes and loose sleeves, his face fierce with the same determination and zeal he knew himself. He smiled faintly, but then they were separated in the crowd.

The relative darkness and arching height of the great church checked for a moment his enthusiasm. Briefly, he felt again the same wavering he had known more than once on the road to Canterbury. Had not John, his godly brother, spoken in wonder and delight about Christ Church? *Aye, but John was then besotted with a daughter of the neighboring parish*, he thought sourly. How could he make right judgments then? Did not all the world look fair when Jane looked kindly on?

The soldiers in Sandys's troop jostled impatiently at his back as more and more of them entered the vaulted doorway behind him. He heard a low murmuring in his ears and saw that they were shouting angrily, pointing at statues, windows, and tapestries.

Idols, he thought. And suddenly he was swept forward among them. He found his sword raised and felt himself fill with rage. He shouted, too, and surged forward. By his side again, Culmer waved his sword in equal frenzy, the sleeves of his gabardine falling back to reveal huge, knotted muscles such as Robert had never seen on a minister of God. He felt as if he were shoulder to shoulder with the apostle Paul himself in his war against unrighteousness.

The confusion was short-lived. One of Sandys's men discharged a round of shot, and Robert heard it plainly. The sound echoed round the pillars and ceilings, silencing the troops.

Livesey mounted into the canopied pulpit. "Our orders are to destroy all such idols as do disgrace this shrine. Without fear of judgment ye may destroy it all. This place has become naught but a stable for idols. And the filth and abomination within it are ours to sweep away as God will sweep all away on Judgment Day."

Robert could not catch more than a few of his words, even though he had quickly learned to read Livesey's expressive face. But he had known in advance what the officer would say, and he knew what his own part would be.

With Culmer, forgetting all his doubts again, he mounted the steps to the communion table. Together they overturned it with a crash. A few of the soldiers pressed behind them and tore down the velvet cloth that hung before it. One of them with fire in his eyes, a great Samson of a man from some East Kent farm, ripped the cloth in two between meaty hands and threw it down the steps.

Others began attacking the intricate wooden screen of the tabernacle. They pushed and pounded it with their pikes so that it cracked, crumbled, and fell in splinters to the stone floor. Robert heard little of the rending sound of the ancient wood, nor the shouts of the men in their lust for destruction, but he saw it all, and his heart filled with high joy. They were angels administering God's wrath to a wicked whore posing as a bride of Christ.

Livesey directed some of the men up the narrow tower staircase to the organ loft. Beside Robert, still heaving from the effort of upending the altar table, Culmer touched his sleeve and pointed as the last man ascended the steps. "Come!" he shouted. "Let us break that abomination that it sound no more."

The two men ran after the others. Robert's breath came as fast as Culmer's now. In the gallery they wrenched the pipes from their places. "Cast them down!" Culmer roared in a voice so loud that Robert could hear.

The pipes dropped from their hands to the pavement below the gallery. The larger pipes could not be moved, but some of the men tore up the service books and stuffed the loose pages into the mouths of the pipes. Robert turned over benches and stools, looking for more books, while Culmer broke open the singing men's cupboards and put his sword to their surplices. Round them the broken idols mounted—bent pipes, shredded books, ripped surplices.

Robert stopped to catch his breath. Exhilarated, he leaned over the edge of the gallery and looked into the quire. The devastation below matched that above. Organ pipes hurled by men beside and behind them rained down, and an arras that ran the length of the quire hung in tatters now.

He called Culmer to his side. "Look, brother. They despoil that blasphemous tapestry some say portrays the life of Christ."

Culmer nodded vigorously and shouted directly into Robert's ear. "Aye, 'tis work well done. Hark, how the organs go! Mark what music we may dance to!"

A soldier below them bellowed in a frenzy. "Here be Christ!" Robert could scarcely hear Culmer now, but he saw the soldier point with his sword to a faded image, an untouched part of the arras. Then the man suddenly fell on it, slashing and cutting until the whole tapestry descended in ribbons round his head. A great cheer went up from below.

With the arras down and the service books strewn throughout the quire, the men looked for other objects for their hatred. Watching them, Culmer shouted something that Robert could not hear, then ran breakneck down the spiral stairs to the quire. Robert followed, unsure for a moment what was expected.

Culmer rescued the Bible from its elaborate lectern. Balancing the heavy volume in the crook of one of his strong arms, he waved in his other a sword. Was he exhorting Colonel Sandys's men to be mindful of the Word of God, and to purify God's house? Why else were they rooting out these signs of popery and of Laud's wicked reign?

Several men swarmed to the empty lectern. Robert joined them in slashing and pushing at the rails and seats near it. Carvings split, and the brazen eagle appointed like an idol of Assyria to hold up the Holy Scriptures clanged to the granite flags beneath. Satisfied, they then looked to Culmer for further guidance.

Suddenly Robert took command. Several times during the morning he had noticed the windows, so lofty and inaccessible that perhaps no one had given them consideration. And yet they housed some of the most blasphemous idols of all: Mary enthroned above the moon and stars as spouse of God, St. George, Thomas à Becket in full regalia. . . . Surely those windows should be broken, too.

He flew up the steps beside Culmer and raised his voice as loudly as he would have raised it in the weavers' hall over the clatter of the looms. "Men of Kent! Hear me, I pray you." They stilled for a moment, and Robert caught Culmer's nod of approval. "Hear me, though I who am deaf cannot hear you."

The deafness never mattered less. It was a mark of distinction, almost, a claim on others' attention when he most needed it. He saw that they were listening and grew bolder. "Are those glassy idols sacrosanct, then, brothers?" He waved his arms toward some of the windows. Culmer followed his gestures with rapt attention. "No, I say! And who shall gainsay me?"

"Wait!" One of Sandys's soldiers pushed forward and stood before Robert. His clean sword, mahogany skin, and frayed cuffs indicated a seasoned soldier. "Colonel Sandys has given orders that the windows be not touched," he argued. "'Twould cost blood."

Culmer answered in Robert's stead. "If 'tis no shame to drive out statues and effigies in this place, then 'tis no shame to destroy the windows. They be the fruits of idolatry. They be the occasion of idolatry. See how the men and women of Canterbury worship their Diana?" He pointed to several of the windows in which Mary was pictured, and a great groan went up from the few cathedral officers who had dared remain in the building.

But Culmer's voice rose to a fearful crescendo over the other noise. "Let us do as God bids, not as Caesar bids. Proud Becket shall see his glassy bones on the pavement yet. A ladder! Ho, fetch a ladder."

In wonder, Robert heard the last command, but the men could find no ladders tall enough to reach the windows, and all of them wandered about shouting. He expected at any moment that Sandys himself would reappear and marshall his men for the next march. They were due in Dover by nightfall. Fear gripped him again, for he did not want to cross Sandys. *I must decide now,* he told himself.

Almost forgetting that he himself had stirred the present hubbub, he separated himself from Culmer and the rabble and moved aside to an arched porch that led to steps and side aisles on two sides and to the cloisters on the third. He wanted time for reflection, and this place was empty of soldiers.

He had roused Culmer, that was certain, though the man was already hot in his zeal and might well have recollected the windows himself. But Culmer was a Canterbury man, committed to staying in the city in support of the other godly folk, and in defiance of all who would exalt Archbishop Laud and bring Rome to rule in England again.

But I cannot remain in Canterbury to work with Culmer, he thought.

136

Parliament's army offered much greater hope, a much higher calling than the small work he could do here, drifting in and out of Chilham and always burdened with the affairs of the dwindling cloth trade. But if he stayed faithful to the new army for the length of the war, then there would be the hope of glory and advancement, the respect of men and the praise and adoration of women. . . .

Culmer sat in one pan of the scales, and Livesey and Sandys in the other. The weightier pan trembled and descended, and Robert made his choice. He would serve the parliamentary army against the King for as long as the war lasted, and he would set aside for now all cares for his father, for the cloth trade, for his family, and for what went on in Canterbury. God's wider kingdom was more important.

He reminded himself of the verse his mother had so often quoted at his bedside. *"Whosoever he be of you that forsaketh not all that he hath, he cannot be my disciple."* Well, if John could not obey, and if Isaac had chosen the fleshpots, it was for him to answer the call to righteousness.

He turned and walked deliberately past Culmer and his followers. At last a ladder had been found—a city ladder some sixty steps high. Culmer himself was mounting the rungs, and a hush had fallen as even the most careless of soldiers had refused to make the climb.

I would not venture so high, Robert thought with a shiver.

A man in a surplice stood beside Robert wringing his hands. "Thou'lt break thy neck!" he shouted as he watched the spectacle.

Robert looked scornfully at him. "Nay, he's on his Father's business."

The cleric covered his ears in horror and rushed away from Robert, but Robert laughed harshly and turned on his heel again. Walking purposefully to find Livesey and Sandys, he did not hear the windows shattering under the blows of Culmer's pike.

Robert found his new masters outside the precincts with a group of young dragoons who were dressed as he was. One by one the young men took aim at the statue of Christ that stood in a niche above the cathedral gate. A cheer went up each time the musket fire hit the stonework.

Robert surveyed the scene with cheerful satisfaction. He had made the right choice, and within hours he and the other soldiers would cross Barham Downs. The broken organ pipes would whistle merrily in the mouths of the soldiers, and the torn pages of the service books would be rolled and smoked in pipes all the way to Dover.

Canterbury, Christmass 1647

George

Something about this couple reminded George of Maidstone. The little spark of memory smoldered at the back of his mind but would not ignite. Where had he seen the man? He towered above his wife: wide shoulders, thick, curling black hair, a generous mouth, and freckled cheeks ruddy from the wind. His clothes were immaculately made, and he held himself proudly. Yet clearly the man was not wealthy, else he would have sent a servant to look after the little market booth.

Beside this giant of a yeoman the wife was dwarfed, though she again seemed significant in George's eyes as that flicker trembled in his brain. *I know these people. But when, where, how?*

The woman looked up at him but then withdrew her eyes in haste. He saw fear in them and noticed her twisting her hands under her shawl. She was not dressed warmly enough for the day, though she was wrapped in her husband's jerkin. She could not have been older than her husband, yet her beauty had obviously faded, and she looked dowdy and wan beside him. Two boys, dark and vigorous like their father, chased each other round the booth.

George glanced at Elizabeth, whose eyes were directed toward the discernible bulge under the woman's loose garments. His throat constricted for a moment. After the hopeless years of waiting for a living child, Bess had finally proved more than fruitful, nay, lush as his cherry trees in her generosity. One daughter had followed another in rapid succession. But this poor woman did not look well. She was too frail by half to be breeding again.

His eyes moved back to the man's face. For a reason he couldn't explain to himself, he almost expected to see cruelty and lust, but instead he saw tenderness. The yeoman seemed not to have noticed him at all but was watching his wife anxiously. Before he and Bess passed on, the man caught his wife to him and bent to say something softly in her ear. Her face lighted as she mumbled an inaudible reply. Yes, she had been beautiful once. The memory crackled again, taunting him, but still slipping away.

He guided Elizabeth farther along the road. "'Tis strange, love, but I swear I've seen those two before."

"The tailor and his wife?" She looked up quickly. "The little woman breeding?"

"Aye. He was a tailor, was he? I scarcely noticed what was on his stall."

She curled her lip. "Nay, and I should have known it. Ever an eye for the breeder."

He scoffed. "'Twas not that, and you know it." He turned briefly to assure himself that Anna, Henrietta, and Charlotte still followed close behind. They had left their fourth daughter, Eleanor, asleep in the hostelry, watched over by Nancy. "Nay, but I'm sure I've seen those two before."

"Mayhap, and very likely." Elizabeth stopped and turned back for a moment. "'Tis a small kingdom we dwell in. Perhaps you have tried them, seen them at the assizes."

He shook his head. "Nay, 'twas not that. And yet I know I've seen them in Maidstone somehow."

"Where else but the assizes, then?"

He shook his head again. "'Tis no matter. I'll come back later and inquire of them. They look like plain people—Puritans I mean."

She flung her head back quickly. "Puritans? And he with that great forest of curls on his poll? Never!" She stopped a few stalls away from the tailor's and made a decisive movement with her hand. "Anna, make haste, do! Bring thy sisters along." She lowered her voice. "Husband, I'd like to get some gewgaws for the girls. Aye, I know we've not much to spend on trifles now, but there's so little pleasure for the children nowadays."

George's face fell. Elizabeth wasn't complaining, but lately he had suffered with her. The strife was five years old, with no sign of ceasing, and it was rare for them to make a holiday from Tolhurst Court at all, let alone buy trinkets for the girls. Parliament had reduced the estate now. They had lived meagerly in one of the wings of the house ever since George had returned from Marston Moor nursing a leg wound. And they had sent many of their servants from their doors: the men whistling merrily to join the "cavally men," and the maids weeping bitterly at the prospect of returning to families impoverished by war.

Through all this, Elizabeth had held steady. She had comforted the household and proved a better steward than the man he had dismissed. But her resolution and strength had lately begun to waver, and he wanted earnestly to restore to her some of the gaiety that had been quenched by years of worry.

Business for the county courts had brought him to Faversham just before Christmass. With little to tend to at home but the milking of a few dairy cows, he had decided suddenly to take the family with him. Leaving Tolhurst Court in the care of Matthew, one of his older servants, he had removed the family—muffled in shawls and with hot bricks at their feet in the coach—first to Faversham, then to Canterbury.

Elizabeth, he hoped, would revel in the bustle of the great city. He wanted to see the color return to her cheeks and hear the laughter in her voice again. With money he had safely hidden in a pot since before the troops had ransacked the house, he had endeavored to spoil her. They had the best chambers in the inn and ate from the best board below. While she had been uneasy with this profligacy, asking anxiously how they could possibly afford it, the little girls had blossomed in the unfamiliar surroundings, renewing their parents with their round-eyed wonder and glee.

He looked fondly at Elizabeth as Anna caught his hand, reaching them again with the two younger girls. He leaned to whisper over Anna's head, "'Tis ribbons you want for them, is it?"

"No . . . I . . ."

"Just say it, dearling. They shall have whate'er you desire for them."

Her eyes melted, and her face softened. "I know I've been womanish and fretful about our purses. . . ."

"Nay, just careful, my lass."

She drew her brows together. "Fretful, 'tis true. I say it myself. But as I see all these goodly things, and I think how few delights we've had, I can't help—"

"Nay, nor I. But listen. I've had some gold put by that I never told thee of. So, if you please, no more words about money. Ask what you will." He stole a quick look at Anna, but the child's eyes were averted and her face expressionless.

Light broke on Elizabeth's face so that his innards twisted and turned over. After all these years she could still make him feel this way. Desire, tenderness flooded him in an instant. Why should the wars take everything away? Elizabeth, Anna, and the other girls—they were all he needed.

"Then, George, I'll beg some woolen jackets for the girls—those the tailor had. They were fine indeed, and not the drab colors we are wont to see nowadays."

He hesitated, looking back briefly with a tug of jealousy. Had she looked warmly at the tailor? He frowned. "Not green, I hope."

Her chin went up. He knew she had always loved this color best, though she could not wear it now because the Puritans said it smacked of witchcraft. "And if 'twere?"

"Then I'd say thee nay, sweetheart." He sighed. No, it was the clothes she wanted, not the handsome young man.

Her face crinkled, and he recognized that flare of high spirits he had not seen for months. "Ask what you will?" she mocked him.

He gritted his teeth. "Save *green* jackets."

She laughed naughtily. "Nay, but they were *scarlet*."

"Scarlet! Oh, dear heart, we cannot—"

"Aye." She pursed her lips. "The color of wicked women. Of course, my love, how right you are." Her eyes danced. "Then I'll have to settle for blue, I suppose. There were blue ones, you know."

"A sober blue?" He pictured the dismal color worn by most elderly folk nowadays and felt strangely disappointed.

The corners of her mouth twitched, and Anna gazed up in bemusement from one to the other. "Nay, they were light blue," Elizabeth replied, "the color of the little blue butterflies thou see'st up on the Downs of a summer's day. A novel color indeed. Can we afford—?"

"No more discourse of our purse," he said, cutting her off. "We can, and we shall." He bent to Anna. "A surprise for you girls, my sweetings. Wait and see!" He took Elizabeth's elbow in his hand and steered her back toward the tailor.

They had just turned when Tolhurst noticed a band of yeomen approaching the booth nearest the edge of the marketplace. Some of the men were armed with staves, their faces menacing, but he could not be seriously alarmed when he saw their long hair and bright clothes. None of Livesey's men, these, but King's men. All the same, his grip on Elizabeth's arm tightened, and he stopped. Without thinking, he gathered the three girls close to him.

"There's something ill ado, sweetheart," he said only loudly enough for her ears.

She fixed her gaze directly ahead and licked her lips. "Aye, I see it. But we'll not let it spoil our festival, George? We've waited too long for this."

"Perhaps, but let's bide a moment. We can watch the tailor lest he shuts up shop, can we not?" As he drew her away, the girls followed closely. Absently, he reached for his old sword, but the scabbard and sword were missing. He had long ago given up pretense of wanting to use a sword. His only weapon now, he had once joked to Elizabeth, was his plowshare.

Anna's fingers gripped tightly on the loose folds of his breeches. He looked down and met her eyes.

"What's amiss, my father?" Her voice was low and hollow.

George let go of his wife, bent down, and pulled the child roughly into his arms. "I don't know, poppet. Nothing, perhaps, but we'd better move on."

He guided his family to the steps of the Saracen's Head Inn, so that they had a better view of the market. It was better to be cautious.

He looked first at the tailor and his wife. The woman shrank against her husband, and the two boys had stopped, open-mouthed, to watch the first booth. He followed their eyes to where the yeomen were shouting at the merchant there. The men's voices came clearly over the frosty air, and he noticed that the merchant was frantically packing up his goods.

The crowd jeered. "We'll break your pate and beat your brains out unless you close up here," they threatened. "'Tis a holiday!"

One of them held a football behind his back and another carried a goodwife's basket overflowing with holly and mistletoe. The bizarre mixture of their ugly words and clownish appearance struck him as almost funny, but the laughter did not come. The yeomen had plainly come from the alehouse, and blood might be spilled.

"'Tis not a holiday," cried another merchant from nearer where the family stood. "'Tis an idolatrous festival, not the Sabbath. Market shall be kept open this day as any other. No plum pottage, and no nativity pies."

"Aye, and so it shall," a rich and compelling voice shouted from right beside George. He jerked round to see a tall man in the dark, sober clothes of a Puritan minister move to the top of the steps.

"Culmer! 'Tis that dog Culmer!" The fever of the yeomen rose again, and they seemed to forget the stall holders.

George spoke urgently to the Puritan minister. "Sir, you would do well to quit this place afore the mob sets on you," he said.

Culmer's cold eyes turned on George, spurning him. "Nay, these scoundrels shall feel the pinch of iron on their ankles ere this day's out. Shame on you, sir, for a gentlemen, to favor—"

George felt the color rise to his face.

"Stop, husband!" Elizabeth begged.

Tolhurst's hands dropped to his sides, and he looked at the Puritan with his teeth clenched. "I favor *no* rash or violent man. Neither violent in deed, nor in word. You stir the rabble with your words. Shame on *you*, sir."

The men stood at the bottom of the steps now, ranged round. "Culmer, step down if you dare," they taunted.

Looking out over the ruffians' heads, George saw the merchants hurriedly stowing their goods in barrows and sacks.

Anna's arms pressed round his waist, and she buried her soft strawberry-roan hair in his jerkin, shaking like a hop bine in the autumn winds. Henrietta began to shriek for her mama to pick her up, but Charlotte was flushed and eager to see what would happen. She kept crying for sweetmeats from the stall. He began to curse himself for bringing them out. Why, oh why had he not left them all with Nancy?

"We'll hang up the green at the Saracen's, shall we, gentlefolk?" one of the men bawled. "Holly, and mistletoe, and bay, as at thy country alehouses. Nothing to pay, and 'welcome gentlemen.'"

The others laughed raucously, and the footballer hurled his pig's bladder into the air and kicked it up as it fell again.

"Kick him down, the knave!"

"Aye, kick Culmer down."

"Stone him. He's one of Weldon's bedfellows."

George wavered. He wanted no part of either side, but he couldn't remain where he stood. "Make way, sirs," he shouted, feigning a hearty smile. "Wassail to ye all. Make way for the goodwife and children, pray."

The men parted. They seemed uninterested in the Tolhursts. Surrounding Culmer like hounds round a quarry they had scented for miles, they parted but then came together again, raising their staffs.

Sickness seized him. Could he leave even a hated Puritan minister to the mercy of cutthroats, even Royalist cutthroats? He nodded to his wife. "Elizabeth, make haste and take these children to the inn. Dost hear?"

"But the jackets—"

He stamped his foot irritably. "Come, come. This be no place for women and children. Do as I bid, and make haste."

Anna began to cling even more tightly. "Please—oh, pray, my father, stay not here—"

He clenched his teeth again and with an effort unhooked her from him. "Do as thou'rt bid, daughter. Go with thy mother. She needs thee. Go ye all to Nancy and wait till I come back."

Behind them the shouts grew ugly. Forcibly, he pushed the womenfolk along the cobbles, past the stalls, and away.

And now for Culmer, to help.

But Culmer had gone. He had leaped off the steps with a sword swashing left and right. Now he ran with his black gabardine flapping like a monstrous crow's wings. The mob followed, hounds again, their throats full of revenge.

Tolhurst's chest tightened, and fear closed on the pit of his stomach. Amid all the noise and the crash of the staves, another mob of men ran across his mind: Cromwell's men. Three years earlier he had fought under the Invicta flag with Mainy, Filmer, and Twysden in the name of the King. Marston Moor: far from his darlings, camping under the June and July stars at night, marching and waiting by day. Watching the enemy—like a hideous, invincible machine—range themselves against the army of the King.

He saw them now, Cromwell's men, in their dull colors surging toward him, voices in full cry, mowing down men in the ugliest harvest of all—a fierce July wind blasting a field of Prince Rupert's prime grain. He tasted afresh the bitterness of a battle lost, a battle in which he had fought only on the fringes—fearful, wanting to flee, afraid for Elizabeth and his daughters.

The bitterness of that and other battles, the longing for home—they peopled his memory now. He had escaped from the army without disgrace when a musket wound festered and laid him low. But now the war had caught up with him, this time on Kentish soil.

He saw them scoop mud and filth out of the gutter and hurl it after Culmer. For a moment, his sympathy shifting, he wanted to join the chase. What right had Culmer to say the stalls should open or close? Was Culmer judge and jurate here? Was his ally Sir Anthony Weldon of the Parliament County Committee to declare laws for the spoiling of Christ's mass?

But what right had the mob, either, to pitch Culmer into the gutter as they did now? The man's starched white ruff was caked with filth, one side of his face smeared with it. George saw him open his mouth in protest, heard staffs strike against his back as he wallowed and struggled to stand. Was this murder, then, and was he party to it as a silent witness?

The shouts of rage turned suddenly to cruel laughter as Culmer tottered onto a dry pavement.

"Baptized in foul muck, thou art, Culmer."

"Foul enough for the Devil himself."

"See how we use the man who would spear Christ in the gate and knock out windows in His church."

"Tooth for tooth!" someone else screamed.

The minister's replies were lost in the uproar, and then, whimsically, the mob careened round, forgetting Culmer. George rushed forward as the men fell on the stalls and threw the remaining merchandise to the cobbles and gutter.

This time he could not hesitate, especially seeing the terror of the pale, wispy-haired woman—the tailor's wife.

She screamed high and shrill, her face white. The two boys valiantly grabbed the clothes off the stall and pushed them into sacks. He heard a grating, rending sound and saw the tailor stoop by the corner of the table, the blood pooling in his neck and face as he wrestled with someone unseen under the stall table. Then the tailor straightened, and the table tipped violently to one side.

The tailor held one leg of the table above his head, the nails protruding.

"Let me defend you also!" George shouted. But the tailor did not hear, and he felt more foolish than ever.

Imitating, he bent to wrench off another leg. He tasted bile in his mouth. A Tolhurst defending a Roundhead tailor (or was he?) against a mob of King's men at Christmass. Strange days!

The tailor now saw his intention and shouldered him aside. "Here, take this." And he snapped off a second leg as easily as a twig. Long, irrelevant thoughts skeined through George's mind. *A tailor? This man? Never!*

The tailor shouted above the mob. The men had closed in but were cowed by the makeshift clubs and by the tailor's height. The shouting dwindled. No one else came to their rescue.

The street was deserted now—no Culmer, no merchants, none to buy their wares, just a crowd of grimy men of Kent carrying staffs, a football, and holly. Country fools, more so even than himself. A parody of himself.

"Lay not a hand on me or mine," the tailor warned. His dark brows were fierce, and his eyes blazed.

The man with the holly basket stepped backward, grinning absurdly. "We meant no 'arm, I do warrant 'e, sirs."

"'Twas a sport, 'tis all." The man holding the pig's bladder dropped and kicked it over the cobbles until it rolled into the mire and disappeared. The tailor's two dark-haired sons wistfully watched it sink.

The tailor drew his wife close but did not for one moment loosen his hold on the table leg. "'Tis well, for though I'm selling my wares here, I'm one of your own."

"And I," George found himself saying unexpectedly, gathering courage. Mouths opened.

"Aye." The tailor's voice grew bitter. "Can ye not see I'm but a tailor with a family to feed? Think ye I *want* to spend my holiday in commerce like some prating, busy Puritan?"

George gaped at him, wanting to laugh, but afraid.

"He's a knave. He will trick us," one of the ruffians said.

"Nay, I speak the truth," the tailor answered. "I'm not of Canterbury, as ye should know, but Maidstone. I knew of no mayor's ordinances either for or against."

"He'll trick us," someone hissed again. "Turn 'is table o'er."

"Hush, 'tis turned already. 'E turned it by 'imself."

"Aye, so he did," George agreed quickly.

The tailor gave him a grateful look. "I'd rather sport as ye do, though not with ale and strong drink. But see, my wife's abreeding again. Ye'll not touch a woman that's with child, I warrant." Uneasily, he looked both at his wife and back at George.

"Look at 'is 'air."

"He's one of His Majesty's own."

Others backed away, and George marveled at the man's power over the crowd, at the slavish, dog-like faces of the men standing round them.

"Then peace to thee, tailor, and no offense," ventured one man in the crowd, nodding also at George.

The staves were lowered.

"And peace to you all this Christmass tide," the tailor answered. He, too, lowered his weapon.

George hesitated, then took a step forward. The man backed away, and the woman began to weep more quietly, her shoulders heaving.

"Hush, Mother," one of the boys said. "All's well now."

Isaac

Isaac drew Rebecca close to him. Even the closely stitched sheepskin jerkin and woollen hose he wore were not proof against the wind, and she was shaking from the cold, too, her own garments even more useless than his own.

146

He took off his jerkin, lapped her in it, and bent down. "Thou'lt need warm covers on the bed this night, my darling."

She looked up, smiling. In the cold her eyes were red-rimmed and watery, but the azure of her eyes wasn't dulled by the gray day. She was still his pale princess. "Aye, and I will." She groaned, "Ah, but I would we could be home this night!"

"And I, dear love. But it cannot be." He tightened his arm more closely.

A gentleman passed the stall with his family. He moved with a slight faltering in his steps, but the wife was stately, her red hair parted and braided cleverly across her head. She was tall and wore a cloak of fine Spanish wool. The man, however, cared less for his own appearance; his boots were muddy and his cuffs frayed. They were country folk, then.

The man was no taller than his own wife, stout round the middle, his fair hair thinning slightly, his face watchful, kindly. He had apparently observed Rebecca's pinched face and blue lips and his eyes had dropped quickly, but not rudely, to her belly.

He shut his eyes briefly, wishing the gentleman away, and then opened them to look at Rebecca again. He saw the terrified, haunted expression that crossed her face whenever a man ran his eyes over her, and he clenched his teeth. The man meant no harm. And what man could avoid a second glance at Rebecca, especially now she was with child? But as for *Robert* . . . He called down curses upon Robert.

He bent down again. "All's well, my dear. See? The mistress likes our wares."

Rebecca answered him with a reproachful stare, waiting until the family had passed. A string of three little girls in fur muffs and wool surcoats followed their parents.

"Aye," she said, "but not enough to buy." Her voice was bitter.

"Wait. They will. Thou'lt see." He watched the lady carefully as she looked back. Though she called to her daughters, her eyes were on the stall.

"I don't know, love. We came all the way in this cold for naught. What have we sold but a few pair of mittens, some petticoats, and frocks? We do better than this in Maidstone of a Saturday, any week."

"Hush, it won't go amiss. And see how Adam and Charlie disport themselves? 'Tis a good day for them."

Rebecca shifted her weight from one foot to the other and sighed. "Forgive me. I'm ever complaining and peevish."

"Peevish! Nay, we're all starving with cold, and thou'rt abreeding." He gestured to the older child. "Adam, here's a penny. Fetch thy mother some mulled ale over yonder. Quick about it, lad."

Rebecca smiled again. "Thou'rt always kind."

"For I love thee, love thee, little honey." He nuzzled her hair, then let his eyes wander to the family that had just passed. They had stopped again near the top of the market, the wife talking quickly to her husband as the three girls clustered round them, jumping and clapping their hands against the cold.

Three daughters! Aye, some men were lucky. He had sewn three garments for a daughter every time Rebecca had been with child. She had borne two daughters dead, and now, after this one, she would bear no more, neither boys nor girls. It was too much grief. He had promised himself he would live chastely with her from henceforth. He could abide her suffering no longer, and his two sons were good, healthy lads.

The stall was set out with apparel for babes and children, as well as with frocks, surcoats, jerkins, petticoats, and breeches. He prided himself on the fine intricacy and durability of his stitching, in his knowledge of the best cloth, and in the unusual designs. But most of all he loved the soft, decorative work necessary for little girls' clothes.

It made him ache to see that gentleman with three daughters. Not that he begrudged the man his good fortune. About his brother John's age, perhaps, late in life for so young a progeny.

Three daughters. It was the oldest who caught his eye. She hadn't the natural high color and regal air of her mother, but she had inherited the rich, golden-red hair and slender body. She hadn't the high spirits of the middle daughter—and certainly not of his own son Charlie—but her watchful devotion toward her father moved him.

Oh, for a daughter like that! Unthinking, he moved his hand lightly over Rebecca's belly, but she flinched and pulled away. The cord of closeness snapped.

"*Don't,* Isaac."

His hands fell to his sides. "Forgive me, I was . . . oh, thinking of this babe of ours."

She followed to where his gaze had been fixed. "Aye, a girl, God willing." She touched his arm softly. Her hand was blue. "I know, love, what thou thought'st."

"Then why spurn me?" He reached for her gloves and pushed her hands into them.

"I didn't mean to. Thou'rt always kind. I'm sorry, I just said so ere this, didn't I? Peevish, as I said. I cannot help myself."

He shook his head. "Nay . . . but here's Adam. Put thy lips to this, sweetheart. 'Twill warm thee." He held up the frothing mug, then watched, frowning, as she began to sip the brew.

She was right. Their journey to Canterbury had been futile. Only Adam and Charlie had enjoyed themselves, and the cost of the journey had by far exceeded their takings. This was a mistake he would not make again, to come to a town where he was more or less a stranger. It was a risk anyhow. What if his father or Robert—no doubt at business as usual despite Christmass—had come to Canterbury? No, he cared not to think of that.

He looked at Adam. "Son? I think we'll not stay here for the close of the marketing. Thy mother's aweary, and we've made a poor showing of it."

The child's face fell, and he bit his lip.

"Aye, I know. Thou'd like to stay. But 'tis a holiday, and we've had enough. Ye'll help me put it away now, pray."

Charlie pinched his elbow. "I'll help, my father! Let me."

Isaac caught the look of anxiety in Rebecca's eyes as the two boys vied for his attention. *'Tis naught to fret about*, he signaled to her silently.

"Ye'll both help, then. Charlie, fetch the sack." He reached for Adam's shoulder, but the older boy had stiffened.

"Look, my father. Those men mean harm."

With raised voices, a mob advanced in among the booths. Rebecca moaned, falling against him in despair. He caught her to him, anger mounting inside. *Could there be no peace? Not even on Christmass tide? What was their cause this time? What brawl now, on the Nativity of the Lord and in the city of great Christ Church?*

He barked orders to the two boys. They leaped about as he passed them armfuls of clothing, but he did not release Rebecca. Not for the first time, he gave thanks for his own vigor. He would need it today.

He held his breath, every nerve and sinew tensing in his body as the men threatened the merchant at the first booth, then rushed past his stall to the Saracen's Head Inn. He could make little sense of what was happening as the mob began to shout at the straight-backed Puritan who stood boldly facing them at the top of the steps. He pitied the man, but only for a moment. The man's proud, disdainful stance reminded him too much of his brother Robert. *Let them do their worst*, he thought grimly, *but never a hair of my children's heads shall they touch.*

Then he saw the cleric fleeing, splattered ingloriously by mud and finally driven into the stinking gutter. The men cheered and hallooed. The scene was comical yet ugly. They were turning back to the booths.

"Hurry, Charlie, Adam!" He snatched another bundle of clothes and pushed it into one child's arms.

Rebecca began to cry and wring her hands.

His fury boiled over. "Adam, guard thy mother, dost hear?"

The boy nodded stolidly, seizing her round her swollen waist more for his own protection than hers. She sank down on one of the sacks behind the stall and wept, the two boys fussing and cosseting her, beginning to cry themselves.

Isaac lunged at the table, certain now of what must be done. The table leg squeaked, resisting him as the nails splintered the wood and tore away from the upper boards.

Then suddenly someone else stood beside him: the stout gentleman with untidy fair hair whom he had seen earlier but did not recognize. The man shouted to him and began grunting and straining at the other leg, apparently intent on helping him.

The mob approached, sending other stalls toppling to the cobbles, cursing, and berating the stall holders.

Isaac pushed the gentleman away, stiffened his hand, and with a quick downward stroke broke the second leg off the table. Behind him, Rebecca began to scream. Or perhaps she had been screaming before? These moments had gone on too long, far too long.

Rebecca's sobs had subsided, strangely at odds with the festive mood of the inn. An enormous log burned in the hearth, and holly and mistletoe festooned the sills and shelves all round the room. Adam and Charlie sat close to their mother by the fire. As she stroked their dark hair in the firelight, they leaned against her, at peace now. Mugs of steaming cider and ale stood before them all, and in the next room several families were singing carols in defiance of all Puritan ordinances against profane, lewd songs.

He looked round the room, some dim memory stirring in his mind. Had there not been Christmasses years ago before his father and brother had become so strict and his tight-lipped first mother had died? Or had he only heard stories at Mother Mary Snode's knees of years and times before his own memory?

His eyes began to sting. This was another age. England was in winter, a winter that had lasted many years. Only in isolated corners such as this, where they could pay to keep their servants silent, did men dare to flout

Parliament's laws and celebrate Christmass. And Canterbury had seen enough violence for one day. The fierce temper of the filthy Puritan minister, and the fierce faces of the King's men . . . he wanted none of them.

The gentleman who had stood with him in the market watched him guardedly but seemed at a loss for words now that they actually faced each other across a board. He felt he must address him, somehow, but the barriers had come up between them. Himself a yeoman, and this man a knight or gentleman of the shire—a man with three daughters and a queenly wife who wore Spanish wool.

"Sir, I thank you. Rebecca—" He pointed hastily, in embarrassment, with his thumb. "She does thank thee, also. We owe a debt, and I don't even know your name."

"Tolhurst. George Tolhurst."

Isaac remembered his cap and whipped it off, bowing his head. "Then, thank you, Mr. Tolhurst, sir."

"George Tolhurst," the other repeated gently, the skin of his cheeks flushing darkly. "You may . . ."

Isaac saw that the gentleman was even more awkward than himself. He wished the conversation over. But Tolhurst had insisted on providing lodging for them, on helping them carry their goods to the inn where he himself was lodged with his family, on stabling Isaac's donkey, and on setting ale and fruit puddings before them. Adam, Charlie, and even Rebecca had eaten greedily and then retired to the chimney corner.

And now he was left to talk to a stranger to whom he owed not only his own life, but that of their unborn baby. Who could tell whether the crowd would have dispersed had he stood alone against them?

"You may—"

"Nay, sir, I care not to be familiar. But how can I repay you?"

"Don't think of it."

Isaac's mind moved quickly. "You wanted something from my table, did you not?"

Tolhurst's eyebrows rose. "My wife . . . she . . . that is . . ." And he stammered into silence.

Isaac felt compelled to take the lead. "For your wife, perchance?"

Tolhurst looked down, rubbing his hands over his thighs. The breeches were worn, Isaac noticed uncomfortably. And now the poor man was saddled with debts for another family as well as his own.

"For your daughters, then?"

Tolhurst seemed relieved. "Aye, my daughters." A small frown flickered across his brow. "But how did—"

"Your daughters are fair, sir."

"You flatter me."

"Nay, you know they are."

Tolhurst smiled and after a moment said, "As any father knows his own are." He nodded toward Adam and Charlie.

"I noticed your little girls in the marketplace."

"Aye, that's kind of you." Tolhurst's resolve seemed to rise suddenly.

"*Kind!*" Isaac shook his head. Was the man a simpleton?

"Yes, as I said . . . And you noticed my wife, too." The other man smiled with pride. "Everyone does. She was talking to me of your blue jackets. I would have bought them all. We have four daughters. The youngest shall need something of her own one day, instead of cast-offs from the elder ones, though she be but a little hazelnut now. And we saw that thy work will last."

Isaac barely heard the compliment. "*Four* daughters?"

"Aye." Tolhurst flushed again. "God has not ordained boys for us, like yours."

"Nor girls for us." Isaac looked down at the shadowed sawdust floor. "Well, never mind, sir. He knows what's best, I'm sure." The words came of themselves, surprising him. How long was it since he had spoken of God naturally or with any warmth?

Tolhurst nodded slowly. "Then you'll let me buy your blue jackets? 'Twill be a surprise for my wife."

"Buy them? Nay, ye shall have all four. Choose what you will."

Tolhurst stood abruptly and held out his hand. He had hardly touched the tankard before him. "I'll pay thee something, for sure. And the landlord's to give your account to me, as I said. He knows it."

Isaac took his hand and shook it. "I'll send Adam to you in the morn, afore we go."

Tolhurst hesitated. "You—your name? You have not given it to me."

Isaac suddenly felt on his guard. His father's name was far too well known. But then he relaxed. The name was common enough in the county.

"Fessenden, sir. Fessenden."

Tolhurst let his hand drop. "Of Chilham? John or Robert, is it not?"

Isaac looked away, his jaw tightening. "Nay, of Maidstone, as I told the men out there." He cleared his throat, still grateful, but longing to be left alone with his family in the public parlor where they could keep the rest of Christmass without this stranger's inquisitiveness.

Tolhurst looked at him oddly, frowning slightly, but not saying more. "Aye, well, Master Fessenden, God rest ye all this night." He nodded toward Rebecca and the boys. "You've earned a good rest, indeed. And you've two bold sons."

Isaac stood and bowed slightly. "And you have brave womenfolk, sir." He could still picture the oldest girl, her steady eyes like violets and her hair the warm color of russet homespun.

Cambridge, Massachusetts, June 1648

John

John gripped the arms of the chair.

"Some folks have to be tied down," the man confided cheerfully.

That news did not make John feel any better, but he refused the restraining bands gruffly. "I'll bear it, thank 'ee."

Later he was not as sure. The drum of pain beat in his head, softly at first. He shifted in the chair, his mouth stretched wide to admit the other man's fingers and the black pincers. The tooth seemed as embedded and firm as a piece of granite in the hillside, and he groaned.

"Aye, 'tis a stubborn one." The same cheerful voice, sanguine about the pain of another.

Now the drum beat louder. The pincers ground and twisted against the enamel of the tooth. John screwed his eyes shut and tasted his own blood. Neither pain would last long now—neither the immediate, wrenching pain, nor the more chronic, dull ache that had left his face swollen on one side for several days until at last Jane's pleas that he have the tooth removed had availed.

The man's fingers turned and pulled inside John's mouth, sure of their work. Then the tooth tore away from the gum, and with it came the taste of more blood and pus, sharp and foul on his tongue.

"Ah—nasty, that one." Between the pincers, the man triumphantly held the tooth right in front of John's eyes. "Here. Thou'd best rub salt in't and take a syrup of poppy seeds and mithridate, or hyssop and vinegar."

John felt the side of his face. It was bruised and tender, but at least the tooth was out. "Aye." He turned to lean over the edge of the chair and spat into the sawdust on the floor. It was suddenly too much effort to add any more courteous words.

The man proffered a block of salt. John broke off a fragment, crumbled it between his forefinger and thumb, and reached gingerly inside his mouth.

More pain now, but different. The salt was clean on his tongue. It made his spittle run, and he spat again. Then he pushed a small wad of poppy leaves into his mouth. He had been carrying them in his pocket all week to make the pain bearable.

The man stood expectantly. Behind him a child waited with his mother, scuffing the sawdust with his foot, pale in the face and sullen.

John dropped a coin into the man's hand and reached to touch the boy's shoulder. "Thou'lt feel better soon, lad." His voice sounded strange, slightly slurred by his swollen lips and cheek.

The boy scowled at him, unconvinced.

"'Tis kind of you to say so, Goodman Fessenden," the mother said, and she pushed the child forward.

John turned in haste. He did not want to witness the suffering of the child. What if it were Nathaniel bound to that chair and crying piteously?

"Wait, sir, for a bandage. 'Twould take the swelling down sooner."

John stopped on the threshold, his hand going up to his face again. "You have a bandage, then?"

The man pulled a linen cloth from a cabinet beside the chair and tore off a long strip. "Aye, I'll tie it on."

John paused. All of Cambridge would know he'd lost a tooth. But the taste of pus returned to him. "Very well. Tie it on."

The man wound the cloth under and round John's jaw and tied it on top of his head. The pressure on his cheek eased the ache. He replaced his beaver, frowning. What an absurd sight he must look now!

"Come, John, 'tis thy turn."

He swung round abruptly at the woman's word, but she was speaking to the unhappy child, and he slipped out.

John was glad to see the street empty now, especially as he found himself on Winthrop Street, close to where he and Jane had lodged when they first came to Cambridge in the New World. He would prefer to meet no one he knew this morning. But at this hour the men were about their work, the children at their lessons, and the womenfolk within, spinning and baking.

Another house was going up further along the street, not far from where they now lived, and he could hear the men driving the pegs into the walls to hang the clapboards. The sound brought back the sight of the peg-and-tile roof of his family home in Chilham, and for a moment he wished himself back in the Old World.

His gum still throbbed, but he fancied the swelling had already subsided. Reaching into his pocket, he found another fragment of the salt block, crumbled it, and dabbed it gently into the empty socket in his mouth. He winced, but he felt relief. Jane had been wise to urge him to the barber.

He stood quite still for a moment at the edge of the road. Ahead of him the *tchack, tchack* of the hammer went on, and above him the blustery clouds—unusual for early June—churned and rolled from the east. He doffed his hat. "Great Sovereign Lord," he prayed, "I thank Thee for Jane." Immediately, he remembered her as he had first seen her in Canterbury all those years ago. In his eyes, she was as fine and beautiful as ever, her eyes like soft blue wool and her hair like smooth, bleached linen. . . .

He called himself back to the prayer. "And for Thy provision of health to us both." Winter after winter he and Jane had been spared the agues and fevers that ravaged the settlements of Cambridge and Charlestown. Summer after summer, the bloody flux had stolen away children and their parents, but this, too, they had been spared. People came to Jane of an evening, sometimes, to consult about their ailments. She comforted them but claimed no knowledge, and for this he was glad, lest people begin to talk of witches.

"And for our safety, Lord." He bowed his head, no longer looking at the sky. Behind the darkness of his eyelids, he saw Nathaniel again, and he began to frown.

Once again he replaced the beaver, now walking more slowly, his face thoughtful. The child had been an affliction to them both from the first day. What was the Lord teaching them? Was he chastening them for presuming to gainsay His "nay" to their prayers for children by taking the child of others into their home? *No, surely not.* He sighed, wishing himself wiser.

Nathaniel was orphaned four winters after they had arrived in Cambridge. The child had been born to poor unfortunates on a ship from Plymouth. Weakened by fever and months at sea, the mother had died after landfall, soon followed by the father. Jane heard of the infant and begged John to let her bring him home. At last, John had thought, he might have a son, rather than an apprentice, to take over his leather and wool glove business when he yielded up his spirit to Christ's keeping. The cloth trade lay years behind him now, left to Robert and his father.

The child was sickly, though, and needed a wet nurse. Jane had found one close by on Winthrop Street, and soon Nathaniel thrived and came home to them. They had given him their own name. But he was a noisy, fractious, greedy child, and their lives had changed from that day on. Now ten, he had disgraced them repeatedly in their congregation, calling

Reverend Thomas Shepard a fool to his face, and lying to them. John loved the child, nevertheless, and yearned for him to love God in his turn.

He pushed open the nail-studded door of their home and stepped down into the kitchen within. Jane had gathered a handful of flowers from the pasture: blue chicory, spindly buttercups, and some white, three-petaled flowers he did not recognize. She had arranged them carefully in a brass pot, and they provided the only color in the otherwise plain room. *Dear woman!*

Smelling yeast, he looked into the doughbox. She had been baking. A mound of dough was ballooning within. He shut the lid hastily, aware of her silent but definite disapproval. *It'll fall, husband.* Then he clicked his tongue, impatient with himself. By this time in the morning he had usually stitched one glove and sold a pair or two, even in June. What was he doing at home? He stood still again to remember. *Ah, I wanted to write a note to brother Robert.*

He stepped to the sideboard to open the secret drawer where he kept a roll of paper. The stuff was harder to come by in the New World, and he hoarded it away from Nathaniel's marauding fingers.

A piece of slate Jane kept on the shelf above caught his eye. *To the apothy* she had written. Her writing was childish but clear. He smiled. Always she anticipated what he needed, what would relieve him or give him pleasure.

At the table he spread out the paper, sharpened a quill, and began to write. No letter had come from his father in Chilham since one sent the previous autumn—a letter which had not reached him until March. Now he feared that something was amiss. He had sought God's comfort about it but had found no repose. If his father had fallen ill, why had not Robert sent word by the next ship out of Gravesend? Or if Robert and Patience or the family trade had come to grief, why had not his father written to him?

Could the northern battles and bloodshed of which they had all heard have spread south, even to Kent? Had Parliament captured the King at last and taken all England into its own hands? Furrowing his brow, he dipped the quill into the inkhorn. He was glad to be in the Lord's new land, glad to have left the persecution of England, but he could never turn his back on his kin, and he must know what was happening in Kent.

Forgetting his tooth, he bit down hard on his thumb, then cried out. Pain shot up the side of his jaw and across his scalp. He groaned and screwed his eyes tight shut, but the pain passed instantly, serving only as a reminder that he must use more salt and poppy leaves.

To my dear brother, greetings. I trust thou and thy household art safe in Christ's care, but I have heard naught. Kindly send word straightway. And is our father well yet? Make haste to answer me, pray. We continue safely here and by the Lord's grace do prosper—

He grimaced, mentally adding, "Aye, save for Nathaniel," but then went on:

I do meet the ships as they enter the harbor or send my boy to do so. Remember us in thy prayers. Thy faithful brother and servant, John.

He dried the ink with sand, cut the top off the paper, and sealed the letter.

Outside, he saw no sign of his wife or the child. They must have gone out just before his return. He would send his apprentice down to the harbor and would return to work himself.

But in the shop behind their house he found no apprentice, either. A piece of leather lay on the bench ready to be cut, but the apprentice had done no more than open and peg it, stretching it for the cutting. The rascal had discovered his master's absence and gone off. Truly, he was as untrustworthy as Nathaniel!

John gritted his teeth, then winced. "I'll beat that lad," he muttered aloud. But he knew he would relent at the last and let him off. He always did. And the town wardens would do that unpleasant work for him, and more besides, if the lad were caught rolling in the pasture again with one of the selectmen's daughters.

Now the day was wasted.

Irritably, he stopped to use more salt, then strode down Eliot Street. He covered the two-mile walk to the harbor in a short time. There was always some novel sight along the way: new houses going up, or perhaps a church. The settlement was growing, and with it his excitement about the New World. He had been a freeman of Cambridge for seven years now, and proudly so. Some of his fellow freemen had even talked of seeing him into the office of selectman, but that could happen, he reflected, as God willed it.

Down by the wharves, two ships lay at anchor, great wooden shells rising and falling with the swell. The rigging creaked in the breeze, and at the edge of the wharves the water smelled foul and brackish where it was trapped, almost stagnant, between ship and shore. He looked at the more battered of the two with satisfaction. Yes, surely that one had just sailed from the Old World. This time he would know for certain if there were no word from his father. He shouldn't have trusted his apprentice. Perchance there were letters before. He should have come to the ship himself, as now. At least he would know for certain this time.

Inquiring of several seamen as he approached the jetty beside which the ships lay, he discovered that his conjecture was right. The master of this ship was Luke Rolvenden, they said, recently returned from Gravesend and Plymouth. He quickened his pace, smiling slightly. Not only a fellow countryman, but a fellow man of Kent. Surely there would be some news now.

He found a lad to lead him to Rolvenden. The narrow steps and galleys smelled stifling as he went below, but the master's cabin was surprisingly clean and orderly: instruments of navigation set in their places, the books tied into their shelves, and a hammock rolled and tied in one corner of the ceiling. The lad stood aside for John to enter. He ducked, too tall to stand upright anywhere on board, and pulled off his hat again.

The master, bowed over open books and charts, did not look up. John took in quickly the thick mane of grizzled, straggling beard, the stained jerkin round the man's wide shoulders.

"Master Rolvenden, sir?"

"Aye." Still the master did not look up.

"The name's Fessenden, once of Chilham. I think you may have a letter for me."

"Fessenden, you say?" The master's head came up, and John saw that one of his eyes was missing, the empty socket a raw, purplish dent in his face. "Fessenden?"

John was startled by the ugly face. "I have a letter for you to take, too, but first—I am, as I did say—one of your own countrymen." He turned the rim of his beaver uneasily in his hand, not liking the scrutiny.

"*Once*," the other repeated laconically. But then the master pushed aside his stool, reached to some hatches behind him, and lifted one of the flaps. "Aye, Goodman Fessenden, I've a message for thee. Addressed to Eliot Street in Cambridge."

"That's right." His heart began to pound.

The master cocked his head to one side. "It'll cost thee."

John paid him and took the letter. He recognized the Fessenden seal on the outside and bowed. "I'm grateful, sir."

"'Twas one Robert Fessenden did give it me." The man looked curious, still watching him with his one eye.

"Thank you. 'Tis one of my brothers. Fair sailing, I hope?"

"Aye, could ha'e been worser."

"Godspeed, then, Master Rolvenden."

The man sneered. "Good *luck* t'ee, Fessenden. What's a man o' Kent doing on these shores?"

John stooped to duck the door frame. He felt an unfamiliar lump in his throat as he answered, "Sometimes, I know not, truly, but the Lord—"

"Ha!" The master threw back his head and cackled. "A more honester Puritan I ne'er met ere this!"

John scowled and went up on deck again, through the bulwark hatch, and over the gangplank to the jetty. As he stepped over the slight gap, the ship yawed, nearly sending him into the water. How easily he had forgotten the ebb and flow of the sea under his feet on that long crossing! But still clutching the two letters, he hurried to the bottom of the thoroughfare by the harbor and sat down on a capstan.

His fingers damp with sweat, he broke his father's seal and unfolded the letter. Irrelevantly, he remembered that he had not given his own letter to Master Rolvenden. But the ship would not be sailing again yet, and this letter from Robert would doubtless require another reply.

He looked at the top of the paper, where his brother had written *March 1648*, then read on.

Brother:

The news is ill. Our father hath departed this life, and I have buried him with our dear mother in Chilham. I bear all at home when I am not to the war, for Isaac will not and should not return. Mary Snode is sent to Isaac at mine own behest, for Patience and I cannot have her. Our trade is fallen off, thanks to the villainy of the lords, nobles, and servants of Charles Stuart. Greetings to thy wife.

Your servant,
Robert.

He folded the letter. His eyes stung, and he turned his face to the eastern horizon, to where far off from Cambridge the sea curved and blended with the clouds. He wept. Kent was long away. He would never see his father again.

He leaned forward, removed his hat, and covered his face with the back of his hand. He remained still, weeping, for a long time.

Then it came to him that the sea gulls were still circling and screaming overhead and that the water was still slapping and swashing against the harbor wall and under the jetties. He remembered soon the words of the psalmist: *"Deep calleth unto deep at the noise of thy waterspouts: all thy waves and thy billows are gone over me. Yet the Lord will command his lovingkindness in the daytime, and in the night his song shall be with me, and my prayer unto the God of my life."*

He sat up again slowly and opened his eyes. Striking away the tears, and confident of his father's entry into the New Jerusalem, he began to think of his brothers. His mind moved painfully, and he let his head droop.

Puzzled, he tried to recall Robert's demeanor toward their stepmother. He realized he couldn't recollect Robert's ever seeking her out or speaking to her unless it were necessary. But then, he reflected, his brother was a man of few words anyhow, hardly speaking even to his brothers. And to give Robert his due, John had concluded years before that since his brother had gone deaf, the effort of discourse must be great.

He wondered now what sort of a father Robert was to his children. Mary would have loved and cosseted them, just as she had fussed over Isaac. But John could not imagine Robert or Patience tolerating Mary's gentle, soft ways with children—certainly not now that his father was gone. Perhaps that had been the rub between them. His sons Thomas, Nicholas, and Josiah must be growing up apace—please God not as delinquent as Nathaniel—but no doubt they tried Robert sorely, like any boys. Aye, perhaps the children had added unwittingly to the strife.

And what of Isaac? That generous, joyous child had probably not changed as a young man. John could still not believe the news of the May Day brawl or of the hasty marriage to Rebecca Longhurst, news that had reached him from his father. In fact, there were many questions and doubts in his mind about those years in his family's history. Jane had always said that there was something strange about the resolute silence (except from Mother Mary) about Isaac once he had settled permanently in Maidstone.

Isaac—had he been banished, or had he chosen to be? It grieved John that his younger brother never sent news to him directly. Any news he received had come through Mary, and now Mary, too, was banished to Maidstone. *I must pray for them all,* he thought, *and pray that Mary writes me.*

He reread Robert's letter and broke the seal on the one he had just written. It was useless now. He would have to write another.

Lifting his head again and staring across the water, he straightened his back. His father had raised three sons and three daughters and had built up the Kentish cloth trade greatly in his life. He had served the Lord all his life and had lived to be an old man. What more could a man expect?

It occurred to him that had he remained in Kent, it would have fallen to him to try to rebuild the local wool trade. The war between King and Parliament could not go on forever. He was relieved now that this was Robert's lot, not his.

No, his lot, under Providence, was to work for the establishment of a godly city on a new hill beyond the ocean, to bring up Nathaniel in the knowledge and fear of the Lord, and to care for Jane.

Suddenly he longed for his wife. Stifling the renewed urge to weep, he turned back up the steps and went to find her.

The pain in his jaw reasserted itself even through the grief for his father and the uneasy thoughts of Mary, Robert, Isaac, and Nathaniel. It was a reminder, however, that he was alive, though his father was now dead.

Goudhurst, May 9, 1648

George

Elizabeth clung to his sleeves. Her wide brows were straight and low over her eyes as she looked up at him. In the darkness, her eyes gleamed in the uncertain light from the lantern she held.

"I must go, love," he intoned. Beside him, the mare shifted, grazing her hooves on the bricked courtyard, her saddle leather creaking. In the shadows of the stable, one of his servants waited at a distance with another horse.

"George, I'm afraid," she begged. "I dread thy going away, especially now."

"Now?"

"The war . . . the King's rebels riding through . . . and the Roundheads." She shuddered.

"The King's rebels?" He smiled faintly. "Bess, and pray what dost think *I* am? Thou'rt married to one, thyself."

"A very gentle one, though. And not a notorious scoundrel like some of them."

"Gentle to thee, aye," he said grimly. "And no doubt the other rebels are gentle to their own womenfolk, too. But you have naught to fear, sweetheart. All Kent is for the King now. Only Dover holds out for Parliament."

She shrugged and sighed. "Perhaps!" Then she frowned again. "But tell me again how long thou'lt be gone."

He put his foot into the iron and swung himself up onto the mare. She skittered sideways away from Elizabeth, dancing over the bricks and shaking her head until the bridle and bit jingled. George reined her in and leaned forward against the mane to steady her. The old wound in his leg ached. "I cannot say. You know I cannot."

"But the trials could go on for weeks."

163

He pressed his hand against the bags he had strapped onto the back of the saddle. "Aye, they could. Thou'lt have Matthew and young Edmund to look after thee, and the girls to look to"—he dropped his voice—"and you know where I've hidden the little extra gold I've had . . . ? Aye, you'll do well, my love." He saw her eyes fill with tears as she shook her head, so he bent to put his hand under her chin. "What's this? Tears? You're not abreeding again, surely?"

She shook her head again and wiped the tears away on the back of her wrist, laughing a little. "No . . . but, George . . . I can't understand why the committee chose thee—you of all people—to sit at Canterbury. Why? Everyone knows you support the King."

He narrowed his eyes. "No, Bess, you know not what you say. You're privy to what I think, but there be few others I can trust, except my dear friend Mainy, and one or two besides. And we've lain low for years. The Kent Committee hardly knows who I am now—just another justice who's caused no harm, while some are so hot blooded."

"Aye, Lovelace and his fellows."

"Hush, sweetheart." He turned in the saddle. "Mainy is Lovelace's cousin. They both love the King, and we never know who may overhear us." He pinched her cheeks. "And when did you last see a Roundhead here? Hmm?"

She stiffened. "Pray God I never shall!"

"But *when?* Think now." It suddenly became important for her to remember, and for him to press her to be calmer. In the last few months she had seemed less able to think clearly, less able to concentrate on anything except him and the children.

She puckered her forehead and dipped the lamp so that the flame danced madly and the shadows wavered over her face. "Not since the beginning, 'tis true. Five years? Or is it six?"

He felt his advantage and pressed it further. "And why, pray?"

Her head went back again. "Because we paid them off when they took so much of our substance?"

Violently, he wrenched his hand away from her face. "No, never! Never! Is that what you thought?"

"George—" Her voice broke. "These may be our last moments, and we're quarreling. I'm too *tired.*"

He hoisted his right leg back over the horse's tail and dropped down beside her again, full of remorse. "Forgive me! I'm sick with worry myself, and with trying to put a brave face on it. But truly, thou dost not need fear the Roundheads here, nor King's men, neither. Since we did as we were bid by him all those years ago—or so Livesey thought—we've been left alone, haven't we? And yet, none of the King's men privy to my thinking doubts me." He reached out to her and pulled her head against his chest. More than anything, he wanted her to believe him. More than anything, he wanted to believe himself.

"Left alone, you say? Left *alone*, aye," she answered bitterly, her voice muffled by his jerkin. "Alone, but poor."

He tightened his hold of her shoulders. "Nay, even that's not true. Look." He bent and took the lantern from her hand and held it up toward the back of the house. "They can force us to shut half this place, as we've done, and to grow barley for their troops, but this is still ours, and one day the King will be out of captivity in Carisbrooke Castle, and all shall be restored."

Canterbury, May 11, 1648

The chamber was stuffy. George nodded, jerked awake, and nodded again. The County Committee had decreed that they would settle routine matters first, and he found them as dull as the county assizes at Maidstone. He resolved to say little and to keep his seat in the middle bench of the hall, saving his tongue for when he might have need of it later. But as the judge droned on, he found himself increasingly sleepy.

His drowsiness was short-lived the second day. The arrogant, snapping voice of Sir Anthony Weldon cut the air again and again, and more than once he caught sight of Michael Livesey in his place at the hall doors, moving in the shadows like a malignant snake.

Pray God I be not recognized, he thought, but then gave thanks that his hair was scarcer than it had been in the early days of the war. As he looked round he knew he was one of many still faithful to His Majesty King Charles.

He had come a long journey since his first, timorous stand against Livesey six summers before. He would be less afraid, now, to contend with Livesey than he had been then.

The sergeants, Wilde and Creswell, called one case after another before the commission. As the cases ended, George's eyes came wide open, and he searched the room. He caught the eyes of several others, men he knew to be Cavaliers, far more bold and outspoken than he had been in recent years, but—like himself—silent for the present. They were men who had lost land and houses and still stood for the King.

And what have I done, he asked himself angrily. Little in comparison, except for an inglorious skirmish on Marston Moor when he had been wounded, then dragged into the tent to have a musket ball cut out of his thigh and the wound salved and bound; little except an even more inglorious confrontation with the vulgar fellows of Canterbury last Christmass; and little indeed in comparison with the men the Cavaliers had called martyrs for Kent—those who had languished in Leeds Castle since the riots and now awaited trial.

His eyes roamed over the crowded hall. Was it his imagination, or were other eyes kindling as the last case came before the jury? There was a slight stir as men adjusted their jerkins or shifted on the benches.

George disliked Sergeant Wilde instantly. As the accused were penned in the dock, the sergeant's opening remarks about the Christmass rioters sounded bloodthirsty. Had Tolhurst not witnessed some of the struggles himself? Were these men, some of whom were guilty of merely playing football or hanging holly at their doors, the vicious criminals Wilde reported them to be?

Listening, Tolhurst began to scowl. But then laughter broke out as Creswell stood to close the charge. Shuffling apprehensively, Creswell darted a look at Wilde and proclaimed, "God save the King!"

The words were customary but had not echoed in Canterbury halls for years. Moderates and Cavaliers broke into laughter, but Parliament's men rose with a shout of fury.

Livesey ran from his post at the door. "Troops! Send for ten companies this very hour!"

Wilde raised his mace and called for silence, but the laughter spread, turning to mocking and jeering. Some of the prisoners began to laugh. "The King!" they called. "God save His Majesty!"

Weldon rose at the front of the hall. "Ye make mirth?" he screamed over the din, his jowls trembling. "A comedy of solemn justice! We shall adjourn."

"Never!" cried one Cavalier, rising to face him.

Wilde advanced upon the man, threatening him.

George watched helplessly. He might soon be watching tragedy, not comedy.

"Sergeant Creswell! Sergeant Creswell!" Wilde appealed to his colleague.

All round the room, men slowly lowered themselves to the benches, and all attention riveted on the two sergeants.

"Brother Wilde, I am doing as the law bids, and that you know." Creswell's voice was low in the still hall.

"Fool!" Wilde cried harshly. "Old laws, made void when Charles Stuart saw and heard the key turn in the door of his Carisbrooke prison."

The murmuring began again, and George sat forward, fascinated, though his heart still raced with anxiety.

Wilde went on. "There be a statute, the Statute of Twenty-five, and it makes plain our right to arrest and hang the dissident Kentish gentlemen and rogues in this place. Under law of King Edward III, Livesey should bar the doors and hold all fast within."

George rose, among many this time. He felt the blood rushing to his face. All round him, men were hallooing and cursing, and his voice joined theirs. A few other men rushed out, their faces drained and panicked.

"Nay!" Creswell held up his mace and stood slowly. "We durst not apply this statute. These men are not guilty of levying war on their King as the statute intends. They are in no way guilty of such. But if we continue in this vein, sir, we may like to be hanged by your fine statute ourselves. So say no more of Edward III's laws, pray."

George grinned and flashed a look at Weldon. The committee man's face was a sculpture of grim fury, but Weldon could not argue with Creswell. Wilde, too, was silenced. The tension had broken. Many leaned back. For a few moments the case against the rioters proceeded, but George felt a crushing indignation. This was no impartial commission. Only Creswell seemed honest, resolved to play fair. And what of the jury?

He counted them off mentally, most of the faces known to him, men of old families—Edward Dering's son, Oxinden, Harfleete, Hobday, Thornhill, Broadnax—and almost all loyal to Charles. His mouth twisted. *Oh, what a thorn in the side of the commissioners this jury might prove!* Weldon would be bested at last.

Canterbury, May 23, 1648

George lifted a mug of ale to his lips. It had been years since he sat down for an evening at a city inn, except last Christmass with that extraordinary tailor fellow. The homely Star and Eagle Inn, next to St. Mary's in Goudhurst, was hardly a city inn, and not since he and Elizabeth had wed had he felt any desire, or had any freedom, to while away the evening hours over slow mugs of Kentish ale at the inn.

Beside him, Mainy and Filmer flashed him quicksilver smiles, and all round the men's voices rose and fell in excitement.

"The House wanted a verdict . . . Weldon'll have those jurors' heads on a platter yet."

"Nay, the man's stark mad. Who'll stand with him?"

"'Twas contempt of Parliament."

Laughter followed. "'Twas better than any play I ever saw of Mr. Shakespeare's."

"Will Shakespeare? He's long dead, fool."

"Aye, dead, and his playhouses with him, God rest 'em all." One of the Cavaliers crossed himself. "Why talk of Shakespeare's comicry when we can watch our own without fear of being clapped in prison for't!"

"I'm not so sure," a timid man countered. "We may yet join those poor souls in Leeds Castle dungeons."

The others jeered, and George pitied the man, who promptly stood to leave.

"Let him go!" one of the Cavaliers shouted with a toss of his head. "We need no cowards here."

Young Edward Hales of Tunstall leaned forward. He was more richly dressed than any other. "There'll be no talk of cowards." The laughter died away. Hales was one of the few they would all listen to. "Let every man prove his valor. Then we'll see who be the cowards."

George winced inwardly and exchanged glances with Mainy, but Mainy quickly looked back at Hales, and George found himself strongly drawn by the young blue eyes and flushed, eager face. Would this be the man to lead Kent in yet another rebellion?

"Edward Hales is right." The dark-skinned man beside Hales spoke for the first time. He was not a man George recognized.

"And who be you, sir, that we should heed your affirmation?" one dissenter asked.

All eyes turned on Hales and his companion, and Hales spoke. "Forgive me, gentlemen, squires. Robert L'Estrange is here among us. I have awaited his coming for many months now. And he may serve us."

A babble of voices ensued, and George frowned. L'Estrange was a pamphleteer known all over the East of England, but the man was from Norfolk, not Kent.

"How may he serve us, *Child* Edward?" another man shouted scornfully.

168

L'Estrange stood. "I'm willing to draft you a petition, settling once and for all the just deserts and rights of King and Parliament—and Kent. What say you?"

A few of the men jeered; others cheered. George merely groaned. *Another petition!* This game had gone on twenty years!

"Go back to Norfolk, L'Estrange," one man said sourly. "What good have any of our petitions done us?"

Suddenly George was on his feet, surprising even himself, his mind changed altogether by the other man's loutishness. "Nay!" he cried. "Let's not be so proud we cannot take aid when it's offered."

"But on what surety?"

Edward Hales stood, too. "On mine, sir. On mine. You have my word. This man is our ally. Norfolk stands with Kent and with the King."

"Then where is Norfolk?"

"Here!" L'Estrange spat, jamming his fist onto the table so that tankards pitched and rolled to the floor.

George jumped in alarm but then gained courage from the renewed stillness and Mainy's eager look of encouragement.

"Norfolk? Nottingham? Kent? What does it signify what we call ourselves if we be for the King? And what better time to frame a petition than now, when we are all hot, when we are all here and ready?"

"And . . . when I can supply all the arms we need to go in a muster to Westminster," Hales put in.

The skeptic sneered again. "Thou'rt naught but a boy, still smooth on the cheeks! To Westminster, pray? And all of London standing trembling under Parliament's shadows? Phaw! Get back to thy nursery!"

L'Estrange glowered across the table at this opponent. "And get you back to your churchyard, old man. This petition's signed in blood—*young* blood. We want not old blood for this."

George's heart beat high with excitement. Hales and L'Estrange were pitted against only one vocal man. The others, including Filmer and Mainy, remained silent. He wanted to divert the argument. Young blood? His blood was young no longer, but it was rising.

He sat down abruptly. "I believe we should listen to Hales and to Master L'Estrange. Let's hear them out, at least. Kent's never been as resolute, as united as now. Let's hear them out, I say."

Most of the men murmured in agreement.

"Very well," the skeptic allowed, "but let Hales speak, not the *foreigner*, pray." And he, too, sat down.

L'Estrange's mouth twisted, but then he turned to Hales. "Go on, sir."

While the others sat down again, Hales remained standing. "I will speak, then, if't be your will. But I shall speak for Roger L'Estrange, also. The jurors returned *ignoramus*, and the Committee has foundered. I appeal to you as others have done before, since our fathers were delivered from the laws of the Conqueror, and as they and we have prospered in this fair county. Remember the rebels and think of His Majesty over all else. It cannot be the will of God that our King be 'prisoned in the Isle of Wight. We must demand our rights, and his. Once we stood against the king, but now we stand 'gainst Parliament, for it has grown fat by stealing, arrogant by its uncivil army, partial in its laws. 'Tis time to put an end to it and stop once and for all the villainous taxes levied on us all, or else—"

"Fine words! Fine words!" the skeptic cut Hales off, but then seemed to lose his resolve. "Very well, Master Hales. Let Master L'Estrange begin." He leaned forward. "For God's sake let us write this thing down and be done wi't."

Smelling victory, George nodded. He smiled at Mainy and even the skeptic. "Aye, let's write, and then let's gather men and signatures."

"And away to Westminster," Mainy added.

"Blackheath," L'Estrange said. "We should meet at Blackheath."

"Aye, and call men from all Kent to sign," Hales agreed. "Young Dering, you can get your cousins, those of Charing and Egerton . . . and Thanet can bring in the northern villages . . . and there's Barham, and Romney and St. Augustine's . . ."

George felt the smile growing on his own face, and Filmer smiled back at him.

What would Sir Dudley Digges have thought this time?

Burham Heath, May 30, 1648

He had scarcely thought of Elizabeth in the frenzied hours since the petitioners had begun to assemble. The Earl of Thanet had defected, but the Cavaliers had persuaded some of the Canterbury Parliamentarians to join the petitioners. *By now*, George thought, running his eye over the tents, bundles, supplies, and horses that indicated the presence of the absent King's army, *by now there must be ten thousand men at least*.

He and Filmer, with some of the other seasoned soldiers, had spent the first few days collecting arms from the nearby houses without giving offense to the inhabitants. Remembering Livesey clearly and bitterly, he had done the job unwillingly. Now they could only wait until the muster was over and they could move on to Blackheath.

But the strain was still almost visible. L'Estrange, Hales, and the Earl of Norwich (now appointed general) argued hourly with some of the older men about the wisdom of inviting support from Essex, Norfolk, and even from men who had fled to France. Commands and countercommands issued and reissued from one tent after another as each gentleman claimed his prerogative to govern his own men as he saw fit. Meanwhile some of the horsemen were hedged in at Sittingbourne, and others—grown impatient with long indecision—had deserted or laid down their arms at the urging of itinerant Parliamentarians. All was tumult, rumor, and counter-rumor.

L'Estrange passed the tent that Tolhurst, Mainy, and Filmer shared. "The Earl thinks not two days shall pass before the King has his crown again," he shouted cheerfully, reining back his horse briefly.

"I doubt it, Roger." Filmer snorted. "'Tis the work of weeks, not days, much as I wish otherwise."

"Ill-favored wretch you are, Filmer," L'Estrange mocked. "Have ye not heard of the ships that left Parliament's service and seized half dozen of the coastal forts or more? 'Twill be Carisbrooke next, I warrant you. I'm defying Fairfax to keep his men in Blackheath. They'll come to us, no doubt."

A few young men not far away began to sing roisterously:

> *May you unconquered still remain,*
> *Tread down the common foe,*
> *And help the King to the crown.*
> *May ages after say*
> *This noble Kent*
> *Gave the greatest blow*
> *To that cursed Parliament!*

Filmer turned with a faint smile toward the singers. "Dost think we'll truly be champions of Church and Crown, George?" Filmer made a dismissive wave of his hand as L'Estrange moved away.

George shook his head and sighed. He longed for L'Estrange to be right. "Nay, I fear not." He stood and stretched stiffly. The ground where they had been sitting remained damp from the morning's rain, and he was weary of waiting, weary of mud, weary of cleaning again the musket he knew he would never use.

The wound in his leg ached again. "Dover's still in Parliament's hands," he said. "That doesn't augur well. Fairfax is well organized while the Earl of Norwich—" He stopped, hesitant, unsure whether he could voice his doubts, even to Filmer.

Mainy joined them at the opening of the tent. "Aye, the Earl of Norwich . . ." His voice was low, full of laughter.

"—Is like to be a sound man," Filmer said brightly, but his smile was forced. "Son-in-law of Birling Manor—Abergavenny, you know. Hardly a foreigner, George."

The word *foreigner* was beginning to grate on Tolhurst. "What does it matter whether he was born in Kent, or no?" he muttered irritably. "We can only be concerned—" He paused. Others nearby were staring, for he had unwittingly raised his voice. "What our care should be is whether he be able to exercise his office."

Mainy and Filmer stared at him, and Mainy spoke. "He's as apt as any man who's had not experience of war. He's all frolic and pleasant humor, but who can draw together all the fractious men from the Medway towns and every other lathe of Kent?" Mainy's lips curled scornfully. "I know not who else is to lead us, but I've little faith in Norwich."

Filmer nodded slowly. "There is no one else. But you may be right. We must be on our guard. The men of Kent? We know we can count on them, but the others . . . ?"

Mainy's mouth puckered in distaste. "'Tis not that the Earl's from out of Kent, friends. 'Tis what I said before—all fun and frolic. Why, I heard this hour that he had a smuggler as a captain. What sort of general will he make? Is he the match of Fairfax, think ye?"

"Of course not." George laughed. "The Earl of Norwich will make a laughing stock of himself if he seeks to buy off Fairfax's soldiers with money we poor wretches have none of!"

He rested the musket against his leg and wiped his hands on a rag. "Fairfax is too shrewd. He's not in charge of Parliament's men for naught, and he did not choose Oliver Cromwell as his second for naught, neither. He knows what he's about, that man. But as for our Norfolk, I'm not sure."

Filmer stared at him gloomily, and Mainy simply nodded. Tolhurst looked back at them for a moment, retrieved his musket, opened the breech, and sighted down the barrel to make sure it was clean.

Through the barrel he could see a circular patch of blue sky. He remained motionless for a moment, the musket pointing at the sky, the blue circle his only lodestone.

Elizabeth could see that same sky, he reflected. And was she looking up, like him now, only a few miles away, praying for him, perhaps? What would she say? *Thou'rt not in Norfolk's hands, sweetheart, whate'er befalls. Thou'rt in God's hands.*

He put the musket down suddenly and found Mainy and Filmer watching him.

"Clean?" Filmer inquired caustically.

George turned back into the tent. "Aye, clean."

East Malling Heath, May 31, 1648

Robert

Some of the men had gone with Colonel Gibbon to Rochester and Dover, but Robert preferred to remain in the column where he was best known, under Oliver Cromwell. They had marched all day from Wrotham through the Downs to Meopham and at last to East Malling, where they were now camped in thick hazel woods. General Fairfax's scouts had seen the rebels encamped on Burham Heath, but although the local villagers had fled as Parliament's army of seven thousand had swung south of Maidstone, the Royalists seemed unaware that Fairfax was so close.

Battle was imminent now. Robert could not deny it as he lay awake, thinking, wrapped in the ragged bedding he had not carried to battle during the last three years of relative peace.

From the first word that had come to Chilham a week before, he knew that he must rejoin his fellows under Fairfax. Friends of the King were rising all over the county; if he did not stand with Cromwell and Fairfax, who would?

But parting from Patience and the children had been sadder than usual because he had been more fearful. The Royalists outnumbered them this time, and most were fighting on home ground. So Patience had wept sorely, standing at the door of the house with Josiah and Nicholas ranged stalwartly on either side of her.

As his father left, Thomas swung carelessly on the gate, playing foolishly at making a drawbridge. Hannah, timid and shy as ever, held tightly onto Nicholas and gazed up with sloe-eyed awe at her father's buff coat and helmet.

Robert passed Thomas, cuffed him on the ear, then stood in the lane beyond the gate to look back at them all. Thomas was shouting as usual, his mouth open and laughing, but as usual Robert could not hear him. He caught Nicholas's eye for a moment. His second son's face appeared stern and veiled. Duty, not love, kept the child close to his mother now. Nicholas had never cared for his mother as much as Thomas had, but he could be trusted. Thomas, however, was the oldest and should take that part.

Robert turned to face Thomas again. "Go to thy mother, son," he ordered sharply. "You are the oldest and must provide now."

Thomas leaped off the gate, landed in the mud, then wiped his hands on his hose. He motioned to his father that he was sorry. Robert reopened the gate, reached for the boy, and held him close. Thomas meant no harm; he was merely thoughtless.

Over Thomas's wavy hair he caught Nicholas's eye for the second time. Releasing his older son, he watched him bound to Patience's side. Thomas hesitated at the step, gave Nicholas and Hannah an unceremonious push, then put his arm round his mother.

"And you, Nicholas," Robert said, resting his hands on the gate and staring at the mute family tableau only a short distance away, "you, my second son, are charged to keep peace in this house while I am gone. See that Thomas and Josiah do not drive thy mother witless with vain argument. And see that no one oppress thy sister."

Robert nodded to Hannah and in a rare rush of tenderness for his daughter, suddenly hurried back and picked her up. "Hannah, love, be kind and obedient to thy mother as thou always art."

Hannah nodded back, and her eyes filled with tears. Some of Patience's fear had transferred to her.

"The Lord of Hosts is watching over us all, Hannah."

The child nodded back wordlessly and slipped down to catch hold of Nicholas again. Robert searched for Josiah, who was sulking. "Josiah? Apply thyself to thy books, dost thou hear? Nicholas is a man of book-learning already, and there's naught but a year or two between ye. When I come back, I'll diligently examine thee myself." He stopped, his eyes finding his wife's again. Her jaw was set tight. How well he knew that resolve!

"Patience, wife, be of good cheer. We'll see those rascals into prison; then it's home again, and peace under God and Parliament forever."

She held his eyes a moment longer without answering. Although she had never said she loved him, she would stand loyal no matter what the outcome of the battles ahead. She would also rule the household wisely in his absence.

He'd kept her face in his mind as he swung his pack over the horse's back.

Then he set off down the lane with his eyes alert for fellow Parliamentarians he had arranged to journey with. He dared not look back.

Lying now with the rough fabric against his face, he found it hard to picture Patience. She seemed always elusive when he was away, and suddenly he felt horribly alone and empty.

He hunched forward and tried to pray, but the Lord seemed far away, too. He lay down again and shut his eyes. His father, taken away by the Lord, had left a failing business. His brother John had become master of a thriving trade but lived far away on a shore almost as distant as their father's. His other brother, Isaac, was . . . ah, yes . . . giving roof to old Mother Snode. *And Rebecca? Oh—was she still as beautiful?*

Moaning, he turned on his side and opened his eyes to blot out the girl he remembered as clearly from May Day all those years ago as if he had seen her on this May Day. Forgiveness—had the Lord granted him that? He was less certain now than he had been before.

Doubt kept gnawing at him. The deafness had worsened in the last few years, if that were possible. Now even the soft swishing sounds were gone. Stony silence defined his world. He could speak, but even his own voice was lost, and he wondered often if the words still formed themselves correctly or if his speech sounded as clumsy as he often suspected.

Deafness . . . death . . . the disintegration of his family and his trade . . . was anything left? He sighed and looked up at the sky. *The Lord of Hosts is with us,* he thought slowly. *The God of Jacob is our refuge.* He repeated the words over and over until he fell asleep.

Maidstone, June 1, 1648

Under lowering clouds the Parliamentarian cavalry advanced north from Loose. Robert thought only passingly of his boyhood days of riding the same lanes to oversee his father's fullers and millers. *The world seemed lighter then,* he thought, remembering clouds of apple blossoms and hedges white with cow-parsley. But it was already June, and the fruit trees had lost their blossoms and leafed out thickly. The lanes were awash with leaves: the yellow-green of the beech leaves, the uncurling of scalloped oak leaves and the thin grace of long, trailing willow twigs. Only the chestnuts and hawthorn were flowering still. The chestnuts held up cerise and white candles in the gathering dark, and the hawthorn drenched the air with pink-and-white sweetness.

He looked up at the clouds. *Strange,* he thought. *It could not be later than seven o' the clock, yet the sky is as black as at dusk.* Then he looked at the men riding beside him. They rode in silence now, but only a few minutes earlier Livesey had passed through the ranks with the word that the enemy was divided: some to Rochester, some still left at Burham Heath, some to the high ground of Kits Koty, and only two thousand in the city itself.

"They've thrown up barricades on Stone Street," Livesey had shouted, making signs to Robert until Robert understood. "There's only Mainy and Dudley to lead them. The fool Earl of Norwich has fled to Rochester in a fright, and no wonder!"

Maidstone is ours, Robert thought gleefully. He could easily imagine the colonels of the King's fragmented army calling first for an advance, then a retreat. *Indecisive, foolish, irresolute men!* The battle would be over in no time. Fairfax, though stiff with gout today and complaining loudly of their damp quarters on East Malling Heath, would lead them to victory and see the Royalist rebels and scoundrels to prison in Leeds and Westernhanger Castles.

Large raindrops began to splash onto the leaves overhead, then drum on his helmet. He could feel rather than hear the slight vibration of the raindrops on the metal, and he could certainly feel the coldness of the drops that slid down his neck and under his wide collar. He shivered and hunched his shoulders against it. The air became gray with water, and the rain bounced off the summer-hardened road, soon swirling in brown eddies round the horses' hooves.

Then, ahead of the column, he saw the first mound of earthworks raised hastily by the Royalists. Enemy troops were drawn up on either side of the road and beyond the earthworks. The red standards of the King hung limp and discolored in the downpour.

The horses quickened pace; Fairfax must have given his command. In turn, Robert's own heart quickened. The skirmishes at the bridge over the Loose Stream had been insignificant, and until now he had not come close enough to a Royalist even to raise his musket for the aim.

Somewhere a cannon went off. He could not hear it, but he felt the thudding burst of air strike his breastbone. He pressed forward even as some of his fellows fled in panic. *Deserters.* They would be caught and shot unless they returned.

Fairfax's cavalry advanced on the barricades. Muskets fired on both sides, the flowers of flame and smoke blossoming all round Robert as the men fired them. Still the horses pressed forward.

Beyond the earthworks, some of the rebels scattered. In the opening they left, Robert could see—even through the rain—the blurred outlines of the houses and shops at the base of Stone Street. They looked different now, however, for all were barred with logs and planks of wood, and defended by musketeers.

Robert's horse laid its ears back and faltered in the confusion. He had to remind himself that though he could not hear the noise, his poor animal could. But the horse must go forward, so he dug his spurs into the soft flesh, shortened the reins, and pushed forward with the rest.

A great blast from one of the cannons on top of the hill ahead split the air. The ball slit a furrow through the men only a few feet away, and for the first time, sickness gripped Robert's throat. But he dared not pause to look at the carnage beside him. He must move forward, ever forward.

His horse veered sharply to one side, snapping the reins, and dodging back through the cavalry in panic. The animal knew Robert's own fear, then. Frantically, Robert reached to catch the leather thongs in his hand, but the horse turned again and flung its head and neck back so forcefully that Robert looped backwards over the tail and found himself surrounded by the legs of several horses, in danger of a trampling.

The other horses snorted, shied, and reared up, but his own lashed out with its hind hooves and then disappeared in the crush of men and horses.

Dazed, Robert remained where he was. Hands reached down to pull him up; faces and mouths moved in words and gestures he could not understand. He frowned. *What's happening?* He felt strangely drowsy; somewhere in his body a pain nagged at him, but he could not decide where.

One of his fellows was urging him up, so he staggered forward, clutching his musket and bandolier. The houses and shops swayed as another cannon ball ripped down the hill.

Then suddenly, for the first time in years, the world came clear to Robert. The rain eased briefly, and he could see the standards on both sides quite distinctly. Miraculously, he could *hear* quite clearly the roar of the men, the echoing clap of musket fire, the neighing of the horses. He lifted his arms into the rain in frenzied joy.

"I can hear! Livesey! I can hear! Great God of Hosts! I can hear!"

"Out of the way, fool!"

Men surged past him, faces intent, muskets and pikes raised. This was no place to pause. The cavalry had passed him now, and he stood among the foot soldiers.

The cannon roared again and belched smoke over the top of King's High Town. All Robert's fear had gone. Laughing, screaming with delight, he ran forward among the pikemen. "The cannons have given back my ears! I can hear!"

No one listened, but the running men had slowed, and just in front of him his fellow Parliamentarians were fighting the enemy hand to hand. Orders were shouted from both sides, and from cracks in the barred windows came intermittent musket fire and showers of broken pottery. *This is a new kind of battle*, he thought, *fought with new rules*. No open battlefield and ordered charges, this was man to man, Kent fighting Kent in its own county town.

"For God . . . !" a Royalist shrieked, bearing down on him with an absurd broadsword raised ready to club him down.

Still laughing, Robert aimed straight at the man's open mouth and saw him drop to the gutter in a gush of blood. The man's cry still echoed in his head, and for a moment another wave of horror squeezed his innards, but—he could hardly believe it—he had *heard* the man as well as seen him.

"King Charles, and Kent," other Royalists cried.

Maddened shouting broke out all round him, instantly making him dizzy again. The buff and red coats merged, crossed, and separated. Which was the enemy? He paused, half knowing the danger he was in, half denying it, and steadying himself on a doorpost.

Then out of the rabble stepped a Goliath of a man, or so it seemed. The man had lost his helmet, but the thick black curls waving onto his broad shoulders proclaimed him unmistakably a King's man. All round them both, bottles and crockery rained down from the jettied windows above, and the rain still fell in black curtains.

"Traitor!" roared the giant. "Cromwell's fool." His face savage, he raised a thick wooden club in his hands to strike.

Trembling, Robert felt for his helmet, leaped to one side, and raised his musket again. But then he lost his balance, and the houses, sky, and rain-washed street turned a somersault as the other man struck the musket from his hands. Robert staggered up again immediately and stood defenseless yet aware that though he might die, he could hear his enemy's voice.

"Fool, thyself! Then kill me if you will," Robert challenged. Nothing mattered now. "Your King will be dead ere long."

The giant came forward, his eyes slits, his breathing hard. He reached out and wrenched Robert's helmet backward so that the leather chin-piece broke, his collar ripped, and he almost choked. Unthinking, Robert reached forward for the other man's throat.

But then the stranger's face changed and he felt himself abruptly dropped.

"You—!"

Robert stared back, uncomprehending. Was he not to die after all?

"Robert—?"

Suddenly Robert knew the giant, and he saw his own death in the man's eyes.

Isaac

Isaac dealt death with one unerring blow to the other man's head. Then he stooped for a moment to make sure he had made no mistake. Yes, the severe mouth and beaklike nose were the same, but the open, horrified, dark eyes were like none he had ever seen, and he recoiled.

He turned, then, and fought his way up the hill. No one challenged him. The troops were still stuffing the ordnance with cannonballs, powder, and rags. He dodged among them, and in all the panic and darkness no one heeded him as he scrambled over the huge earthworks.

Outside the Crown Inn on the lower end of the High Street, he stopped and retched violently. For two days he had not eaten, and the wrenching spasms of his stomach twisted him with pain and soured his mouth. *I have killed my own brother. My own brother . . . my own . . .* The words corroded his mind and burned as bitterly as the acid in his mouth. But he could not dwell on Robert's death now. As long as the battle raged on Gabriel's Hill, and as long as darkness cloaked the town, he would have a chance of escape. No, he could not think of his brother now, only of reaching safety. He had seen enough of death for a lifetime.

He began to run toward the river. He heard the ragged, frantic sound of his own breathing as well as the musket fire and shouts of battle behind him. How was he to escape now? All the bridges were held by Cromwell and Fairfax, and yet to stay in the town or go back down Stone Street was certain death. He could not even hide in his shop; that would never be safe either. The battle was all over for him, anyway. *I have killed my own brother. . .*

At the edge of the Fair Meadow Isaac hesitated again. The expanse of shadowed grass and trees looked eerily quiet. Roundheads might well be hiding there to ambush the unwary. But no, they had come up from Loose, funneled into Stone Street and Gabriel's Hill where the King's men waited. There was no reason why he should be caught here.

On the bank of the river he shed his boots and jerkin, dropping the club he had clasped unaware all the way up Gabriel's Hill. If only he could cross here, then again near Wateringbury, he might be able to reach Rebecca and the children without meeting the enemy soldiers who were spread out all over the southern edges of Maidstone, Loose, and East Farleigh.

He looked down at the black river water. In all the rain it was angry and swollen. No, he could not swim across; it was foolish to think so. Reclaiming his clothes, he went back a little way and sat under a linden tree with his back pressed against the bulbous trunk as the rain dripped unevenly from the branches and leaves above.

The familiarity of the sound steadied him, and the noise of the siege faded somewhat in the watery night. From up in the marketplace the courthouse clock chimed ten, answered then by All Saints' Church and St. Faith's Chapel.

He put his head on his knees and wept. It was the second time this year he had wept. When their third living child, born only a few weeks earlier, had died, he cried then, too, after years without tears. He had wept for Rebecca's loss. She had longed so deeply for the little girl child who had died . . . as others had died before. But he had wept, too, for the unnamed child herself, buried now in St. Mary's churchyard in Goudhurst.

Goudhurst. It was a long way to Goudhurst. But he had taken Mother Mary, Adam, Charlie, and Rebecca to Goudhurst for safety some time earlier. Now he must somehow find his way there from the Fair Meadow.

And he wept here also for the silent May Day dancers who years before had skipped and laughed on Fair Meadow under the same sky, then sunny, that now spouted rain on his bare head.

Thirteen years. He shut his eyes tightly, caught his breath, and pushed away the scalding grief. Yet he could never forget the day he had fallen in love with Rebecca, the very same day Robert had stolen her from him. *Stolen.* The word was right and fair. Robert had stolen not only her maidenhead; he had stolen her joy, her laughter—even her beauty. Ever afterward, she had been as thin and cowering as a hungry rabbit in the winter woods round Chilham. Always cold, always fearful. Robert had stolen her from him, and the girl who skipped on Fair Meadow under the May sunshine was buried, as it were, at her father's old house near the

Shambles. Another Rebecca lived on as his wife, a Rebecca he loved as much but who was no laughing Queen of the May garlanded with honeysuckle and cherry blossoms.

He clamped his teeth hard together. *This was all Robert's doing.* Then he remembered Robert's last look of horror again, remembered that the man he had killed was his own brother. The tears burned his eyelids, and bitterness rose into his mouth again.

The cannons roared from the High Town. Were they still fighting? How long would the battle drag on? How long would he be safe here?

Pushing himself forward painfully, he lurched onto his knees, intending to stand and walk again, though he did not yet know where. But as soon as his knees touched the yielding softness of the sodden grass, he bowed his head and found himself praying.

For years, angry with Providence, he had spoken few words to God. The God he had known as a child was the hateful, fierce God of Robert and, at times, of his father. But now he was talking to the God of his stepmother, Mary: the loving God who forgave and understood and called him His son. Could this Almighty God forgive even murder? He shuddered.

But I did not know 'twas Robert until . . . I did not know . . . Oh Lord. . . .

He crouched down farther, the rain running forward on his neck and up into his thick hair. Then a picture came into his mind of the thin, sharp-faced woman, Patience, whom Robert had wed. They had borne children, he knew, for Mary had written lovingly of them all: Thomas, Nicholas, Josiah, Hannah. *Little ones, fatherless ones. I promise thee, Oh God, that I shall care for them. . . .*

He scrambled up and wiped the mud from his hands onto his breeches. His own sons would be fatherless if he did not find a way back to Goudhurst. He strode toward the Medway again.

On the bank he paused to listen. Thinly through the rain he heard the sound of men's voices and the crackle of musket fire. He could not go back.

He threw his jerkin aside but held his boots aloft. *I must swim with these boots, somehow, please God.* But he knew they would fill with water and sink, so he tied them upside-down inside his belt. Then he plunged into the water.

The cold rush of it took away his breath. He rose to the surface, gasping. Immediately a swell surged up and slapped him under again. He thrashed blindly, surfaced again, and struck out for the far bank, praying he would not flounder into quicksand or marsh on the other side. All round him the water pulled and swirled; every lift of his arms begged desperate effort. The boots turned over and began filling with water.

Their weight pulled him down. He wrestled with his belt, slipped under the water again, then managed to wrench it off. Instantly the boots disappeared in the flood, and he buoyed up with renewed freedom and energy.

In the dark he strained to see the far bank. It seemed nowhere near. Was the water sending him downstream to Allington? He flailed wildly in a sudden panic, but then his bare feet touched sand, and he propelled himself forward with his last strength.

His head struck a wooden surface. More in surprise than by choice, he reached up and found himself bobbing madly with his hand on a craft moored by the edge. Pulling himself hand over hand round the prow of the small vessel, he discovered the mooring rope and held on tightly to its twisted, swollen fibers. Never had a rope offered so much security. Never had he thanked God as he did now.

On the lee side of the boat he floated in the rising and falling water with his feet grazing the river bottom. His heart clamored and his teeth chattered with excitement and cold, but he knew that neither Roundheads nor King's men could catch him now. He could regain his breath and make his way back in the dark.

He hung in the water for several minutes until he felt calm again; then he heaved himself up onto the bank by the rope and sat dripping by the capstan. His body felt unutterably heavy and spent. For a moment he leaned sideways. Sleep was a cordial he longed to sip, but he could not risk discovery by daylight on the edge of a river. He must walk to Goudhurst and evade the Roundheads all the way.

Standing, he swayed, braced his feet against the capstan, and turned his face toward the southwest. There would be a climb up into the Weald, but he must ford the river again and skirt round Linton in case Fairfax's reserves were camped there. He could perhaps reach Goudhurst by dawn if he moved with stealth.

The rain had stopped. Maidstone and the fighting, dying men lay miles behind, a world away from the fragrant, drenched orchards and lush fields of the Weald where he walked now.

An overpowering need for sleep sapped his ability to think and move. He stopped at a gateway and leaned against it. His head immediately dropped forward, but his chin jarred on the top bar and brought him harshly awake.

He shook himself and trudged on, but within moments he knew he could go no further; he must find a hedgerow or hovel and curl up in it, damp or not, for the sleep of his life.

The gate, he thought dully. *I'll go back to the gate.* He turned, hauled himself over it and stumbled down the long, banked-up rows of earth between the hop poles. The wet earth squeezed up between his toes, feeling soft and kind after the rough stones of the road he had followed for some miles. Somewhere in this hop garden would be a hut where the farmer sheltered or kept his balls of twine, or somewhere a stack of hop poles he could set round him as a hiding place.

Between the ragged rain clouds above him floated the moon—pale, swollen and waterlogged as a pig's bladder football on the end of a jester's stick-and-bells. While giving meager light in the blanketing darkness, it did give comfort. He lifted his face to his new solace and trudged forward again until he came to the end of a row. For an instant he thought of following the ditch a few rows to one side, since he had walked down the central row—the row where he would most likely be discovered. But he was too weary now to take those last steps, and so he sank down where he stood. Insensible to the cold raindrops that clung to the leaves round him, he dropped into the long furrow of sleep.

He might have been asleep for a moment or for an hour—he did not know how long—when a violent tug on his bare foot sent him bolt upright, shouting in terror.

"Don't move! Don't move or thou'rt a dead rat!"

The farmer. In the dark? Something cold and hard was piercing his side, right against his ribs. He froze.

"Thy name? What art thou?" The voice was sharp.

Isaac's body was now twisted into an awkward posture. He wanted to shift but dared not. In the dizziness of a sudden awakening his head hardly seemed to belong to his own body, and the voice issuing from the darkness, equally disembodied, seemed unreal.

The cold point twisted against his skin. "Answer me, you scoundrel!"

This time as the other man's voice rose shrilly, Isaac heard something else: fear. "I'm but a tailor . . . of Maid—of Goudhurst, sir." He heard the same fear in his own voice and was surprised.

"A tailor! Then what in—?" The voice stopped, and the sharp metal moved away.

In spite of himself, Isaac smiled. Was the man a simpleton? Would he believe anything he was told? "Aye," he replied. "I was caught in Maidstone against my will."

"Maidstone? Then what art thou, I say? Speak, or thou'lt taste this musket."

"You'd slay an unarmed, unshod man, sir? Fie, for shame."

"But I cannot see thee."

Isaac quickly drew up his legs. "Then may I stand, sir?"

Back came the tip of the musket in his ribs. "Nay. Stay where thou'rt, *and tell my thy name.*"

"Fessenden, sir."

The other man let out a hoarse cry. "Fessenden? Of Chilham?"

Something in this exchange of words was familiar. Isaac struggled with the memory but lost it. "Nay, that was my father. He's dead, sir. Died a fourmonth ago."

"Of Maidstone then . . . and Robert's thy name?"

Isaac felt a convulsion run through his body and found his face contorting in anguish. "Nay, 'twas my brother . . . died this very night fighting . . . for Lord Fairfax."

The musket dropped suddenly, the stock ringing against a large pebble on the edge of the ditch. Then Isaac heard a clumsy movement as the other man dropped down beside him. The man's breathing quickened, and his face came so close to Isaac's that he could feel the breath on his face. "Then you are Isaac Fessenden? Of course, the *tailor* Isaac, but I knew not you were of Fairfax's persuasion."

Isaac's fear had left him. He shifted so that his body was straight again. "I'm not, sir. I'm for His Majesty."

"Ah—" The other man's breath expelled faintly. "That's good." He gave a shaky laugh. "But I mistook thee for a Roundhead! Nearly killed thee, Master Fessenden. Do you remember that riotous day last Christmass in Canterbury?"

Somewhere in the top of a tree a nightingale rolled out its song. Isaac searched the darkness with his eyes; the light was coming, and he wanted to look this strange, foolish man in the face. "Of course," he answered guardedly.

"And George Tolhurst, to whom you gave the little blue coats?"

His own breathing quickened. "Tolhurst? Yes, of course I remember." Wasn't there a squire Tolhurst in the village of Goudhurst he'd never seen? Could this be the same man?

There was a moment's silence except for the breeze rising in the hop leaves. "'Tis I, George Tolhurst, for His Majesty likewise."

At dawn, reassured by each other's company and by their distance from the town, the two men walked across country under the inverted, pale green bowl of the sky. As they exchanged stories, Isaac discovered that George had fled with Mainy when the outcome of the pitched battle became apparent. The Royalists had been driven all the way into St. Faith's churchyard.

"Many of us fled," Tolhurst admitted. "We have wives and children, and the King wasn't coming to our aid. We must wait for his pleasure or his end, I suppose. But I lost my horse and some of my friends, for we were all scattered. Hales, L'Estrange—they fled, too, though I know not whither. Brockman is killed, and Norwich retreated to Greenwich."

In return Isaac related his own tale, and as light shortened the shadows of the hop poles round them, he saw the sadness lengthen on his companion's face.

"Your own brother, Master Fessenden?"

"Yes, sir."

"Ah, poor lad," Tolhurst sighed. "You must tell me of all this—if you will."

"Yes, sir, I shall."

Tolhurst stopped and faced him. "Hold, you may be a yeoman by birth and have lost your boots, but though I'm a gentleman farmer, I've lost my horse—which is a good deal worse, I lay. And under the King we are brother soldiers, and under God, brothers." He blinked, and Isaac smiled at his companion's dancing eyes. Clearly the man was rarely given to such long speeches. "So have done with this 'sir', pray."

Isaac laughed. What a strange, affectionate man he was! "So I shall, then . . . George."

They walked on in silence for a while, Tolhurst limping slightly. Isaac limped, too, for his feet were cut now, even through the calloused skin. With every step painful, he could not help wincing. To distract himself, he began telling Tolhurst about his brother, even about Robert's betrayal of Rebecca. Now that his brother was dead, and this man could without a doubt be trusted, he found relief in telling another what had happened.

Tolhurst listened carefully, asking a few pointed questions and murmuring in sympathy. "You cannot condemn yourself," he said at last. "Until the helmet came off, you didn't know who the man was, and cannot therefore be blamed. No man alive would have done other than you did, Isaac."

Isaac felt his throat swell as if he would cry again in response to such generous and spontaneous pity. Embarrassed, he stopped, picked two ferns from the hedgerow, and busied himself soothing his feet with the leaves so that he would not have to look into Tolhurst's face. He could not bear to think of Robert any more.

Tolhurst, perhaps knowing Isaac's humiliation and revulsion, kept walking, though more slowly, his steps still faltering. "But what came you to Maidstone for? You said you were caught there. Surely you did not go to the muster in Penenden Heath or Burham Heath?"

Isaac quickly shook his head. "Nay, I knew nothing of what was ado until I came to Loose this morning . . . no, last morning." He rubbed his eyes and crinkled his brow. "Lord, I know not even what day it is. I was about my business—nothing untoward—fetching cloth at the mills there. Lo and behold the whole village was astir with word of Fairfax's coming."

"And you joined the King's men?"

Isaac shuddered and started walking again. "I've had no great love for the other side—no, not even when those idle Royalists would attack my stall in Canterbury last Christmasstide. But I'm a family man, and my father was one of the godly folk, and I never thought to fight with any man . . . until my brother turned against me, against Rebecca. Then I hardened my heart against him and against all his kith and kin among the Puritans, wanted none o' them. I'm for the King, through and through."

He thought of his stepmother suddenly. "There be only one Puritan I trust—" Then he remembered John, to whom he ought to have written immediately when their father died. "Or mayhap, two."

Tolhurst's brows rose in inquiry.

"Aye, my father's second wife, Mary. She lives with us now that Father's gone. And my brother John, though I've naught to do with him these many years, as he's away to the New World." He was abreast of George again.

"And your goodwife? And the boys? And your stepmother?"

"In Goudhurst for the while. My wife's family lived there once. They're safely lodged with cousins until the war in Kent subsides."

George looked surprised. "I'm surprised I did not hear of it. But this is good news! We shall be neighbors!"

"For a short while." Isaac looked down, frowning, uneasy with the other man's warm appraisal and reluctant to give away his own uncertainties. "But it cannot be for long, sir." He felt that Tolhurst's apparent liking for him could not possibly last. Gentlemen, even farmers, simply did not speak this way to yeomen.

"Call me George, pray."

"Not for long, George," he repeated ruefully, smiling again; Tolhurst's grin was contagious. "I have my shop in Maidstone."

The other man shook his head. "You'd be safer in Goudhurst for now. So would your sons. There's no telling how long Parliament's folly and the King's imprisonment will endure."

Isaac scoffed. "No, but your Goudhurst tailors won't welcome another, and I have built up my trade. I cannot but return when there is peace again. I have too many to feed now."

George looked troubled. "I'd be glad to serve thee in any way I could."

They limped on side by side, their eyes fixed on the climb ahead to the sleeping village of Goudhurst.

Goudhurst

A thin child sitting in a window seat by the front door saw them, or one of them at least. Throwing down her handwork, she disappeared from the window, then flung herself out the front door, running wildly down the brick path toward them. Her hair was a golden-red cloud round her head, and the breeze blew it back as she ran under the early morning light. Her cheeks flushed pink as chestnut flowers.

"Father! Father!"

She had not properly seen Isaac, and his throat tightened painfully again at the look of intense love and longing on the girl child's face. What did he know of little girls?

George squatted on his haunches as his daughter flew into his arms. Standing a few paces behind them, Isaac noted the breadth of this man's back, the ridges of muscles across his shoulders. *Whatever this Tolhurst is,* he thought, *the man is no weakling or coward because he loves his family more than battle.* It was an unexpected thought slipping between the leaves of his mind, there and gone.

As George rose painfully, still holding his daughter, Isaac noticed that one of his legs was positioned oddly. Had the man been injured?

"Thou'rt looking at my Marston Moor leg," Tolhurst said wryly, following the gaze.

"Aye, forgive me."

"Musket fire. 'Twas messy. But I was lucky to get out alive at all, I suppose. So many were cut down, and it rarely troubles me." The dazed, bemused smile Isaac had seen on his face as he stood up had gone now, replaced by the distant stare of memory. Then the eyes focused again. "However, Isaac Fessenden, enough of war for this day. And thou'rt uneasy thyself, I see, on those poor torn feet. Come, my wife will dress them for thee ere—"

"Nay." Isaac backed off. George was hospitable, but Isaac did not belong at Tolhurst Court. The little girl's cool, direct eyes told him, *Go away. I want my father to myself.* And the thought of her tall, queenly mother bathing his feet—no, it was not possible.

"Indeed, you shall stay. Your way lies another mile or more, does it not? And we'd not suffer even a beggar to go from our gate with feet as cut as thine." George's hand came out to him. "Pray, be not proud."

Not knowing why, Isaac let his eyes go to the girl's face again.

Her eyes dropped, and the color in her face deepened. She bobbed a curtsy, and Isaac suddenly wanted to laugh at this formidable little piece of womanhood. "Please stay, sir, as my father wills it and you are his friend."

George chuckled. "Well spoken, my Anna."

Isaac looked from one to the other, wooed by their unabashed courting. George: solid, almost bovine in the stoutness of his body, grinning amiably at him with pleasure and—something else—relief, perhaps, that the Kentish war, though lost, was over. Anna: slight, violet eyes, her coppery hair round faintly freckled, pink skin. How beautiful she would be as a woman!

His own sons passed before his eyes: Adam and Charlie, both about her age. And Robert's, though he had never seen them: Thomas the rascal, Nicholas the scholar, Josiah. . . . They must be only a little older. Lucky the young men of Kent growing up to court so fair a maid as Anna Tolhurst! Especially if in time to come a yeoman might court a gentlewoman!

"Very well," he answered them at last. "I thank you."

"Then my wife shall wait upon thee," George said.

Anna looked at him timidly, her eyes scanning his tired face, muddy clothes, and bloodied feet. He wondered uneasily how he appeared to her.

Part 3
man and maid

"Madam, I will give to you the keys of Canterbury,
And all the bells of London Town shall ring to make us merry—
If you will be my love, my one and only dear,
And walk along with me everywhere."

"Sir, I'll not accept from you the keys of Canterbury
Nor all the bells in London Town to ring and make us merry.
And I won't be your love, your one and only dear,
Nor walk along with you everywhere."

"Then Madam, I will give to you a pair of boots of cork.
One was made in London, the other made in York.
And I will be your love . . ."

"Sir, I'll not accept from you a pair of boots of cork,
Though one was made in London and the other made in York,
And I won't be your love . . ."

"Then Madam, I will give to you a little silver bell,
To ring for all your servants and to make them serve you well,
And I will be your love . . ."

"Sir, I'll not accept from you a little silver bell,
To ring for all my servants and to make them serve me well,
And I won't be your love . . ."

"Then Madam, I will give to you a handsome oaken chest,
Enwrought with gold and silver, and jewels of the best,
And I will be your love . . ."

"Sir, I'll not accept from you a handsome oaken chest,
Enwrought with gold and silver and jewels of the best,
And I won't be your love . . ."

"Then Madam, I will give to you the embroidered silken gown,
With nine yards adropping and atraining on the ground.
And I will be thy love, thy one and only dear,
And walk along with thee everywhere."

"Then Sir, I will accept from you the embroidered silken gown,
With nine yards adropping and atraining on the ground.
And I will be thy love, thy one and only dear,
And walk along with thee everywhere."

Cambridge, Massachusetts, Autumn 1653

John

The green light of early Boston twilight capped the houses and cottages of Eliot Street. In the scullery, Jane Fessenden was scouring the bowls and tankards they had used at supper time, and John sat hunched over the table in the kitchen. He was reading the Scriptures, poring over the book of Amos as the light failed round him. He was too tired to get up and light the candle.

The clatter of trenchers ceased, and Jane stepped back into the room behind him, wiping her hands on her apron. He looked up for her quick smile. She was bending now to find her sewing in the basket by the chimney.

"Thou'lt go as blind as Robert was deaf, if you don't light a candle, husband," she reproached. "And so shall I, what's more."

"Light it for me, pray, Jane. I'm weary altogether." He glanced over at Nathaniel, who had flung himself on the settle and now lay there, his face puckered into a disagreeable scowl. John straightened his back and cleared his throat. "Up, Nathaniel, lazy boy, when thy mother enters the room."

The boy's only concession was to swing his legs to the floor and sit forward with his elbows on his knees. "What do you wish me to do, Father?" he grunted.

The words were polite enough, but the boy's tone heightened John's irritation. He motioned for Jane to sit beside him, then looked back at Nathaniel. "Thy mother's toiled all day and still has sewing to do. You can light candles, at least."

Nathaniel's eyelids slid half-shut, and John saw his jaws tighten. "Aye, Father, I shall." And he took a taper from the chimney piece, lighted it in the fire, and brought it to the candles.

John watched his sullen expression with a strange mixture of pride, anguish, and doubt. Nathaniel had grown tall, with a thick, muscled body and large hands that could nevertheless stretch and sew wool and leather deftly. *Could.* But John's anguish arose because of the boy's strong-willed and careless behavior. If he did not have his way, he sulked, worked slowly, and was rude to those who traded at the tanyard and the shop. What kind of future did the family have in this, its only son? The lad was still young, true, but by now he should be trustworthy, upright, and diligent.

Nathaniel was none of these things. John sighed. "Thou'rt waiting to speak with us, perchance, son?"

Nathaniel's hand stopped over the last candle so that the flame licked up the taper to his fingers. He gave John a cold stare and did not seem to notice the flame. "No, Father."

"Foolish boy," Jane said in a low voice. She bent forward and blew out the spill. "Thou'lt hurt thyself. And thy speech is discourteous. Amend it, pray. Come, you may join us as we read."

Again John looked at Nathaniel's face and saw hostility in his eyes before the lids came down and veiled it. He remembered, suddenly, the family Bible readings in Chilham. How impatient had his younger brothers been to hear the closing amen from their father! He frowned slightly, looking back at the closing pages of Amos before him. Could he condemn Nathaniel for the same impatience?

Nathaniel paused by the fire and dropped the last piece of taper into the grate. They kept only a low fire at this time of year, for the coldest weather was still a month away.

"Well, will you join us, or no?" John asked.

The boy stiffened. He stood silently, his eyes leaping first to Jane, then to John. "If I have a choice, no."

Jane's head went up so sharply that John felt the bench beneath them shift slightly on its legs. "A *choice*, Nathaniel?" she said mildly. "Why, of course you must choose."

"But choose to read, that's what you mean, is't not?"

"Thou'rt an insolent pup, Nathaniel! No, that's not what thy mother means at all. You must choose now. Thou'rt old enough." John caught his lower lip hard under his teeth to bite back other words. He doubted that even now, after years of gentle teaching and example, the lad understood.

A triumphant smirk glittered in Nathaniel's eyes. "Then I'll be off . . . nay . . . *forgive me.*" He bowed to Jane. "Pray excuse me, Mother, but my brethren bade me meet them on the Common, and I promised I'd come there by seven o' the clock." He reached up for his surcoat where it hung behind the door.

John knew that Jane longed to ask why the boys of the church were meeting on the Common in the dark, but he also knew that she wouldn't ask. He slowly eased himself up and faced Nathaniel. *At least I am still the taller.* "For what purpose, pray, Nathaniel?"

The lad swung open the door and laughed bitterly. "To make *choices*, Father. I bid you good night."

The room was silent for only a moment; then John groaned. "Much as it pains me, that boy shall feel the rod for this."

Jane's face fell, and she swallowed so loudly that John was afraid she would break into weeping.

"We've been too soft with that hot-blooded youth. And now we live to regret it."

"Will he go awenching, think you? Is that what he intends?" She shivered.

"I'll not wait long to see."

"But thou must rest. Thou'lt not go out in the dark, surely, when evil is abroad?"

"Jane! Jane!" He smoothed back the thinning gray hair only half-covered by her cap. "We must trust God, who is abroad day *and* night." He pointed to the cupboard by the door. "See, he left the lantern. Were he truly going to the Common, he would have taken it. He'll be off somewhere else, and I off with the lantern myself. But shall we continue reading the Word of God to Amos?"

Jane moved to the bench opposite him. Her face was lined now, though the skin on her cheekbones was still taut, and many of those lines were drawn by laughter. He still loved her. She smiled back at him. "Aye. Read on, John."

He cleared his throat. "I was in the seventh chapter."

"The visions?"

"Indeed." And he began to read, slowly and low at first, but he heard his voice gathering in power:

"Thus he showed me: and behold, the Lord stood upon a wall made by a plumbline, with a plumbline in his hand. And the Lord said unto me, Amos, what seest thou? And I said, A plumbline. Then said the Lord, Behold, I will set a plumbline in the midst of my people Israel: I will not again pass by them any more: And the high places of Isaac shall be desolate, and the sanctuaries of Israel shall be laid waste; and I will rise against the house of Jeroboam with the sword."

The words filled the room, hovered, and hung heavy in the air round them. He stopped and glanced at Jane, whose head was now bowed, her eyes obscured by the curving edge of her cap. Then he looked back at the yellowing page and continued into the next chapter. *"And the songs of the temple shall be howlings in that day, saith the Lord God . . ."*

A tiny sound from Jane's lips arrested him. In amusement he looked to see if she had hiccoughed, but her hand covered her eyes now and her mouth contorted oddly. She was crying, after all, almost choking to hold back the sobs.

"For shame, love," he reproved her gently. "What ails thee, now?" He stretched out his hand toward hers, stroking the chapped skin and murmuring softly.

In answer she let out a gulping wail.

"Ah, don't, sweetheart—" He levered himself up and came round to kneel beside her. Pulling her head against his shoulder, he repeated the words, "Don't, don't . . . what is't?" several times before he could make sense of her reply.

"Nathaniel, 'tis Nathaniel," she finally managed, her eyes streaming with tears, which he tried to wipe away. "I foresee the Lord's judgment on him, too. All his wild ways. I know things about him I dursn't tell even thee."

"What things?" He grasped her wrists and shook them. "Why didn't you tell me?" He was surprised at the anger in his voice. "*What* things?" he demanded again.

His wife's hurt, tear-swollen face reproached him, but she answered directly this time. "He's told me of a maid he means to wed when you've loosed him from his apprenticeship. A maid he said you'd not approve, though I know little enough of her."

"*What* maid?" He let her go and stood up. "Wed? Phaw! 'Tis utter nonsense. I'll whip sense into that boy if it's the last breath I draw doing it. Fifteen! Apprenticed! And he's got a wench!"

She reached out a restraining hand. "Nay, John, wait. Thou wast but twenty thyself."

He turned away furiously and bit down on his lip. Dimly he realized that he had never been so angry. The emotion drained and frightened him; he did not want to be mastered by it. He drew a long, unsteady breath and relaxed a little. "Aye, but—"

Jane looked up anxiously. "Thou wast far wiser than Nathaniel."

He shrugged. "Wise in choosing thee, aye, but not in other ways, mayhap." He frowned at her. "But do you know this maid?"

Jane's eyes slid away from him. "By name only. She's Owen's daughter—serves at the ordinary."

He ground his teeth together and reached for the lantern. "I might have known as much! She's unlikely a maid, drawing ale in that abhorrent place. I'll fetch him out for lying and wenching, so I will."

The lantern shed only a feeble pool of light on the cobbles below his feet, and every time the salty wind gusted from the harbor, the light wavered and shuddered. John clutched its swinging handle tightly and beat the ground firmly with his staff to make sure of his way.

He passed a drunken couple asleep in a doorway. The long forms of their outstretched legs and tangle of skirts caught his eye only just in time to prevent him from falling headlong over them. He drew back for a second, hearing the sharp intake of his own breath. Holding the lantern quite near their faces he could see that they were young, the lad scarcely older than Nathaniel. But their cheeks were ingrained with grime, hollowed out under the cheekbones. The girl was snoring, and the sharp smell of sour ale rose to his nostrils. He sighed heavily. Could this be happening in Cambridge already? Homelessness, hunger . . . ?

He went on more slowly now. The alleyway stank of vomit and cats so that his gorge rose as he groped his way forward. He regretted not having gone the longer way over the Common, especially since Nathaniel might have gone to the Common after all, though he still doubted it.

A gust of fresh air heralded the end of the alley and the more open area of the square where he expected to find the boy. A few flickering candles in drafty windows faintly showed the uneven outlines of the crude hovels built only a few months before. Other lanterns bobbed round him in the darkness, but they were veiled, and he felt strongly the presence of evil, stealth, and men who would not want to be known to walk abroad in this part of town at night.

"Good night t'thee, Goodman Fessenden." The voice sounded civil but seemed to come out of nowhere, somewhat slurred.

He held his lantern aloft and searched the darkness with his eyes. "Good night, friend," he answered hesitantly.

"Aye, John, you've naught to fear." The voice broke into a cackle. "'Tis only poor Gronwort, thy neighbor from Sussex."

Out of the darkness appeared the vacant, witless face of the man they all called "Gronwort o' Bedlam," though the name had become affixed to the man more through pity than scorn. Having seen his wife washed overboard on a gale in the great sea crossing, Gronwort had lost his wits the same day. Everyone in Cambridge was kind to him, giving him bread and simple tasks in the summer, and a bed in the outbuildings or stable in the winter. And now here he was, wandering in the darkness with no lantern.

"Alas, poor fellow." John gently took his arm. "You should be in bed long ere this." Voices rose in the ordinary—curses, and shouting, and the sound of splintering furniture. John's stomach churned with anxiety.

"And you also," the other replied so quickly that John almost doubted the tales of Gronwort's weak wits were true.

John held the lantern higher again. "I'm looking for my boy, Nathaniel. Hast thou seen him? You know him, do you not?"

Gronwort had scythed down a field of tall grass for him earlier in the year and for part of the day had worked with Nathaniel. But would he remember?

Gronwort's tongue lolled out of his mouth, wet and pink like a dog's. He rubbed his hands together. "Aye, I do."

John shook his arm with slight impatience. "Then have you seen him? Pray, tell me."

"I'm thirsty, John Fessenden."

"Ah, you'd like—"

"A jug of ale, sir."

John dropped his arm. "I don't buy ale, Gronwort. You'll have to excuse me."

"And leave me maundering in the dark, neighbor?"

John hesitated, trapped by his own pity and by his concern for Nathaniel. But he would have to go into the brawling ordinary, anyhow, if he wanted to find the boy, for he was now convinced that Nathaniel must have gone there. So he reached slowly into his pocket and drew out a coin. "Here, friend. This will buy you what you want. And will you look for Nathaniel within and report to me?"

Gronwort took the coin and stumbled away without answering, but John knew the man had understood and would, even in his beclouded state, seek out Nathaniel. Then he remembered. "Wait, Gronwort!"

"What is't?" The disembodied voice, now annoyed, came from farther away, toward the orange lamps of the ordinary.

"Do not tell him, pray, that you seek him. And have a care. The place is ill."

Gronwort cackled again and slapped his sides in glee. John heard the thwack of his hands on rags and flesh, then another mirthless cackle and a burst of song:

> *"Back and sides go bare, go bare,*
> *Both foot and hand go cold.*
> *For sure I think, have I good drink,*
> *No man can do me harm, boys,*
> *No man can do me harm—"*

The ordinary door creaked open, and Gronwort vanished within.

John waited, growing cold, and doubting his own wisdom. If Nathaniel were not in the ordinary, he had lost time and money both. And if he were in the ordinary—he shifted unhappily from one foot to the other—he might have to search the place himself, after all.

He leaned his back against the side of a hovel and prepared for a long wait. He found himself praying, no longer afraid, but sorry, longing for the souls of benighted men who hid their faces without, and hurried within the ordinary to carouse the night away and wake in the filth and squalor of an alleyway in the bleak morning. He remembered the couple he had seen, too, and prayed for their souls, as well. Then he lost account of time, and ceased to notice the noise of the square.

As his senses withdrew, it seemed that Cambridge was no longer the haven of light, peace, and freedom he and Jane had envisaged. Cambridge was not the city on the hill they had sought. The realization weighed on his mind as he recollected his early dreams among the brethren in Leyden. Things had soured there, too.

It wasn't only the square that seemed dark; suddenly all life seemed oppressive, wearying, and dark as the harbor under massing northeasterly storm clouds. First his father had died, and his own brother Robert had sent Mary away. Then, soon afterward, Robert had died, fighting for Cromwell in Maidstone . . . six years ago, now. *A wasted life,* he thought. Mad Englishmen! Could they never be content unless spilling one another's blood!

And now Isaac had turned sullen, rarely sending news. Mary—faithful Mother Mary—had written that Isaac was exhausted with working to feed his own as well as Robert's family; that Isaac openly argued with Patience each time they met; and that he now claimed allegiance with some of the more outspoken of the Cavaliers, including a certain Squire George Tolhurst, of Goudhurst. All this, she said, troubled everyone, even the gentle Rebecca.

Mary had written to him, though not so often recently, that Isaac sometimes suffered days of black melancholy. On these occasions he would shut himself up; she had heard him grieving, she recorded. Only a ride with the donkey cart to see the mysterious Squire Tolhurst would avail.

Was Isaac perhaps unwisely entangled with another woman?

John put his hand on his brow, wanting to wipe away all the questions. His father . . . Robert . . . Isaac . . . Nathaniel . . . the young couple in the alleyway . . . would none of them find the peace he wanted?

A man and woman muffled in heavy cloaks brushed past him and pulled the ordinary door shut after them.

Peace . . . silence . . . there was silence now. In the dark the lanterns had stopped bobbing. Even the ordinary lay quiet with no one coming or going through the door. Just heavy silence. He stiffened. The silence loomed heavier and more fearful than the tumult before. He must know where Nathaniel was!

"A bowl. Fetch a bowl!" a woman's voice within shouted.

He walked over and lifted the latch of the door. By the faint light of guttering candles, he could not immediately discern the faces within. The place reeked of Virginia tobacco, rancid tallow, and ale. He stood still, his head light with anxiety, his eyes straining. *Nathaniel?*

A face pressed close to his in the haze of smoke: distorted, ugly, gibbering. It was Gronwort's. Tears made greasy furrows down the man's cheeks, and a groaning cry bubbled out of his mouth. The devil-may-care song of a half hour before hung between them in mockery:

"For sure I think, have I good drink,
No man can do me harm boys . . ."

Other men crowded round, hands waving aimlessly, shoulders shrugging. The air hummed with confused voices as in a choking nightmare. John wrestled with the fear and darkness round him and called out, "God 'a mercy! Where be my son?" He grasped Gronwort's collar and shook him, terrified now. He wanted to strike the man out of his babbling folly, but even as he shook him and saw the eyes widen in fear, he relented and checked himself. *Is poor, crazed Gronwort at fault?* Nay, he was only playing messenger.

Abruptly, John released him. The men caught Gronwort as he staggered backwards, his crying redoubled. John felt his heart go cold, chilled by the disorder and dirt in the room. "Will no one speak to me save this poor wretch?"

"Goodman Fessenden, are you not?"

Ah, a sane voice, though gruff. "Aye, and looking for my son, if any know of him." He looked round accusingly, his eyes resting on the tall, rough man who had spoken. A sailor by the look of him: weathered, with great knotty hands and only one eye—fierce and raw. Vaguely familiar, somehow.

"I know naught of thy son, Fessenden," the sailor said harshly. "But I lay there be a lad here in sore trouble."

"It *is* young Fessenden," another observed.

The crowd of men parted to let John through as the sailor led him by the arm to the back of the ordinary. Gronwort followed closely, his hands waving wildly and the loud lament continuing, but John hardly noticed him now. Though the ordinary was not large, he felt as if they were walking down a long, tree-tangled Wealden pathway in the dark. He longed for light at the end.

Instead, someone lay on a cushioned settle with his head in the lap of a buxom middle-aged woman whose hood was thrown back, though she still wore a cloak. He formed an impression quickly: she was decently and modestly dressed with a neat cap and a high-necked dress—a godly matron, by her looks. Then why was she in this den of wickedness?

She bent over with a sop in her hand, wiping the battered face so near her own. A bowl of water close to her feet was red with blood, and her cloak was splattered by it. She seemed to be whispering comfort.

He stared in disbelief and dismay. Nathaniel? Was he dead? No, the lad was sorely injured. Trembling, he rushed forward and fell to his knees by the woman.

"What ails thee, Nathaniel?" His voice came out in a strangled cry. He scarcely recognized it. The swollen eyelids flickered but did not open. John reached for the boy's shoulders to shake and revive him. Surely this was some nightmare.

"Nay, doan't thou tooch the puir lad, sir," the woman begged him, her speech thick with a north country accent he did not know. "'E's been abrawling, this wild boy, so 'e 'as."

"But 'tis my boy!"

The woman continued stroking Nathaniel's face and wiping away the blood. He stared at her, half bewitched, half angry. Who was she to cradle his son? Ah, but Nathaniel was not his own son.

"Then pray, sir. Pray as you've ne'er prayed to this day. Beseech the Almickel tae spare the puir laddie, for he be nigh untae death."

Behind him the circle of onlookers shifted uneasily. Hats and caps came off, and the men in the corner stopped gaming to watch. A shiver ran through John's veins so that his skin pricked and the hair on his arms stood on end. Would God perform a miracle in this hellish place?

He poured out prayer after prayer. The words flowed out like the minister's preaching on the Sabbath. If Nathaniel heard, and if the onlookers understood, they gave no sign. Nathaniel's life passed before John's eyes: the wailing babe handed to him after the shipwreck; the laughing, carefree child who skived off the lessons and his work in the tanyard and shop; the sullen, ugly youth who had left so rudely this evening.

As he prayed, he kept his eyes on Nathaniel's face, alarmed that the blood was still flowing fast from the wound on his temple. Could the woman not stanch it?

His prayers died on his lips, and he wrenched the kerchief off his neck and pressed it over the wound. "Why? Why, Nathaniel?" he begged.

The boy's eyes opened for a moment, unseeing. Yet he seemed to hear, trying to answer at last.

"'Twas a fight o'er some lassie," the woman interposed mournfully. "A worthless, scur'lous minx."

John pressed harder with the kerchief. The bleeding seemed to be slowing. But the boy's face had turned ashen, his lips blue. John hardly took in the woman's words.

"The other lad's gang awa' by noo, nae doot."

This he heard. "Away?" John leaped angrily to his feet. "Did none arrest him?"

The men stared at him like dumb, foolish sheep.

"Did none—?"

"None!" the sailor spat out. "For 'twas this boy that struck the first blow. Unjustly done, too, as all here will tell thee."

The others mumbled in assent, and John looked round, horrified. He looked back at Nathaniel. The boy was open-eyed again, one hand raised, his face full of terror. Then a thin stream of blood trickled out of his mouth. His eyes rolled backward. His hand dropped.

Painfully, John wrote to Patience.

Madam—

Nathaniel, my foster boy, has died. I pray thee, send my brother's son Thomas to me if that you can spare him. But if, since he be the eldest, you had rather send Nicholas or Josiah, I pray thee do so. I trust Isaac our brother still cares for thee and thine, as would I, were we dwelling still on your shores. My greetings to thee, sister, and to Isaac's family also. May God keep ye all.

Your kinsman,
John

He sealed the document with the same familiar seal his father had used on bolts of Fessenden cloth in Chilham forty years before, and he addressed it to Widow Patience Fessenden of Chilham. The letter would go out on *The Venturer* at the next tide.

Maidstone, March 1655

Isaac

Isaac pushed the needle in and out of the cloth, his fingers moving fast, but his mind moving faster. The rebels would see him handsomely rewarded, George had assured him, if he joined the new rising for the King. And as he sat at work above the shop, Isaac wondered how else they would survive the year.

Patience had died of a fit soon after the news of her son Thomas had come from the Bay Colony by way of Dartford: Thomas had been lost at sea. A foolish accident, the captain had reported. Foolish and unnecessary. The young boy, bent on showing his mettle to the other sailor lads, had climbed the mizzenmast in high seas. The waves had come up and snatched him. Like Nathaniel, the boy was gone. He would never serve John in the New World.

Isaac had gone by cart to Chilham to fetch Robert's orphaned children—Nicholas, Josiah, and Hannah—to Maidstone. Nicholas was a steady, clever lad, a boy who would work hard. Isaac liked him and trusted him as he would never have trusted Thomas, for Nicholas could be relied upon. The boy had cherished and comforted his sister, Hannah, as she grieved for her mother and brother, but then Mother Mary and Rebecca won all their hearts, and the sorrow was eased.

But how was he to feed so large a family? Mary ate little and worked hard,

203

even as an old woman, but Rebecca was breeding yet again and could do little.

He sighed. *Breeding again.* He could not leave her alone! It shamed him, but he could *not*. In Goudhurst, seven years before, she had borne yet another girl who had lived. Isaac named her Anna, for George's child, but the baby died about the same time as King Charles in the harsh winter of 1649. Died—like the rest of them. And since then, every babe had been stillborn. He did not expect otherwise.

He thought of Adam and Charlie, his own sons—big, hungry lads now— as well as Robert's sons and his niece, Hannah. So many to feed!

If only John had stayed in Chilham! Perhaps they would all now be living off the fruits of the Fessenden woolens. No, too much had changed. There had been bad harvests for six years. The war had destroyed the roots of trade in England, and the old cloths were no longer in demand. Parliament had spoken against unnamed "ills" in the wool trade, created ordinances to forbid the export of wool, and encouraged only the largest wool masters to produce. Cromwell, once so plain in russets and homespuns, now affected the dress of French courtiers and smiled upon his daughters decked like princesses in silken finery. *The turncoat! I'm glad I'll none of him!*

And many followed after Cromwell. The clothes Isaac sewed for the gentlefolk nearby were of finer stuff than his father had ever imagined. Ah well, as long as he still had cloth to sew, and people still wanted clothes to wear, he would find a living somehow. Adam was good with a needle, too, and Rebecca, when she felt well enough—

But he needed more money than they could earn, and he would never go begging or send Robert's children to the poor house.

George's proposal was tempting indeed. He could overlook the fact that all the Cavalier plots in Kent had failed thus far. This one would be different. The plot of 1654 was wild and ill-advised, right under the nose of Cromwell's favorite, Governor Thomas Kelsey. But though the Governor of Kent was watchful now because of it, George was convinced that the King's men stood a better chance this time. Tolhurst and his Cavalier friends had asked Isaac, then, to serve as a captain of their infantry, and they had promised him a rich recompense.

"'Tis thy bearing and height, Isaac," George had said warmly. "You're a King David in the frame of Goliath. Come now. Kent has need of thee."

"I wonder at you, George," Isaac had said easily as the two of them walked round the leafless orchard one Sabbath afternoon. "Thou wert ever a man of peace."

"And still am," George agreed. "But how can we live quietly as long as kings are beheaded in our own realm and houses are plundered and estates are sequestered and men like you must feed two or three families at once?"

"Aye, and the Committee allows lawlessness—"

"Then Isaac, the risings *must* continue."

"I'm glad Nicholas, my nephew, cannot hear thee!"

"He's a canting Puritan, is he?"

Isaac would not have accepted harsh words, even of Robert's children, from anyone but George Tolhurst. He laughed bitterly. "Yes, yet no. Not in the mold of his mother. There's a fineness about him I cannot describe. I like the boy. He and Josiah know not what to make of me, I lay, for I'm so unlike their mother and father. But Nicholas is only eighteen. Unformed yet. He'll change—if he needs to." He spread his palms and dismissed the boy. "That's for God to dispose, not me."

They stopped under a few dead brown hops that had been left to dry and die in the wind since last autumn—hops that would, George said superstitiously, assure the growth of new plants in the spring. "For God, aye, thank goodness! But, Isaac, to the matter at hand. Have you considered?"

"Yes," Isaac replied, "but not for long enough. And I must talk to Rebecca. You understand?"

"Aye. Of course you must."

"If aught went against me and I were killed, or imprisoned, Rebecca would surely die. Robert's girl Hannah is but a little thing, scarcely as old as thy Henrietta. Could I leave her in the care of four green boys and a woman too old to do—"

"And could I leave my womenfolk even in the care of my wife?"

That was the question that had stayed longest and most painfully in Isaac's mind. George was willing to sacrifice his life and risk everything in a rebellion, even though Elizabeth, too, had been unwell with a mysterious flux that kept her indisposed whenever Isaac came to Goudhurst.

And now as he finished a seam and nimbly turned the garment right side out, he weighed the consequences of pledging himself to yet another rebellion.

Rebecca's eyes widened. "Surely, sweetheart, you cannot go again?"

She was frightened, and his resolve weakened. They sat in the light of a single candle in the kitchen. Above them, the rest of the family slept the long winter night; only Mary sat by the fire with them, her chin on her sunken breast, her cheeks sucking in and out with her faint breathing.

He had waited for a quiet moment to talk with Rebecca, intending to tell her that indeed he must stand beside Tolhurst with the Cavalier rebels. But she would not listen.

"You cannot, love," she repeated, her face drawn, her hands turning and twisting on her small lap. Above her knees, another coming child curved its back toward him. He leaned forward and stirred the fire, not daring to meet her gaze. *Live, child, live,* he prayed silently.

He cleared his throat at last. "I was talking with George just last Lord's Day. The men of Kent need me."

She laughed sadly. "Need you to rot in Leeds or Westenhanger—or worse, since thou'rt not *gentlefolk*? Aye, they surely need thee, Isaac, but not as *we* need thee. Pray, do not join them, love. The Cavaliers are rash, wild young fellows. I cannot believe George Tolhurst thinks otherwise." She stopped, and he saw on her face a struggle deeper within. "But . . . but . . . if you must. . . ."

He looked up quickly as her voice died. She did not weep easily unless she was afraid, but when she did weep, the tears were his undoing. "Nay," he murmured. "I doubt you can spare me." He sighed. "But I feel as torn asunder as an old smock. George pressed me so—"

"And flattered thee, no doubt." She smiled slightly, but he knew she was uneasy with his friend George, and he had accepted that long ago. He sighed again, shifting on his stool. "But 'tis such a pity, wife. The King over the water is to land with his court ere long."

"So they say."

"And the plot is well arranged and cannot fail."

This time she did not answer. She didn't have to, for he knew her thoughts. *Yes, so thou hast said before.*

He shrugged and dismissed the rising. "Well-a-day, Rebecca. So be it. I'll not leave Maidstone but bide here, safe I hope." He watched her face soften and relax a little. "Anyway, dearling, the babe's nigh now, and I'd rather be at hand."

Then he retreated into silence, staring absently at the fire, and Rebecca took up a calico coif she was sewing for a gentlewoman on East Street. Isaac could not bear the thought of sewing more. His eyes were tired after a day of close stitching on red stammel petticoats, and he wanted to work out in his mind what he would say to George about the captaincy.

For a moment he debated deceit. What if he were to go to Canterbury or

Chilham for cloth and be gone a day or two? Rebecca would never know—unless he died or were shut up in prison. But he rejected this idea at once. He had never lied to her before and would not now. Perhaps Providence was using Rebecca to warn him. His angel . . .

Rebecca caught his eye and then went on with her sewing. He stood, suddenly hungry and thirsty. But it was not food he wanted; Mary had served them an ample stew that night, the result of a neighbor's gift of a chicken. No, he was unaccountably and deeply thirsty—as he had not been for years—for God.

"Where's the Bible?" he asked gruffly. In spite of Mary's gentle reproof and Nicholas's repeated requests, he had not read it aloud to his family of an evening for so long that he could not remember where it was kept.

Mary stirred, blinking her eyes. "The Bible, Isaac? Is that what you want?" She made as if to rise, but she was weary and slow these days.

"Nay, Mother," he restrained her. "I'll fetch it myself."

"'Tis in my chamber, Isaac." Mary's old face looked rueful. "On the shelf, under my *Herbal*. Mind you, don't wake Hannah."

He laughed. "Fie, you thief, Mother Mary!"

Rebecca laughed, too, and he felt a wave of love for them both. "Then may I fetch it down, fair ladies?"

"By all means." Mary adjusted her shoulders, sitting more upright. "Will it please thee to read aloud?"

He looked uncertainly at her. "Aye, I shall."

In a moment he was settled again with the heavy book open at Psalm 42, a candle at his elbow.

"'As the hart panteth after the water brooks, so panteth my soul after thee, O God. My soul thirsteth for God, for the living God: when shall I come and appear before God? . . .'"

At the end of the psalm he fell silent.

He had dreamed the night before of a deer. In his dream he had been running from an unseen foe through a dense wood that looked uncannily like the hop garden where he had met George again all those years ago. But instead of meeting George, he had run face-to-face with a reddish-brown doe. She stopped with her hooves in a dried watercourse, her head jerking up, her eyes wild. Then he became the pursuer and she the pursued, bounding over the thickets and brambles and bines until—in the quirk of all dreams—she vanished.

Sitting now in the quiet of his own house, he felt loss and hunger. What did the deer mean? Not given often nowadays to melancholic ramblings, he hardly knew how to answer the puzzle, but he bowed his head anyway and sought God.

Warmth began to fill him. He felt flooded by a calm and completeness he had not known for seven years. If it were right for him to join the rebels and rise against Parliament, nothing would impede him. If it were not, God would make that clear.

His hands still covering his face, he smiled slightly. It had been so long since he had thought in this way, of God as his guide and shelter. God had too long been his adversary, the One pitted against his will and desires. But Mary knew, though she had lost both the men she loved and now her grandchild Thomas, that God was not *her* adversary. And John knew, though he had lost his foster son, that God was not *his* adversary.

Had Robert known that? He who had been bent on proving himself righteous before man and God, though both knew otherwise? Had Robert known that God was not *his* adversary? *Hush,* an inner voice bade him. *That is the Almighty's concern. Hush.*

"Hush!" Mary's cracked voice roused him suddenly. Had he fallen asleep? "Hark, do you not hear—?"

"Footsteps on the path," Rebecca said anxiously.

Isaac stretched and yawned lazily. "Naught to fret about."

Someone pounded on the door. "Open, friend!"

Rebecca dropped her sewing and jumped up. "'Tis Kelsey's men come for thee, dearling." A spool of thread unraveled on the floor at her feet, and she stiffened like a weft thread ready to snap.

"Nay!" He laughed, pulling back the lock and the doorpin.

A stranger stood on the threshold muffled against the cold. Isaac caught the stink of horse sweat on his clothes. A *messenger*—but he was alone.

"From George Tolhurst," the man said breathlessly.

Behind Isaac, Rebecca sat down again. She was still fearful; he knew it without even turning round.

"Come in, then," Isaac beckoned. "Have you a seal or letter about you?"

The messenger stepped in and threw back his cloak. Isaac recognized one of George's older servants. "Aye, a letter from the Squire."

"Fetch ale and a bite of bread for this man, Rebecca," Isaac said absently. He had already begun to scan the letter. "Sit you down—Matthew, is it?— and eat, will you?"

Isaac shook his head at his friend's awkward handwriting. The words were blotted, the script running over invisible downs and dales in the paper. The flourishes looked absurd.

Friend:

Penruddock's Rising sall not bee. Sir John, Edward Hales, and Thos. Culpeper bee all arrested, and the magazine is disclosed—and all is lost. Tufton is to the Tower. I sall lie low, not being charged. Howbeit I may be called to sit at the assizes when they be tried. A foolish spectackle indeed!

Thy servant,
GT

Isaac looked up at Matthew. "You know the import of this letter?"

The servant stared back with bulging eyes and fat cheeks. He was stuffing himself with half a cottage loaf Rebecca had set before him. Isaac laughed, his voice sounding oddly merry in the still, tightly woven room.

Mary leaned forward in her chair. "For sure he knows, son, whate'er it be."

Isaac smiled vaguely back at her. His eyes returned to the servant's. "Then . . . say naught of this to anyone."

The man swallowed noisily, then stammered, "No . . . not no one . . . neither, sir . . . but—"

"But?"

"My master bade me take this word to others in Maidstone besides your good self. You must let me go, I pray."

"Go then, and peace be with thee, old Matthew."

Standing at the open door, Isaac watched Matthew's dark cloak blend into the darkness of Mill Street. In a moment he heard the clatter of hooves on the cobbles, and the man was gone. At least for now, Isaac would not have to stand for Kent.

Maidstone, August 1656

Nicholas

My cousin Adam is a dullard, Nicholas thought. Of course he would never have said that to anyone—except his brother Thomas—if Thomas had lived. Different as they were, he could always tell Thomas what was on his mind. But not Adam and Charlie (though they were his age), and not even his brother Josiah.

It was easier for Nicholas to talk to Isaac than to anyone except his grandmother Mary or his sister Hannah. And though he loved Hannah, she hardly counted.

It was curious how he had drawn closer to his uncle. Isaac only occasionally read the Bible and acknowledged God, and Nicholas guessed that religion was barely more than a hollow shell to him. Isaac had little sympathy for everything his own parents had stood for. *But death makes strange bedfellows*, he reasoned, and now here were Robert Fessenden's children in the family and care of Royalist Isaac—the uncle rarely mentioned in the Chilham household, the uncle he had scarcely known existed until the great dark-haired man had come to offer help to his mother and eventually to fetch them to Maidstone and close the house when his mother died. Isaac—sometimes withdrawn and fierce, sometimes full of merry laughter and joy—the uncle he had come to respect and love.

Isaac was merry today. He seemed carefree, glancing sideways as they walked along East Street on the Sabbath afternoon. It had been raining all morning and the road was pitted with evil-smelling brown pools. But Isaac had put on a clean jerkin in honor of his friend and had talked in excitement all the way up the High Street.

Nicholas caught the excitement, too, wondering at this paragon of kindness and goodness they were soon to meet, and at his inclusion in the jaunt. There was nothing untoward about Adam's going; he was Isaac's older son, after all. But for him to go—!

Adam plodded silently beside Nicholas. He rarely spoke, and when he did, he was neither courteous nor churlish. At home Adam watched over his mother with the ferocity of a terrier but otherwise showed no strong emotion.

How different Nicholas knew himself to be! He could see why Adam and Charlie petted and loved their mother—she was such a frail, gentle woman—but he had never felt so protective of his own mother. And for most of his childhood, his father had been away either on errands for the cloth trade or off to war. Isaac, however, was always nearby, either at home or in the shop—and wanted to be.

Nicholas glanced at Adam again, then at Isaac. Had Adam noticed what a risk his father was taking on the Sabbath afternoon? For Isaac was whistling "A Kentish Man I'm Proud to Be" as clearly and saucily as could be. It was enough to set a man's teeth on edge! He knew the words well enough from the brazen boys at the grammar school who sang it deliberately under their masters' noses in the Corpus Christi Yard, usually earning a cuff for their wickedness.

All the same, he couldn't stop smiling in delight at his uncle's roguish behavior, and at Adam's dogged indifference. It was as if Adam noticed nothing. Was that because all his care was toward work? Because already he was finished with his tailor's apprenticeship? Perhaps, for his cousin cared nothing for learning as he himself had grown to care.

But—*no.* Nicholas corrected himself. Who was he to accuse his cousin of dull-wittedness? *Not all the important learning of this world falls between the covers of a book*, his grandmother Mary had said when he was little.

He often remembered these words. He had heard her say them again, in fact, since he and Josiah and Hannah had all been reunited with her early the year before. But he was not sure, yet, whether he quite believed her. He had read and reread *Eikon Basilike*, morbidly preoccupying himself with the death of the tyrant Charles Stuart. His mother had long ago forbidden the book and twice had tried to burn it, but he had secreted it in a cubbyhole in his chamber. Isaac had read it now, and they had argued over it, his uncle vehemently taking the part of the dead tyrant.

Nicholas had reveled in the debate, though they could never agree, and Adam had sat by open-mouthed as the discussion became more heated. Now Nicholas wanted Isaac to read John Milton's rebuttal of the book, *Eikonoklastes*, certain his uncle's wavering faith would be strengthened and that he would view the King differently. But they would only argue again.

"Would that we had ten pound a year to send thee away to Cambridge,

Nicholas, to make a gentleman scholar of thee the way we ought," Mary had once said.

Now he sighed. Small hope of that! Instead, since he was no hand with a needle like his cousin, he was out early on messages and business for his uncle: usually delivering garments and collecting payment for the work. His time for books was snatched on the Sabbath or occasionally at home of an evening if there were candles enough in the house for him to read by after dark. He sighed again.

The whistling stopped. "Sad sighs, nephew Nicholas." Isaac's dark eyes twinkled at him, a question in them.

Adam made a grunt of acknowledgment and continued walking at the same pace, only now a few steps ahead. Nicholas fell in beside Isaac.

"Not sad. I was musing on books, 'tis all."

"Ah, indeed." The corners of his uncle's mouth turned up in his warm, mobile, expressive face. "And what was the end of thy musing?"

"That I want no end to books."

Isaac laughed.

"And does Sir George . . . does he care for learning?"

Isaac threw back his head. "*Sir George?* Oh, fie, he won't know what to do with thee if you talk to him thus. He'll not brook a title. Squire George, George the Farmer—those names suit him better. And as for books? Not a straw does he care, I'm sure. His wife's the one for books, I warrant. Or was, anyhow."

All this puzzled Nicholas. "But is he not a justice of the peace in this county? How can he make laws if he cannot con his books?"

"Oh, he can con his books well enough. He did it as a lad, you may be certain. But justices pay little heed to *books*, I fear. That's for the clerks of the town . . . but thou'lt see for thyself in a moment." He reached forward to touch Adam's shoulder. "See, Adam? There's where we stop. He's lodged at the inn there."

They crossed the highway cautiously. Although this far from the marketplace the streets were more wholesome, still the men did not want to dirty their best clothes in the mud.

A stout, ruddy-faced man with sparse flaxen hair stood under the arch of the courtyard looking up and down the lane. Nicholas only half observed the man, wondering with increasing curiosity about his uncle's friend. But then Isaac made a small exclamation and flashed him a smile before loping ahead toward the archway.

The stranger saw him coming and stepped forward. "Isaac!"

"George! My dear George!" Isaac cried excitedly. The two men gripped each other's hands and stared hard at each other.

Nicholas stopped dead. Something was wrong. Was this well-fed countryman Sir George Tolhurst, knight of the shire? Surely not. He could not—could never be George Tolhurst. Sir George was a dashing prince of a man with curling lovelocks and soulful eyes, having the coolly imperious look of a Charles Stuart or a Richard Lovelace—someone he would not like but would admire. This surely was not the Royalist who had rescued his uncle from the hop garden after the battle, who had taken him home to Goudhurst and washed his feet like the Good Lord Himself. *This* man— George Tolhurst? He wanted to laugh. It was too impossible!

"Adam, Nicholas! Don't stand there woolgathering and gawping. Come hither." His uncle had turned now and summoned them into the inn. Adam obeyed without a word. As Nicholas followed, with his eyes fixed on Tolhurst's wide back and uneven gait, his head spun, trying to adjust his previous ideas about his uncle's friend.

This fellow—red-cheeked, broad, and having a slight limp as he moved—why, he was scarcely more than a bumpkin!

Nicholas knew he must hide his surprise from Isaac, but perhaps he had already failed, for while they passed through the flagged entrance corridor, his uncle kept glancing over his shoulder, looking anxious, as if Nicholas had been indiscreet.

Once again, as the four men settled in a small, low-ceilinged parlor at the back of the inn, Nicholas reproved himself. The man was kindly. That was clear. He called for ale from the taproom for them all, though it was strictly forbidden on the Sabbath, then sat staring at Isaac without a word, a happy grin splitting his wide face. Adam, meanwhile, sat looking at his boots. Nicholas watched them all, intrigued, but wishing he had someone else to speak to about it all.

At last Isaac introduced Adam and Nicholas to Sir George. There was a moment's confusion as Tolhurst mistook Nicholas for Isaac's own son. Adam wasn't in the least offended, which surprised Nicholas.

"He's like to his father, is he?" Tolhurst asked Isaac after a long stare in Nicholas's direction—not of rudeness, only with a puzzled curiosity.

His uncle paled. "Nay, see for thyself."

Tolhurst grunted. "He looks like a son of thine own, I'd say."

Isaac just smiled in return, and Nicholas's heart lifted. For all their differences of opinion, he would have been proud to have Isaac as a father.

Tolhurst then dropped his voice with a searching look at Isaac, and said, "May we speak freely, friend, when—?"

Nicholas stood up, his face flushing in indignation. "Of course you may, sir." The heat carried into his voice.

Isaac looked dismayed at the outburst, the muscles in his face tensing. "Be seated, nephew, and do not take offense." He turned his attention back to Tolhurst. "Yes, George, his father was a parliamentary man, as you rightly know. And Nicholas is a godly fellow, too. But he's our friend. Say on."

Nicholas subsided into his seat but did not feel at ease. They spoke as if he were not in the room, or as if he were a hunting dog whose pedigree had to be wrangled over before he could lie in the master's hall. He resolved that he would not like Tolhurst if the man were so suspicious and hasty in judgment.

A maid brought ale into the parlor at that moment, and everyone's spirits rose.

"Fetch my daughter from her chamber, pray," Tolhurst instructed the maid. He put a halfpenny into her hand, and Nicholas wondered at this largesse.

Dropping a curtsy, the maid withdrew. Isaac leaned back in his seat and drank deeply of the ale. The Fessendens rarely drank it these days, not because of any scruples like his father's, but because Rebecca had been unlucky in her last two years of brewing. This ale was frothy and redolent of last year's best hops. Nicholas, not used to it, had nevertheless learned to like it. Adam drank deeply, too, and caught Nicholas's eyes over the top of the tankard: the first spark of life all afternoon.

"You brought your daughter?" Isaac asked.

"Yes, Anna. Dost thou remember her?"

Isaac nodded. "Of course I remember. The eldest, and like her mother."

"A comely maid, yes, and like Elizabeth—fair to look upon—as she was before her illness, poor wife. But Anna's not like her mother in other ways." Sir George looked over at him. "She'll make good company for your two lads as we talk a while."

Nicholas drummed his fingers on the table. He did not want to be condemned to the company of a fat, spoiled country girl when he could listen to the men's converse. And Adam was no fit company for anyone today, either.

"How go the assizes, George?" his uncle asked.

"Oh, dull, compared to last year past, that is."

Isaac's eyebrows rose quizzically.

"'Tis all petty nonsense bent to send a man to sleep. Breach of the Sabbath. How many strokes of the birch should such-and-such a one have for the wickedness of playing the viol on the Sabbath in a public house . . ."

"Thou must be hard put not to laugh, thyself."

George set his tankard on the table. "Oh, I often am. Little men amusing themselves by making mighty rules. Assizes? No, 'tis a *trial*—for me, I mean."

"And there are more inns closing, I hear."

"Indeed. Dens of sedition and iniquity." His voice rose in mockery.

"'Tis a wonder this one's open, then," Nicholas interposed. Seeing his uncle's face, he instantly regretted his words and hung his head.

Tolhurst seemed not to hear. "The usual run of conycatchers, gamesters, drunkards, and players. Vagabonds and gamblers, I understand, must be stopped ere they dupe the poor, but drunkards, poor souls, I feel sorry for 'em. Who has not drunk too much at least once in his life? And strolling players—what harm in them, unless they've gulled the poor with all the mummeries? All they do is dwell in their own giddy fantasies. I like a good 'George and the Turkish Knight' myself, or a fine side of Morris dancers." He laughed lustily. "Instead, I'm supposed to see 'em into the stocks."

"You whited sepulcher," Isaac teased.

Nicholas watched this interchange with bemusement.

"Ah, quoting Scripture at me, are you now, you rogue?" There was a smile on Tolhurst's face.

"But how can you sit there imposing Puritan laws when you don't believe them yourself?"

"Because 'tis best if I'm thought a conformist, Isaac. Best for my family, and best for Kent. At least you know there's *one* honest King's man on the assizes, should you ever go to trial, Isaac. There I'd be, and few now to connect me with rebellions or Charles Stuart."

Nicholas's mouth dropped. This man was a turncoat! Whose side did he really serve, and who was tricking whom? And why did Isaac therefore trust him? He shook his head, trying to clear it.

He noticed then that a young girl had come in. How long she had been in the room, he did not know. *Tolhurst's girl?*

She sat in the corner only a few feet away, her needlework in her lap and her eyes down so that all he could see of her face was a broad brow and straight nose. Adam sat staring at her, his color heightened and his hands folding and unfolding on his knees as he watched her sew. She was no fat country maid.

She was beautiful. Her hair shone red-gold in the afternoon light, and her skin looked as pale as milk. Nicholas could not help staring.

"Not like that, if you please, mistress—" Adam said softly, standing up and gesturing toward her sewing. "You'll prick yourself and bloody the linen with the needle that way about."

Nicholas wanted to laugh at his cousin's concern for the stitching. For himself, he could not take his eyes off the girl's face.

Anna looked up at Adam, ignoring Nicholas altogether. Her eyes were a pale blue-violet, soft as fading bluebells in the chestnut woods round his Chilham home. "Will I now?" she said vaguely. "And what would you know, young sir?"

Adam looked nonplussed, and from the other side of the room came talk and laughter. Nicholas only half heard now.

". . .an abhorrent feast to be stamped out lest England fall again to popery," Tolhurst said.

"Oh, no! 'Tis Canterbury all over again, George. Dost thou think, because thou art virtuous, there shall be no more cakes and ale?'"

George laughed at Isaac, and somehow these words were familiar to Nicholas. He could not place them right away . . .

"Will Shakespeare." Isaac laughed back. "Sir Toby Belch, I think. Probably the only quotation I remember from my schooling, save the Bible."

George only shrugged. Nicholas was surprised his uncle could quote Shakespeare, but he quickly forgot again and looked back at Adam and Anna. His cousin was kneeling at her feet now, one hand holding the needle and the other grasping her sewing. As she bent forward to see what he was doing, their heads were almost touching: Adam's dark and curling like his father's, and hers soft and fine.

Nicholas felt a strange pang. Anna had not even acknowledged him. He watched Adam in annoyance, divided between wanting to win the girl's attention and wanting to take part in the men's discourse. He had not come here with his uncle to chatter about fine stitching!

"You mentioned last year, George?"

"Aye, surely you were in Maidstone a twelvemonth ago?"

Isaac frowned. "Yes, as far as I remember."

"And the name of Sondes—that means something, does it not?" Tolhurst sipped his ale noisily.

"Sondes . . . Sondes . . . was he not the sheriff?"

"The very one. They took his house away—Lees Court—in all the sequestrations . . . though he's done better than any of us at restoring his fortunes, except in one regard, poor soul."

"And that?"

Nicholas lost interest in Adam and Anna as the men's conversation became far more compelling again.

Tolhurst bent forward to answer. "His son Freeman—last year it was—slew his own brother."

Isaac flinched as if he had been struck. Tolhurst, seeming afraid he had blundered, began to stammer. "Isaac, no . . . pardon me . . . this was an affair of the heart."

His uncle made a guttural sound but seemed unable to reply.

"Very ugly, it was. Jealousy. Killed him with a cleaver and dagger while he slept at home."

Isaac shuddered, and Nicholas caught an anxious, hunted look as it passed between the two men: a message his uncle had flashed out silently and the other man had understood. A warning.

"They were both in love with the same woman," Tolhurst said slowly. "Their father couldn't tame Freeman." He looked down. "The assizes tamed him. Saddest case I ever sat on. He was hanged at Penenden a year ago this month."

The room fell silent again. Adam was watching his father now, the needlework having slipped from his hands. Anna looked up, also, her eyes fixed on Nicholas's, seeing him for the first time.

He gazed back at her. She looked as frightened as he was. At the same time he felt angry. How could anyone love a woman enough to kill his own brother?

"Both in love with the same woman," George mused again in a sad voice.

Anna's eyes held his, wavering now. Her forehead puckered into a slight frown.

Home again later that afternoon, Nicholas waited until all the family was out of the room—except Isaac, who often sat reading on the Sabbath. He moved so restlessly in his seat that at last Isaac looked up.

"What is it, nephew?"

Nicholas hesitated, but then poured out his tale. All the time, Anna's face swum before his eyes. He longed for her, he said.

"Don't be foolish, lad," Isaac said gently. "What would we have to offer?

And what would she? In all the reversals of Royalist fortunes, her father's been in and out of penury scarcely different from our own—though she is the eldest, and will be dowried, no doubt."

Nicholas clenched his teeth tightly. "And Adam? I suppose Adam's already spoken for her?"

Isaac shook his head as though befuddled with ale. "Adam? Nay, he's not got a mind for maidens yet a while. And just as well. Nicholas, dear nephew, thou'rt being rash and hasty. You must not think of it."

"Because I am a Parliament's man?" He knew his voice was bitter.

Isaac shook his head, impatiently this time. "Nay . . . no . . . that's naught. But thou'rt a yeoman."

"And is not Sir George, at heart?"

Isaac smiled sadly. "At heart, yes. But he would never hear of it. If thou hast a mind for wooing, Nicholas, you must woo elsewhere." He rubbed his brow with a tired expression. "Again I say, Anna Tolhurst is her father's oldest. She'll marry a fine gentleman, and when King Charles the Second returns, she'll be a great lady, perhaps at court. Her mother is as tall and fine as a princess. Not for the likes of a Fessenden."

No sympathy in that quarter, Nicholas realized. Then could he speak to Hannah? She at least might advise him on how a sweet young maid should be won. But no, Hannah was scarcely sixteen, and no one had yet come awooing her. She could not help . . . and perhaps might even speak of it.

Then he must talk to Grandmother Mary.

He found her out in the small shop's garden late that evening picking herbs. She moved deliberately now, but her deft fingers did not hesitate over which sprigs to pick and which to leave.

He watched her unthinkingly as he talked. She hardly seemed aware of his voice, but he knew she was listening. She stood still once he had finished, and her eyes misted.

"Ah, Nicholas, this story is one I've heard before."

"My father—?" No one spoke of Robert in this house, and he liked the rare occasions when he could mention his father to Mary.

"Nay." She looked away, uncomfortably, he thought. Her smile seemed forced as she went on. "Thy father wooed thy mother away from home, mostly." She lowered her eyes, apparently recalling the courtship. "And your Uncle Isaac did the same. I knew little of Rebecca until I came to Maidstone after your grandfather died." She sighed. "And a finer, sweeter wife he couldn't have chosen."

Nicholas wanted to ask more about his parents, but she clearly desired to vouchsafe no more about their wooing. It seemed strange to him, all the same, that people never spoke of his mother the way they spoke of Rebecca. He looked down. But why was it strange? Hadn't he only a moment ago been thinking himself of his aunt's sweetness? And he had never received much affection from his mother . . .

"Then, pray tell me who's been telling you tales like mine?"

His grandmother went back to her picking. The shears snipped, and the piles of lavender, mint, borage, and fennel grew higher in her basket. "You remind me through and through of your Uncle John. He was about your age when he fell in love."

Nicholas's face grew hot. "In love, Grandame? Did I say that?"

She laughed. Her gums were almost toothless now, but she still looked lovely, he thought. "Nay, son. You didn't—in so many words. But why would you be talking of wooing if you be not in love, Nicholas? 'Tis a strange, wicked man that prates of marriage without love."

He blinked. "You loved my grandfather, then?" The old man had died soberly and quietly, a solemn event made more so by his own father's solemnity and grief. But Nicholas could not associate his grandmother with the drooling old man he remembered. Love? Was it possible?

Mary set down her basket and took him by the shoulders. Her hands were spotted with large brown freckles and twisted with age, but they were still strong. "Yes, I loved him. It wasn't just a matter of convenience, you know, no matter what thy—what anyone said or thought. And he loved me, too. Loved me as much as thy uncle loved Jane—and still loves her, no doubt."

"Then tell me, pray, how he wooed her."

She laughed again. "Oh, 'twas a curious wooing. Once he'd set his eyes on her, he was all fire but no resolve. How was he to get her from her uncle? A blackcoat in Canterbury he was, high and mighty, though he kept her poorly, John always said. But he hardly saw her before he'd made up his mind." Mary looked up at him sharply. "It was the Almighty's will, Nicholas. And you—have you prayed and sought God?"

He hung his head. She always asked the most difficult questions. But they were the questions he knew he had to answer, the right questions.

"No, I see thou hast not. Well-a-day—" She sighed. "'Tis a hopeless case, I'd say. She a gentleborn maiden and thou a penniless orphan dependent upon thine uncle. You had best think no more of her until you get a trade and settle yourself—if she's not wed by then."

He groaned at the simplicity of her summary. "And in the meanwhile?

How shall I see her? How shall she know I want to acquaint myself with her?"

"Acquaint thyself with her? Oh Nicholas, thou'rt a comical lad!"

He spread his hands with a shrug. "But I know not what to say, how to—"

"Let's see now. Does she sew well?"

He frowned. "Perhaps, though Adam thought—"

Mary was all business now. "And does she speak wisely?"

"I hardly heard her voice, madam."

"Not so good. And does she read?"

"Oh—!" He let out an angry exclamation. "Oh, I do *not* know. It was just that she looked—in such a way—" How could he explain?

She smiled. "Your Uncle John, again."

"Pray, no more questions or comparisons!" he said in exasperation.

"No more questions, then. But I see no remedy, Nicholas. You must meet her again ere her father returns to Goudhurst. It could all be vain fantasy—and her father's a Cavalier."

He held up his hand. "No more obstacles, either, pray. How shall I meet her?"

Mary considered. She turned the lavender slowly in her fingers. "Her mother's ill, I heard Isaac say. I might make up some cordial for her and send her some of these herbs. By thee."

"And my uncle?"

"He shall know of it, of course, and I think he will relent. He loves thee dearly. Sir George is his friend. And times are changing, when with no more kings, I suppose, a merchant's son may look upon a gentleman's daughter."

The basket of herbs, however, was not enough, he decided, nor was the flask of cordial. He wanted to take Anna something of his own. It would be a sign between them.

But what could he take her? He owned nothing except a share of the bed with his brother, and the clothes and boots he wore. He knew not what had happened to his father's remaining things, which had gone to Thomas, and his mother had left little except her Bible and a house of spotless furniture that had all been sold to pay the last of the Fessenden debts to weavers, dyers, and fullers.

Leaving Mary out-of-doors in the fading light, he went within. Josiah was already asleep, but Rebecca was softly talking with Adam and Charlie below stairs. He passed them and mounted the stairs slowly. Then he remembered Culpeper's *Herbal.* Mary had presented it to his mother some years before, but the book had lain unused on an attic shelf. Mary reclaimed it after Patience died, and she still referred to it, though not often.

He ran heavily downstairs again. "May I give her thy *Herbal,* Grandmother Mary?" The words came rushing out.

She did not answer immediately but came back into the house first. He lighted a candle to show her way up the back steps. At last she said, "Thou'rt hasty, Nicholas. I doubt she'll accept it." She sighed. "But you may try. Take it, and welcome."

"The master's to the assizes," the maid at the inn assured him insolently. "But his daughter's above stairs, I lay."

He took a deep breath, resenting the girl's rude, suggestive grimaces. She tossed her head so that her bodice shook with the weight of her breasts, and he knew the display was intended to provoke him.

He looked away. "Then tell her—" His voice sounded odd: tight, and lower than usual. "Pray, *ask her* if she will receive me in the parlor where we sat yester afternoon."

The girl eyed him wickedly and wiped her hands down the greasy sides of her skirt so that her hips showed plainly beneath the stained, coarse material. "And what wilt'ou give me to do thy bidding?"

He stood up straight. "A box in the ears if you won't, and a sprig of lavender if you will."

Laughing, she turned to the stairs, and he crossed into the inn's parlor. To his dismay, it was not empty. Two heavy gentlewomen sat gossiping in the corner. They rearranged their skirts when he came in, preened themselves slightly, but then went on with their loud discourse. *Perhaps,* he thought, *'tis as well we shall have older folk about.* Disappointment nagged, but he would make the best of it.

The women inclined their heads as Anna Tolhurst came in—a slight acknowledgment for the daughter of a respected man, albeit a man not so rich now as he once was.

Nicholas stood, bowing, only half aware that he was holding the basket so tightly that the dry rushes were squeaking against his palms.

"Pray do sit down, sir," Anna said stiffly. Her voice was quiet but a few tones lower than any he had heard in such a young woman. It was cool, like music, and her patched silk skirts rustled like faint waterfalls. With her came the scent of sandalwood and pomander; she was altogether lovely to him.

"I've come to bring—" The words failed, and he began to stammer. "That is, these herbs . . . and . . . I've brought a cordial . . . for . . . I mean . . . for your lady mother. And 'twas my grandmother that did send me." Seated again, now opposite her, he leaned back, half laughing, glad to be shot of the speech he had rehearsed in his head all morning.

She was nodding, her eyes soft and yet amused, timid and delighted—all at once. He had a curious feeling that she had not heard one word he had said.

"For your mother," he repeated stupidly.

"Aye, so you said. 'Tis very kind of you, Master Fessenden."

He looked desperately at the basket and felt her eyes on his face. He was even more afraid than before. He searched for the right words and found none. "My name is Nicholas," he murmured at last.

"And mine is Anna."

Still he clung onto the basket, not knowing how to proceed.

"May I see?" As she stretched her arms toward the basket, he noticed under the soft material of her bodice the gentle swell of her breasts and the fine curve of her shoulders. She seemed to be drawing and draining him as if he were a draft she drank with her eyes. He felt unbalanced.

"Of course," he managed. But then he remembered the *Herbal* and pulled it out. He passed her the basket. She was not looking at it anymore, however, but at his face. Her cheeks were flushed and her eyes anxious.

"And there's this. I brought it for thee." He heard the strange note in his voice again and the oddness of the word *thee*. It was a word Isaac used to Rebecca, not one he himself had ever used to a woman.

"Oh, but I cannot accept . . . my father . . ." Her face was pained, and he was afraid he had offended her. He moved to the edge of his seat. Her face wore such an agonized expression that he wanted to make her smile again. From the other side of the room, the two women sent them frowning looks.

"Anna . . . I know not how to say it, sweetheart." His voice and body had begun to shake. "But this is all I can give thee now. Will it please thee take it?" He felt confused, overwhelmed by the love that took possession of him.

She leaned slightly toward him. He gave in to his impulses, fell forward onto his knees, and laid the book in her lap. She was shaking her head, speechless, her eyes watering. A wave of impressions flooded into his mind: that he was wrong to be wooing without consent, wrong to be alone with her without her father's knowledge, foolish to have chosen a maiden so far beyond him. And it was all in vain. She was accepting the book, but she was not accepting him. He had overstepped the bounds of courtesy and had disturbed her.

He stood up and backed away from her. He felt as he had felt as a child when reproved by Mary for disobedience.

"Forgive me, Anna." His hand was on the door. "I'll think on thee."

He turned and went out. In the courtyard outside, a crowd of unkempt men gathered for a cockfight. The cocks, restrained in baskets, were crowing loudly. He felt sick with loathng and disappointment.

Goudhurst, September 1658

George

His field was already plowed for the barley sowing. The brown furrows lay as straight and even as links in chainmail or threads in linen. He whistled and sang as he stepped over them.

> *And when the dogs of war growl loud*
> *I'll quit the Weald and be a proud—*
> *A Cavilally man!*

The mild afternoon sunshine touched his shoulders, and he was glad to be alive. Cromwell—"the Protector" they had called him, poor man—was dead, or so the Kentish news asserted, and England was weary of Puritan zeal. The rumor mills in Kent ground out the word that the beheaded King's eldest son, Charles, now across the water, would not tarry long; and soon the county—the entire country—would be restored!

He sighed and hoisted his hop hook on his shoulder. Life was good. He had the estate back to order again, and Tolhurst Court was not as poor as it had been at the end of the war. For the first time in many years, no Roundheads had come demanding corn or malt from the harvest. The hops were drying in the oasts, there had been no plague of damson-hop flies this year, and the hop burrs had been big and fat with pollen.

And not only the hops. Elizabeth was with child again. This strange event had shaken them in the early spring. Eleanor, the youngest, was thirteen, and they had long ago ceased to expect more. Elizabeth was almost to the end of her child-bearing years now, and she had been ill for several years with a persistent flux.

"'Tis like to be a canker, sir," the physician had told him.

Then suddenly, this spring, when after a cold winter he had taken her to Tunbridge Wells for the waters, the flux had stopped as mysteriously as it had started. They had rejoiced and thanked God, but fear had followed fast on the heels of joy, as Elizabeth's body began to swell.

"The canker," she had cried. "'Tis the canker, George, after all."

And looking at her face, then growing thinner, he had feared as much. But no, more joy awaited them, for now it was quite clear that the swelling in her belly was a living, moving child. When she had first felt the quickening, early one morning in May, she had come running out into the courtyard weeping for joy, her red hair streaming down her back and all her reserve before the servants forgotten in her moment of discovery.

He laughed aloud, thinking of it now, for Elizabeth was plump and rosy again. She was carrying this child more easily than any before: comfortable, cheerful, young again.

He began to hurry as he neared the kitchen garden. Anna was strolling indolently under the cherry trees, but he did not want to talk to her. Since Elizabeth had been with child, all his delight in his eldest daughter had been replaced by care for his wife. In return, Anna had withdrawn. She irritated him often, seeming to prefer the company of some of the servants—especially the two kitchen maids who tended the herb gardens—to that of her own sisters. But what of that? Soon she would be wed and would have a husband to wait on. He clicked his tongue impatiently. Yes, it was time she wed.

He frowned and scratched his jaw. *Ah, but there's the rub! Will she be wed?* She had proved stubborn about a short betrothal to William Frittenden, the man they had chosen for her. She wanted to wait.

He looked away from Anna and could not even bring himself to bow or smile. But his other daughters rescued him as he mounted the steps to the courtyard. Henrietta, Charlotte, and Eleanor had been playing at bowls, and a spaniel bitch was chasing and barking round their ankles in high excitement.

"Hush up, Maria!" Charlotte scolded. She ran to her father. "Oh, thou'rt dreadfully hot, Father. Take some water, pray." She wrinkled her nose at him.

He wiped away the sweat on his forehead. "I shall. I shall. What's ado, ladies?"

"We're playing at bowls, as you can rightly see for yourself," Eleanor said pertly.

"No we're not, goose," Henrietta argued. "We have ceased and were just agoing to send Matthew for you. Our mother has need of you."

His heart constricted. "She's ill?" Even now he worried about her.

"Nay!" The girls began to giggle. "She's sent for the midwife . . . thinks her time is come."

His temper rose, and he heard the snap in his own voice: "Oh, why didn't ye tell me?"

His daughters stared back, wide-eyed and flushed with excitement. The spaniel stopped barking and sat down on the bricks with its tail swishing back and forth in the dust. But George could not be angry; the girls had all been longing for this day.

As he hurried to the scullery door, Henrietta caught his sleeve. "Is there nothing we can do, Father?"

"The midwife's bidden?"

"Aye."

"Then nothing, but tell Nancy to heat water quickly. And get thy oldest sister inside at once. Thy mother's well, I know, but—" He did not bother to finish what he was saying.

Elizabeth was sitting in the great family bed upstairs where they had first lain together. A maid hovered in the doorway, wringing her hands in distress. George dismissed her with instructions to bring in the midwife as soon as the old woman arrived.

He leaned over the bed, kissed Elizabeth's forehead, and adjusted the bolsters. "It's time, is it, already?"

She nodded, her eyes glittering. "I'm certain 'tis a son. I've never felt so sure and strong ere this."

He smoothed the folds of the loose linen gown round her shoulders and looked lovingly at the rounded curve of the baby pushing up the sheet. "Son or daughter, it matters not, so you be well."

"I'm well." Her voice dropped lower, and he saw the feverish joy of motherhood that he had never expected to see on her face again.

"Then I'm content," he said.

"Sit, husband, wilt'ou, whilst thou may? I'd like thee by me, till the midwife comes at least."

He settled on the edge of the bed and took her hand. Every so often she held his harder, and he watched her face contort as a pang gripped her body. But she did not yet cry out.

"Art sure, dear heart?" he asked uncertainly. "You have had false pangs ere this—then nothing."

Another pain crossed her body like a harrow turning up earth and twisting it over. There was no doubt this time.

"Yes," she whispered, smiling dryly as she saw his doubt melt away. "Yes, I'm sure."

"Then there is nothing—?"

"I want to talk for now. 'Tis easier than the other babes, except when the pain passes me. I want to talk."

"Then we'll talk. But rest, dearling, for what is to come." He remembered Charlotte's birth in particular, though Eleanor's had been more recent. The child had seemed to tear Elizabeth's body in two and at birth was as red and resentful at being brought into the world as a fox cub pulled unsuspecting from its lair. Red and angry—and leaving Elizabeth wracked with exhaustion. He did not want her so exhausted this time, and he said so. "Thou *needs must* rest, dearling."

"I know." Another pang tightened its hold, and she moaned this time. But as soon as it had gone, she brightened. "Then *you* talk. Talk to me of Anna's wedding."

He shut his eyes for a second and almost leaned against Elizabeth before remembering her condition. "Ah, Anna." He opened his eyes again and frowned.

"You look so troubled, love." Elizabeth touched his brow lightly.

"I am, for her sake. Anna and I—we've hardly been able to speak to each other in latter days."

She looked at him sharply. "That's unlike your Anna." She always called her *your Anna.* "Why? Have you offended her?"

"Not that I know of. At first I thought 'twas just a fit of womanish temper, but it passes not away—rather grows worse."

"I am dismayed I haven't observed—oh!" Her hand tightened on his again, and her face paled. She doubled over, her breath coming hard and ragged and her face prickling with sweat.

Sweat broke out on his own brow as he remembered Charlotte's birth again. He murmured in compassion but felt utterly helpless. "'Tis bad, is it?" he whispered a moment later when she flopped back on the bolster with her eyes shut.

She did not answer immediately, and when she did he saw that her lips were slightly cracked. "I've a terrible thirst, George."

Glad of an errand, he leaped up—too quickly, for she opened startled eyes to him, wide with fright. As he had many times before with this wise and beautiful woman, he felt a clumsy fool. "I'm sorry, love. I'll send Nancy for water. She's boiling water anyway." He stumbled over the door frame and stood at the top of the stairs. "Ho! Nancy!"

There was no answer. Instead he could hear the drone of a wasp in the window and the girls' voices from below stairs, giddy with joy. *Damme!* he thought angrily. *Can't they be still?*

Rushing into the hall below, he ran headlong into Anna. Her face was pink and her skirts were stained here and there with purplish-red splotches. In her hair was some leaf or other, and her hands were full of greenery. He opened his mouth to rebuke her for unseemliness but then swallowed the rebuke. She of all his daughters would be most help with Elizabeth if the babe came untimely, before the midwife. He could not cross her now.

He plucked the leaf out of her hair and made himself smile. "Anna, sweetheart, thy mother—" Her blue eyes were soft, and he realized painfully that all the constraint between them was on his side because of William Frittenden.

"I know—is in labor," she said quietly.

He was flustered at the plainness of her words. What could she know of the pangs of childbed and the sufferings of women? "Nancy's not about. I sent her off to heat water. Mayhap you'll wait on us a while?"

Her eyes lighted, and he saw a joy in her that had been quenched for months. "I shall, Father. Pray forgive my graceless dress, but I knew my mother was brought to bed, and I was gathering leaves for her."

"*Leaves?* Have you lost your senses?"

Anna laughed and dropped a curtsy. "Nay, I've been getting raspberry leaves for her. And I need hot water and honey to make a cordial for her. And cumfrey—"

"Raspberry leaves? Cumfrey?" His head reeled with bewilderment. "Well, you shall speak of it ere long. Come, the women are in the scullery. Make haste, for I cannot leave your mother for long." He turned and ran back up the stairs, forgetting about the cold water.

He found Elizabeth bolt upright in the bed. She had flung back the sheet and torn off her gown. The bed was soaked, water dripping to the floor. He saw her in all her beautiful and terrible womanliness and loved her as he had never loved before—loved her as fiercely as she loved this little being that was battering its way into the world through her body. Her face was intent, eyes wide open and fixed on the end of the bed. She neither saw nor heard him, nor could she speak. Her hands were like claws on the side of the bed, stiff and white as she crouched forward and dug her nails into the flock mattress. But for the moment she was not crying out. She had become somehow inhuman, yet altogether human.

Her body convulsed and shuddered as he stepped to the foot of the bed.

Fear rose in him like a sickness. "Oh, my dear Bessie! Whatever shall I do? How shall I help thee?" The sound of his own panicked voice only frightened him more.

At last she seemed to hear. She looked at him as if from a long way off. "The midwife," she ground out from between clenched jaws. "Oh, *fetch the midwife!*"

Then two things happened at once: the tension in her body eased for a moment, and she seemed plainly aware of his horror and fear. She bowed her head over her knees, drew them together, and tried to pull up the sheet, as if ashamed.

He reached forward quickly. "Nay, do without it if thou'rt better this way. Think you I'm dismayed to see you naked, dear heart?" He leaned against the post of the bed.

A ghost of a smile touched her lips. "I know thou art, but—God help me—" The pain seized her again, cutting off her answer. She bore down again.

Something was different now, for her cries and groans had turned to roars, and her face suffused with blood. He thought he had never seen her so bright and so alive, yet so aweful.

He came to the head of the bed and put his mouth against her ear and his arm round her back. He found himself wanting to shout and gasp with her. "Lean hard on me, Bess. Lean hard. The babe is nigh coming."

Suddenly Nancy and Anna were in the room—Nancy the old nursemaid who had waited on all the girls since their babyhood, and now was pressed into service in the absence of a midwife; and Anna, who had never before seen childbed, now to see her mother naked on the bed, shouting in pity and joy to birth her child. He had not heard them enter, and lost all track of time, except that punctuated by the waves of tension in Elizabeth's body. She was falling asleep between pangs now, limp against him, eyes dazed and surprised when she woke after these brief intervals to push down again. He wondered if he was falling asleep himself, for the sun seemed to have lengthened the shadows a little.

Anna placed a cool cloth over Elizabeth's forehead and helped support her each time she bore down. Nancy hobbled, muttering, round the bed, until at last Anna sent her out. "Go, Nancy, pray—"

George saw the old woman's unhappiness and her relief. But then Anna softened her words. "Perhaps the midwife is tarrying or Matthew is waylaid. I beg thee, send and see. This babe won't wait for anyone."

He looked at Anna gratefully. Her face was just a few inches from his own, separated only by the red stream of Elizabeth's unbound hair and her hot, straining shoulders.

"Well said," he whispered. "Nancy's not a one for childbed. Never was."

Anna did not smile back, but her eyes held his steadily, saying *All will be well, do not fear.* He drew courage from those steady eyes.

But then Anna moved abruptly, and he noticed that the tone of Elizabeth's cries had changed. The lapses between the waves of pain had grown longer, and she had relaxed.

Anna was facing her mother now, her hands on Elizabeth's feet. He was surprised at her bravery and sympathy; she seemed to know quite naturally what her mother needed.

"Push down, dear Mother! I see the babe's crown."

He almost let go of his wife's shoulders, seeing for the first time that he was faint-hearted and cowardly in comparison with a woman. Would the midwife *never* come?

Elizabeth was gasping, crying, laughing—all at once. Then with a final heaving, shuddering push, the baby was born, and she sank back against him. Anna's hands reached out, swift and somehow knowing, gathering the wailing child to the cloths laid out in the wooden cradle bedside the bed weeks before—gathering, and lifting the baby onto Elizabeth's distended belly.

He leaned over to see the baby's form, but she was too quick for him. He eased Elizabeth gently down and covered her legs.

"I have a brother," Anna whispered. Tears began to pour down her face. "Thou hast a son! Look, Father, oh, look, my lady mother!"

Elizabeth reached forward feebly and rested her arms on the baby's loosely covered body. Another thin, mewing cry splintered the room, and George's own breathing became uneven. He fell to his knees, his face pressed against Elizabeth's damp skin, and he wept for joy.

When he came fully to himself again, the midwife had come and was busying herself about the room giving directions to Elizabeth to suckle the babe, and to Nancy—now that the birth was over—to remove the sodden bedding. His son was properly swaddled now, and the midwife rambled through her mysterious rites with all the haste and mumbling of an old village priest saying the mass. George stood up again.

The midwife looked at him suspiciously. "Fie upon you, Squire Tolhurst, weeping like a woman by your new baby's bed. You've no place at a birthing, sir. Get you gone—you'll bring ill luck."

Elizabeth raised her eyes from the baby's face: serene, madonnalike—all the lioness in her gone now. The child was suckling noisily at her breast, and George swelled with pride. "Superstitious cant, Goody Medhurst," Elizabeth said firmly. "I'll have none of it here. But for my husband and my daughter, this babe would have had rough passage. I thank thee not for thy lateness."

The old woman's face turned scarlet, and her cheeks puffed out like a toad's. "Aye—" she spat. "Yon babe's faster on his little feet than I on mine in my dotage, I lay. But I'm here at your bidding now, am I not? And there's more yet adone." She looked spitefully at Anna, who now stood apart with her hands clasped, watching hungrily, waiting to be of further service. George wished he could hold her, to thank her for her calm resolve, but he guessed she would spurn him now after his months of indifference.

"This lass 'ere, now, is she good for nothing but astanding and agawping?"

For the second time that day he felt his temper rise. "You're speaking to my eldest daughter. Hold your tongue, and do your work. She has a cordial."

The old woman looked cunningly at Anna. "A cordial, have you? And what be in't, pray?"

Anna came forward with an uncertain look at him to which he tried to respond with silent encouragement. "'Tis raspberry leaves and cumfrey, ma'am. I read in Culpeper's 'tis the very thing."

George saw the midwife's startled and grudging recognition. The old woman's face changed. "Ah, you're wise, then, lass, after all. Aye, thy mother hath need of this." She folded back the lower part of the sheet, and he saw with dismay that there were new blood stains on the fresh linens. "See, there is still blood aplenty." Was there a glint of evil or triumph in her eyes because she was still needed? "The suckling child should assuage it, yet—"

He looked anxiously at his wife, but she was completely absorbed. He prayed that she had not heard and pulled the covers back quickly. Then he drew the midwife aside into the window alcove for a moment. "This bleeding—" He felt unsure of himself; hating her, yet needing her counsel. "—all's not well?"

"She *will* bleed," the old woman said laconically. "They all bleed, as you would know, were husbands midwives, as you be not! And she *will* bleed."

He took her shoulders to shake her in impotent fury, but she pushed him away; her arms were muscular and strong like none he had seen on a woman, and he was suddenly afraid. "What do you mean?"

"The cordial will help. Fortunate for you your daughter's wise. But the blood is heavy. You were best to your knees, squire, and mayhap look for a wet nurse."

He returned to the bedside, shaking slightly. *No*, he thought slowly. *No, the woman has lied.* He looked at Elizabeth's face—pink, unaware, and happy—and at the baby's. *My son. My first son.* The hair was dark and wet, the crinkled face shut against the sudden light but at ease in the warmth and comfort of his mother's milk. The child was well. The mother was well. *All would be well.*

He turned away. The voice inside him was a chant in the dark.

Anna followed him out into the upstairs corridor and put her hand lightly onto his shoulder. He looked into her face, then away again.

"How did you learn from Culpeper's *Herbal?*" His voice seemed to be swallowed in the stifling heat of roof timbers and narrow walls in the unmoving autumn evening air, and he leaned exhausted against the wall.

"'Twas a gift, my father—" She broke off.

"From whom?" he asked, thinking of her friends the serving maids, and wondering where maids had money nowadays for such extravagances.

"From—from the Fessendens."

He hardly registered surprise, but then the name penetrated, and Isaac's face came vividly before him.

Isaac, he thought. *Matthew must go for Isaac. But why? What can Isaac do? No physician he, to stop the bleeding . . . All shall be well . . . Rebecca . . . has she not just on St. Mary's day in harvest time gotten herself a child again? So I think I heard . . .* He struggled to remember. *And if the child be not alive . . . for she lost many before . . .*

"Anna," he said unsteadily, straightening his back again.

She looked back at him, and beads of moisture broke out on his upper lip. She was afraid, and he didn't understand why.

"Anna, before you speak to your sisters—and I want you to tell them, for I shall sit here and wait upon your mother—I want you to send Matthew or Edmund to Maidstone this night. I shall have a letter for Isaac Fessenden, the tailor. Did you not mention him ere this?"

His mind was confused now. How had Isaac come into his thoughts? "I may have need of Isaac." He stopped, frowning, almost broken with weariness. "Or of his goodwife. I think . . . I think . . . she has kinsmen hereabouts and may not mind to come with him anyhow—" He knew his mind was browsing, and he tried to tug it back with the reins of his will. "So bring me a quill and a paper, and send Matthew here."

She heard him out, and he knew she was thinking—quick as her mother—about the meaning under the words. "I shall, Father, but—"

He dropped onto a chest beside the stairs and leaned back on a tapestry Elizabeth had sewn in the early days of their marriage. "But what, Anna?"

"Matthew is old and slow, now. Can you not—"

"Then send Edmund. It matters not." He stared at her, still pleased by her usefulness but puzzled by her look of determination.

She swung round so that her skirts lifted, and he caught a glimpse of petticoats, lace, and a slim ankle. Her face was transfigured with joy.

Nicholas

"You *shall* go with us, Nicholas," Isaac said. "I'll be glad of someone with me on the lonely way home."

"And Adam? Should he not—?" Nicholas grew uncomfortable, knowing he himself was his uncle's favorite (though unresented by the others) and not wanting their birthright.

"No, I cannot spare Adam or Charlie from the work. Thou'rt good with the donkey, too, and Rebecca's still not strong."

In his mind's eye Nicholas saw his uncle in the cart with his arm round Rebecca: the strong and the sweet. He groaned inwardly. *I need my own.* "Yes," he said aloud. "She needs thee. I'll gladly go with thee."

One of Isaac's large hands suddenly came out and caught him by the sleeve. If his uncle's hands had not been accustomed to the ways of soft, yielding cloth, the garment would have torn, but Isaac was gentle. Nicholas looked up to see his uncle's eyes, dark and liquid as they looked into his own.

"It is good for my dear friend George," he said slowly. "I have long wanted to return the thanks I owe him. Now I can. And I know it is good for thee, also." His face crinkled into laughter. "Good, is't not?"

Nicholas felt himself redden. Since he had confessed his love of Anna to Isaac, his uncle had relented and even sometimes encouraged him by bringing news of her. But now he was speechless. He had not seen her for two years.

"I said, 'twill be to thy advantage, perhaps, to accompany us, Nicholas."

"Aye." He looked up, marveling at Isaac's understanding, and moved. "But how can I repay *you*, my uncle?"

Isaac abruptly let him go and turned away. His voice was harsh. "There's naught to repay, Nicholas. 'Tis I who pay a debt—to thee."

Anna

A hush had fallen on the house today. Nancy had bidden Henrietta, Charlotte, and Eleanor keep to their chamber, and they fretted in the heat. Only Anna had been left to her own, and she wandered restlessly in and out of the house. She heard the murmur of her mother's and father's voices from time to time, from behind the shut door of their chamber, or the cry of the baby, so she knew all was well. But where was the rejoicing they should expect, and why had her father not sent to the church to have St. Mary's bells rung in thanksgiving?

All the joy of yesterday had vanished in the chill breath of this morning's early fog as it rolled up the Weald and curled round the cherry trees. So what if Edmund had been sent for Isaac Fessenden and his wife? What good was that to her? It was Nicholas she wanted, but *he* would not come. And in the meanwhile something was oddly amiss above stairs, and no one would speak of it.

She must find out. She had held that child, seen his minuscule toes and fingers, felt his flailing, crying, wet body next to hers for an instant before she wrapped him. She had seen the strange little buds between his legs— buds that meant manhood: minute, frightening, beautiful . . . her *brother*.

She bit down on her lip, willing the child to live. Would he die? Was this the cause of the hush and secrecy?

She *must* find out.

She pressed urgently into the kitchen where the wenches were dressing fowl for dinner. Odd how the round of maids went on while their ladies bore sons in the chambers above. Martha would know.

The frightened girl, drawn from the kitchen into the courtyard, where they would not be overheard, began to blubber. "He doesn't want thee frighted, lady. We mayn't tell any o' ye a word."

"Martha, come," she coaxed, hating the honey in her own voice. "I'm not frightened like my foolish sisters. Was I not at the birthing?"

The girl stared stupidly. "Truly, I don't know."

"I was, so tell me, pray."

Martha could not answer but led her with faltering steps to the outbuilding where most of the household linens were purged. Piled inside on the flagged floor were bundles of bloodstained sheets.

The maid burst into tears.

Absently, Anna reached into her pocket, found a comfit for her, then sent her back to the kitchen. Alone, she stood and stared at the bedding.

She did not remain there long. Instead, she gathered her skirts and ran back into the house. Raspberry leaves and cumfrey had failed. She must find something else. Oh, would that she herself had the knowledge of a Culpeper!

Book in hand, she returned to the courtyard. Her sisters' voices chattered like sparrows in their chamber above the back kitchen. They seemed as unaware of her relative freedom as she felt uninterested in their incarceration. Instead, she leafed slowly through the book, her eyes staring blankly at the neat drawings of fumitory and foxglove, bittersweet and bryony.

Then she clapped it shut. There was no comfort in it. She must see if she could encourage her mother, instead, with ordinary cordials to make her cheerful. She could not stop the bleeding, perhaps, but she could at least cheer her.

Dropping the book into the deep pocket of her skirt, she went thoughtfully down the steps to the kitchen garden. She would collect fennel, St. John's wort, and knapweed—she counted them off on her fingers. The weight of doubt and sorrow lifted slightly under the late morning sunlight as she began to gather what she needed.

The smell of drying hops came on the air from the oasts. She knew her father was pleased with the harvest and was glad, but she could think of nothing else for very long except the bloodied sheets. She looked round unhappily. Under the cherry and hazelnut trees the wavering beams of sunlight were hazy with motes of dust from the wheat harvest: everything was golden and still.

Everything except Anna Tolhurst, she thought, snapping off a twig sharply.

She set the herbs aside and walked beyond the trees to the dovecotes. One hen, fat and sleek, was sunning itself at one of the tiny entrance holes. The rest, shy as ever, secreted themselves somewhere within. She heard the occasional flutter and soft calling. Above her the wild woodpigeons in the poplars that guarded the hop gardens called to their tame cousins below, but the doves remained. A cart rumbled somewhere down the lane.

She sat down under a poplar and let herself drift, neither hearing nor seeing anything clearly. The book in her pocket lay heavily against her thigh. She pressed her hand on it and felt the warmth of book and fabric under her palm. Then without moving her hand, she shut her eyes.

The book was the strong back of Nicholas Fessenden, hard and warm under her fingers. Her arms were round him, and his round her, pressing into her own back, pulling her close to him. And if she screwed her eyes tightly shut she could see—not her wooer, William Frittenden—but the face she had seen only twice, the face that was as stamped on her memory now as Culpeper's perfect drawings. It was his face—his dark, searching eyes and small nose, his crinkling black hair cut short like a Roundhead's— that stopped her at every turn when her father spoke of marriage.

She turned her head and began to weep. The crying had been pent up too long, and it took her by surprise. Since no one could see her, she let the tears flow where they would, her hand moving slowly over the book he had given her, his face receding further into the abstraction of grief.

At last she opened her eyes.

The reality was shattering. She screamed and jumped to her feet.

The very face she had seen, with her eyes closed, was leaning close to hers. Now, as she leaped up, she was almost as tall as the young man who faced her.

"Anna Tolhurst?" He seemed unsure, and she remembered her tear-stained face and wiped it quickly with the back of her hand. She felt vulnerable, stripped before him because he had seen her crying, so she kept the back of her wrist over her mouth and just stared.

He stepped back, and she could see that he was afraid of offending her. "It *is* Anna?"

She let her hand drop and pushed it into her pocket. There was the book, still hard and warm. "Yes." It was all she could say.

He laughed suddenly, his hair bobbing backward and his teeth very white. "Am I a ghost that you scream and stop your weeping to stare? Or am I just hatefully ugly? Pray tell me, if so, and I shall leave you."

Ugly? She stared all the more, still speechless. *No, he is the fairest man I have ever looked upon!* "No, no," she said stupidly.

"Then what?" He frowned but then seemed embarrassed. His eyes sought something else, and he pointed to the pocket that was now stretching the cloth of her gown. "What—is this? Don't you know 'tis too heavy a thing for such fine stuff as your dress?"

She found herself smiling at his carefulness. "Aye, but see what it is." And she pulled out Culpeper's *Herbal.*

His face changed. The laughing youth became the ardent lover. "So you do read it?"

"Read it?" Her voice was steady now but faint. "I read it daily. 'Tis never far from me, and I know it well." She was answering unthinkingly now, her tongue moving without command while her mind sifted the questions. *Why had he come?* "Sir, how did you find me?"

He pushed his hands inside his jerkin with a slight swagger that she rather liked. "I asked thy father's maids." He shrugged, his eyes never leaving her face.

He had matured and grown more serious, but she could tell by his closely barbered hair that he was still a Parliament's man. How could she tell him directly that she was glad to see him? Absently she noticed that the poplars had already dropped a few triangular yellow leaves at her feet. How could she tell him—? She raised her eyes.

He was still watching her.

Her heart began to hammer loudly, and her voice sounded cracked. "Why have you come?"

He did not answer with his voice but with his hands, stretching them out. His hands were large but finely boned.

She stepped back a pace but was angry with herself for doing so. However, once it was done, how was she to step forward again? "My father sent for your uncle and his wife, but not for you, did he not?" she blurted at last.

His hands returned to his jerkin but with slightly less assurance now. He breathed a heavy sigh. "Aye, but Isaac had need of me. And so, I think, Anna Tolhurst, do you." He looked at her so piercingly now that she began to tremble. "But I do speak out of turn, I fear," he went on. Moving away, he leaned against the tree nearest the one where she had been sitting. "For I hear you have another sweetheart. Perhaps I was mistaken, but I thought you had understood—"

"Understood what?" she begged. His bitter tone was unfamiliar.

"Never mind it . . . but is't true? If 'tis, I should go away and trouble you not."

She sank down on the grass beside him on her knees. "Nay, I'm sorry, Nicholas. Do not say so. I do not have a sweetheart." She shook her head, now as earnest as he. "But I am betrothed. My father—" She averted her eyes. "My father arranged it because he and my mother. . . ." She could not say the words *had no son.* He would misunderstand her now. But the mention of her mother was her undoing, and she began to cry again.

"Then heaven forgive me." He bent toward her as if to raise her up. "May I not kiss thee, then, as a farewell?"

She did not think of hiding the tears this time. Let him think what he would! But she could not betray her family by letting him kiss her. She scrambled up quickly and brushed the dead leaves off her skirt. "No . . ." she said sadly. "No, I think not." She made herself walk away.

His voice followed her, an edge of desperation in it. "Then I should never think of thee more as a sweetheart?" He spread his hands, and all the remaining bravado had gone out of his voice and face. "I do not know if I can bear that."

The words cut into her. She turned. "Your mind is free, Nicholas; your heart is free to think as you like."

"And so is thine, Anna."

"Then we shall be thinking the same," she said softly.

Up in the courtyard the spaniel began to bark, and Charlotte's loud voice called imperiously across the gardens. "Where *is* she, Henrietta? Dost know? *Anna!*"

Her sisters were evidently out-of-doors at last. She did not want to be found with Nicholas. "I must go now," she said quickly, turning away again.

He reached her before she knew it. In the cushioned grass under the trees his footfalls made no noise, and he caught up with her before she had taken five steps. Seizing her shoulders, he pulled her gently round to face him, so that her eyes were level with his chin but only a few inches away. "Don't leave me like that, sweetheart. I beg thee."

She tried to pull away, but it was a half-hearted attempt, and he knew it.

"Thy sisters—aye, I know," he said softly. "That's what thou'rt fretting about."

She moved her shoulders slightly and looked straight into his eyes, seeing her own reflection in the dark pupils. He seemed to take her into himself, all of her, as she wanted to take him to herself.

Neither of them spoke for several moments. Then he let her shoulders go and slid one hand round her back and with his other hand lifted her chin.

Is it so easy? she wondered, if there were time for wondering. *It's just as I thought of him.* She leaned toward him, slowly allowing him to draw her forward, slowly letting her mouth go up to his. Then he was kissing her, and she was engulfed in the tide of her own blood as it rushed to her face and sent her heart hammering again. Her knees weakened. He smoothed her back with his hand and pressed close against her until she felt they had become one being.

But then she awoke. The excited barks of the spaniel came nearer, and behind the dog, her sisters.

She fought free of him, fear overcoming passion. "I *must* go now, love."

"Aye, go. But I shall see thee again. Rebecca is to stay awhile." His voice sounded strangely calm to her own frantic mind.

The spaniel suddenly leaped onto her skirts. She was strung so tight that she struck the dog down with a shout of anger. "Away, foolish dog!"

The spaniel dropped its tail and cowered in the grass. Nicholas reached down to stroke the animal, apparently glad of the diversion. His face was flushed.

Anna cringed at the sound of her own rage. She walked forward to face the inevitable Charlotte, but although her back was now turned to Nicholas again, she was as aware of his hard, warm body against her own as if he still held her. No daydreams, these, and her heart sang out. She was loved by— and loved—this man of Kent.

Goudhurst, October 1658

George

This morning Elizabeth had not spoken distinctly to him. She seemed able to hear him clearly enough, but her speech slurred, and she drifted in and out of a deep sleep. It wasn't an easy sleep, but something heavy and drugged, as if the midwife had mixed too strong a syrup of poppy seeds for her. When she did awaken, it was usually only to loll about clumsily on the bolster. She had ceased asking for little Edward now, too; her mind seemed shadowed and confused. A few days earlier she had asked faintly for Charlotte, and he had sent for her, only to watch the poor child sent away again. *"Nay! That's not my baby! 'Tis a full-grown wench. Bring me my baby!"*

But her weeping entreaties had stopped the same day, and she seemed to have forgotten not only about baby Edward—who was now safely feeding in Rebecca's arms at the other end of the house—but also about their daughters. She wandered in and out of her childhood: one day she was a girl again, and the next day Livesey's men were sacking Tolhurst Court. And every day the blood flowed on, a thin, scarlet nightmare. Her life was seeping away.

He realized as he watched at her bedside that he had relied on her even more than he knew: her cool judgment, her quick mind, her ability to see to the heart of their trials. And now she was leaving him, slipping away as surely as the poplars were losing their leaves. Now he would have to decide everything, solve everything, dispose everything. He bowed his head. *I am too old to do these things without her.*

Then there was the matter of Anna's marriage. He would have to get the banns called. Yet, was there need for haste? He had Edward now, and—he smiled to himself—Edward was growing apace. The estate, what was left of it, would not have to be settled upon Anna. He must go to Chancery and change his will. Anna would marry well, certainly, but it was Edward who would come into the estate: a son, not a daughter.

He turned his eyes again on his wife's white face. Her eyes were closed and her breathing shallow. *How could he think of Edward, Anna, Frittenden, and the estate at such a time?* A choking sensation blocked his throat, and he was furious, suddenly, with the demands of death. *How could his own heart keep beating while her blood was trickling from her body?*

He moved the linens aside tenderly, willing the blood to be an illusion, an evil from which he might escape. But no. The same hideously familiar stain of fresh blood. *God's wounds! Would nothing assuage it?*

He pushed the covers back in place so roughly that Elizabeth's eyes opened. She made the words *Dear love* with her lips, then slept again. He cried out in despair and leaned his head against her. Though he could feel her ribs, she was still warm. *Dear God in heaven, let her live. Let her live.*

Unbidden, William Frittenden's face returned to his mind. If Elizabeth died, Anna would be beside herself with sorrow. Even when a horse or puppy died she grieved bitterly. But for her mother? Yes, she needed a man to comfort her.

Frittenden was courteous and well bred. He played the lute and viol charmingly and attired himself in the satins and lace of Cromwell's sons-in-law, now (curiously) the fashion again. Such refinements struck George as somewhat frivolous, but Frittenden was good humored and well-to-do. *Needs must,* he thought to himself. *And Anna must.*

Had he said it aloud? No one stirred. He kept his head where it was, still feeling the warm bed linens against his brow, and he thought of Anna. Somewhere in his mind a faint warning wriggled like a maggot on a hop bine. *What was it?*

Anna did not want Frittenden. Perhaps she wanted someone else. But whom? He could not remember.

His mind strayed back to Edward again, curled in Rebecca's arms, and to Rebecca herself, growing plump on the sweetmeats and fruits of a countryman's autumn table, the rest from the demands of her own family. Edward had smiled at him today—or was it yesterday? Puzzled blue eyes clearing into a beatific twinkle, and the little mouth pursing, trembling into a gummy smile, then a chuckle. Edward. . . . But there was a shadow standing behind Rebecca, falling over the face of his child.

Nicholas Fessenden. He did not like the youth and wished Isaac had not left him with Rebecca. Though like his uncle to look upon, Nicholas was too saturnine by half, glowering at him, serious like his father Robert—not to be trusted. He would send for Isaac to fetch him home. No, he did not need to. Nicholas could quite well go home by himself.

"Oh, George—"

His head went up and he shook it, trying to think. Had he been dreaming?

Elizabeth's eyes were open wide now. She was straining forward. Quite clearly, she said, "The butterfly is on her hair. See it?"

He frowned, afraid now. "Yes," he murmured, not understanding at all. Any words to comfort her.

"It will fly away."

He squeezed her hand hard, nodding dumbly as she shut her eyes again.

Nicholas

Make thyself useful, Isaac had instructed him. But how?

He sat thoughtfully in the cramped room above the stables that he was sharing with one of the servants. That in itself did not trouble him; he had never slept alone since he was a child, and he was used to low ceilings and crowded spaces. Yet his aunt was housed in comfort. She was his only tie with home—or what he called home—but he could not see her. Nancy took meals to her in the nursery, he found out, and Rebecca either did not or could not ask to see him. He felt shut out, neglected. Tolhurst, courteous as long as Isaac had remained, had withdrawn, and spoke churlishly to him now.

Worse still, he had scarcely seen Anna since that first day out under the trees. He had no idea what she might be thinking or feeling, no idea how to find or approach her. From time to time the servants at table in the hall spoke of her and of Frittenden, her betrothed, but they were disinterested, and all the talk was of the mother, who was dying now. They did not speak of Rebecca, but he guessed she had won favor, for everyone said how fat and healthy the new babe was growing.

Anna he saw only in the distance, as she walked with her younger sisters, or occasionally at the high table at the end of the hall when the family took their meals with the servants. But she seemed as distant as a princess, and he dared not go to her.

Tolhurst's servants stolidly refused all offers of help, so Nicholas felt impotent as well as lonely. For the first few days he had perused the

Tolhurst library, though there was little to his taste. If it weren't for Anna, he would gladly have gone home.

Following his thoughts down one path and then another, he at last decided he would risk trying to talk with Anna again. But whom could he trust? *No one.* All the servants stood steadfastly with their master.

He jumped up with sudden resolve. Finding a quill and inkhorn, he wrote carefully:

My Aunt Rebecca,

I wish to go home, for I can do no good here. But first, I pray you, will you speak to Mistress Anna on my behalf? As you have ever loved mine uncle, so do I love this lady.

He set down the pen, and ink splattered everywhere. Despair seized him. *Rebecca cannot read!* And moreover, if she could, whatever could she say to Anna that he could not say quite as well himself? No, it was a foolish idea to put a note in the basket of food Nancy carried to Rebecca from the hall. An utterly childish thought! He must find some other means to put a stop to fantasy and vain hope.

He banged the chamber door behind him and clattered down the wooden stairs to the stable yard. Edmund, the fellow who had ridden to Maidstone with the plea for Isaac's help, was raking muck out of the stable and shoveling it into a cart.

Nicholas hesitated. "May I not help thee, Edmund?" He judged the fellow to be about ten years his senior. Throughout the week, Edmund had been sullen and resentful of him.

He kept shoveling now, grunting with the effort, not looking up. "Aye, there's a shovel back of the manger." It was the most friendly word he had given so far.

They worked side by side. Nicholas was unaccustomed to such drudgery and soon felt his back aching and his arms trembling, but he went on, his teeth clenched in resolve. He would not be the first to give up.

"Thou'rt a good worker, Master Fessenden," Edmund said at last. His face was streaked with sweat and muck, but he was grinning, and Nicholas knew he'd gained an ally.

He nodded breathlessly. "And you—you're a Hercules."

Edmund looked back blankly. "What?"

"Thou'rt as strong as can be. That's what I meant. And quick, too."

Now Edmund looked embarrassed. "Well-a-day, so art thou." He seemed to be sizing him up. "How should you like to take the master's mare out in my stead? I was late rising this morn and am behindhand in my work. No 'arm'll come; she's gentle as a lamb but wants her head, and thou'rt a man good with horses, so I've heard."

The length of this speech, as well as the content, took Nicholas completely by surprise. "I don't know who told thee tales of me. I doubt they spoke the truth." He frowned. "Would you not let me do your work here while you take the mare yourself?"

"Not I! Matthew would have me in the stocks for't."

"Nay!"

"He would, though." Edmund stepped into the stable and came out with a bridle. "Here, you've been looking peaky. A ride will be the thing. Take it."

"But if I damage the mare?"

"You shan't."

Nicholas straightened his back. "No, I shan't." He looked back into the stable. "But what horse is that?" An unfamiliar animal was stalled there, and he heard the steady grinding of the horse's jaws and the rustle of hay.

"Oh, that? 'Tis young William Frittenden's beast. He's here acourtin' our lady Anna."

Something snapped in Nicholas's mind. He turned angrily. *Would Anna betray him? No,* reason argued. *No, for she as good as said she loves me.* He tightened his fists. *The lass is straitened by her father's wishes. Poor Anna!* Still, the thought of Frittenden's presence at Tolhurst Court made him desperate with jealousy.

He flung himself onto the horse's back so violently that she started, and Edmund shouted a warning. But now Nicholas needed a gallop as much as the horse did.

Within a few minutes he was out in the lane with the breeze in his face and the strong legs of the mare striding under him. He held her hard at first—she should know who was master—for he knew she was accustomed to a heavier weight on her back and might be skittish. At the gate he turned her away from the village and rode southeast along the lane.

He was reminded for a moment of errands for his father round Chilham, and of errands his father had done for his grandfather before that. And where was the Fessenden clan now? Poor or dead. And where was he going? He knew not where. And what if, please God, Anna were free to wed him, how could he support a wife? How indeed! He was not even apprenticed, and now that Adam was of age and Charlie almost so, and both had sweethearts already, they would soon want their cousins out of the shop and out of the house.

The mare started at the sound of a squirrel chattering in the chestnut tree. Several nuts descended in front of them, and she shied. "Go then!" he cried, loosening the reins. The mare began to pant with excitement, and her hooves thudded and thundered below. They set off at a gallop.

It was then that he knew what he must do. With the whole blue Weald spreading out before him under the faint mist of autumn, he knew what he must do.

He bent forward, gathered the reins closer, and laid his face to one side of the rising, falling, straining neck of the horse. The wind in his face and the flying strands of mane almost forced his eyes shut, but through the cracks between his eyelids he could see the windmills of Cranbrook in the distance, and he kept his eyes on them.

Cranbrook, Goudhurst, Maidstone, Chilham—all he had known as a boy and as a young man must be left behind. He would take his brother Josiah and go to the New World. If they worked for their Uncle John, who wanted sons, he would have the means to send for Anna and to provide for her in the Bay Colony. Would she come? Could she leave her betrothed?

He turned the horse before reaching Cranbrook. Now that he had made up his mind what he wanted, he felt hopeful and carefree. If he could show himself worthy to Anna's father, all might be well, after all. He must simply give his heart's desire into God's hands and let it rest there.

He clattered into the stable yard and threw the reins over the mare's head as he slid off. She was lathered and trembling. In the stable he rubbed her down, covered her with a cloth, filled her manger with hay, and went to look for Edmund.

The place was deserted. He called up the stairs to the loft, and he called across the gardens. Edmund did not answer. There was no sound but the calling of the doves and pigeons and the wind in the poplars.

He rushed across the kitchen gardens, his eyes cast down so that he would not miss his footing on the courtyard steps. He saw the hem of her dress barely in time to avoid hurtling into her. *Anna.*

"Nicholas!"

He stood only a step or two below her. For a moment he forgot entirely about Frittenden. "Oh, my dearest girl—" His arms went straight out to her.

She drew back. "Oh, no, thou canst not come nigh me. William is here. I should be—"

He looked properly at her face for the first time. It was red and swollen with weeping again. He backed away. She would never be his. His hands dropped to his sides, empty. "Forgive me. I had forgot."

"No, you don't understand. He is hateful and jealous. I have told him to go, but he will not. He badgers and pets me till I am beside myself, and my father encourages him. So I bade him go—" she said again. "But since he will not, I have left him standing."

He reached up hesitantly and touched her cheek. "There are always tears here, Anna. It isn't right."

She wiped her face with a kerchief, and her voice was bitter. "Those tears are not for William, for I despise him!" Her face crumpled, and she covered it with the kerchief.

"Anna, can we go aside? We shall be seen, and I would comfort thee, love." Tenderness overcame him, and he took her free hand and led her back among the cherry trees. She was weeping loudly, trying to catch her breath. Behind a clump of hazel bushes he put his arms round her.

"I was looking for thee," she began. "I could not bear to stay in the house more."

It did not matter now that he stank of the stable or that her face was distorted and raw. *She has looked for me!* "Did he hurt thee?"

Her head tossed up. "Aye, this morning, early, he did." Her face reddened. "Pinched my arm and . . . and put his hand—" She stopped.

His rage returned. "I'll make him cry mercy if he—"

"No, Nicholas!" Her voice was steadier now. "He'll not be touching me again. 'Tis not that man makes we weep so. My mother . . . my mother . . ." Her head sank onto his shoulder.

A crowd of questions clamored in his head. She had died? And how was he to console her when he knew not how men and women of the King's party consoled themselves in time of grief? But then he ceased trying to unravel the tangle. His love for her swept everything else aside, and he tightened his arms round her again.

"Thy mother?" he whispered, his mouth beside her ear.

She did not need to answer; the renewed sobs told him.

"Then God will comfort thee, dear Anna. And so shall I. Come." He stroked the hair from her forehead and lifted her face to his. He was surprised to see a slow smile breaking in her eyes. "What?"

"Aye, I grieve for my mother." She was struggling between tears and joy.

"Sorely, as you should."

"But there is one good—one good come of it—God forgive me for thinking so, for my father will not."

He was puzzled by the change in her. "What, then?"

"I shall be able to give the nay to William now. We shall be in mourning, all of us, and 'tis not decent—Nicholas, thou wilt abide here?"

He was bewildered and half laughed, "As long as thy father suffers me, and as long as my aunt—"

"Rebecca has no need of thee. My father has told me he likes thee not, but will you stay?"

He looked down, misery descending like a shroud. "How can I?"

"Your aunt Rebecca, I've heard her say you have kin hereabouts." The high color returned to her face.

"Dear, sweet Anna, yes . . . but . . ."

She was reaching toward him this time, and the tears had started again. "Pray, I beg thee, do not go! But oh, I am wicked to be thinking thus when my mother lies above stairs, dead."

Groaning, he bent and pressed his mouth slowly and gently against hers. For a few moments they clung to each other, then sank down among the yellow hazel leaves. He did not let her go but raised her so that she lay against his chest, out of the damp grass, with her face now against his neck. "I love thee . . . Anna . . . as I never thought . . . to love any woman on earth." The words came out in breathless fragments between kisses. "I want thee . . . for my only love . . . my wife . . . though I know I am not worthy."

"Oh, but you are worthy," she said hotly. "Every bit and more worthy than . . . than . . . and I do love thee in return."

He laughed to hear her indignation and began to kiss her again. They lost all account of time, knowing only kissing, comforting, and each other's warmth.

When he first became aware again, a flock of pigeons was whirring up in fright, a dog was barking.

Anna's father stood over them, his face mottled with anger. He reached down and grabbed Anna by the arm. "Get up, you slut! So this is why you've played so coy with William, is it?" He pushed her away from him so that she staggered backward against a cherry tree and stood there panting.

Then he went for Nicholas. The first blow fell on his cheek. "Get up! Lollygagging with my oldest girl when her mother's scarcely cold, would you?" Tolhurst struck him again as he was rising.

Nicholas lifted his hands to defend himself, but Anna had begun to scream, and shame suddenly struck him harder than any man could.

He fell to his knees. "Mercy, sir," he said. His body stiffened, ready for the next blow, but it did not come.

Tolhurst went to his daughter. "Anna, sweet, pray come in with me, do." His voice was conciliatory, wheedling, and Nicholas hated him.

Tolhurst picked up his daughter, then turned to Nicholas. "You'll be gone by morning. I count your uncle my friend, and you even bear his likeness in your face, but you have brought disgrace on him. Trouble not my mourning household, nor my daughter, or you shall pay dearly."

Anna was struggling in her father's arms. "No!" she cried. "No, my father. 'Tis *I* will pay dearly." She was distraught now.

Tolhurst set her down and shook her. "And so you shall if you ever come nigh this lad again. Come with me."

A dangerous look came into her eyes. "If you command it. But I swear to you upon my soul that I shall never, never wed William." She broke free and ran away through the trees, but her voice floated back. "You have your son, now, remember."

The last glimpse Nicholas had of her was the gleam of her red hair among the yellow leaves. He passed Tolhurst without a look and walked back to the stable yard. Bright sunshine washed down over his head, but he was mired in the blackness of despair.

Goudhurst, December 1658

Isaac

Isaac had sat in the great hall of Tolhurst Court before now and had not felt awed by it, but this time it seemed different. The harvest had been good, his friend was prospering again after the long years of scarcity, and with Rebecca's continuing care young Edward thrived. Yet the man sitting opposite him by the fire was old and unhappy. Blessed with harvest, house, a son, and lovely daughters, he nevertheless lacked the one thing Isaac had: a wife.

Although a fire roared in the chimney and the bells of St. Mary's pealed in celebration of Christmass Eve, the room lacked both warmth and music. Outside the leaded window the sky hung dour and gray over the bare hills. Isaac shivered and drew his stool nearer the blaze.

George, however, did not move. With his head bowed and his back bent, he cradled a mug of sack in his hand. From Isaac's place on the other side of the mantel, he could see the top of Tolhurst's head; it was almost half bald, threaded with white. Isaac watched him and shared his dull pain.

Part of him wanted to see George as Nicholas had appraised him: bitter, obdurate, jealous of his daughters. He could understand Nicholas's view, but he had known George too long to see him as anyone but the gentle, unassuming squire of Goudhurst—now broken by grief. And if his own wife had not already given three months to the babe Edward (and promised another year, at least, until the child was weaned), he would have felt as if he had betrayed his friend. He would never completely comprehend the conflict between George and Nicholas.

At last George's voice came, muffled by the loose jerkin against which his head had sunk. "I suppose I'm sorry for the lad—a mite."

"Then—?"

"No, Isaac," George mumbled, still not looking up. "Come now, Master

Tailor. How well does silk do, sewn together with frieze?" His hand moved idly to the coarse stuff of his jerkin. "Shall the silk not tear?"

"Aye, thou know'st it will," Isaac conceded cautiously. "But you do Nicholas an injustice. He is no rough village simpleton. He has more book learning than your village priests had, I shouldn't wonder, before Old Noll threw 'em out."

"He's his father's boy: a Roundhead."

Isaac leaned forward and sipped from his mug of sack. It was no use saying, *Sit up, George Tolhurst, and harken to me,* for he would not. Yet Isaac wished the older man would at least meet his eyes. "George, yes, he's a Roundhead—if that means aught these days. Half the Roundheads are turned Cavalier, and this-way-that-way. I couldn't keep Nicholas in my house, or his brother, were they canting brethren of the kind you—we both—hate. He's but a lad."

"Aye, an unformed lad." George's voice sounded dry and unconvinced.

"Young as I was when I met Rebecca. Young as my brother John was with Jane—whom you never met."

George looked up at last. "Nay, 'tis not his age that I oppose, nor even, in truth, his politics. And were he thine own son, Isaac, I'd give her gladly to him." He drank deeply of the sack and stared at the floor beams again.

Isaac felt his throat tighten, and his next words came out choked with emotion. "He's not mine own, but never was a lad closer to me than Nicholas—and dearer than either of my own two sons—though I would never confess it to anyone."

George shook his head. "Thy brain is addled by the sack I gave thee."

"Nay, I speak the truth."

"But he was your *brother's* son, he that betrayed thee, betrayed Rebecca. The one I saw and never will forget that first day of May. He was a—"

Isaac held up his hand. "I know what he was, well enough." He dropped his voice. "But I was his murderer. Thou sit'st with a murderer, George."

A tiny smile flickered round George's cracked lips. "Nay, I sit with an honest gentleman."

Isaac half laughed. "A yeoman. A tailor. Phaw! Away with all the flattery." He laid his broad hands palms down on his knees and studied them. "George, I beg you, as you love your daughter, let her come to him! If 'tis a matter of money—"

"No! 'Tis *not* a matter of money. 'Tis his father, as I said. She's my eldest daughter, and though he's your eldest and dearest nephew, she shall *not* come to him." He stood up, but his body shook, and he had to lean on the mantel for support. "This is my last word on't, Isaac. Say no more, I pray thee. Come, thy wife is languishing for thee, I've no doubt." His voice softened. "Go and see her. An old man needs his solitude by the fire."

Isaac stood, facing George. Neither man spoke for several moments. Then Isaac put out his hand to George's shoulder. "Bless thee, good squire," he said.

He went out through the arched doorway to the hall and to the door of the parlor, where he knew the womenfolk were sitting, for he could hear their voices. He recognized one from among the others: low, musical, full of joy, very like her mother's.

"Oh, Edward! What a poppet! Rebecca, let me have him a while, pray." That was Anna.

Then Rebecca's voice—soft, more fluting: "Pray, do, mistress. I believe I heard the cart but a few minutes ago. Isaac may be here to see me." She would be blushing.

All the girls laughed softly. Then the door came open and closed again just as he approached to knock. Rebecca hesitated on the threshold, then flew into his arms. He held her, rocking her to and fro. "My dear love. Oh, how I have longed for thee."

"Come, then," she whispered.

And he led her above stairs to the small, warm room they had given her beside the nursery, where a cradle, now empty, stood beside the bed.

Maidstone and Chatham, 1659

Nicholas

Nicholas had never doubted that he would see Anna again, but he thought that God must have another design for his life. When Isaac had finished speaking with him, he went out into the back of the inn where the Fessenden donkey was stabled, and he spent an hour furiously combing and brushing the animal's coat. All the while it stood patiently still, eyes glazing and mouth slavering with delight at all the attention. At the end he thumped it on the rump, bolted the stall, and went back home as if nothing had changed.

But everything had changed.

In the summer, Isaac had advised, he should set sail with Josiah for the Bay Colony—but without Anna. As Isaac had told him Tolhurst's words, his soft brown eyes sad with sympathy, he had urged Nicholas not to give up hope.

"If she loves thee, as you say, then it will not be for naught. Set yourself up with brother John and see if Anna's father doesn't relent when he hears how great a merchant you've become."

But words like these did not comfort him at all. What if their ship were blown off course by an early gale and he never reached Boston Harbor? What if John fell ill and could not teach his trade to him? What if—?

But a soft inner voice calmed him. *"Trust also in him; and he shall bring it to pass"* . . . *"This is the way, walk ye in it."* He must simply abandon himself, and Anna as well, to the Providence of God.

In this way Nicholas went on stolidly with preparations for the voyage. Everything took longer and cost more than expected, and in the end they were delayed in their departure until early autumn, as he and Josiah had to find journeymen's labor to pay their way. He thought and dreamed of Anna often, but she was usually in the back of his mind: a lovely room to sit in or scene to contemplate when he had moments alone.

Rebecca ended her service in Goudhurst upon baby Edward's first birthday, and one of George's servants carried her home to Maidstone in the coach. The little boy was fat and cheery and had weaned himself, she said. Rebecca now glowed with health, and Isaac, in reflection of her, seemed renewed also. In payment for her nursing, the whole family now ate well and had goods in store.

Nicholas pressed her for news of Anna. She would give little.

"Is she wed?"

"Nay, indeed not!" Rebecca laughed.

"Betrothed, then?"

"I hear she is."

"To the same man as before?" His teeth clenched as he thought of it. "And does she know I go to the New World and would take her there?"

"Truly, Nicholas, thou must not set thy heart on her, love."

Sighing, he left her to her sewing. After that, he had wrestled with God until he found a measure of peace again.

They were to sail from Chatham. Isaac would make a festival day of it: his cousins, Hannah, and all of Isaac's family would journey over Boxley Hill to the docks, Isaac said, and see the great ship sail in full furl down the estuary. Only Mary, too old now to make such a journey, would stay behind to mind the shop.

Josiah, filled with excitement, babbled and laughed all the way. For Nicholas, there was only a dull ache about the parting, and an increasing, deadening certainty that he would never see Anna again. This he tried to push from his heart as the family made the slow journey northward. Hannah, Rebecca, and Isaac rode in the creaking cart with their bundles of clothes and a small hamper of books. Adam, Charlie, and Josiah strode close behind.

Nicholas walked at the donkey's head exchanging an occasional word with his uncle and an occasional glance with Hannah, whose soft eyes brimmed with understanding. But most of the way he kept a loose hold of the bridle, stared at the chalky road under their feet, and thought bitterly of the man who opposed his dearest wish.

They passed under the tangled trees and over the peaty ground of Boxley Woods, then emerged again at the top of the hill into open farmland. After the dim early-morning light under the trees, the mist rising over the napped stubble of the golden fields was almost unbearably white. But then a breeze sprang up, and the fog blew away.

The donkey pricked its ears and quickened pace, and Isaac and Rebecca began to sing an old sheep-shearing ballad:

> *We'll pipe and we'll sing, love*
> *We'll dance in a ring, love,*
> *When each lad takes his lass*
> *All on the green grass,*
> *And it's oh—to plow,*
> *When the fat oxen graze low,*
> *And the lads and their lasses*
> *Do sheepshearing go.*

Their voices—hers sweet and high, his deep and somewhat out of tune—were merry in spite of the song's sad cadences, and Nicholas turned briefly to look at them.

Isaac: forty-five now, and in the peak of his strength, not a gray hair among the black curls, his eyes bright, his face broad and honest. Ah, no wonder everyone loved him!

Rebecca: diminutive beside him, yet with a strength of her own since she had nursed little Edward Tolhurst; her cheeks glowed pink in the freshening wind. Again, no wonder she was loved! Even on the verge of becoming an old woman by many people's reckoning, she was still lovely.

And yet—he checked himself gently—Rebecca had been the daughter of a fiery preacher, so he had heard, and here she was singing pagan songs!

What was it, then, about both his uncle and his aunt that he loved so much? They acknowledged God, though not in his parents' ways. They helped each other and gave to others: to Tolhurst, to Nicholas himself, to Josiah, to Hannah, to Grandmother Mary . . . though not as the godly folk would have done it.

Unaware, he stopped on the track. The donkey tossed impatiently and wrenched its head from his grasp. Surprised, he walked on. *Not as the godly folk would have done it. . . .*

His mother's face came before him: her carefulness over detail, her insistence on obedience, however harsh, her watchfulness over the family purse. Was there perhaps a lack of generosity in her? If so, he had never knowingly thought that way about her.

He threw another look over his shoulder at his uncle. That was it! Isaac had always reminded him in his stature of a Goliath, but in his nature of a David: dignified, almost kingly, but with the spontaneous gaiety and generosity of spirit of the David who had danced his way into Jerusalem. He was indeed a king of Kent—lordly but lowly, poor but giving all he had.

Nicholas turned his face back to the north. Yes, Isaac was a good man. Would John, the elderly uncle he had never seen, be as kind?

They passed down through Canny Fields and uphill into Rome Lane, which was flanked by more farms and a few cottages, until at last they reached the near end of the High Street, marked by the Little Crown Inn. A farmer driving sheep and cows to the public stocks blocked their way, so they moved more slowly now. Nicholas could see over the crowded heads of the bleating sheep and the plodding cattle to the posting-house. A tide-coach stood outside ready for its journey, and the High Street bustled with prosperity.

Chatham was foreign to Nicholas. Neither a mannerly Wealden village with the grace and beauty of Chilham or Goudhurst, nor the busy, bricked marketplace of Maidstone, spacious and established. It was something quite different—a naval town just come up from a wattle-hut village: noisy, squalid, in the making as a place of shipbuilding. Shops for carpenters, ropemakers, and ironsmiths lined the thoroughfare. Everywhere hammers clanged on anvils. The smell of hot tar hung in the air. Chatham, some said, provided such safe anchorage that it might one day be more useful to their naval vessels than London.

Looking round as they continued along the High Street, he doubted it.

Not that he had seen London yet, nor ever would if he went to the other side of the ocean, but Chatham seemed like a groveling, sniveling serving man. In the New World, so he had heard and read, there was freedom and space. But here, even where their supposed hope for the future lay in daring naval enterprise, he saw only an old world of dirt and degradation. Aye, it was just as well he planned to leave England.

He smiled quietly to himself, then laughed aloud. *A groveling, sniveling serving man!* What a fantasy! What a foolish, proud conceit! He had read too much of Tolhurst's Cavalier poetry broadsides, perhaps, to be thinking in that way of a town he did not know.

"Beyond that church yonder," Isaac called to him. "Follow down the hill. Hold the beast hard, now, Nicholas, as 'tis steep, thou'lt find."

Underfoot, the cobbles became more slippery and uneven, and strange smells, rank and putrid, oozed up from the gutters and the docks. He had to look down to see where he was stepping to avoid leading the donkey into the slimy ditches on either side of the street. Their progress slowed still more.

"Are you sure, Isaac, that you want that donkey down this-a-way?" Nicholas shouted back.

"Aye, go on, son," his uncle encouraged. "Adam, give thy cousin a hand. Charlie, Josiah, hold ye onto the cart lest we all tip out."

Rebecca's voice floated unhappily over all the commotion. "Could we not walk, love, and leave the cart at an hostelry?"

"Nay, we haven't enough to pay for such a thing, sweetheart, as thou should'st know." Isaac's reply sounded strained.

"Please," Hannah begged, "let me walk with my brother!"

Nicholas heard her voice and grieved for her. *Poor Hannah!* He wished she could go with them, but she would be safer with Isaac and Rebecca. He would miss her.

He signaled to Adam, and they steadied the donkey, waiting until Hannah, assisted by Charlie, had climbed down. Nicholas felt her small hand press into his free hand as she came to walk beside him.

"Thank you, Nicholas." She smiled faintly up at him.

"Thou'rt welcome, but won't you foul your petticoats?" He tugged the donkey forward again and noted with disgust a pair of dead rats in the gutter.

"Never mind if I do, silly."

He looked at her quizzically. Her voice sounded light, but though she made a brave face of it, he knew she was as sorry to part from him as he was to lose her.

"Hannah—?"

"What?" She turned her pale face upwards to search his.

He knew that he had sounded far too serious and that she was too young to bear the weight of his own sorrow. All the same, he knew she would understand. "Wilt'ou do something for me, Hannah?"

"I'll try. Yes, indeed, I shall do anything you ask." Her voice was pert, but unsteady.

He squeezed her hand. "If any word should come from Goudhurst . . . from the maid there that I love . . . you will find a way to send word, won't you, my sister?"

She returned his inquiring gaze with wide, frightened eyes. "But our uncle is to do that. You know I cannot write more than a word or two. Or Grandmother Mary shall send—"

"No, no!" He gave her hand a little shake. "Isaac and our grandame I can count on, but if anything should befall, can I count upon thee as well?" He spoke softly, his face close to his sister's so that Adam might not hear.

Hannah's eyelashes lowered. "You may, dear Nicholas." Her voice was wistful. "Ah, would that I had met this maid of thine!"

He warmed to their conversation, hardly noticing that the wharves and the sluggish waters of the Medway at ebb tide lay not far below them now. "Thou shalt meet her, Hannah, of a surety." He wished he could believe it, himself.

She pouted slightly. "But thou shalt never meet my sweetheart, I fear."

He threw back his head and chuckled. "Thine, little one?"

"Little one? Old, wise brother, I'm barely littler than thee."

"And big enough to have a dozen sweethearts. But somehow, pretty sister, I doubt—"

She sighed. "'Tis true. I do not have one."

"God has a husband for thee, Hannah."

She smiled shyly. "I hope he has."

"And a wife for me, too." He pictured the red hair among the hazel leaves and the face of the woman he had not seen for a year but had loved for three.

Isaac

The ship was laden already with provisions. She nevertheless rode high in the water, a stately vessel with four masts and seven sails, now furled, and pennants of gold fluttering from the mastheads. The brass cannons on the forecastle and main decks gleamed in the sunlight, and on the ship's prow the figure of a white horse leaped forward toward the mouth of the river. That horse would ride the waves all the way to Boston Harbor and into the Charles River of which Isaac's brother had written. She would carry Nicholas and Josiah away forever.

The master had rung the last bells, and the seamen were swarming on the ropes. The ship would sail as the tide rose. On the wharf Isaac and Rebecca put their arms round the two boys, wept over them, then bade them go.

Shouldering a hamper, while Josiah clutched their bundle, Nicholas looked over his left shoulder at the ship. "It will wait long enough for us to say a prayer together," he said in the calm voice Isaac loved and always associated with him.

Nicholas glanced at his sister, for Hannah was crying.

Isaac nudged Rebecca, and she put her arm round the girl. Then he took off his hat, feeling awkward, suddenly. "Go on, Adam, Charlie," he said uneasily.

His two sons bowed their heads and pulled off their hats.

Nicholas's voice came softly against the noise of whirring cables and clanging bells. "Father of heaven," he prayed, "we commend ourselves to Thee upon the deep. And we commend to Thee our beloved sister, Hannah, and our cousins Adam and Charles." His voice wavered now, thick with sorrow. "I pray Thee, keep my aunt and uncle and all their dear ones unto Thyself. . . ."

Isaac held his breath, his eyes shut. His nephew had stopped, as if he could say no more. He heard with surprise his own voice continuing for Nicholas, "And keep Thy servants Nicholas and Josiah safe. May Thine eye, Lord, be ever upon John and Jane also, and upon the maid Anna . . ." He hesitated. "And upon her father also."

"Amen," Josiah answered fervently.

"Amen," the others replied, more slowly.

Isaac straightened his back, donned his cap, and gripped Nicholas's shoulders for the last time. He felt hot, suddenly, with the heavy heat of early autumn hanging in the fetid dampness of the dockyards, and he longed to be on the open uplands again, away from Chatham and the stinking Medway. "Go now, nephews," he urged.

They stood watching as Nicholas and Josiah mounted the gangway. Wavelets slapped noisily against the gunwales as the tide began to flow. Above the ship a few gulls circled or dived for debris on the incoming water while the sails unfurled for the voyage. Josiah turned once to wave, but Nicholas never looked back.

Heavy-hearted, Isaac lifted Rebecca and Hannah into the cart again. He felt empty and sad without Nicholas to lead them back the way they had come, but he knew Hannah felt the loss even more deeply. As he settled Hannah into the cart, she seemed light as a bolt of muslin compared to his newly plump wife. Hannah's face was now bright pink as well as unhappy, and as she arranged her skirts, he caught sight of a small red welt on her ankle. He looked away quickly; she would be embarrassed if she found him looking at her ankles. Besides, she had complained of no discomfort.

Thinking no more of the women, he gave the reins to Adam, and with Charlie's help turned the donkey back uphill toward the church. It would be night before they reached home again, and hunger gnawed at his stomach. The bright day seemed suddenly forlorn and overcast. The shop would seem cheerless when they returned. The excitement of this festival day had all evaporated.

His back to the wharves, he saw no more of the fluttering pennants and leaping fair horse. Instead, everything they passed seemed foul. Chatham smelled and looked close and evil. The donkey's ears were laid back against its neck, and the poor beast was panting, its eyes bulging and its back wet with sweat.

"We must find a clean watering trough," he called back to Rebecca.

"I thought I did see a well by the church," she answered.

"Aye, I believe you are right. And I'm ahungered. Are ye not, too?" He could hear Hannah crying quietly in the cart, but he did not want to look back and shame her, so he kept his eyes on the church. "The lass is, for sure."

"I'm forgetting, Isaac," Rebecca said, "but I brought some apples, and Hannah baked some pasties for us all. Will it please thee stop?"

Isaac laughed, glad of her thoughtfulness. His head had been so full of Nicholas, Josiah, and Hannah's sorrow that he had not given a thought to food for the donkey, or even for himself. He wiped his upper lip and his cheeks with his sleeve. "Aye, but let's get to the church first."

At the top of the hill he cranked the iron handle of the churchyard pump. The water came in a fast, cold rush, and he filled the tankard he usually kept on his belt for a journey. They passed it round, gasping with pleasure and relief. He saw no need to use the well water; winching up the bucket would take more time than he wanted to spare at the moment.

In the short shadow of St. Mary's they sat still and ate the pasties. A few seamen swaggered past, eyed Rebecca and Hannah lasciviously, then noticed Isaac and glanced elsewhere. Though the sailors, reeking of tar, ale, and sweat, were hardly inconspicuous, the women did not even look up from their food.

A rat crept out from behind a tombstone, frisked its tail, and vanished into a hole. Another, or perhaps the same one, came out of the same hole a few moments later, crouched down, and dropped dead where it had just stood. Isaac shuddered. Chatham was indeed an unwholesome place.

"Come, dearlings," he said. "Let's away home now."

They set out along the street again and soon traveled the open air of the Downs farmlands.

Goudhurst, October 1659

Anna

Anna waited until the house was still and dark, then sat up with her arms round her knees and watched the moon rising slowly over the thin mist outside. No word had come from Nicholas in answer to the messages she had sent with Rebecca, but she knew without doubt that he still loved her.

If only I had gone to Maidstone with Rebecca, she thought over and over again, *I might have hidden without* . . . Without what? At this hour of night her thoughts were unformed and desperate. Surely Nicholas knew that they could not wait longer. William was arriving on the morrow to claim her; the year of mourning for her mother was over now by several weeks, and she could refuse her father no more.

She felt trapped. In the year since her mother had died, her father had become more and more a stranger. He wept openly for Elizabeth, ignored even her brother Edward, and spent most of his time out-of-doors with the laborers. It was harvest time, true, but he had become slovenly about the house and allowed his new steward to behave just as carelessly. He cared not if they brought dung, straw, and mud into the hall on their boots or if the spaniels leaped onto the table to eat the food off his trencher. Her father drank too much sack and snored shamelessly over the table. He made no pretense of keeping the Sabbath or praying in his private chapel. He had become a stranger—a crazed stranger—but a stranger with power over her future.

The night before, driven to despair, she had bowed to him and agreed he could ask the minister to arrange the marriage to William. He would not wait anymore, especially now that Henrietta and Charlotte both had wooers. He wanted to see her wed first, he had said on one of his clearer days, as was proper for a gentlewoman in the county. Her life was sealed up unless she could find an escape.

She saw no way but to flee to Nicholas. There was a risk in that, certainly, for his uncle was her father's friend. But surely Isaac was a merciful man and would spare her if she cast herself on his mercy and told him that her father was beside himself now? All she had heard of Isaac from Rebecca convinced her he would be kind.

She had laid her plans shrewdly, trusting no one. At first she had thought of asking help from Martha, one of the serving maids, or from Edmund, who had liked Nicholas. But she could neither take them with her nor leave them to face her father if he were crazed or in his cups. No, she had decided, it was better to fend for herself.

The previous night, soon after the discourse about William, she had lain awake as long as she had tonight. Then she had crept out of her chamber, down the back stairs, past the privy, and into the kitchen to where she knew her father had long ago hidden gold in an unused pot. All the way along the passage, down the stairs and back again, she had been frightened by the sound of her own breathing, by the creaking beams of the stairs, and tonight it was the same. Last night, nevertheless, she had achieved her errand; and she would tonight, as well.

Shivering, she took off her shift, poured water from the ewer that stood ready for the morning, splashed her face, and bound her hair tightly in an old kerchief of her mother's. In the glass that hung by the window, she caught a glimpse of her naked body, white and unreal by moonlight. *What if he does not want me as his wife?* In the dim light of her chamber, she felt her face grow hot. *What if I am deceived, and he does not even want me as his love? Should I make him a potion of mint and vinegar, or of onion and dog's mercury?* She shook her head sternly. No, such thoughts were devilish; she needed no false props. He loved her, wanted her as his wife, and would protect her. Still shivering, she pulled on her oldest petticoat, then hooked her bodice and dress.

In her bride chest she found a stout pair of pattens and a heavy cloak of her mother's. Then she took out the bundle of clothes and small bag of gold that she had hidden under the bed. Inside them she wrapped her prayer book, Culpeper's *Herbal*, and some scraps she had saved from the table. The gold she tied inside her dress where it could not be seen, all except a few smaller coins that she put in a little purse at her waist.

She stood still for a moment in the middle of the room that she, as the eldest, was entitled to keep to herself all her life. She had once loved the room's privacy and coziness. Now it felt like a prison, and she was not going to change one prison for another in the bed of William Frittenden. She shuddered. He was gracious, a skilled horseman, and he was wealthy. But his insipid smiles and elaborate courtesies left her cold. She would never be his wife—so she had vowed a year ago, and so she intended now.

A woman walking alone by day would attract attention, she had decided, and these bright nights lit by a full moon were clear and beautiful to walk in. She knew the way as far as Marden at least, and after that, she supposed, she might find a carter who would carry her farther north. It would not take her above a day to reach Maidstone.

She took a last glance in the glass. Her eyes were far too bright, dancing at her from her pale face. She would be safer, perhaps, if she streaked her face and hands with dust like a poor traveling woman going from one farm to another for the harvesting.

Outside, she wet her hands in the dewy grass, rubbed them with a little earth, and smeared her face. Then, pulling the cloak tightly round her, she trudged out of the gateway of Tolhurst Court and turned up the village street. She did not look back. No one passed her. An owl dropped silently out of the church tower and swooped past her into a grove of yellowing horse chestnuts. It came so close that she heard the whir of its feathers and felt the downrush from its wings.

In places the road led through coppices and under trees, where the moonlight shone feebly. In other places it dipped down into misty hollows and she had to take off her pattens to ford the stream in her path. But she walked on steadily, exulting every time the path led her uphill so that she could see the dark countryside spreading out before her under the wide sky.

Marden was hushed and shuttered, except in the tavern, where lights glared and the sound of revelry broke the air. She hurried past and on into the countryside. The land was more open beyond Marden: farms and apple orchards on either side, and clumps of chestnut, beech, and ash by the roadside. The soft breathing of cattle and the strong smell of sheep hung in the damp air.

She stole an apple from a tree near the road, then continued. Her spirits rose high as she thought of seeing Nicholas. Each time he entered her mind, her heart quickened and a smile came to her lips.

At a crossing in the road she hesitated, unsure of her way. There were milestones either side, but in the scarce light she could not read them. The moon was setting, the sky that peculiar shade of indigo that suggests dawn is not far off, and she wondered if she should wait to ask for the help of another traveler before going on. But she had seen no one and dared not cast herself on the first knave who passed. The night seemed darker now than before.

Noticing a gate in the hedgerow beside her, she climbed over it, careful not to tear her petticoats. In the field ahead, she could make out the vague outline of a small hut or shed, a shepherd's hut no doubt. She trod forward carefully, glad of the pattens in the wet grass, until she could see clearly the white weatherboards on the side of the hut. Even though its low roof had long ago collapsed on one side, it would afford shelter until daylight. It seemed deserted.

The hut stank of sheep dung and old, worm-eaten fleeces, but it was dry. When her eyes became accustomed to the gloom inside, she could see spindly grass pushing up here and there on the earth floor. A small creature scuttled across the floor to gather the crumbs from her loaf as she broke pieces off it. She felt dusty, dirty, and a little afraid, but by now she was too tired to dwell for long on how she felt. Wrapped in the cloak, and with her head on her bundle, she soon fell asleep.

As she awoke to the drenching of a broad beam of sunlight through the broken roof, one wall of the hut appeared to be wrenched off, and an old man's face peered in on her in surprise. She blinked in utter bewilderment.

"Well I never, maidy! Tut! Stir thyself, and get up out of my barn. Fie, shame on thee!" The man, apparently a shepherd, had broken teeth and a crabbed, leathery face.

Shocked into wakefulness, she pulled the cloak round her more securely and opened her mouth to scream.

"Fie! Out on thee!" the shepherd shouted angrily. Then his face softened. "I mean no harm," he said irritably. The wall swung wider now, and she saw it was not a wall after all, but another door. "And I trust you meant none, neither. In my barn, indeed."

She shut her mouth and expelled her breath loudly. The man was just a foolish shepherd, an old laborer like her father's man, Matthew. No wonder he was surprised to see her. Awkwardly she sat up. "Forgive me, sir, I did mean no harm. Tell me what o'clock is't?"

"Why, 'tis broad afternoon, lass."

Anna groaned and jumped up.

"What art thou? A lass or a lady? For you do speak like a lady."

"I—I'm a lady's maid, but I lost my way last night and came in here to bed." She bit her lip. *I have never lied before that I can remember,* she thought.

The shepherd put his hands on his hips and twisted his face grotesquely. "A likely tale, but never mind."

She pulled her things together, her mind whirling. *Barn* he had said, but surely this was only a hut? Should she offer to pay him for her night's lodging, or would that only arouse suspicion? And could it truly be the afternoon? She must be on the road quickly, or her father might come looking for her.

She came and stood beside him at the door, and he stepped aside for her. She blinked in amazement. The door led to a huge, dark-beamed barn that she had not even been able to see the night before. She recoiled at the same, strong smell of sheep. Her night's lodging had only been a lean-to on the side of the barn!

"Why dost start and stare so, maidy?" The shepherd laughed. "Ain't you never seen a shearing barn afore?"

Eager to be gone before she betrayed herself, Anna pulled up her hood and lowered her eyes. Perhaps the damage was done; he would have seen her face clearly as she was waking. But she had to do what she could. He must not remember her; she must not say anything out of the ordinary.

"Nay, I'm not from these parts," she muttered.

"Whither bound, then maidy? Haste, now, for I've a hundred sheep from the staple this very day to drive into my fold."

His tone betrayed pride in his purchase. "Aye, God speed to you, then. I did not mean to trespass. Can you show me the way to Maidstone?"

The shepherd looked curiously at her, then pointed up the lane. "That-a-way. Walk till you come to Linton. 'Tis not so far. And you'd best wash your face there, as you be a lady's maid, for you're fair besmirched from this place—not fitten for a lass of your breeding." He clicked his tongue indignantly. "What'd your father say if he saw you thus?"

Her heart leaped into her throat, and her head felt light for a moment. But looking at the old shepherd's face again, she could see that the question was fanciful. He did not know her father, of course, but was himself probably the father of daughters. The question required no answer in any event, and she scrambled over the gate and off down the path he had shown her.

By the time she reached Linton, hunger gripped her and the bundle felt heavier every step she took up the long Linton Hill. Carters, shepherds, and an occasional post messenger passed her, but all seemed to be going toward the coast, away from Maidstone. She decided to stop at the Bull Inn and buy a pennyworth of bread and ale as any other traveler might do.

No one paid her any attention first, and she kept her hood up deliberately. Sitting in the corner of the parlor, she listened to snatches of discourse to discover a fellow traveler who might bring her the rest of the way to the town. Though it was long past the noon hour and far too early for most country people to sup, the inn was crowded and noisy.

"'Tis them prisoners they've been sending down from the pesty Fleet in London, I reckon," one man said.

"Nay, 'tis those filthy soldiers from York, I warrant thee. They've brought 'un with 'em."

"It makes no sense . . . not since thirty years . . ."

"Nay, 'tis Maidstone itself."

"Aye, venomous, scurvy place it is."

Anna's heart contracted uneasily. What sedition was being planned here? Why would the men of Linton speak so harshly of their fellows in Maidstone? There was so much she did not understand! Never had she heard men talk this way of the town where Nicholas lived and where she had gone sometimes for the assizes with her father. She bit hard into the bread, kept her eyes down, and listened intently.

"Nay," a softer voice argued. "'Tis a fine market town, and the half o' ye never set foot in't! 'Tis Chatham that's to blame, and the whoreson seamen there."

"Chatham? Where's that?" jeered a fat man. "We've never heerd of Chatham." All the men laughed.

The soft-voiced man directed his words toward Anna's corner, suddenly, and she knew without looking up that she would have to answer. "Yon maiden there—she's heard of Chatham, I lay." The voice was wooing, smooth as silk, and she shrank inside.

"By name only," she murmured.

"What's that? Speak up, lass."

"By name only," she repeated.

"Pretty voice," he wheedled.

She did not look up.

"Let her alone, Martin," the innkeeper shouted. "What wert thou saying about Chatham, anyhow?"

The parlor became hushed. All Anna could hear was the sound of her own quiet chewing on the coarse bread that now tasted like wool to her, and the slurping of the men over their ale.

"'Tis where the plague's acome from," the man called Martin declared. "I'll wager any man."

"Can't prove it either way," another argued.

Anna barely heard what followed. *Plague! In Maidstone?* Fear clutched her round the neck. Grabbing her bundle, she rushed out of the low doorway and immediately retched in the road. Shaken, she sat on a stool by the door and tried to take slow, deep breaths. *Plague, plague . . .* The word clamored endlessly in her ears.

She saw someone standing beside her, a man with torn, dusty breeches. She would not look up but remained hunched over, waiting for doom to strike. It would be Martin, the man who had singled her out.

"What ails thee, lass? Abreeding, art thou?" The voice was different: rough, but not unkind. The man held out a tankard of cold water, his hand dusted with some fine, white stuff. Flour? Perhaps he was a baker. . . .

She took the water without sitting upright but kept her free hand firmly round her bundle. "Thank 'ee, no." She sipped, spat, and sipped again. The joy of the moonlight the night before had disappeared into the terror of harsh October daylight. She floundered between the hated world of her father in Goudhurst and the unfamiliar—now threatening—world of Nicholas in Maidstone.

"Thou'rt bound for Maidstone?"

She was not sure whether to answer.

"If you are, and you mind not the wares of a fuller's cart, I can take you there."

At last she looked up at the gray-haired speaker, his forehead lined, and his face drawn with pity for her. She nodded gratefully. "Aye, and I can pay you, too."

"No need for that. Come, let's be gone before the wolves come out." He gestured to the inn with his thumb, and she could not help smiling a little. "I have sacks to leave in Loose," he explained, "then on to Maidstone by tonight. Will it serve?"

They jolted along under the trees and up the lane to Loose. The fuller's donkey was slow and lazy, but the fuller himself was kind and companiona-ble. "Don't fret about the plague, lassie," he said when at last he set her down at the Market Cross. "Just mind where you stay and what you drink. You know where you're bound?"

She hesitated. Even this dear man might unwittingly betray her. Then she remembered where she had first met Nicholas. "Aye, to meet my master at the sign of the Cock." She hated lying to the fuller, but she could not trust anyone.

The fuller frowned, and she wondered if she had blundered. "Well, have a care, then, love."

She waved and turned away. Though she had been to Maidstone many times with her father as a child and knew her way quite well, she did not want to go where there might be pestilence, and she did not even know exactly where the Fessendens lived. She trod carefully but quickly. Darkness descended again, and a band of thick mist rose from the Medway. *Nicholas, I shall soon be with thee, Nicholas, love.*

A tall man with a muffled face banged heavily into her so that her bundle fell heavily to the road and split open like an overripe plum. She cried out indignantly, then something in his posture and voice struck her as familiar.

"Forgive me, ma'am. I moved in haste." He stopped to retrieve her belongings, then dropped them as if burned. "Oh, I cannot—"

She stared at him fearfully. "Whatever is the matter?" She now bent down herself to pull the bundle together again. The books were still safe, she saw with relief.

"'Tis the pestilence," he said, backing away. "All my womenfolk have the plague. Pray, forgive me."

She reeled as she heard the deep, clear voice. The words meant nothing to her. *Isaac. Isaac Fessenden. My father's friend. Nicholas's uncle. . . .* Trembling, she said aloud, "Sir, are you not Isaac, the tailor?"

He was still backing away. The cowl round his neck and face had slipped slightly, however, and she could see the man's dark, curling hair beneath. His likeness to Nicholas made her hungry with longing.

"What do you want of me?" She heard fear in his voice this time. He did not know her.

She pushed back her hood and shook out her hair so that he gasped in recognition. "I have come to see you, to find Nicholas," she said.

His hands went together as if he were begging for his life. "Oh, mistress, but you don't understand. Did you not hear what I said? You cannot bide in this place. My household is all shut up lest we spread the plague. I myself—" He lowered his voice, but it was ragged with emotion. "I myself should not be abroad, but I must fetch Doctor Cox or Doctor Bennet . . . Rebecca is so ill . . . you cannot bide here."

Her heart constricted with dread. "Oh, I had no notion!" Her hands flew to her mouth. "And Nicholas? Is he well or ill?"

Isaac's eyes glazed over with pain. "I pray you, let me go for this doctor. Spare me—"

She grabbed his sleeve, but he shook her off and started to run. Was he afraid to answer her? "Wait! I have gold. Will that fetch the surgeon faster?"

But he had left her standing, a gold coin held foolishly in her outstretched hand.

Swinging round, she looked helplessly for guidance and hope. She walked on, taking the way she knew: past the upper and lower court houses, past the Shambles—where the market was held—and down to the Rose and Crown Inn. Just behind the Rose and Crown stood another inn where her father had sometimes stayed during the assizes. The innkeeper there might remember her and tell her where to find the tailor's house. But as she dragged herself wearily to the tavern door, she became aware again of how dirty she was with mud and chalky fulling dust. The innkeeper would laugh if she said she was Anna Tolhurst.

She waited by the door, leaning against the door frame in utter exhaustion. A serving maid came out, eyed her coldly, and started to slam the door shut again when Anna pushed the gold coin into the girl's hand and closed her fingers on it. "Gold for thee," she said hurriedly, "if thou'lt tell me where Isaac Fessenden's shop is."

The maid looked cunningly at her as if Anna were a simpleton. "Mill Lane," she snapped. Then she snatched her hand out of Anna's to close the door.

Anna ran back up toward the marketplace. She did not care now about mud, or footpads, or plague, or anything on earth. Her pattens clattered and slithered on the cobbles until she found the top of Mill Lane and slowed to look at the signs above the doors. *Cablewright . . . Smith . . . Baker . . . Mason . . . Tailor.*

She beat the door with her fists, but it seemed barred fast from within. Weren't they expecting Isaac's return?

As she pounded again, her bundle fell to the doorstep, and she began to weep.

Then she heard the sound of bolts and bars moving, and a young man whose face she did not know opened the door a hand's breadth. As the door moved, the smell of sulphur or some other foul smoke penetrated the air. Her disappointment, however, was more bitter than the sulphur.

"'Tis I, Anna Tolhurst. Is not Nicholas here?"

"We have the plague."

The word was becoming familiar, no longer so terrible, somehow, now that she was near him. "I know. I saw Isaac."

"My father? You'd best go away." He began to close the door again.

She jammed her foot in the crack, wincing as the door hit her. "I beg you, tell me, is Nicholas here?"

"Nicholas?" The young man sounded doltish and slow. "My cousin? Or do you want Dr. Bennet? He is Nicholas, too."

"Oh, your cousin! Please, please—"

"He's gone. Last week. What do you want? Who are you?"

"I told you! Anna Tolhurst."

His face registered recognition for the first time. "Are you not of Goudhurst and Squire Tolhurst's house? What are you to Nicholas?"

She withdrew her foot painfully. "I'd thought to be his wife, one day, and cousin to you." She leaned against the wall outside and wept again.

Maidstone, Autumn 1659

Isaac

Isaac found her on the doorstep when he returned. The shop door was still barred as he had bidden Adam to bar it, and the Tolhurst girl huddled over a bundle of clothes outside.

He could not be angry with her for long (anger borne of fear, not directed toward the girl) for he remembered the flash of red-gold hair as she pulled back her hood, and for a moment he saw her with Nicholas's eyes.

"Poor lass," he said, bending over her. "But what am I to do with you? We're sick of the plague. Several households nearby are likewise, and this is no place for you." Then he remembered Rebecca tossing feverishly upstairs. Panic seized him again. "And my wife—the doctors are both ill themselves. Neither one can leave his bed." Scarcely aware of what he was saying or doing, he stood above her, clenching and unclenching his hands.

Anna looked up, her face smeared and marked by runnels of tears, and she shook her head in dumb misery.

"I must look to my wife, maiden, do you understand? Have you enough money to find a safe house to lodge in?" The words came out unthinkingly, and he immediately regretted them. But what was he to do? He could offer no hospitality, not even to the daughter of his dearest friend. Yet how could a squire's daughter, a lovely one at that, put up at a hostelry by herself and not be molested by the men of the town? "Have you—?"

She stood up suddenly. Much taller than Rebecca, she looked taller still by the tilt of her chin and the straightness of her bearing. "Yes." Her face cleared slightly. She seemed ashamed of her stricken appearance. "Yes, I have gold. But I cannot use it." Her hands went together in supplication. "I beg you, let me lodge with Nicholas's kin. I'll cause you no trouble and will see food on your—"

"*Food?* You're mad! Moonstruck!" He stared at her and lifted his hand to knock and bring Adam to the door.

She caught his hand in her own, and he was surprised at the strength in her hands and in her voice. "No, not just food on your table," she burst out, "but physic as well. I know something of healing. Please, please let me in."

He shook her hand away but made no further attempt to raise Adam yet. "Let you in to your death, mistress? Nay, your father is my friend."

Tears started out of her eyes again. "Rebecca did not tell you? You're *nothing* to my father." She shook her head. "Nor am I. Nor is even little Edward, the babe your wife nursed so tenderly as her own. . . . My father is crazed, beside himself. We are nothing to him now."

The words penetrated, and Isaac's shoulders slumped forward. He felt hot all of a sudden, and wrenched the clouts away from his face and neck. Tiredness washed over him, and he leaned heavily on the doorpost.

Her voice continued—that low, bewitching voice he remembered in her mother, the same voice that had captivated his nephew. "I shall look to Rebecca, sir, I assure you." She pulled something out of her bundle and waved a book under his nose.

But Isaac's head had begun to swim, and he had no strength left to argue. "Come in, then," he said without lifting his head. "At your peril. No one can leave this house again until the angel of death has passed over it. Neither can you."

She did not answer immediately. Then her voice seemed to come from a long way off. "But I must gather herbs."

He did not hear much more. The shop doorway, the girl's face, the dark lane—all rushed in a dizzy whirlpool round him. He felt his grip on the doorpost loosen. His vision darkened, and he sank down under thundering waters.

When he awoke again, it was only for a few moments. He became aware of burning pains in his back and pressure under his arm and in his groin. He lay in his bed, alone, and the room was smoky with a strong smell he could not recognize. Blinding light poured in through the window, piercing him like arrows; he turned his head. *Rebecca?*

He struggled to sit up, but his head pounded as with a thousand fulling mallets. His body seemed disjointed, floating like an old, unraveled garment on a foul pond. The smoke cleared for an instant, and the face of a woman who was not Rebecca blocked out the swords of light that sliced into his eyes.

"Oh, shut the curtains," he moaned.

"You must drink this water. 'Tis sweet and cool."

How did she know his throat was burning? He floated away again, this time under the water. It was stagnant, thick and green, yet it roared in his ears like a tumultuous waterfall. The roaring grew and grew, and he felt he was fighting for his life in the raging filth round him.

He opened his eyes again and saw his own arms and legs flailing in the darkness. A stranger stood beside him with a candle in her hand. The candle flame seemed to burn his eyes, and he shut them. At the sound of a woman's voice, he opened his eyes again. The woman and the candle had moved, the candle now at the foot of the bed where it would not hurt him. But then the woman came and stood beside him, her hair unbound and beautiful in the faint light. She stretched out her hand to pull up the covers.

"You must be covered," she said gently.

"But . . . I am hot. . . ." He felt ashamed of his nakedness before this woman, but his body was burning, and his mouth was swollen and tasted foul. "I am hot. Tell Rebecca . . . tell her to bring me a drink."

Immediately the woman slipped her hand under his head, cool and strong, raising it up, and she pressed a phial of something sweet and thick against his lips. "Drink it," she instructed.

He could not remember whether he had drunk it, but when he opened his eyes again, there was a twilight in the room and the phial stood beside him, now empty. The same woman—he remembered her face now, though not her name—was standing in the corner of the small room with her back to him. He heard the sound of water poured out: not the black waters of his nightmare, now, but fresh, real water.

She turned round, a jug in her hand. "I must wash you, Isaac Fessenden, and salve your sores."

"Who are you? Where is Rebecca?"

"Rebecca is with your mother Mary. Remember? Both were ill."

"And they are well?"

She did not hesitate. "They are well. But I am here in their stead—your physician, if you will. I must wash you." She caught her lower lip under her teeth as she squeezed the water out of a strip of clean linen.

"I'll do it myself, woman," he protested, shaking his head. But the motion made the room dip round him again, and he retched into the flock bedding.

"I have washed you before, Isaac." She pulled away the fouled bedding and rolled back the sheet.

He did not dare move. The water felt lukewarm on his tight, burning skin, and her hands were light but sure. He looked down, ashamed again, though he did not know why. *Thou hast the longest, strongest, kindest body of any man on earth,* Rebecca always said. But now it looked swollen in places, flaccid in others, and dark lumps marked his groin.

He let his head go back with a moan. So the pestilence had come to him as well. He screwed his eyes shut.

"I must lance these, you know," the same woman's voice said, "or the venom will consume you."

Floating on the hideous pond of his half-dreams again, he no longer cared. "Do as you will," he mumbled.

She raised his arm first. He opened his eyes to see her face only inches from his own, her eyes narrowed with concentration on the ugly mass under his arm. "You will feel pain," she warned, and he heard her swallow.

He did not trouble to answer her, and she continued. "I have a salve of cuckoo pint and ground ivy. You will *not* die, Isaac." He felt the knife probing, then a release of pressure, followed by a hot plaster that stung and soothed him at once. He moaned again.

"There! Now the others." Her voice sounded triumphant, half on the verge of laughter.

"What is it to you?" His teeth began to chatter violently. Then the black tide came up again and carried him away. Swallowed up in it, he rolled over and over in the wet darkness like Jonah in the belly of the great fish. In the sea of sickness that enclosed him and that he enclosed, he heard a bell ringing over and over again, and a wild voice crying, "Bring out your dead." He was carried out on the clang of the bell and the surge of the waves, and he had died.

Later when he woke again, it was full daylight, and the room was empty. He heard the voices of Adam and Charlie below stairs, and the low, musical voice of the strange woman answering them. He remembered the hideous black lumps but felt no pressure now, and the fever had left him. *I have not died, after all.*

He tried to sit up, but he was still too weak. He waited, but no one came, so he eased the bedding back cautiously and looked down at his body again. There were neat poultices in his groin, and his legs looked thin as sticks, his belly hollow so that his ribs stuck out like the timbers of a half-built ship in the Chatham dockyard.

Chatham . . . His mind was clearing now. How long had he lain ill? Three separate pictures formed in his mind: the red mark on Hannah's leg;

the dead rats in the gutter; and the sad, resolute face of young Nicholas as he left for the New World.

Then he remembered the strange woman below stairs and knew who she was at last. The plague bell rang outside again, and a cart rumbled up the lane. "Bring out your dead!"

He did not know whether to weep for himself or for the woman.

Cambridge, Massachusetts, January 1660

John

Five years of waiting, hoping, and praying had brought a double reward: a fair wind at Christmass time had carried not one of his nephews, but two. The Almighty had not blessed him with sons—unless he counted poor, benighted Nathaniel—but both his brothers had been generously endowed, and now both Nicholas and Josiah had come to him. Steady in the faith, eager to work and learn, they were turning his old age into a time of peace and joy.

Jane, inconsolable after Nathaniel's ugly death, now moved more swiftly about the house. Even on these mornings of deep frost and falsely bright winter skies, she sang as she stirred the fire in the morning.

His mind was full of plans now: plans for the work of the tannery and the gloving business, and plans for his two nephews. Nicholas, the stronger of the two boys, was learning the trade more quickly than his brother, but Josiah was clever with the glovemaking itself and kindly with the customers. To Nicholas he therefore entrusted the oversight of the tanning yard, the account keeping in the shop, and the trading with Indians and trappers who came seasonally to sell to him. To Josiah he entrusted the day-to-day management of the shop and the glove work.

Both lads already thrived in their labors, but Nicholas puzzled John. Sometimes on the Sabbath as they sat cozily by the fire and Jane read aloud to them all, he fancied that Nicholas's eyes wandered away, and the boy's chiseled face became melancholy and remote. He thought he remembered in Robert's face such moments of withdrawal, though Nicholas generally reminded him far more of young Isaac than of Robert. But the boy's sadness puzzled him.

How old is the lad? Aye, going on twenty-four, and still not wed! John had come to see all men's trials in terms of their need of womenfolk. A *man's not a man without a woman beside him* had become his most favored saying to fellow selectmen and other Cambridge freemen.

Jane only smiled when he said as much to her. "So thou'd make a married man of him when he's scarce set foot on the new land, would you?" She bent to blow out the candle by their bed.

"Aye, I would." John pulled the quilts round his shoulders and enfolded Jane in his arms as she came to lie beside him. Before they came upstairs, she had warmed the bed with hot bricks from the fireplace.

"Josiah's as likely to need a wife himself, is he not?" she asked, laughing a little.

"I suppose so, though he never casts an eye on the maids as our Nicholas does."

"Nicholas plays the lecher?" In the dark, her voice was loud with surprise.

"Hush! Nay, I never said so. But he looks hungry, ne'ertheless, poor lad. Think now of the young women of our fellowship. Is there a proper maid for him, not betrothed and goodly enough to look upon?"

Beside him, Jane lay silent, but he knew by her quick breathing that she was still wide awake and thinking carefully. At last, she said, "Aye, there *is* such a lass."

He squeezed her. "Say on."

"I'm thinking of John Cheney's girl."

"What? Margaret? Oh, she's but a thin hop pole of a girl. And far too young for Nicholas."

"Dost think so? She's of age, I'm sure. And John, dear, you've not been looking at the lasses lately, that's quite clear, for Margaret's as sturdy as I am."

He ran his hands over her breasts and belly under the coarse material of her shift. "Then she'll do," he teased. "*Sturdy?* What a word, sweetheart! You be not *sturdy*—"

"And thou art shameless." She pushed him gently away. "Give o'er."

"Not while I have a sturdy wife."

Her arms held him at a distance. "Wait, we're speaking of Nicholas, not of ourselves. And though he wants a wife, he wants his sister, also," Jane reminded him.

"His sister?"

"Aye, have you not heard him speak of Hannah? She sounds to be an honest maiden. Could we not bring her hither, too, to be with her brethren? She must be lonely without them."

He considered. Sons he had always wanted, but the responsibility of a daughter? That might be another matter. "Aye, she must be lonely. I'm sure Isaac's good for her, but he's not quite of our persuasion nowadays, and mayhap she feels neglected at times. And if God gives us the means to bring her across the sea, why not? But, Jane, Nicholas wants a wife more . . ." He lay quiet for a moment, then asked, "Shall I broach the idea with him?"

She hesitated again. "He's not straightforward like Josiah. I don't mean he's devious, but thou'lt need to be tender with him. I shouldn't wonder if he'd been crossed in love."

He clicked his tongue impatiently. "Oh, trust a woman to dream up such a thought! Very well, you speak to him, then."

"Good!" she exclaimed. "I shall, my love."

He gathered her into his arms and pushed away the shift. "Will she be as good to him, think you, as you are to me?" he whispered.

Her answer came more slowly this time. "I hope so, John." She touched his face in the dark. "Poor lad, I hope so."

Jane would have spoken to Nicholas the next morning, had not a letter come in by sea. A messenger had carried it up at dawn from the harbor since it was marked *For John Fessenden, on Eliot Street, most pressing.* Jane brought the letter straight to the table where John, Nicholas, and Josiah were breaking their fast with a bowl of hot cornmeal.

"Best open this, husband," she urged.

The arrival of any letter was cause enough for surprise. Nicholas's spoon rattled into the trencher. "'Tis my uncle's hand. I pray nothing be amiss."

John looked across the table at Nicholas's inquiring face, silently wishing the boy less earnest.

Jane came and stood with one hand on the shoulder of each of their nephews. "He probably sends to see that ye be safe arrived," she said gently.

He broke the seal quickly and scanned the letter. As he did, the cornmeal rose into his gorge again, and he felt the sweat start out of his face.

Nicholas rose to his feet and leaned over the table, but Josiah's face was passive. "Is it our sister?" Nicholas asked. "Has aught befallen Hannah?"

John shook his head slowly, but his mind had gone numb. "Nay. Hannah hath been—she hath been ill." He stumbled over the words; they would not come right. "But she is well, and she has come, that is—will come to us ere long, at the summer's end, God willing."

The blood leaped into Nicholas's face. "Oh, but that is good news indeed!"

John reached for his beaver. On cold mornings he wore it even indoors, and now pulled it off roughly. "Aye, good news. But there is more, and ye must broth brace thyselves like men."

Nicholas flinched. "Is it Anna, then?"

"*Nay!*" His voice was sharper than he had intended. "Nay," he repeated, more softly. "I told thee, she is well."

"Uncle John," Josiah broke in, "he means *Anna*, not Hannah. Anna is his beloved."

Jane caught John's eye, but he was upset now, and he looked again at the letter. "There *is* an Anna mentioned, I see, but I know not—I confess, I am befuddled and thought he meant thy sister. But listen, and wait." He took a deep breath. "Mary, our good stepmother, and thy grandmother, has been taken to the Lord. And Rebecca, Isaac's sweet wife—" He heard the quaver of his own voice and felt tears prick hot against his eyelids. "Rebecca, also. Of the *plague*." His teeth ground together so that the last words came out harshly.

Except for the sharp intake of Jane's breath and the hissing of the firewood, the room was silent.

One of Nicholas's hands clamped onto John's wrist, and the other whipped the letter from his hand. "Forgive me—!"

John watched him scan the letter frantically, his lips moving slightly. Then Nicholas turned to Josiah. "Our sister lived through the plague. Our cousins somehow escaped it." His voice turned bitter. "Isaac cared for them all until Anna, my Anna, came. Now she, too, is at the door of death."

John watched the interchange without fully understanding. Josiah's arm went round his brother's shoulders, and the two turned to each other and wept. "My Anna . . . now she is at the door of death."

"Who is this girl, this Anna?" Jane asked softly. She had not moved from where she stood, and the three figures were now locked together in sorrow.

John retrieved the letter from Nicholas's hand to look at the date. *Ye 10th Octobre* was scrawled below Isaac's enormous signature. More than three months had passed.

Nicholas raised his head to Jane. "I forbore to tell ye of her as I had so little hope. And now I have none."

John could not answer. What if he had lost Jane at the same time in their young lives?

At last, Jane said, "The Almighty *is* merciful, Nicholas. He knoweth all things, and all things are in His hand. He will bring Hannah to us, I believe, and you can console each other." Her voice was unsteady, but John marveled at her discernment. "I know not of thy Anna, but if it has pleased Him to take her unto Himself, she is indeed at rest now."

Nicholas stood up abruptly and pulled on his worsted surcoat, wool cap, and thick mittens. Then he went out.

John got up to follow but sank down again on the bench. Nicholas was not Nathaniel to go running to the ordinary for comfort.

"Let him be, my Uncle John," Josiah said after a moment. "He has loved that maid for many months now and hoped—in spite of all he said—to have her to his wife one day."

John nodded. "Aye, I can see that." He pushed the letter across the table and sighed. Though he had loved Mother Mary, her death did not disturb his own settled life. It was Isaac's life that was shattered; it was Nicholas's life that was shattered.

John wrote to his brother Isaac:

On a drizzling morn this month, our nephew Nicholas was married to Margaret Cheney of Cambridge. Reverend Thomas Shepard did perform the ceremony, with Josiah and I to witness. Margaret is a chaste maid. They will live a godly and sober life, so rest you that we have done all we can for our brother Robert's children.

Our greetings to Hannah, whom we hope to welcome to this house in the fall, should she set sail when you receive this paper. We shall hope to find as good a wife to Josiah and husband to Hannah, so please God.

Brother, we grieve for thee and thy dear Rebecca. Of the maid Anna I know not what to say, save that Nicholas has grieved full sore for her, but wants a bride, so is wed. May God rest that poor maid. God save thee, dear my brother Isaac.

He signed and dated the letter, *March 1660, John Fessenden,* then decided to add a postscript:

I have taken thought to another matter. If there be naught to keep thee in England now, would you not come hither, bringing our niece Hannah with you?

Maidstone, Summer 1660

Isaac

Isaac had become quite used to Anna's ways now, since she had recovered. She had made herself indispensable to him, driven, no doubt, by a false sense of debt for her lodging: a "safe" lodging that had almost cost her her life. She polished, scrubbed, and washed more vigorously than any woman he had known or heard of, and there was no more sickness in the house after the plague, even when the fierce spring fevers in Maidstone carried off many other families.

But Anna could not stay forever. Adam and Charlie were bringing brides to their beds later in the summer; the rooms above the shop would be crowded again, and summer was the best time for journeying.

They heard nothing from Anna's father, and they rarely spoke of him now. Whenever his name was mentioned, shadows crossed Anna's eyes, and he knew that all she wanted was to escape Kent and go to Nicholas again.

It troubled him to realize that he was delaying in arranging the young woman's passage. He grieved deeply for Rebecca, but Anna was unwittingly filling her place at home. He had resented her at first. *Nicholas's sweetheart. George's daughter*—she meant little to him except as someone belonging to other men. *But she has healed me. I owe her my life.*

More and more, her delicate skin (had he not seen her entire, when she was ill?), her mass of angel-like hair, and her laughing eyes entered his dreams. On mornings after such dreams, he was abrupt with her as she spoke happily about Nicholas and of the coming voyage. But when he spoke harshly, she only pricked herself and bloodied the sewing so that he grew all the more enraged.

It was not as a seamstress that she filled Rebecca's place, then, for she would never sew well, he thought. No, she was "all things to all men"— that's what his father would have said. She was sister to Adam and Charlie, prodding Adam out of his dull discussions, teasing Charlie when he ranted about the delights of his sweetheart, doctoring them with physic when they were low, comforting him when he cried for Rebecca. She was, he suddenly realized, exactly what Mary had been to his father.

But that, he thought, entailed more than he could contemplate. *She's Nicholas's sweetheart*, he reminded himself. *I must find another wife.*

The end of May brought word from London and Kent that the King would return at last from France.

"We should go and see the King ride in," Charlie insisted one afternoon when they were shutting up the shop for the day.

The smell of finely seasoned mutton drifted in at the back door of the shop. *She's made a meal fit for a king again,* he thought, forgetting—as they all had—that he himself had taught her how to prepare food. She cooked it now with as much discrimination as she made cordials and poultices. Even the most commonplace of foods set his mouth watering.

"My father, I said we should go over to Barham to see the King," Charlie persisted, hands on hips.

Isaac saw himself at the same age: black, curling hair bouncing as he spoke, brown eyes shining. Is that how Rebecca had seen him, fallen in love with him? *I'm woolgathering.*

"Charlie, I'm sorry, I was thinking of thy mother."

The boy's face had schooled itself to seriousness. How could Isaac expect his sons to understand his muddled feelings about Rebecca, about Anna. . . .

"Dost not think 'twould be a fine thing to see the King, my father?"

"Yes, 'twould indeed." He gripped himself, concentrating. "Let's think now. I was but a lad when the last King came to the throne, but I believe thy uncles went to see him ride in." He met Charlie's eyes. "Aye, 'twould be good to see him for ourselves." He laughed suddenly, unexpectedly. "And it would be good for the King to see us, too, do you not suppose?"

Charlie, mystified perhaps by the sudden change from reflection to merriment, smiled back absently, and they went back to the kitchen.

The outer doors stood open, and warm air breathed in from outside. Remembering the plague of last autumn, Isaac silently gave thanks for the blessing of open doors and windows, for the freedom they had with the passing of the pestilence to go in and out as they pleased.

Anna stood by the fire in a patched apron of Rebecca's. She was tasting the meat, and steam curled round her pink face. She looked young and beautiful, and Isaac felt again a surge of resentment that he must give this girl to Nicholas—even to Nicholas, whom he loved so. He wanted to touch her flushed cheek with his fingers. He wanted to kiss her.

She left off stirring and crossed the room close to him but not looking at him. She was quick like that, not patient (unless someone were ill) nor timid like Rebecca. Now she was reaching up to the dresser, and she pulled down a folded note from behind an upturned milk pitcher.

Her voice jolted him uncomfortably. "There's a letter, Isaac, from someone. . . ." Her face was red now, right to the roots of her hair. "I think from Nicholas, or from thy brother. Does it say when they expect us?" She threw an eager look across at Hannah, who was separating curds and whey on the other side of the room. Hannah's face shone equally brightly.

"Oh, open it, do!" Hannah pleaded.

He broke the seal and glanced at the writing with a heavy heart. *Now they must go at last.* They had never complained of the waiting; he had marveled at that, but now they could wait no longer.

Our nephew Nicholas was married to Margaret Cheney . . . Brother, we grieve for thee. . . . Of the maid Anna I know not what to say. . . . Would you not come hither?

His eye jumped from phrase to phrase, but he could make no sense of the letter. "'Tis from John," he muttered, not looking up.

He read it again, more slowly, and his hand began to shake. "Hannah." He swallowed hard. "Thy brothers expect thee forthwith. I shall see to it tomorrow."

He was aware, suddenly, that Anna was standing close to him, her breathing quick and uneven. His eyes traveled reluctantly from the letter to her clasped hands and to her face.

"And me? Do they not know that I shall journey with her?" Her eyes were wide and frightened. He hated to see that look of fear in them. She was not a woman to be afraid.

"No." Did she know how difficult that word had been?

Her hands fell to her sides. "Then—how so, Isaac?" Hurt and puzzlement clouded her face now.

"My brother and Nicholas—all of them—they believe thou didst die of the pestilence, my—"

Her face flamed, and she threw out her arms. "But I didn't!" she shouted. "I am alive!" She began to laugh wildly and spun round the room.

He leaned forward and dropped his head into his hands. The rough paper of the note scratched his cheek. His joy was her destruction, and he could not look her in the face.

"Anna," he said at last, and she stopped her dancing. "Anna, my dear love, Nicholas—Nicholas is wed to another."

Hannah was due to sail from Dover. After his experience with Chatham the year before, Isaac had decided to arrange her voyage from another port.

She would travel with an elderly cobbler and his family, neighbors from Mill Lane, but no one else would accompany her.

He presumed Anna would not want to go with them to Dover. She had spoken vaguely of finding employ with an apothecary in London but otherwise had said very little since John's letter arrived. So they had left her to herself, Hannah tiptoeing in and out of the chamber they shared in the attic. Though Isaac heard her weeping many times, she spurned all offers of comfort.

On the morning of Hannah's departure from Maidstone, however, he found her dry-eyed in the kitchen at dawn—just as she had been in the past—making broth. He sat at table, saying nothing, watching her as she moved about. Familiar with every curve and line of her body now, he ached to hold her, as much for himself as to comfort her. But she would have none of him, of course.

At last he ventured, "Anna, are you sure thou wilt not go with us to Dover? I believe Hannah would be sorry if you didn't, though I . . ." He let his voice die. It would be foolish to say that he would understand if she did not choose to go.

She turned her violet eyes on him. "I meant to go all along, Isaac. 'Tis painful—that's all." She shrugged. "But 'tis painful for thee, also, to see the last of thy kin save thy two sons go away forever." Her voice sounded hollow as if she were reciting what someone else had asked her to say or lines she had rehearsed for a pageant.

With his eyes he drank in the pale skin of her neck that showed above the partlet, the tilted roundness of her breasts, the slenderness of her waist— she was too thin now, he thought. He was struck speechless.

She caught his wandering eyes and began to stammer. "I said, I shall go. But then I must—" She turned away and began to stir the broth again, her hand moving in quick circles. "I feel I'm here on sufferance. 'Tis time I were gone." Her shoulders were taut, and he could not see her face.

He stood uncertainly. "Thou'rt *not* here on sufferance, Anna," he grated. "Thou art my—"

"I know—thy dearest friend's daughter." The bitterness in her voice made it sound even lower than usual.

He waved his hand helplessly. He could not say what he wanted to say. It was futile to speak of it at all. He sat down again. "We may well see the King on his way if we make a good start." He would begin on a new tack, he decided, and he tried to sound matter-of-fact.

She was ladling broth so hastily into the bowls that some of it spilled hissing into the fire. "Aye, so Charlie tells me." She sounded steadier again.

He rose to lift the broth onto the tables. Hannah's eyes were sparkling as she came into the room. "Aye, there's the King coming, and I'm agoing t'other way."

Isaac welcomed her interruption. "Foolish King! He should make thee his Queen, Hannah. Then we'd keep thee in England."

Hannah laughed. "Nay, I'd keep *ye*. Take all the gold of Parliament and give it to the people. His poor Majesty shall have none anyhow."

Charlie came down the back stairs. "Hush, cousin," he shouted. "What a way for a woman to talk! What would you know? And I thought thou wast a Roundhead, anyway, like thy—"

Isaac caught his eye, and Charlie swallowed the last words.

Hannah seemed to notice nothing amiss. "I was, ere I came here. 'Tis listening to thee and my uncle that's changed me. Now I'd love to see the King, wouldn't you, Anna?"

Charlie scoffed. "Fine Puritan thou'lt make in Boston!"

Anna smiled faintly. "Oh, she'll regain her wits there," she said.

Isaac breathed a sigh of relief to see them sparring as usual, but Anna would still not meet his eyes.

The Dover road was lined with timber, merchants, shepherds, fullers, and other travelers. The heat shimmered up from the chalky track as it had done thirty-five years before on Barham Down when King Charles I had picnicked there on his own way from Dover to Canterbury, as it had shimmered thirty-five years before when on one side of the hill John and Robert Fessenden and on the other George Tolhurst had watched the new King ride to be crowned in Canterbury.

Dover, Canterbury, and all the towns in between made holiday of the day. The road was decked with flowers and banners; musicians brayed on horns and trumpets; and men—dressed in liveries, chains, velvet, and cloth of gold—marched to and fro, puffed with their own importance.

In the crush of people, Charlie, Adam, and Hannah had drifted away with the cobbler and his wife. Isaac watched the spectacle without feeling he was part of it. The splendor could not touch him as long as there was a banner of silence between him and Anna. He was aware only that she was near, aware—though he did not dare look straight at her—that her eyes were fixed forward on the road. She might have been blinkered.

But suddenly he no longer minded what she thought or did not think of him. He looked at her directly. The sunlight drew a circlet of copper round her hair; her back was straight and unafraid. *This is the woman who nursed me back to life. This is the woman who thought she lived for Nicholas but now is dead in her heart because, save God, she has no one. And this is the woman, young though she be, that I want as my wife.*

Slowly, so slowly that he scarcely felt his own movement, he put out his arm toward her. She did not move—he hardly expected her to move—and her eyes did not shift. He hesitated, but then, remembering the great crowd round them, grew bold again. His hand reached her waist.

Her head turned, her face questioning, surprised.

"Anna?"

She nodded almost imperceptibly.

"Wilt thou come hither, then?" He did not move his hand or force her, but she seemed to understand.

"Isaac—"

The people round them had begun to shout, but he did not notice, his eyes watching her mouth say his name. "Anna, I love thee. I know I am but a tailor—" He spread his hands, letting go of her again.

A small blue butterfly had settled on her hair and sat there basking in her warmth and in the sunlight falling on them both. She smiled suddenly, as if she had heard the words before. Her eyes shone warmly, and she came nearer.

He fitted his arm round her waist again and drew her close, as he wanted to. The pounding of his heart obscured all other noise round them. They looked at each other, and Anna rested her head against his arm.

Then they both turned their eyes toward the road. A cavalcade was riding past: proud stallions and gray mares stamping and tossing, bridles ringing. The tall, dark-wigged new King Charles passed only a few feet from where they stood. He waved an enormous plumed hat, and Isaac found himself calculating ridiculously the length of felt that had been used, and the size of the peacock from which the feathers had been plucked.

"A free Parliament! A free Parliament!" some rogues shouted.

A sardonic grin twisted the King's face, and he reined in his horse almost directly in front of Isaac and Anna. The crowd fell silent in embarrassment.

"Pray, be quiet," King Charles said clearly, his voice clipped like a Frenchman's, "and ye shall have both King and Parliament." He laughed and waved his hat again. "Ride on."

Isaac threw back his head and laughed with him.

Historical Note

Home on holiday in England in 1974 from America, I discovered something that made the hair prickle on my arms and that set me thinking about another novel: Jim's ancestors and mine had lived near each other—some of them in the same Kentish village—in the seventeenth century. A useful book written by one of Jim's relatives—*The Fessenden Family in America*—gave us a few clues. My mother's family supplied others, and soon we found ourselves trying to read parish records and churchyard tombstones.

History led to speculation as I realized that the Fessendens had been Puritans and (I surmised) the Tolhursts had been King's men. It wasn't long before Jim and I were sitting in a restaurant in Cranbrook and I was outlining another novel on the back of a red paper napkin.

Back in the States the red napkin went into a drawer with other such scraps of paper and was for a while forgotten. Ten years later, Jim's work brought us to Kent again, and here we remain. I wrote this book looking out of a succession of windows in and around Maidstone, the county town: one looking north to the Downs, and the other two looking south toward the Weald.

Men of Kent tells the story of three generations of the Fessenden family and two generations of the Tolhursts. The lives of its characters are rooted in history, but this is not a history book. I have changed history only where I had to for the purpose of the story, though of course I have embroidered history, too, and have inevitably looked at it through my own particular set of prejudices.

The places mentioned, and many of the minor characters (Sir Dudley Digges and Sir John Mainy on the Royalist side; and Sandys, Livesey, and Weldon on the Parliamentarian/County Committee side) are as true to life as I can make them, relying on county records and Civil War accounts both contemporary and modern. The daily life of Kentish gentlemen and yeomen—their homes, their way of conversing, their songs, their dependence on cloth and hops—these were all real, and I have tried to reproduce them faithfully here.

But as I said, this is not history, and at times history would not work as a lively story. Hence I have changed somewhat the birth dates and names of the Fessenden family (Robert's wife, for example, was Mary; I preferred to avoid the confusion). In history, John Fessenden Senior was a glover, not a clothier. He fathered two sons: John, who married Jane Tritton of Chilham at the same time as his father remarried—to Widow Mary Snode; and Robert, who fathered a large family, including one son who was lost at sea, a daughter Hannah, a son Nicholas, and as many as four other children (John, Mary, Elizabeth, and Jane). Nicholas Fessenden went to the Bay Colony of Massachusetts in 1674 (1660 in my story) and fathered seven sons. I have made some guesses about what took him from England, though history relates with certainty that he did go to work with his Uncle John (a glover) in Cambridge, Massachusetts.

The destruction of Canterbury Cathedral actually took place over two successive summers, 1642 and 1643, but again, I have compressed the events into one to avoid too much repetition. Similarly, the plague struck Maidstone severely in the 1630s, but did not return until 1666, not 1659 as in my story. But since there was indeed severe sickness in Goudhurst in the late 1650s, I simply transposed this to the county town. Correspondence between a gentleman and Samuel Pepys in 1665 documents what *did* happen in Maidstone during the terrible plague years.

Many people in Kent to whom I have spoken raised their eyebrows in surprise when I said I was writing a book about the Civil War in Kent. Surely nothing happened *here*, they said. Nothing could be further from the truth. The Kentish tradition of rebellion asserted itself quite vigorously during the century—first in protests against the imposition of heavy royal taxes, then against the demands of Parliament. And no government, regal or Roundhead, could afford to ignore the strategic importance of Kent, standing as it does between France and the rest of Britain. Kent had to be silenced! Rebellions of the 1640s and 1650s were often ill-planned; to the modern eye they seem somehow quaint (as in the case of the Canterbury Christmas riots of 1647) or foolhardy (as in the case of the Battle of Maidstone in June 1648, when the rebels ended with their backs to the wall of St. Faith's churchyard or hunted down in the nearby hop gardens). But whatever else may be said about Kent's history at the time, it cannot be said to lack color!

Chronology

1603	James I becomes King
1617–1618	*Book of Sports* defies Puritan concern for the Sabbath
1620	*Mayflower* sails for the New World
1625	Charles I becomes King
1626	England at war with France and Spain: forced loans extracted from gentry to support the King
1628	Petition of Rights: Sir Dudley Digges William Laud appointed Archbishop of London Dr. William Harvey discovers blood circulation
1629	Charles I's fourth and last Parliament before the Long Parliament (of 1640) Royal Charter issued for Massachusetts Bay Company
1633	William Laud appointed Archbishop of Canterbury
1634	Laud clamps down on Huguenot (Strangers) worship in Kent Ship Money (taxes) first levied to pay for royal vessels; opposed by Kentish gentry
1636	Severe plague in London
1640	Charles I calls Parliament forth first time in eleven years: the Long Parliament
1641	Groundswell of anti-Parliamentary feeling in Kent
1642	Charles I enters House of Commons Bishops removed from House of Lords Theatres closed by order of Parliament Kentish Petition against Parliament drawn up at the Star Inn, Maidstone First Civil War begins Canterbury Cathedral desecrated by Parliamentary troops Battle of Edgehill

1643	Royalists in Sevenoaks, Kent, attempt a rising in support of the King
	Parliament increasingly anxious about Kentish loyalties to the Crown
	Canterbury Cathedral desecrated a second time
1644	Battle of Marston Moor
1645	New Model Army (Parliamentarian) formed under Fairfax
	Kent Country Committee increasingly anti-royalist: raids and sequestrations become commonplace
	Battle of Naseby: Fairfax and Oliver Cromwell defeat Charles I
1646	First of six consecutive poor harvests
1647	Charles I flees to Carisbrooke Castle and is later imprisoned there by Parliamentarian forces
	Celebration of Easter, Whitsun, and Christmass banned by order of Parliament
	Christmass riots, Canterbury; rioters imprisoned in Leeds and Westenhanger Castles, Kent
1648	Further Kentish Petitions against Parliament
	Trial of Canterbury rioters
	Kent rises against Parliament
	Battle of Maidstone: Charles I's supporters defeated; end of Second Civil War
	Trial of Charles I
1649	Execution of Charles I
	Poet and essayist John Milton publishes two books arguing against the monarchy: *Eikon Basilike* and *Eikonoklastes*
	Oliver Cromwell appointed Lord High Protector of England
1652	Maidstone witch trails
1653	Four men indicted for playing unlawful game of football in Maidstone
1655–1656	Alehouses closed by order of Parliament
1658	Oliver Cromwell dies
1659	Severe epidemics in Goudhurst
1660	Charles II returns from exile in France and is crowned King in Canterbury
1665	Severe plague in Chatham, Maidstone, and London
1666	Great Fire of London

Selected Sources

Brooke, Iris. *English Costume of the Seventeenth Century*. London: A & C Black, Ltd. 1977. Reprint.

Burnham, Paul, and Stuart McRae. *Kent, the Garden of England*. Tenterden, Kent: Paul Norbury Publications, 1978.

Chalkin, C. W. *Seventeenth-Century Kent*. London: Longman's, 1965.

· Coward, Barry. *The Stuart Age*. London: Longman's, 1980.

Crouch, Marcus. *Canterbury*. London: Longman's, 1970.

Davies, Godfrey, *The Early Stuarts: 1603–1660*. (2nd edition) Oxford: Clarendon Press, 1959.

Everitt, Alan. *The Community of Kent and the Great Rebellion 1640–1660*. Leicester: Leicester University Press, 1966 and 1973.

Gardiner, S. R. *History of England*. (vol VI).

Glover, J., *The Placenames of Kent*. London: Batsford, 1976.

Heaton, Vernon. *The Mayflower*. Exeter: Webb and Bower, 1980.

Jessup, Frank W. *A History of Kent*. London: Phillimore & Co. Ltd., 1978. Reprint.

Lambarde, W. *A Perambulation of Kent, 1570*. Bath: Adams & Dart, 1970. Reprint.

Lodge, E. C., ed. *The Account Book of a Kentish Estate, 1616–1704*. Oxford: Oxford University Press, 1927.

McLeod, Kirsty. *Drums and Trumpets: The House of Stuart*. London: Andre Deutsch Ltd., 1977.

Sichel, Marion. *Costume Reference 3: Jacobean, Stuart and Restoration*. London: Batsford, 1977.

Who's Who in Kent. Worcester: Baylis and Sons, Ltd., 1935.

Winnifrith, A. *Men of Kent and Kentish Men*. Folkestone, Kent: Parsons, 1913.

Wright, Christopher. *Kent Through the Years*. London: Batsford, 1975.